Semper Fidelis

Squire of Middleham

C J Lock

DEDICATION

'Tempus omnia monstrat'

This motto is often attributed to Francis Lovell, and although it appears to have been used by different branches of the Lovell family, it cannot be said to be one he personally used. That being said, in dedicating this book to the memory of Francis, 1st Viscount Lovell, I hope that in relation to both himself, and his much maligned friend Richard III, it comes to pass and we do find that...

Time shows all things

FOREWORD

'Semper Fidelis' is, essentially, the same timeline as featured in 'Desmond's Daughter,' only told from the perspective of Richard's friend, Francis Lovell.

Why, you may ask?

Isn't that just re-hashing the same thing over again? Well, yes, and no.

There are many places in 'Desmond's Daughter' where the events take place 'off stage.' Caitlin does not witness these, may not even have heard of them second hand, but they happened all the same. She was not present as her children arrived at Middleham. Nor was she there when Anne gave birth to Richard's son. Or later, when the news reached the royal couple of his death. She played no witness to many key events in Richard's life, which is where this storyline can now shed some light. Some scenes will be familiar, cropping up in the story here and there, as we hear how Francis saw them. We find out when he first became attracted to Caitlin, and how that burgeoning affection played out over the ensuing years, encompassing love, hate, frustration, jealousy and tragedy. It is the story of one man's continuing loyalty, as a slew of powerful, external forces did their best to pull him from his chosen path.

Francis Lovell is both an enigmatic and shadowy figure. Shadowy in that we only get various, tantalising glimpses of his life in documents such as the Calendar Patent Rolls and the odd letter written in his own hand. Enigmatic in that there is so much we don't know for certain. We don't know his character or motivations; not even how, or when, he died. Myth and legend fill the void, but most opinions see him as a capable, dependable and loyal friend of Richard Plantagenet. Yet, even when and where this close friendship was formed cannot be certain, but however it happened, it seems undeniable that at some stage in their lives they met and formed a close friendship which lasted until Richard's death in 1485. And beyond.

After that, apart from almost managing to murder Henry Tudor in York and his role in the Battle of Stoke Field in June 1487, he disappears. No doubt to die sometime, but when and how?

Drowned in the Trent, starved in a vault, fighting abroad in a foreign army? Or peacefully, in his bed, long forgotten by those who once stood at his side. Those readers of 'Desmond's Daughter' will already know my take on this so the ending will be no surprise.

Although the story of Richard III is dramatic enough in itself, there are many areas where authors take dramatic licence. There are places where, for reasons which sit best with the storyline, certain minor facts are changed. Indeed certain suppositions are made. In 'Semper Fidelis' this is no different. In fact, it applies even more so.

I have, as far as I can, stuck to the facts as they are known, but with a figure such as Francis Lovell, this would make sparse material for a book. Where things have been changed, or subject to invention, see the detail in the Author's notes, and I say - 'Mea Culpa,' for any who find this annoying. Yet this is a work of fiction. The Francis Lovell who exists in these pages is the one who roams my mind. Nothing else.

I wanted to make Francis a real man, with true dilemmas and challenges, failures and successes and if we just laid out the facts, there is hardly anything there to go on at all. Wherever he rests, I hope I have done him justice

Table of Contents

ACKNOWLEDGMENTS

My sincere thanks and appreciation to the Richard III Society who hold a wealth of information about all things Ricardian, including the main protagonist of this story, Francis Lovell.   My apologies to anyone who has waited for ages for me to respond to an email because my head is almost permanently stuck in the 15th century and finally, the person I couldn't do this without, my beta/proof reader Amanda Geary

BOOK 1
Loyalty and Love

1. WESTMINSTER PALACE
June 1468

"Tom?"

Tom Parr jerked up his head quickly, looking somewhat flustered as I strode towards him across the bustling courtyard. It was a fair morning, summer just beginning to bloom, and although I had recently returned from a trip to Greenwich, my mood was more than a little subdued. Once again, my bird, my prize possession, flatly refused to hunt.

Despite my best efforts, and believe me there were many, she showed no interest at all. Not even when I knew she must surely be more ravenous than any one of the beasts in the Tower menagerie. Serenely graceful in flight, it was a sheer delight to watch as she soared up into the heavens, her dark, feathered wings stretched out majestically against the sky. Yet instead of seeking out prey, she mostly ignored it, seemingly absorbed in the sheer elegance of her ability to swoop and glide at will. Try as I might, I could not entice her into the hunt, yet neither could I give up the challenge. She was the first real possession I had ever owned and I was not about to relinquish her. At least not yet.

Not that I was a pauper. Far from it. My family had a long and noble lineage, owning lands spread around the country from north to south. Yet at the time my father had died, I was too young to benefit from any of it. Instead, I found myself thrust into the service of one of the noblest families in the land where I was to receive the training and education aimed to prepare me for my inheritance. At the express will of our sovereign King Edward, I became the ward of his most valued counsellor and cousin, Richard Neville.

The great and mighty Earl of Warwick. An experienced knight and soldier. A hardened warrior who had fought at the side of the king's father, and who had helped the king himself to win a bloody, snow bound battle at Towton seven years ago.

It was a battle which ousted the Lancastrian regime that my own family supported, and transformed a scion of the rival House of York, Edward Plantagenet, into King Edward of England. He was only nineteen years old. And a king!

My family's fortunes turned like the tide and in short order, in fact with somewhat breathless speed, I found myself married to Warwick's niece. She was a timid young girl who was pleasing enough even, I supposed, if taking into account that she was around half my age. That done, and my future decided on the whims of kings, I was summarily packed off to one of the earl's primary fortresses. A massive, slate- grey edifice rooted in the rolling green hills and dales of the wild and desolate north. It was a place called Middleham Castle.

I have to admit, when I first rode underneath the arch of the eastern gatehouse, I had no idea how attached I would become to those cold, forbidding walls. Of how the bonds formed within their towering shadows would determine the course of my path in life. On that first day I only remember being sad, lonely and afraid of what was to become of me - the son of a family with Lancastrian ties, with blood bonds to a house which had risen against the king.

That was seven years ago and as a child, I had no part in it, yet the stain still seemed to linger. Now, I had been brought to court by the earl himself, in the company of my fellow henchmen, with the aim of practising our courtly skills within the confines of a royal palace. Everywhere you turned there were people. Each hall and chamber was stuffed full of an array of churchmen, nobles and ambassadors, all attended by a plethora of servants and courtiers. Fording through them was like being smothered by a pillow drenched in sickly-sweet spices. There was no air. Eyes were sharp, ears skillfully honed. Moistened lips murmured secret words that only those especially chosen could determine.

I knew very little about the men of the court, their faces were a blur, their names unknown. It was something I expected the next few weeks would resolve, as one thing I was sure of was that no one could survive this seething sea of political expediency if they did not learn fast. Learn who to trust, who to befriend, and more importantly, who to avoid!

It was enough to make me turn tail and hurtle back to the wild, clear spaces of the north, if only I could. Having survived my early years at Middleham, despite the constant trials which had seen my Lancastrian leanings stripped away day by day, like cook stripping an onion in the castle kitchens, I had grown to respect and honour the House of York. It was in their service I now toiled by the hour to make myself the best squire, the best knight, that I could. I often wondered if my ancestors would be turning in their graves.

Yet, something completely unexpected happened which had eased my way into these hallowed halls. I had, quite by accident, acquired a secret weapon. I had made a friend of the king's youngest brother, Richard Plantagenet, Duke of Gloucester. I can truly say unexpected, as he was uncommon amongst the young squires who were crafting their skills at the lectern and tiltyard. He was quiet, serious, with a rare smile which imbued a sense of warm satisfaction if you caused it to appear by word or deed. Studious and attentive, he held a deep well of thoughts behind penetrating grey eyes, and to my astonishment, he had found my company to his liking and after only a mere hour at his side, I felt the same.

Since that day, we had formed a firm bond of friendship and both of us seemed to recognise, without ever acknowledging it out loud, that it would tie us together for life. Call me a fool, a dolt or an imbecile if you will. I can only tell you what I felt. What I knew, and still know, to be a certainty, as sure as one day death will claim us all. It was as simple as that, for me.

It was Tom, another friend and one of Richard's squires, who was now skulking round the stables suspiciously as I returned Lark, my aptly named falcon, to the mews. His lean face flushed sunset red when he saw me and it was then I understood that he was up to no good.

"Francis! Where the devil did you spring from?" He cast a quick, cautious look over his shoulder towards the stables as if fearing, or wishing, to be overheard, before returning his gaze to mine as I halted before him.

Lark danced fractiously on my wrist, moving restlessly from one foot to another. I reached up to caress her downy breast with one finger and she settled immediately, her head still alert under the leather hood. Recovering a little, Tom gave a short laugh, his high colour receding as he sought to steer the subject away from his loitering presence outside the stables.

"Surely you are not still trying to get that bird to hunt? Take some advice from me! Give up! It's beyond time to find a new one."

To a certain extent his ploy was a success. I couldn't help but look at her standing so proudly on my gauntlet. Wings the colour of autumn acorns, her breast creamy white, spotted dark here and there, like royal ermine. She was a beautiful creature, but I just couldn't make her do what she didn't feel like doing and in a small way I admired that, despite my frustration. As she was my first experience with anything of the female gender outside of my mother and sisters, I was fervently hoping it wasn't a pattern that was likely to reoccur!

I shrugged carelessly, as if her shortcomings mattered little, even though the smirking grins of the other henchmen rankled more and more each day. My friend and fellow esquire, Rob Percy, was the worst, which was made all the more galling by the fact that his bird was like an arrow in flight, and it always, always,

14

hit its mark.

"I'll keep her as a pet," I answered with a bravado I was far from feeling, hating myself for the twinge of embarrassment that pierced my innards.   "There are other birds more suited to the hunt than she."

Tom accepted this, although he didn't look overly convinced but he seemed to catch a glimpse of something behind me and his lips twitched involuntarily.

"Speaking of hunting... " he murmured softly, lowering his head as if in greeting to whoever he had seen approaching. He refrained from finishing his thought and I turned, half expecting to see Rob having followed me to the mews so he could goad me for my failings in the art of falconry. Yet what I saw caused me to lose all breath from my body, so unexpectedly that I almost gasped aloud, as if an invisible fist had punched me in the stomach.

A figure approached all right, but it was in no way the annoyingly mocking Rob Percy. It was a young girl, and even before she dropped her hood as she came to a halt before me, I knew without question she would be a beauty. When she did finally reveal herself to me, I had to avert my gaze swiftly and look back at Tom to prevent from betraying a sudden rush of confusion.

With the sun behind her, catching light to hair the shade of an autumn forest ablaze with fire, she stood bathed in a golden halo of radiance. As I turned my head back slowly, narrowing my eyes against the brilliance of this vision, emerald green eyes reached out and harnessed my heart as surely as two hands clasping around it and claiming it for their own. My chest tightened in response, as I floundered, hopelessly, hardly knowing if it were still day, or if night had descended as I stood, enraptured.

My throat closed up and I swallowed quickly, hoping to recover my former composure, still not understanding how a mere girl could have such a devastating effect on me. Things were happening inside my body that I had, for certain, never experienced before with this intensity and certainly not in such a public place.

"Tom, what's this?" I asked him, speaking quickly to cover my own embarrassment and hoping my voice remained steady. "Clandestine trysts in the stables? Surely you can do better than that? This lady is far too fair to be courted in a stable yard!"

The girl said nothing, keeping her brilliantine gaze fixed on mine. I longed for her to speak to me, wanting more than anything to hear her voice and know she was not some angelic vision and I a gibbering fool. Never could I recall ever having seen anyone who appeared so perfect in my eyes, not even the queen, who most men said was the most exquisite of women, a true beauty who had captured the heart of a king.

There was only one flaw. She appeared to have a cut on her bottom lip, which was slightly swollen. Yet even that only gave her pout even more allure. The wound made me stare at her mouth much more than was decent, I was sure. At my goading, Tom flushed even brighter and looked down at his boots, lowering his voice with his head.

"'Tis the duke my lady is here to meet, not I!"

Before any of us could react further, that very duke, the king's brother and my own good friend Richard, Duke of Gloucester, stepped out of the stables, cloaked and booted in readiness for a journey. To say I was startled was an understatement, for I had no idea how long he had been in there. Or if he had been hiding, or waiting. Yet just one look at his face gave me my answer.

His usually sombre expression was lit from within and with unexplained dismay, I saw a light kindle in his dark grey eyes as they too met those of our silent visitor. My own breath shortened even more at the sight of their wordless greeting and my head began to spin a little. They knew each other, that was for certain.

"Thank you, Tom," Richard said simply, folding his gloves in his hand slowly. "Get the horses would you?"

As Tom scurried away, visibly relieved it had to be said, at this command, Richard turned to me, but his eyes were still firmly fixed on the girl as if he was afraid she would disappear should he look away for one moment.

"Francis, this is Lady Caitlin Desmond, a lady-in-waiting to the queen. She hails from Ireland and is lately come here at the king's request."

Desmond! The name brought me up sharp as if I had been doused in freezing water. He must have seen me start as his eyes finally met mine, albeit briefly, before looking back at his prize, a shy smile curving his usually serious mouth.

I regarded her then with a mixture of comprehension and fascination. Everyone at court knew the story of Thomas Fitzpatrick, the Earl of Desmond, and the king's one-time close friend. Accused of treason, of seeking to make himself a King of Ireland some said, he had been executed on the orders of the Lord High Constable, John Tiptoft, the Earl of Worcester. Not only that, but two of his young children had also been murdered at the same time.

Yet the true facts around such a shameful crime still remained frustratingly unclear. As if lips that knew the truth were too ashamed to make the words real. Many whispered that there was, in fact, no treason. That the Earl of Desmond met his fate because he incurred the wrath of King Edward's queen, Elizabeth. For certain, the order that led to his death seemed to have been given when the king was not at court and the gossip ran that when he found out what had happened to his friend, he was incandescent with rage.

Now, the daughter of that unfortunate earl stood before me, regarding my friend with a lambent gaze. It was the loss of a father at an early age that Richard and I had in common and it struck me then that he may also have sought, and found, the same solace in this winsome girl.

"My lady," I inclined my head in greeting, finally finding my voice. "'Tis a real pleasure and an honour to meet you. I will

17

leave you in the duke's hands as I need to get Lark back to the mews." I felt my tongue almost tripping over my teeth and with my stomach churning nervously as I spoke to her, I was worried I may garble or appear dim witted if I spoke too much. I nodded my head in tacit acknowledgement to Richard, who was still smiling fondly at the girl and almost forgotten that I was there. "Dickon."

Sure that I had outstayed my welcome, I turned away and headed towards the mews.

"By Jesu, Lark!" I whispered under my breath as soon as I was sure I was out of earshot, talking to my bird as if she understood every word. "Now there is a sight to truly make my heart soar as high you do!"

Before turning the corner, I looked back for a moment, wishing more than anything that I had heard her speak fair words. That I had heard those sweet lips speak my name. Tom had now appeared with Richard's chestnut bay and a smaller palfrey, silver-grey, which I knew to be Richard's true favourite colour for a steed. Tom danced away again, his duty done, winking in my direction mischievously, but I still found it hard to tear my eyes away from Richard and the girl.

They stood very close together, and at one point he reached up and touched her cheek, a simple gesture which made me feel unaccountably uncomfortable to witness. Then I realised why and my face flushed, heat radiating upwards like the noon-day sun and I headed off to the mews quickly, my mind full of what I had just seen.

We had trained together, learned scripture, struggled with the courtly etiquette that was required of those destined to knighthood and suffered a range of humiliations and triumphs which had solidified the close bond between us. Now he had a lover and I wondered if that would change anything between us.

Particularly knowing that if I had but seen her first, I would have done anything to make her mine.

2. WESTMINSTER PALACE
June 1468

I returned Lark to her perch in the mews, still unable to shake off the vision of the girl who had just ridden away with Richard, her eyes dancing in the recesses of my mind like fireflies. Although I knew him to be my true friend, and that I should be mindful of how fortunate a position that privilege afforded me, it did little to prevent a sharp stab of jealousy, immediately followed by the bitter taste of guilt.

Richard had always bested me at the quintain and the butts, and we were matched in swordplay, but never had I grudged him his skill, for I witnessed how hard he worked to perfect each craft. Oft times he left me sweating, short of breath and crumpled on my knees in the dust, longing for the respite of a cleansing bath and hot supper.

Yet, it was not unusual for him to challenge me to just one more bout, or one last charge, his restless energy pushing him further than many of the henchmen who also served out their time at Middleham. Even when roundly beaten, never was there a ghost of bad feeling between us, no matter how sore and tired I became. But today, for the first time, some evil spirit stirred within me, filling my mind with envious, uncharitable thoughts and whilst I hated myself for them, there was nothing I could do about it. The more I tried, the less I could do to stop myself from feeling so utterly wretched.

Still giving myself a good talking to under my breath, I settled Lark down on her perch, only to catch the pitying gaze of the Master of the Mews out of the corner of my eye as he attended diligently to King Edward's splendid gerfalcon. It was obvious he was another who considered flying Lark to be a waste of time, and at heart I knew this to be true, but still could not bring myself to give up on her just yet. Patience, I told myself each time she stepped onto my leather gauntlet with dainty, yet sharply clawed, yellow feet, even knowing it to be all but fruitless.

Leaving her to rest in the mews, I stepped out through the door, squinting up at the sky which was now clearing to a brilliant blue, washing the courtyard with so much light that I almost didn't see Tom waiting for me outside. He pushed himself from the wall, throwing down the stalk of hay he had been chewing on as he waited, crushing it beneath the heel of his boot.

"Did you know the earl was back?"

His question was almost casual and I answered with a shake of my head. The earl had not stayed long in the city after our arrival and I had no idea where he had been since then, although that in itself was nothing to remark upon. A man of his status had business all over the realm, but the knowledge that he had returned served only to darken my mood further.

"I had better go then," I sighed heavily, looking over towards where the royal apartments towered over the inner ward. Many times did I have to act as either cupbearer or page to the earl and I would find myself severely chastened if he looked for me and found me missing. The mere fact that I did not even know he was back would be no excuse should I be found wanting in my duties. Tom was nodding in agreement, almost sagely, his eyes still on the ground.

"He's with Clarence. They looked on some determined business. The king's brother was as sour as I have ever seen him."

That revelation made my heart plummet even more. This was just not turning out to be the best of days and there were many hours yet before Compline. George, Duke of Clarence, was the middle brother between the king himself and Richard. Endowed with King Edward's golden brilliance, yet none of his charm or shrewdness, he was a somewhat shallow fellow, I found. Not at all like Richard. And much the worse for lacking his qualities.

George smiled constantly, which instantly made me mistrust him, whereas my friend was rare to flash a grin. Tom laughed loudly as he looked up and caught the expression on my face.

"He's a pain in the arse and that's the truth! Struts about like he's the king himself. I don't know how they put up with him. The man's a prig and a bore!"

I looked around quickly, hoping there was no one close enough to hear Tom's careless words, no matter how truthful they may be and I thumped him on the arm, ignoring his scowl at the gesture.

"Hush, man! Watch what you say! As it stands, His Grace is the king's heir and powerful enough to have you clapped in the stocks outside the city walls!" He looked suitably sheepish at my admonishment which I had given only to protect him and I flashed a rueful smile. "I have to go." Tom shrugged casually and looked over to the gate, hitching up his belt with purpose.

"Sooner you than me." He knew just how fortunate he was to serve the king's youngest brother and not any one amongst the coterie of nobles who swam around the court. Ignoring his sly grin, I walked away, only to turn at his next words, which hit me like a hurled rock. "She's pretty though, is she not?"

My heart stopped along with my feet and I looked back over my shoulder. The sun was high in the sky, burning down on the top of my head, as if my very hair were aflame. Like hers. I knew of whom he spoke, but asked anyway, as innocently as I could.

"Who?"

"The lady Desmond! My lord's lady."

His cheeks flamed on the words. It seemed he too could not bring himself to frame the term "mistress." Yet we knew all too well from what we had seen that Richard had already bedded his Irish angel.

"Yes, very pretty," I agreed, as pleasantly as I could under the circumstances, before striding off to attend to the earl, pretending it didn't matter at all, hoping that if my head told my heart that enough times, it would make it true.

3. WESTMINSTER PALACE
June 1468

As the day wore on to its inevitable end, I found myself in the very last place on earth I wanted to be, back in the stable-yard pacing backwards and forwards, waiting for Richard to return from wherever he had wandered that morning.

My anticipated attendance on lord Warwick had not been required in the end. After making haste to the king's privy chamber, being advised on the way by a helpful page who had seen the earl and the duke head off that way, I had been met only by a closed chamber door through which raised voices could easily be heard. Mostly for their resonant timbre, but occasionally the odd, angry word also escaped through the ancient oak.

Two of those very words made my blood run as brackish as the River Cover in spring. Rebellion and betrayal. There were more mumbled words, harder to hear, but which certainly touched on a French alliance and that was when the air was rent in two by a bellow so loud, I knew it could only have come from the throat of the king.

"Treason!"

With that, the door had been wrenched open with some force and George had burst from the room, his face suffused with anger, both hands clenched into bloodless fists at his side. If I had not managed to step back quickly, the sheer impetus of his exit would have knocked me down to the floor as he stalked away, indignance fuelling his every step. He left a stunned silence in his wake and without really thinking what I was doing, I had peered into the chamber, only to find myself connecting directly with the fiercely blazing eyes of the king himself. That unexpected encounter had led me to my current task, waiting for his younger brother to return from his lover's tryst, knowing for a certainty that I would once again be forced to look into a siren's gaze which had dogged my path since earlier that morning.

As I waited by the stables, my agony was only to be

prolonged and I suffered both enquiring stares and complete disinterest from the merchants, men-at-arms and courtiers who crossed the courtyard as my vigil continued. I caught a brief glimpse of Clarence through one of the archways, talking heatedly to Sir William Hastings, one of the king's most steadfast friends.

George was as animated as ever and for as long as I had him within my sights, his lips did not cease moving, his manner almost affectedly earnest as he talked and talked, waving a hand in the air occasionally to illustrate a point. Hastings, tall, dark-haired, still retaining the agile build of a soldier, even if just beginning to thicken with age. The elder statesman had his head bowed, giving every impression of listening intently, although his eyes were scanning the scene around him, ever alert. The collar of his Chamberlain's office glinted harshly in the sun, nestling in comfort against the thick sable trim of his dun velvet robe.

Whether it was my sheer boredom or some random flight of fancy, he fascinated me. The king's friend. A man who had fought at his side and been well rewarded with estates and the highest office in the land. He was Lord High Chamberlain. No one gained access to King Edward without the express permission of this man. I wondered idly what it felt like to wield such power. What secrets he knew, what decisions he was privy to. What quality he possessed that made Edward trust him, above all men.

As they passed out of sight, I remembered something else. Hastings was married to Warwick's sister, Katherine. I wondered what George's business with the king's chamberlain could have been, particularly that which had been conducted in plain sight. Even as little as I knew, it was for sure that George never made a single step without a purpose. So what was his design in courting Warwick's brother-in-law?

So distracted was I by these thoughts that Richard and his lady were almost upon me before I realised they had even ridden through the gate. One thing was for certain, I did not need to be told anything to know that the invisible bond between them had drawn even tighter, like a knot in a fine piece of silk. It was written all over their faces.

Richard frowned when he spied me waiting, the brief joy I had glimpsed on his face, disappearing in an instant. Guarding his expression as always, he slid from his mount with ease, tossing the reins over to Tom, who had appeared from nowhere, his ability to hide in plain sight becoming somewhat alarming. I wondered how long he had been hunkered in the stables, watching my discomfort, and enjoying it.

"Is this a welcome or something more sinister?" Richard threw the words over his shoulder as

by now, he had reached up to aid his companion and she was slipping down from her saddle in a rustle of silk, her small, gloveless hands white on his shoulders, the contact almost intimate in its closeness.

As I stepped up, she turned around to face me and for a second I feared that the heat in her gaze would dry the words at the back of my throat, leaving me dumb. She was looking at me more directly than she had done before and the interest in her gaze caused my throat to close like a gate at curfew. Her lips were parted, tenderly pink and moist, as if she was about to speak, but she did not, for which I was at that moment most thankful. I swallowed hard, wishing I had a drink handy to moisten my tongue and help me talk rather than stand gawping as I was beginning to fear I would.

Somehow, it worked and I looked at Richard directly, still aware of her attention, like a flame against my skin.

"The king is looking for you. He's in a foul mood, I warn you now. George and Warwick are back with news of a rebellion in the north."

"Rebellion?" Richard's answer was swift and terse. I saw him bite the inside of his bottom lip almost nervously.

"The king's apoplectic," I answered with a nod, remembering Edward's face as he had yelled at me across the chamber, asking where his "loyal" brother was. "Coming so close after the conspiracy in Kent. You had better get over there."

Richard said nothing for a moment, but directed his attention to his hands, stripping off his gloves quickly before uttering a simple response.

"I see," he answered quietly, before raising his eyes to look at the girl by his side. Not a word did he speak to her but she inclined her head, and for the first time I heard her voice.

"Your Grace." Taking her leave without being prompted, she inclined her head. The flaming braid of her hair cradled her neck and she spun away, walking quickly towards the royal apartments, showing an incredibly mature understanding of the situation. We both watched her leave, enveloped in her dark green cloak which billowed gently in the breeze, the soft lift of those two words still caressing my ears. I inhaled deeply, feeling better able to breathe now that she had departed.

"Where did you find her?" I tried to keep my voice casual, echoing the light, easy friendship that we had developed so long ago and was rewarded with a wry grin.

"In the service of the queen. For the moment."

He was still watching her, his grey eyes speculative as I gave a low whistle, a totally natural reaction to the situation, bearing in mind her lineage.

"Well, they won't be easy bedfellows. I take it she knows..." I stopped abruptly as I saw him shake his head, once again looking down at his gloves now that she was out of sight.

"No. She knows nothing of it. Edward brought her here for no other reason than he could. He placed her in the queen's household. Jesu knows what he was thinking!"

I was shaking my head too now, more in amazement at Edward's folly than anything else. So, not only did the poor girl not know how her father had met his fate, she had no idea that she was also at the whim of the woman who many blamed for his death. Well, those who were brave enough to express an opinion, mostly whispered, mostly outside of these walls.

Tom had led the horses away now and we fell into step alongside each other, matching our strides, heading in the direction of Edward's privy apartments. I was still mulling over this recent revelation.

"I can't imagine the queen was particularly pleased to have the girl foisted upon her. She dispatches one Desmond only to find another appearing in his place. Poor girl!"

Before this, I had been so taken aback by her sheer beauty, that I had hardly given a thought to the circumstance that found her here. She was the daughter of one of the queen's bitterest enemies. Of the man who had come the closest to causing a fatal rip in the passionate bond which saw Edward spurn the advice of his loyal advisers and marry a Lancastrian widow. One had to wonder how the girl spent her days within the queen's inner circle. That was just as much a mystery to me as the lady was herself.

Richard gave a grim grunt of assent as we reached the staircase.

"Well, not for much longer if I have my way."

There was a dark determination in his tone which I had heard many times before, usually when he had set his mind to a particular course of action. Before I could ask him what he meant, he cocked his head my way and gave me a direct look. "I may have a job for you in a day or two."

His expression was as enigmatic as his words and so I just shrugged in acceptance. I didn't mind doing anything to help him, in fact it was an honour to know I had his trust. There was only one thing I would really struggle with, and he knew it.

"At your service Dickon, as ever. As long as it doesn't involve anything to do with those infernal hounds of yours."

With a curt laugh, he slapped me on the back heartily as we reached the top of the stairs, turning into the passage which lead to the royal apartments.

"Frank, you really should change your cognizance!"

I laughed too then. It was an old joke. I had chosen lupellus, a wolf-dog, as my badge. Taken from my family's crest even though I had no real affection for dogs, I just thought the animal looked both noble and fierce. It was to the eternal amusement of my friends that Richard's hounds took absolutely no notice of my complete indifference to them and followed me everywhere when their master was not around. It was if they thought I had food scraps secreted in my clothing.

Sometimes annoyed, I was, secretly, mostly flattered. Surely it was a sign that they acknowledged me as one of Richard's closest friends, and therefore a member of their loyal and obedient pack. It gave me a sense of belonging that I had very rarely felt at any time in my life until I reached Middleham, four years ago.

4. WESTMINSTER PALACE
June 1468

It is the privilege of those who are chosen to serve royal princes that they gain access to the most powerful people in the country and often see things that others can only ponder on. Although my own lineage was far from common, the death of my father propelled me into the very inner circle of the Yorkist court. It was a consequence of that unfortunate tragedy which had ensured that King Edward had not only seen fit to charge me with finding his youngest brother and bringing him hence, but also meant he batted not an eyelid as I entered the room with Richard, my task completed.

Edward was lounging back in a chair, in fact, the term sprawled fitted better. His long, well muscled legs were spread out before him and he was seated at an angle, one elbow resting on the arm of the chair, fingers curled around a burnished gold goblet engraved with the York falcon and fetterlock. In front of him was a chess board, a few of the pieces lying on their side, as if tumbled from their place by the action of him kicking out when he slumped backwards.

He looked up as we entered, lifting the goblet to his lips, surveying us carefully over the rim. Richard stepped forwards whilst I kept my distance, remaining with my back to the door, understanding that Edward may still ask me to leave, especially if his mood had not improved. I thought it prudent to allow myself the opportunity to make a hasty exit should he want to talk to his brother alone.

Standing before the golden colossus that was our king, my friend made a stark comparison. Much more slender, darker haired, his hands long and fine boned. Edward had soldier's hands, large and capable; fingers just made to grasp the hilt of a sword. Yet I knew from experience that his brother's hands, although appearing more scholarly, were just as adept, even though the similarity stopped there. They were, in fact, different sides of the same, glittering York coin.

"Where have you been?" Edward growled, placing his goblet down in the middle of the chessboard, upsetting a black knight who rolled around noisily. "I had to endure the unexpected company of our cousin and brother alone. I would have welcomed your support."

I couldn't see Richard's face but I caught the slight bow of his head as he looked down, then up again.

"My apologies, Edward. Had I known you needed me I would have been here. As it was, I didn't even know George was back at court. If... "

"You didn't answer my question. Where were you?"

Edward gave him no time to answer and the accusatory tone in those words caused me to bite my lip. His unexpected visitors had obviously rattled him as his relationship with Richard was usually a markedly cordial and affectionate one, much closer than that enjoyed by the middle York brother, George. But then George was the most flamboyant member of the family, always striving to be the centre of attention, be it by word or appearance. He well knew that he was the heir to the throne, and he never tired of letting everyone else know it as well.

God help us, I reflected thoughtfully, watching Edward and Richard trade glances across the room, when the queen produces a son. George had already made his feelings about the queen's family crystal clear, and there had been some dangerously heated exchanges between him and her eldest son from her former marriage, Thomas Grey. If things carried on as they were, it promised to be a pot-boiler of a summer, which in itself would be entertaining in one way or another. Not the least for Rob Percy, one of our Middleham companions, who found such tensions endlessly amusing.

"Greenwich." Richard answered the question after a short pause. That revelation surprised me as much as it did Edward but I must have hidden it well as the king immediately pinned me to the door with a speculative gaze.

"And left your usual companion behind? So, what business south of the river was so pressing that you disappeared for half the day?"

Whatever it was that had been bothering Edward now seemed to be the least of his worries and his face creased into a knowing smile. If I knew Richard half as well as I believed I did, he would be most unhappy about being the subject of his brother's interest. Especially as that interest involved a girl. He was the most private and reserved person I knew, whereas any of the other henchmen in our small, select company would have been openly bragging about their conquest from the ramparts and giving it additional colour in the telling. Richard's response was assuredly calm and measured but then I often forgot he was well used to his brother's mercurial moods and he answered with studied patience.

"Edward, you sent for me. I am sure it was not to discuss how I spend my time. If you did, I can give you chapter and verse on everything I have done since I came down from Middleham. If that will help?"

There was a brief silence where Edward just looked at him, grinning, before he unfolded his massive frame, rising from his chair. In one smooth move he swept up his goblet, walking forwards towards his brother with casual ease.

"No, not every day, Dickon. Just today. What were you about today?"

I could see him standing before his brother, a good two heads taller, drinking slowly from his cup, the amusement in his eyes all too obvious. He was teasing Richard as he alone knew he could. There was one advantage to this in that he seemed to have completely forgotten his earlier anger – but whether that was a good thing or not it was hard to tell. I thought that sometimes George could do with someone putting him in his place and the best person to do that now seemed to have found a new distraction.

My discomfort increased markedly, even though I knew the king meant no harm and was only entertaining himself at this brother's expense. Richard didn't often blush. There was, it had to be said, very little for him to blush about, but to me it was completely obvious what had occurred down the river. It was written all over Caitlin Desmond's face. A look I was finding very hard to banish from my mind.

Richard began to shuffle his feet and I just knew, even though he still had his back to me, that he had begun to fidget with his finger rings, a somewhat distracting habit of his. I would not in a million years have wished to be under the intense scrutiny of the king's all-knowing eyes, and so I had no choice. I joined the fray.

"Your Grace?" I stepped forwards with a short nod, and Richard's head whirled round. His eyes latched onto mine, brimmed with warning, causing me to swallow before I continued, yet continue I did. "His Grace was helping me. I have a troublesome hawk and he kindly offered to try her out. The Master of the Mews commented that it may be the handler and not the hawk that was the problem and that despite all of my efforts, she had set her mind not to respond to me." I tried to look as shamefaced as I could, having no idea if my ploy would work, admitting to my inadequacies in the sport I loved so much. It was a blatant lie of course. I had blithely spoken an untruth to the king, but the words leapt out of my mouth before I could even judge the sense of them. God knows why I felt such a need to spare my friend's blushes, it was just an instinctive reflex that I had no control over and now I waited for the consequences, whatever they may be.

Edward peered over Richard's shoulder and barked a short laugh before wheeling away casually towards the sideboard. He refilled his cup with relish and turned to regard us, leaning back against the table. There was something about him which would naturally make all eyes gravitate in his direction, even had he not been king. It was a quality in him I envied, apart from his golden, good looks and an ingrained self assurance that was so natural, it was almost captivating. Self consciously, I reached up and rubbed at the cleft in my chin.

It was an odd thing, passed down from someone back in the annals of my earlier family and I had spent many a younger year trying to stretch it out, which only resulted in hours of my pulling ridiculous faces at a glass. Despite my efforts, it doggedly became more defined as I aged. My mother had remarked that my face would grow into it, but I had no idea what that meant.

"Nice try, Lovell," Edward grinned taking another deep drink of his wine. "A bit short of the mark maybe, but as I know your bird is female, I think we are not too far away from the truth!"

I shrugged then and Richard sighed, his expression softening as he turned back towards his brother. I had tried, and lied, but Edward had accepted it with good grace. Richard was his own worst enemy; he shouldn't let Edward get to him. He enjoyed it too damn much.

"Thank you Frank, but my brother knows full well why I was at Greenwich. It's the only place to get any peace or privacy – at least whilst the court is at Westminster." He paused and pulled his shoulders back, raising his chin defiantly. "Yes, Ned, I was with a girl. Now you can congratulate yourself on the accuracy of your finely honed senses, would you mind doing me the favour of telling me if you have acted on the other matter I asked of you?"

Edward smiled easily, his eyes dancing, more than pleased to have been proved right but, unfortunately for Richard, he still hadn't finished with him. He was having far too much fun and prodding his brother about matters he knew Richard would move heaven and earth to keep private, coupled with the fact that teasing his brother was providing a welcome distraction from his earlier troubles.

"Ah, the fair Lady Desmond! You're a spoilsport Dickon and no mistake! No sooner do I invite a wild beauty to grace my court, you have to get all righteous and demand that I send her away again!"

My ears pricked up immediately. Send her away? A strange feeling clutched at my innards. If I had a girl such as her staring at me the way she did Richard, the last thing I would be doing is sending her away!   It made no sense at all and I held my breath, waiting.

Richard walked over to the sideboard then and Edward watched him closely as he filled a goblet of wine for himself. Turning, he gestured to me but I declined. This was getting far too interesting and I fully intended to keep a clear head.

The two brothers stood side by side, the easy familiarity between them now very much in evidence, which caused another stab of envy. There was a lot that I envied my friend for it seemed.

"You didn't invite her here, you brought her here, Ned, there is a difference." He took a sip of his own wine, keeping his eyes on the contents. "She's unhappy. Desperately unhappy. You do realise she knows nothing of what happened to her father?"

Storm clouds passed over Edward's face and for a moment I shivered, but it was thankfully fleeting and the smile soon made a welcome reappearance, like the sun returning to the world.

"I am sure you are more than making up for that brother, although you have barely known the girl a week. I admire your skills as a courtier, I never knew you had it in you!" He drank deeply again. "Even if it does run in the blood."

"Ned… "Richard gave a heavily resigned sigh. "Please?"

The king's laugh barrelled around the chamber as he threw a conciliatory arm around his brother's shoulder.

"Fear not, Dickon! I have to say I admire your choice, even if the speed of your courtship took me by surprise, so perhaps I do have to thank Warwick for his efforts in your training, in more ways than one."

Richard and I both frowned at the same time, although it has to be said his was one of forbearance more than mine, but Edward waved his hand airily.

"No matter. I am about to repay him the favour. Your Lady

Desmond will join his household at Warwick as one of the Countess's ladies-in-waiting. No doubt this will at some jointure lead to her being ferried up to the god-forsaken north, but then that can only be to your advantage." Edward bowed to Richard with exaggerated ease before performing an easy saunter back to his chair, where he threw himself down with a loud sigh, his face a study in self-satisfaction. "Well? Do I hear a, "My heartfelt thanks, Your Grace?" in return?"

It was all I could do to smother a grin. Richard was taking all of this jocular discourse with amazingly good grace and as he lowered his chin down to his chest, I noticed his own smile of amusement. Not answering immediately, he took a slow sip of wine, making his brother wait. The easy camaraderie was something I had witnessed before and I admit, was another addition to my list of enviable traits. My family ties consisted of two sisters, Frideswide and Joan. And a bride. Richard was the closest I had ever come to knowing what it was like to have a brother.

For a moment, any pleasure I felt at watching the play of princes subsided, thoughts turning to my own predicament. My wife. A young girl half my age with hair like flax and innocent, sapphire blue eyes. Anna Fitzhugh was Warwick's niece, and as far as I saw it, just another way to connect his family to mine in a way which could not be easily undone once I reached an age where everything that was mine, truly became mine. And much there was. I was most probably the richest pauper at court.

"Only if you grant me one more favour." Richard's voice cut through my thoughts at a particularly timely moment, just as I was beginning to wonder how appealing a vast fortune may seem to the young, emerald-eyed daughter of a disgraced Irish lord.

"Another favour?" Edward chortled. "Have you not as yet thanked me for the last one? By God, Dickon, do you grow as acquisitive as George? For nothing I do for him seems to settle his restless nature?" Despite the humour there was a ring of steel to those last few words and Richard looked up quickly, alert to the change in tone, so subtle it could have almost gone unnoticed.

"Forgive me, brother, for I do thank you truly for attending so promptly to Lady Desmond's plight." He half turned then, placing his cup down on the sideboard. "Only this boon may be more to your liking. I would like to go to Warwick Castle myself – for a few days, no more." He paused in anticipation of an answer. Unable to see his face fully, all I knew was that the two brothers were speaking, in their gazes, words they had no cause for me to hear. The beaming smile returned to Edward's face as he raised his goblet in his brother's direction.

"What an excellent idea! Warwick himself is due to return there any day now, with his family I do believe. What better place for his ward to be when he arrives home?" He drank deeply before setting the wine down at his side. "And of course, you can then introduce Lady Desmond to the Countess... and her daughters."

That was when I covered myself in shame as I laughed out loud, only to be silenced by a look of steel from my closest friend as his head flew round in my direction once more. Everyone at Middleham knew that the earl's youngest daughter, Anne, had a soft spot for Richard. It was obvious. The way her eyes followed him in the hall, how she often appeared in the bailey at times when she should really have been with the ladies reading or sewing. The constant frowns of concern whenever Richard appeared with a graze or bruise following our more heated bouts of training in the yard. It was an unspoken acknowledgement, but all of us there saw it plain. How Anne Neville would take to the pearl-skinned beauty that was Caitlin Desmond turning up in her home was anyone's guess.

"My apologies, Dickon!" I offered shamefacedly, watching his lips form a familiar thin line of forbearance before he turned back to Edward who was now laughing uproariously. Whatever had caused his earlier bad mood, his younger brother had certainly lifted his spirits without even trying.

"I must admit it is to my surprise that you should turn out to attract as many fair ladies as myself." He followed this with a grudging shrug. "Well... almost. Yes, you may leave for Warwick Castle immediately. In fact, I insist, now that the value of the visit has been brought home to me. In fact, Lovell there can escort your fair lady to meet you there once arrangements have been made, for whilst we have been having this rather enjoyable conversation, the queen has been dismissing her erstwhile servant, who seemed to be most negligent in her duties this morning." He paused then, giving me a crafty wink which caused me to bite my lip again. "At least to the queen."

Richard raised his hands in defeated supplication while I struggled to suppress a grin.

"Enough Ned! You have had more than enough mirth at my expense today, but truly, I thank you for this." Once again he turned in my direction, but this time he was smiling too. "And as on so many things, we certainly agree on the escort. "

Edward stood suddenly, yawning, his arms stretched out wide making him appear even larger than he was.

"Indeed! A safe pair of hands Lovell has – except when beating me at chess! Now, I feel I may need to go and mollify my wife, having seen fit to disrupt the balance of her household. I always find a bit of light seduction can avoid a scold!" As Edward strode from the chamber with a languid gait, Richard was surveying me thoughtfully.

"A safe pair of hands. How very apt, Frank!"

However my hands felt, my heart was sinking. Safe? God's blood! If only he knew what I really thought every time Caitlin Desmond's face rose in my mind like a spectral angel, he'd be locking me in the Tower rather than sending me off to spend several days in her company. Yet I smiled back at him winningly. In truth, what else could I do?

5. WARWICK CASTLE
June 1468

How can I begin to explain the delicious torture that was now my lot, riding next to Lady Desmond as our small party made their way northwards through the forests towards Warwick? From the moment I met her in the courtyard, I felt like a lack-wit simpleton, gabbling on inanely no matter that those around them had long lost interest in anything they might say. She, on the other hand, regarded me distantly, not even a ghost of a smile making an appearance on her lips.

The day began badly when I appeared to upset her right from my very first words, which was as far from my intention as it could possibly have been. For some reason she had been expecting to travel just a few miles to the earl's London residence of Le Herber and I wondered if the queen had somehow led her to believe that she would not be leaving the city. I couldn't think why else she would have thought it.

Her crestfallen expression when I told her we were actually to travel much further, in fact leaving the city walls and indeed going to Warwick Castle, was extremely hard to witness. She had asked me how long a journey it was and had then fallen silent, seeming to lose herself in thought.

Standing next to her then, as the usually brilliant eyes dulled and pearly white teeth sank into her plump bottom lip, her sheer sorrow was almost my undoing. It took every ounce of of my self will to refrain from offering her comfort, by either touch or word, knowing it would be neither seemly or accepted. Instead I turned my attention to assisting her mount the waiting silver-grey palfrey, and attending to my own pale steed and begin our journey.

The first two days were the most difficult. She stared

straight ahead, hardly looking at me and seemingly far from inclined to make conversation. I remember trying to pass the time by pointing out all the different birds we saw along the route, with a mind to the fact that she was hardly well travelled. Although she looked at everything I drew to her attention, I could see it interested her not at all. By this time, I was so disturbed by her total solitude, I almost told her that the secret I had been sworn not to reveal. That Richard had gone ahead and she would indeed meet him at Warwick, hoping to see the life spark back into her empty gaze. But I had been expressly forbidden to speak a word of it, just in case plans had to be changed and Edward called him back to Westminster.

Her subdued mood finally began to melt about half way through our journey, much to my intense relief, as I was beginning to fear that once we had reached Warwick, she would never wish to be in my company again. It came about when I had completely exhausted my limited knowledge of flora or fauna, animals and insects and so, I began to talk of myself. If nothing else, I hoped it would pass away the next few hours. For when we rode in complete silence, I found it even harder to keep my mind from descending into dangerous waters where I sank deep, drowning in the depths of those remarkable eyes, wondering what it would feel like to press my lips onto hers, to feel her warm, sweet breath whisper my name.

Oh, I was more than aware how futile and stupid these thoughts were, but so addled was my head from spending such time in her company, that it began to wander down paths which I had never so much dreamed existed. So, it was to keep my sanity only that I began to talk of the death of my own father and how I came to meet the duke who was now my friend. And it was as easy as that. As I talked of my family, the death of my father and how I came to arrive at Middleham, she began to look at me, rather than at the road. Finally, she smiled, and began to ask me questions and was, in all things, exceedingly fair.

By the time we rode across the bridge and under the massive

gatehouse of the castle, I felt we had begun to form at least the bare beginnings of a real friendship. Her gold-fringed eyes regarded me with trust and thankfulness and I had to admit that I felt totally unworthy of her attentions. Yet, I also knew right then that I would never carry out any act that would cause her to look at me in dread. It was a silent pact I made with myself for if I could never hold that face in my hands and express my love, I would ensure that no sorrow ever filled those eyes on my part.

As her gaze alighted on Richard, who had somehow ensured he was the very first person she would see upon her arrival, I knew that any hopes I held for more than that were doomed to be thwarted. He turned away from Rob who stood at his side, and as he and Caitlin looked at each other, a desperate feeling of hopelessness gripped my gut. I had, I decided, better get used to it. There was a bond between them now that no man should have the right to break, and certainly not when one of them was my closest friend. It wasn't right, even if I was the type of man who would deliberately try to steal another man's possession, and even then, I didn't think I was.

She halted her palfrey in its tracks, completely taken aback by the sight of Richard standing there in the bailey. As he had planned, it was the very last place she had expected him to be. I wheeled Fides, my sturdy mount, around to face her and she looked back at me, wondrous eyes bright with tears.

In that once grateful glance, I almost – almost changed my mind, wondering if I really tried, could I wrest her from Richard's arms? But it lasted only for a fleeting second and I held up my hands in supplication, hoping she wasn't secretly cursing me for my duplicity.

"He swore me to silence! I was not to breathe a word in case he was called back to Westminster before we arrived." I flashed a quick glance over to Richard, who was talking to Percy again, although his eyes never left her face. "He was concerned for your welfare and safety on the journey." I had to grin then, remembering something Richard had said back in the city. "He wished you to travel in a safe pair of hands."

Richard touched Rob on the shoulder and, turning, began to walk towards us, his face wreathed in a smile. But, Caitlin was now looking at our other friend.

"Who is that?" her voice was almost a whisper.

I looked at Rob and he threw me a quick wink. I grinned, hoping she had not noticed.

"Oh, that's Rob," I said gaily. "Rob Percy. You'll like him."

Richard had reached us by then and my presence was no longer required. I gave a quick nod in his direction, but I may as well have been invisible as I directed Fides around and cantered over towards where Rob was standing, watching Richard with interest.

I slipped from the saddle with ease almost before Fides had halted, and threw my reins over to a waiting groom. Out of the corner of my eye I saw someone emerge from the entrance to the great hall to greet them, but then turned away. After so many hours in her company, the pain of watching her depart with another man, no matter that it was Richard, was too much to bear.

"Well, there's a turn up!" Rob was still watching them as I fiddled with my gloves, taking much longer to strip them from my fingers than the task warranted. If I strung it out long enough, by the time I looked up, they would be gone. True enough, as I turned to follow his gaze, there was only the grey palfrey, being led away towards the stables. "Who is she? I had no idea Dickon had..."

His words trailed off as he frowned, dark brows forming an arrow above clear blue eyes.

"I think the word you are looking for is Mistress." I paused then, wondering for a moment how much to tell him, before deciding there was no point in secrecy now. Richard's assignation here in broad daylight had put paid to that. He was hardly hiding her in the shadows after all. "And before your eyes fall out of your head, she's Lady Caitlin Desmond. Natural daughter of Tom

Desmond." I watched his eyes widen. "Yes, that Tom Desmond."

"Well, I'll be damned!"

"No doubt about that!" I remarked casually, looking up at the sky where the sun was beating down on us with unbelievable ferocity, bleeding the yard of colour. "But why are you so surprised? He's a royal duke. He can hardly consort with scullery-maids and tavern wenches. The lady has the noblest of Irish blood, and was a lady-in-waiting to the queen until recently."

Rob scratched his chin speculatively.

"I am more surprised that he's brought her here! Warwick will be back tomorrow, and with the girls. That's surely bound to be awkward."

I laughed then, as we stood there together in the heat, beginning to feel the need for a good drink.

"Anne, you mean? Well, we all know she's a bit sweet on him, yes, but... Rob?"

His expression had changed as I spoke, as if a realisation had dawned.

"Of course! You won't know! I am sure Dickon will tell you, once he has a free moment that is!" He grinned, before his face composed once more. "There was one hell of an argument apparently. Warwick approached the king again, pressing for him to reconsider the marriages for his daughters. Edward flatly refused. Outright. He told them he was even more set against it than he had been before. Apparently, George hinted that he would wed whom he damn well pleased, just as Edward had done. You can imagine how that went down!"

I shrugged diffidently. It wouldn't be the first time Edward had shunned Warwick's marriage plans. After all, hadn't that been the biggest scandal of court a few years back? The earl had worked diligently to negotiate a brilliant foreign marriage for the king, which came with a cast-iron French alliance. Unfortunately, Edward had other plans and had announced, in front of a full council at Reading, that he had secretly married already. Not only that, but his bride was older than him, a widow and a Lancastrian.

I was surprised Warwick hadn't died of apoplexy on the spot! I patted Fides on his strong, muscular neck as the stable lad walked him away.

"The earl should take care. The king seems different these days, not so easy going as he used to be from what I gather. But then, he should also not snub my lord of Warwick. After all, without his help he may not even have gained the crown."

Rob snorted his contempt loudly.

"It's gone way past that! If you thought dispensing with the Savoy marriage was a punch in the gut, refusing to let his brothers marry the Warwick sisters is more like a dagger in the back to the earl. There was quite a heated exchange. Warwick accused Edward of promoting the interests of Woodville commoners above those of the nobility. After all, how else are his daughter's to become duchesses? Can you see the earl settling for anything less?"

The sun went behind a cloud and the air cooled. For a few seconds, it was almost cold. I couldn't believe such a change could happen so quickly but my thoughts had drifted back to that afternoon at Westminster when George had stormed out of Edward's chamber in high dudgeon.

Anne and Isabel. I tried to swallow but somehow my throat felt swollen, thinking of the two young faces I knew so well. One of them particularly well. Rob was nodding, looking up at the castle windows.

"Warwick has taken it very badly, by all accounts. After all, marriages are a touchy subject with him. Anyone would think Edward was doing it deliberately."

Rob was right. Not only had Edward spurned the French marriage Warwick had arranged, he had also married one of the queen's young brothers to Warwick's aged aunt, the Duchess of Norfolk. Now, he was refusing to grant his daughters the boon of a good match, which was only to be expected by the quality of their birth. It had not crossed my mind before, after all, I hardly paid heed to my own marriage so tended not to dwell on the matches of others. I too looked at the upper windows then, sighing.

Somewhere, behind one of them, Caitlin Desmond walked, settling in to her new home. Tomorrow the rest of the household would arrive. It wasn't Warwick's reaction I was thinking of then; it was Anne Neville's.

6. WARWICK CASTLE
June 1468

I did not rest well at all that night. Rob and I had spent the afternoon in the tiltyard with the Harington boys, and all three of them had bested me at the butts, much to their enjoyment. Rob had quipped that I had best find myself a woman to assist in the sharpening up of my shooting skills and James Harington nearly fell over laughing.

It was a common jest, to compare our burgeoning skills on the field with those of the bedchamber, not that many of us had much experience in that area. Well, apart from Rob, it had to be said, him being a few years our elder. Something he rarely let us forget. He had spent the better part of the previous year at Middleham trying to encourage me to "earn my spurs" with an accommodating tavern wench of his acquaintance. How I sorely regretted then letting it slip that I had not as yet bedded a girl. He never let it alone from that moment on and whilst once it had been quite amusing, the constant reference to my education in the ways of the flesh was beginning to rankle.

To be honest, until recently, I had not really given much thought to it, not since the circumstances of my marriage, which had been more of an embarrassment than an event. The girl was barely six years old but I had seen the sly winks and nudges as we walked from the chapel hand in hand. I remembered her small, cool hand in mine, a veil of golden hair streaming over her shoulders, periwinkle eyes glancing up at me shyly once or twice during the banquet that followed. It had been a grand affair. Even the king had attended, but that did nothing to salve the burning resentment which I had begun to feel taking hold of me.

My sister Joan had tears in her eyes, although to this day I was unsure as to why. It was a strange thing to find your allegiances change overnight and all of us had been somewhat surprised at the speed in which we became entrenched in Yorkist policy. Even though I was relieved that my new bride was too young to take to the marital bed, therefore sparing me the shame of the usual wedding rituals, I still found the whole day awkward and disturbing.

Since then, whenever I saw a pretty face, any feelings I had were instantly washed away by guilt at the thought of Anna, my bride. It did not take me long to understand that guilt and passion were unhappy bedfellows. It was a struggle that was to haunt me through all of my early days at Middleham. As an orphaned Lancastrian dumped into the middle of a Yorkist household, waking each day had been a fight of its own, never mind the trials of the tiltyard. That had all changed once Richard made it clear that I had, remarkably, found favour with him. From that day, I attached myself to his cause with a fierce determination, which had not faltered once, until I looked into the eyes of Caitlin Desmond.

These thoughts ran through my mind the next morning as we assembled in the bailey waiting for the earl to return. It was warm, almost unpleasantly so, which was adding to the dull throb that threatened to split my head into two like a cleaved apple. Even the ale taken as I broke my fast had failed to help and the rye bread had stuck in my throat where it still seemed lodged like a river rock.

Richard had not supped in the hall last night and neither had Caitlin. Their very absence had brought into my head visions I did not particularly want there and so I did the only sensible thing. And of course, my Tantalus was always there to keep my cup filled to the very brim. Yet as Rob poured more and more ale, his own hand remaining infuriatingly steady no matter how much he himself downed, all it did was increase my dolour. Not a single imagined image was dulled, in fact, only sharpened.

Her eyes haunted me, glowing in my mind like fireflies. Her

hair bound me against her in a skein of flaming cord, yet even that pain was delicious. Her mother-of-pearl skin cried out for my touch and I longed to trace a finger down her throat, across her chest and down into the mysterious hidden shadowlands that lay beneath her gown. It was a torture of my own making and all Rob did was grin, thankfully believing my mood to be a result of my shameful performance that afternoon.

He had not guessed that the cause for both my predicaments was the same and I was glad of it. The desires I had would remain my closely guarded secret. I had no intention of ever letting Rob, Tom or, God forbid, Richard, ever suspect how I felt. Quite how I meant to achieve that was a different matter. I just knew it was a fight I had to win, and in time, praise God, the pain would ease.

So my head pounded like a tabor and the sun threatened to break through the hovering clouds as we waited around somewhat restlessly. A sharp nudge almost cracked my ribs caused me to scowl as Rob leaned toward me.

"I hear it's tilt yard practice again later this afternoon! Can you take a second beating in two days, I wonder? By the looks of you - I think even one of the pot boys could best you today!"

My lips formed a sharp retort that was never to see life as Richard appeared at the entrance to the great hall. He glanced over quickly to where we stood but it was not my friend who kept my attention, not for more than a breath. Behind him, accompanied by Miriam, one of the more statuesque ladies-in-waiting, was Caitlin, and the world began to wheel!

It was not so much that her dress of shiny, grey silk, give the impression of an angel clad in silver plate - it was her face. Lord have mercy! My throat dried and I feared I would never again have enough spit to speak. That I should ever live to see that look on the face of a woman whom I had recently bedded.

If I had lived to be five score and ten, I would not have the words to describe what I saw, only that she was lit from within. Burning with a flame that imbued her with as much radiance as the sun itself and I prayed that she would not look at me for fear it would be my undoing, but she did.

"Holy Christ!"

At first I thought I had spoken aloud and my face burned hotly, then I realised that the oath of appreciation had in fact escaped from Rob's lips.

"Is that not a vision to soothe the very soul?"

Richard began to make his way towards us, walking with a determined stride and if I wanted to be whimsical, I could say a certain liveliness to his step.

"Lady Desmond?" I asked quietly, ignoring the stab of jealousy that pricked me at his words.

"Well, I was thinking more Lady Shaftesbury, but now you come to mention it...!"

A flood of relief, mingled with despair, flooded my gut as it sunk in that he had been talking about Miriam, who now stood protectively at Caitlin's side. Rob was assessing her with a speculative appreciation that began to worry me. He had an ease and charm that I could never hope to possess, and the brazenness of Satan to go with it. Thankfully he had no time to say more as Richard halted before us, his manner as serious as ever.

"You two look as if you are up to no good." His eyes then flicked towards me, his mouth quirking in a sardonic grin. "Although, I have to say Frank, I have seen you look better. Are you ailing?"

These words were greeted with a snort by Rob.

"Only in his aim. I keep telling him Dickon, he needs to find a way to relax. It's no good if the archer is more tightly sprung than his bowstring, if you get my meaning!"

As I threw him a contemptuous glance, causing only more hilarity, Richard looked down at his feet, his own colour rising slightly, before regarding me with amusement from beneath his lowered brow.

"Well then Rob, you should be a true marksman by now. Remind me of that fact, will you, should we ever end up in a real conflict." He paused, and looked towards the gatehouse. "Which could be sooner than we think."

I took the break in our discourse to glance over at Caitlin just as she moved her gaze from Richard to myself and I offered her the smallest of smiles. Any further conversation was halted as the earl's party began to clatter over the bridge, riding into the bailey rising dust and noise with their passing. The earl rode his magnificent steed as proudly as ever but there was another with him who bested him in his efforts to portray himself as a prince of noble blood. And that was an actual prince of noble blood. Clarence rode with him, every inch a royal duke, in manner and in appearance.

I saw rather than heard Richard's sigh, but what I did catch was the desperate look thrown over to him by Caitlin. Fear filled her usually lambent eyes and something in my chest began to tighten. Why on earth would she be frightened by the arrival of the earl? She had been sent here to serve his family, certainly, but during our travels she had expressed no worry at all over being bound to the Neville household. As I watched with heightened interest, she turned her head back towards the party who were now disembarking and then it made sense. Of sorts. It wasn't the earl causing her concern. It was George. a realisation which was confirmed by a whispered curse which drifted over Richard's shoulder.

"Jesu!"

Without looking backwards, he retraced his steps towards the hall, much more slowly than he had on his first passing of the same path.

"Dickon!" the earl bellowed loudly as he drew closer to them. "There is news from court! A rider caught us just south of Warwick!" His words rang around the bailey like a noon-day bell. No one could have failed to hear a word, and some inner demon told me that this was exactly what he had intended.

"Good news I hope?"

Richard's words were quieter, and he came to a standstill, inclining his head in greeting to his brother. "George. An

48

unexpected pleasure." I didn't catch any other exchange between them, but in any event their greeting was cut short by the earl who seemed greatly at pains to let us all know his news.

"Depends on your outlook," drawled the earl, removing a parchment from his belt and waving it dismissively in his gloved hand. "The queen has miscarried. The succession is still not secure. It seems she could bear sons for the Lancastrian traitor, but not for the king."

I heard the whistle of Rob's breath between his teeth as he stood beside me. As if a spell had been cast, not a soul in the bailey was moving, every last one of us attentive to the earl's arrival and in some shock at the pleasure in his voice which sat decidedly at odds with the gravity of his announcement.

"As yet," Richard answered, quietly but just as loud in the deafening silence that surrounded us and I held my breath. The expected riposte did not appear and the earl disappeared into the hall, followed by the countess, Isabel and Anne, who I saw only briefly as they moved in his wake.

After the earl's departure from the bailey, the activity around us began to return to normal and it became impossible to hear what was being said between them, but the whole scenario made me feel uneasy both for Richard and for Caitlin. Whatever was going on it was affecting her markedly and even if I had been chained to the ground, it could not have stopped me moving over to join the tense little group.

As I reached her side, I saw Miriam's hand tighten on Caitlin's arm. Richard's back was rigid, and I could almost imagine him reaching for the dagger at his belt in answer to whatever slur George had flung at him. George was grinning languidly, his eyes passing between Richard and Caitlin and then back again. The man was insufferable. Not that I had known him long, just long enough to work that much out for myself. There was only one way I could think of to prevent the two of them going for each other's throats in view of half of the castle servants. There needed to be a distraction, of sorts.

Taking a deep breath, I leaned closer to Caitlin, trying not to lose my head in the sweetness of her fragrance. Placing my mouth as close to her ear as I dare, I whispered three words.

"Go to him."

It was her response to my prompt that endeared her to me even more and gave me just a brief glimpse into a heart that was braver than mine, and as full of love for Richard as mine was for her. Without a moments hesitation, she removed Miriam's restraining hand gently and stepped forwards, bestowing on me a look that almost took me down to my knees in awe. I watched as she took her place by Richard's side, appearing every inch their match, any anxiety she felt only visible in the tautness of her hands which held onto the skirts of her gown as she sank into a small curtsey

"Your Grace."

The emphasis she put on that simple greeting was almost devastating and it took every inch of will I had not to grin. George, however, continued to smile. A hard smile that didn't reach his eyes.

"Lady Caitlin, how good it is to see you again! I must say, you look exceedingly charming today and your beauty seems to have increased with the passing of the seasons. But yet, there is something about you." He paused, for effect and I began to get very uneasy over the way he was talking. "What say you, Dickon? Don't you feel that Lady Caitlin seems to have blossomed? Unfolded, like a summer rose, where before there was only a tightly furled bud? Just as beauteous, nonetheless, but with promise of a greater flowering to come. Either it is the clement Warwickshire air or…. I would swear…"

"Bastard!" The muttered curse gained me a shocked gasp from Miriam but I was beyond caring. Their backs to me, I could only guess how they were reacting to this public outing of their relationship, and knowing Richard as I did, I knew he would take it hard. He guarded his privacy jealously, and all of us who shared his trust knew it well. It was a trust we gambled with at our peril.

George laughed harshly, the sound grating in my ears and making me want to punch him, hard. My fists even clenched of their own accord.

"Fear not, little brother! Your secret is safe with me! How could I bear to see young Anne's face should she discover that you have managed to place your mistress into her very own household? You are either exceedingly clever, or particularly cruel, I must say! I didn't realise you had it in you! I admit, I did begin to wonder, when I discovered that Edward had so suddenly removed a particular thorn from the queen's side. I remember remarking to our cousin, there was only one person at court who would be able to achieve such a feat." It was then that the forced geniality disappeared as his eyes narrowed, fixing his brother with an almost hostile glare. "It seems there is nothing you ask for that he will not grant you. Maybe you yourself should have asked for Anne's hand in marriage and not left it to our cousin."

Richard's retort was calm. Deathly calm.

"At least one of us sought to remove the lady from her unfortunate situation rather than try to take advantage of it." Once again I began to feel that there was something I had missed. Why was George so at pains to vent his ire on Richard? Was it Caitlin? And if so, why? I strained my ears even further, desperate to understand the play that was unfolding before me.

"Poor Dickon! You really don't have much experience in the way women use their feminine wiles do you? The lady waited for a brave knight on a white steed to rescue her, like in the old chivalric tales of Arthur! How fortunate that she found you, such a willing sap, to fulfil her hearts desire."

On those words, he stepped through the doorway and left them both standing together in silence. Caitlin looked at Richard, but his head was slightly bowed, and my heart went out to her. Even though I had no real understanding of what had just taken place, I crossed the few paces between us, trying not to notice Caitlin's flushed face and anxious eyes.

"Trouble, I assume?" Trying to lighten the mood, I peered

51

through the door into the shadows. "Wherever George goes, there has to be something amiss. What is it now?"

Richard shook his head, biting his bottom lip as Caitlin stood looking at him in silence. There was a silent plea in her eyes that he just didn't see. Almost as if he was deliberately trying to avoid it.

"It's nothing, Frank. Just trying to bait me as usual. You would never believe how close we used to be. I don't know him of late. He seems more..." Richard looked at me then, lost for words. Or preferring not to speak them.

"Royal?" I asked innocently, yet meaning every word of it. It was an old jest, one a few of us had shared over the table in the hall at Middleham. George was the king's heir, until the queen gave birth to a son. It was something none of us were allowed to forget. Not the grey walls and sodden tiltyards of Middleham, no, not for George. He glittered away at court, basking in the approval of his mother and the reverence of the household.

"He's not all bad," Richard admitted, very generously I thought. "Arrogant, I give you that, yes..." He seemed reluctant to say more and so I changed the subject "

"'Tis sad news, about the queen." I dared to look at Caitlin for the first time at close quarters and she glanced back at Richard, fussing with the sleeves of her gown as she spoke.

"The last time I met with her, she seemed to be unwell," she said somewhat hesitantly, and it was all I could do not to get lost in her eyes. " I remember, it was a very hot day and she appeared to be ailing."

Richard looked at her fully now and finally smiled, although I could tell his thoughts were elsewhere.

"Warwick seemed.... unmoved." I ventured quietly. Richard looked down at the ground, kicking away at it with his boot, sighing as he raised his head up, empty-eyed.

"I think he still lives in hope that Edward will see sense, especially if he does not have a son before too much longer. He still harbours ambition in France." He looked directly at me then, as if he had been reading my mind. A talent he seemed to have where I was concerned. "And of course, George is still his heir."

Any further discourse was cut short as Miriam appeared beside Caitlin, her expression full of anxiety.

"Your Grace, we should go inside. Lady Caitlin should be introduced to the countess without delay."

"Of course," Richard agreed instantly, flashing her a smile. "Would you take Lady Desmond into the hall? I have some business to attend to before I join the earl."

He gave the barest of nods towards Caitlin and even I had to admit to being more than a little taken aback at his sudden coolness. Almost an eagerness to depart. I saw disappointment, and not a little hurt, bloom in her eyes as he turned away from her, encouraging me to fall into step beside him.

We walked away, and I was consciously aware of her watching us leave. Richard leaned his head towards mine.

"I know you have had hardly a moment to pause for breath, but can you have everyone ready to leave for Westminster after breakfast tomorrow?"

I couldn't help but stop dead at these words. No sooner had Caitlin arrived and he was going to leave her already? It was also obvious that there was some tension between the girl and George. Yet Richard was seemingly about to abandon her to his dubious intentions. His arm came around my shoulder then, firmly reassuring.

"Yes, I know. Believe me if I could I would leave you here to keep an eye on him, but Edward wants me back. He seems unusually restless presently. There is something on his mind that he appears to be unwilling to share, as yet."

I pondered on this for a few moments as we walked on. Edward had been very keen for Richard to come to Warwick, so what had changed? What had been the purpose of such a brief visit?

I turned my head to look at Richard's profile, which to be fair, didn't give much away. If he was distressed at having to leave

Caitlin behind, it was hidden behind other, more pressing concerns. I envied him the ability to be able to so completely separate different aspects of his life.

"Dickon, does Edward know George came here with the earl?"

As I should have expected, we were on completely the same track. That knowledge, as always, gave me a great, inner satisfaction as he turned towards me with a knowing look in his eye.

"Well, he will when we return and tell him."

7. WESTMINSTER PALACE
July 1468

"Lovell, you are a black hearted knave!" Although I wanted to smile, fear prevented the muscles in my face from responding normally.

I raised my eyes slowly and found myself pinned by the penetrating green-gold glare of the king. At that precise moment I envisaged that furious stare blazing out from behind a visor slit and I shivered. Memories of the bloodshed at Towton were still all too fresh in the minds of many at court. Of those who had followed this man on the quest to avenge his father's death and seize the throne that was his rightful inheritance. A vengeance that left over twenty-eight thousand men dead in the snow, if the chroniclers told true.

"Checkmate," I replied nervously, followed by a suitably subservient, "Your Grace."

Edward threw himself back into the chair, still not releasing my gaze from across the chessboard where my black knight had done its work.

"I thought you were over-reaching when your bishop took my queen, but I have to say this is the ultimate in betrayals."

Although I knew well that Edward liked a jest, his words were hard as stone. For the barest of seconds, I wondered if anyone had ever been executed for treason by the game and play of chess. I admonished myself silently for not having thought of that before I agreed to this game. Usually, I pushed hard to win only to fall back at the end, thus allowing my sovereign to maintain his dignity. Today, for some reason, there had been no inner Angel staying my hand.

"You do know," he drawled lazily, be-jewelled fingers reaching out to an ornately figured goblet by his side, "that you have taken advantage of your sovereign?"

The frown creased my brow before I could stop it as my mind worked furiously to figure out where he was going with this conversation. Edward was a more than genial host, most of the time, but when crossed, he had a fury to scorch the earth. I sank my teeth into my bottom lip, hard, before replying. Warwick may be my Lord and master, but that was at the whim of this colossus who was eyeing me with speculation. I decided the best course of action was to play dumb. After all, it worked for Percy all the time.

"How so, Your Grace? For a king to be taken by a knight could do no better than to look for the tales of Lancelot and King Arthur, for there was never a better example of chivalry, even though they were both set against each other for the love of a fair maiden."

It was his turn to frown then as a cloud passed behind his gaze. It was only brief and thankfully followed by a smile as his eyes finally warmed, making me also heat up as a vision of Caitlin rose in my mind like a spectre. His full lips pursed thoughtfully.

"You will advance far, Francis, your lineage notwithstanding. Yet, I feel a duty to caution you." He took a deep draught from his goblet before fixing me with his eyes once more. "Considering you have no father to guide your hand."

No father and no fortunes at the moment I thought silently, but without rancour. Warwick profited from my estates and would do for some time to come. It was the way of things - and the pleasure of kings - to reward thus.

"I value your advice in all things, Your Grace," I offered humbly. "I know how truly fortunate I am to be in your service."

He snorted then, his laugh as loud as his temper sometimes

"In Dickon's service more like!" He saw my raised brows and waved his free hand airily. "Oh don't mistake me! I readily see that my little brother is assembling quite the coterie of followers. In fact, " his tone softened to match his reflective mood, "it gladdens my heart. He was never one for casual company, not even as a young boy. Our father's death affected him more than any of us. I know not how but he seems to attract those who value loyalty and a certain moral standard." He grinned widely then. "Although I am beginning to wonder about you!" He nodded towards the chess board pointedly. "You do know you would not have triumphed had I not had a head like a baited bear this morning?"

It was utter rubbish and he knew it. We both knew it, but I inclined my head graciously.

"It goes without saying, Your Grace. I could see your hand trembling above your rook and took full advantage. I am sure you will not begrudge me one single victory."

Lowering his eyes, he picked up my white knight which had been challenging his king.

"No, of course not. This once. You understand strategy Francis, and I hope you will use this to serve the House of York well. Rebellions and unrest still simmer abroad, stoked by those who feel their efforts on my behalf have not been properly ... rewarded." He placed the knight back down, knocking it onto it's side with a finger. "My brother may have need of you as the years pass. I hope you will not find your loyalties unduly tested." He picked up his own rook, examining it as if it was somehow alien.

"Tested?"

"Pick a side Francis and cleave to it." He paused, his lips puckered in thought. The ebony chess piece held between his fingers, his eyes still fixed on it as though it was some strange beast he needed to identify. "No, that's wrong. Pick a man, Francis, for all men are forged by their values and beliefs, and it is those which determine their actions. So, if you choose my brother, make sure it is for the right reasons, and bond them to you as truly as your own."

Strong, powerful fingers curled around the piece in his hand, obscuring it completely from view, held fast within the king's massive palm. This was his guidance then, but was it also a test? Why should I choose Dickon above Edward? Was that it? It was hard for me to work out his purpose but there were not many men, I was certain, who would be given such personal advice from their king. It had to mean something and at the thought of that, my throat dried up like a shallow river-bed in summer, making my next words hushed.

"Should I not cleave to my king, Your Grace?"

The grip on the chess piece tightened, but his voice remained soft.

"By swearing to serve my brother, you serve me. By becoming his bondsman in all things, you become mine." Suddenly, he released his grip on the rook and it fell onto the board, scattering pieces in the wake of it's fall. Only the king remained standing. Edward grinned easily and sat back in his chair once again. "Power can be a seductive force, Francis. Warwick is a powerful man, but do not under-estimate Richard. He is young, but then, so are you. He needs men like you at his side, even that reprobate Percy!"

I laughed then and began righting the chess pieces, returning them back to their familiar places on the board but in one swift move I didn't see coming, he leaned forwards and grasped my wrist, stopping my actions. I had been about to assure him that Rob was harmless, but the strength of his fingers stopped me. Whatever this was, it was serious business and once again I looked up into his intense stare.

"Have you chosen your man, Francis?"

For a few seconds, I didn't now what to say. He knew full well that I was Richard's friend, but as for anything else, my actions were dictated by the earl. Despite my association with the king's brother, he was my master. Edward knew it. He had made it so! I had even had to ask permission to travel back to London with Richard. Even though his move was at the king's request, Warwick could have detained me had be wished. I gave him the only politic answer I could

"I have, Your Grace. Although my colours are inevitably those of my Lord of Warwick, my loyalty has already been won by

His Grace of Gloucester."

The grip tightened as his eyes narrowed and a spark of fear burned bright for a second, and not just because I worried he may break my wrist with his infernal strength. I felt a bead of sweat break out on my upper lip.

"And if you had to choose between the two? What then?"

My answer was as swift as it was honest. I had no need to consider it.

"My loyalty lies with Richard, Your Grace."

"No matter what prizes you are offered?" The grip was vice-like now and I did my best not to wince. Something was obviously troubling him, that much was plain. But no matter, my words were my honest truth, that much was made easy for me.

"Money may purchase a man's sword, Your Grace, but cannot buy a man's heart."

Suddenly, the force released at the same time as Edward's face creased in pleasure, his eyes shining brightly. My words had satisfied him it seemed, and it was a great relief knowing that I had been able to speak the truth. Had I needed to be false to get that same reaction, I think my sleep may well have been long in coming that night.

"Well, said! I take it back! A knave, you are most definitely not! And now you shall prove it to me once more! Set up the board Francis, and this time beware! My head is feeling much clearer than it was therefore any advantage you may have had is long fled!"

As Edward raised his goblet back up to his lips, I began to pick up the pieces once more, arranging them in order, ready for the fray. This time, he would win. I had no doubt of that at all.

8. MIDDLEHAM CASTLE
September 1468

It was only as I sat with Rob Percy, nursing a sore wrist, that I remembered it was the same one which King Edward had held within his grasp a few weeks ago. We had returned to Middleham shortly after that exchange, sent here for the rest of the summer and the days were now beginning to shorten, shadows growing long as we ended our practice in the yard. It had been an unusually hot day, one of many over the last few weeks, and clouds of dust raised like a fog as Richard attacked Rob Harington relentlessly, with one lethal swing of his sword following another, causing him to retreat, his own blade a useless defence now as his arm weakened. The constant chiming of steel against steel mimicked St Akelda's bell.

As Harington finally fell to his knees, beaten, Percy thrust his own sword back into it's sheath with a flourish.

"Well, that's three of us he has seen off today. I don't intend to be the fourth. Something has stirred his blood and no mistake! Poor Harington! Last of three and still forced to his knees!"

I had to admit there was something in that. Richard seemed to have gained the stamina of ten men and despite his easy going manner, today, he was a force to be reckoned with. When his visor was up, his expression was its usual relaxed, if serious, self, yet once it was slammed shut, there was no mercy. He had defended my own attack with such ferocity that at one point my right wrist had doubled back, causing a stab of pain to shoot up my arm, weakening my grip. It was only a momentary lapse, but it was enough. Richard saw it, had sliced towards me in one smooth stroke and watched as my weapon performed a slow arc in the air, before falling into the dust.

I watched him help Harington up, his helm under his arm now, his face sweat-streaked, yet he was grinning mirthlessly.

"There have been more rumours out of the south," I murmured softly so as not to be overheard. "I think they are beginning to trouble him."

Rob grunted. A noise that could either have been assent or disagreement.

"He needs a woman."

"He has a woman!" My answer was hotly defensive and I knew it. Caitlin Desmond was never far from my thoughts, despite that she still remained at Warwick Castle with the countess and her daughters. Every day I had both hoped and despaired that the countess may take it upon herself to bring her girls to the northern stronghold. It was a strange feeling, to long for something so much yet fear it at the same time.

"A fat lot of use she is at Warwick! He needs to plunge his sword into something more willing before he breaks someone's arm!"

His last words were also softly spoken as Richard and the defeated Harington approached us, Rob limping slightly on his left leg where he had gone down on the hard-packed ground.

"Well done, Dickon!" Percy grinned as Richard reached up his hand, pushing away the hair that was plastered to his damp forehead. "You've had a good day!"

"And a distinct advantage, I think. You had all been hard at it before I joined you." He threw his helm on the ground at his feet. "Francis, you should get that wrist looked at." He drew his brows together in a familiar frown, his eyes on my hand.

"That was some force you hit him with Dickon, by Jesu!" Percy admitted with obvious admiration. "You should tell us your secret!"

Richard quirked a fleeting smile but said nothing more, stripping off his gauntlets quickly.

"What delayed you?" We were all wondering, so I thought it only sensible to ask. He would have no qualms in telling me to mind my business if he wanted to.

"Warwick. He rode in this morning."

My ears pricked up even though there was no indication in Richard's tone that this was in any way unusual. Although those poor unfortunates who claim to have second sight, or an ability to predict the future, always scare me, I couldn't help my gut from almost turning in on itself, but I had no idea why. My throat tightened, making it hard to ask the next question in my mind.

"Is he alone?"

"If you mean is my brother George with him, the answer is no. He travels alone. The household are still at Warwick." He bent over then and picked up his helm, settling it under his arm. "He is on a progress around his fortresses. Pontefract, Sandal, Penrith..."

A strained silence fell across our small group. It wasn't George I had been enquiring about, but it was an excellent cover to my feeble attempt to find out if Caitlin was now within these very walls. It was Harington who finally aired his thoughts.

"Is he fortifying them?"

Richard gave him a smile, which failed to reach his eyes. It was, I knew, meant to be reassuring, but instead came as only a diversion.

"We must always be on our guard against the Scots, Rob. Their border Lords never fail to exploit the weakest link in our defences should they spot it."

Harington wasn't fooled for one moment, but winced as he moved his weight from one foot to another.

"I was thinking of somewhere closer to home."

Richard's response was swift as his face closed in, eyes sparking like granite.

"You should not listen to gossip, Rob. I thought better of you than that." He paused, squinting up at the sky. We traded loaded glances as he studiously avoided ours. "He has sworn his loyalty to his king. He has even written to him assuring him of his continued service and decrying the actions of those who are attempting to stir up dissent."

Knowing how stoically Richard was in defense of his kin, I remained silent, even though I suspected there was no smoke without fire. The earl had been in high dudgeon ever since Reading when Edward had produced his new bride, Elizabeth Woodville. In one master stroke destroying months of hard negotiation with France. Negotiation carried out by Warwick himself, and designed to provide England with a firm alliance.

Warwick had stood by Edward's side, both before and after Richard's father, the Duke of York, had been mercilessly killed in battle at Wakefield. Fuelled by anger, Edward had forged a path to the throne with steel and blood, winning battles so decisively, his conquest of the old king could not be denied. The sight of three suns rising on the dawn of the battle at Mortimer's Cross seemed to prophesise his triumph, which was then sealed in the snows of Yorkshire at Towton.

Skilled though Edward was, one had to wonder if any of this would have been possible without Warwick's support, no less the men that he brought with him under his banners. He won the crown by right of conquest and by right of inheritance from the lines of Clare and Mortimer. Eventually, the old king had been captured, and to this day languished in the Tower, no doubt immersed in prayer as he had long ago lost most of his wits. Warwick had been there at each step, advising, guiding his hand. Then, one day, the tide turned.

As I heard it, and it came from one of Warwick's men who had accompanied him on one of his many visits abroad, the King of France had joked that there were two kings in England. For Warwick, it may have been the most costly jest ever, and the most galling. To have years of allegiance cast asunder by one careless remark. Or, not so careless for those who knew King Louis well. Not for nothing was he called "The Spider King."

As diplomatic as Harington and I remained, Percy displayed no such skill.

"Well, to be fair, he needed to after that Wenlock business.

Did anyone actually believe he wasn't behind it?"

Richard lowered his head with an agonizing slowness. Inside, my chest tightened as I saw the look he directed at Percy, yet he didn't speak a word. We were all aware of the rumblings in the south. Of the story of the Kent shoemaker who had been passing letters to Lancastrian exiles in France. When discovered, the man had implicated Lord Wenlock, one of Warwick's trusted friends. Somehow, they had both wriggled out of any guilt, yet the smell of suspicion remained. In answer to this, all Richard did was turn on his heel and leave us, standing in the autumn sunshine, watching him return to the keep. It was a few moments before Percy exhaled heavily.

"I am thinking that the answer to that was no."

The day had a sour feeling to it, and I was glad to leave the yard, not even bothering to seek out the surgeon, thinking to soothe my hand in cold water instead. The incident, harmless as it had been, was unsettling and I wasn't sure why.

Looking back, it was all too apparent. This was the first time Richard was to have his loyalty tested. His cousin had taken him into his home, schooled and trained him, welcomed him into his family and forged a relationship almost as close as father and son. But Edward was his brother, and his king. The three of us may not have said as much that afternoon, but we all knew it. If he had to choose between the two, there was only one winner.

9. MIDDLEHAM CASTLE
September 1468

Supper in the hall was an unremarkable affair, despite the presence of the earl within the walls. With his family still in the south, he remained absent from the hall, as did Richard. Rob and I could only conjecture that they were closeted somewhere together, or being served food privately in their chambers, either together or alone. It had to be said this behavior was unusual for Richard in particular, as he usually enjoyed the company of his friends. With us he could truly relax, drop his guard and put down the mask worn by all of those whose movements were constantly scrutinized by others. In this wise, he was as far from his brothers as was the sun from the moon.

It therefore did not take me by surprise at all that our paths crossed later that evening, after the sun had sunk down low beneath the battlements. Crossing the newly installed covered bridge linking the former private chamber to the newly refurbished rooms along the southern wall, I made my way to a favourite vantage point on top of the south-east tower. Not that there was anything in particular to see. There was just something about the rolling landscape and the site of the old castle on William's Hill that made me feel a strange sense of peace. I had begun escaping up there not long after my arrival at Middleham, when the taunting of the young Yorkist henchmen had been at its worst.

There had been those who had made it their mission to make my life as uncomfortable as possible. This included acts so childish as slipping frogs into my ale and spooking my mount during training to tying my family name to a hog's head and using it for target practice at the butts. Friendless, at that time anyway, I had found a way to breathe the fresh northern air and admit to myself that although I loved these sprawling northern lands, the people were another matter entirely. It was the slur with the hog's head which had lead to my meeting Richard. His disgust at that one act had been so complete, the squires who had committed the act were expelled from Middleham without either delay or fuss. They just disappeared.

It was not until a year later that I found out that they had been truly dispatched – to the earl's garrison at Calais. When I registered my surprise, Richard had merely arched a brow, commenting that if they enjoyed baiting southerners so much, they could test their mettle on the French. So as I emerged from the darkness of the tower onto the battlements, I supposed it should not have surprised me to find my usual hiding place occupied. Richard had beaten me to it, and was leaning on one of the merlons, staring out at the turquoise sky as it deepened into night, the fresh breeze lifting his hair back as he stared out at nothing, or so it seemed.

Although I thought my approach silent, I saw his head turn slightly, suddenly understanding his solitude had been broken.

"I wondered how long it would be before you made it up here. Are you alone?"

I came to a halt by his side. His profile was set, sternly, and I knew then that although he would never admit it, he would be glad if the answer was yes. I had a feeling he was not in the mood for the affable, jocular humour that some of the men, such as Rob, brought with them like so much baggage.

"Just me, Dickon. The day I let Rob know how often I come up here is the day my only haven loses its allure. Before I know it, there will be fifteen of us up here playing cards and dicing."

I saw the corner of his mouth lift up.

"And a goodly half of them tavern wenches from the village."

I couldn't help but laugh out loud. Despite the lightness of his tone, he still managed to colour his words with a tinge of disdain.

"Well, that is Rob for you. But then, he has the advantage of some years on us. Something he never lets me forget." I picked up a pebble from down at my feet, tossing it in my hand. It was ragged, ill formed, but sparkled in the light of the torches. "You were missed in the hall."

I watched as his lips pursed ruefully, his shoulders rising in a shrug.

"The earl had not captured enough of my time earlier today, it appeared, and asked me to sup with him."

"He could have done that at the high table," I replied casually, still tossing the stone in my hand, its cold weight giving me some strange satisfaction when cupped in the palm of my hand.

I had always found it difficult to be idle, which had led to me mastering the lute at a young age. For myself, it was always merely a distraction, although others told me that I was quite good. Well, Anne Neville had told me I was quite good, whereas her sister Isabel, always haughtily aloof, had merely sneered. There was something about Isabel which left my heart completely cold, whereas Anne was like a little bird. Fragile, with a bright eyed beauty. Her every movement was light and delicate. In the absence of my sisters Frideswide and Joan who remained at Titchfield, I regarded her as my sister and felt an unusual protectiveness towards her, an emotion I knew Richard shared.

"It was women who were the subject of our conversation earlier," he said quietly, his eyes still fixed ahead. "The earl wants me to press Edward on the subject of his daughters' marriages."

"To?"

It was only then that he turned his head to look at me, his eyes dark and troubled.

"I think you can guess." Turning towards me, he leant back on the stone wall, torches flaring in his eyes. "I wish he would give up this madness. Edward is still touchy on the subject of Warwick and marriages. Even if it does make complete sense, and his girls are the most suitable matches in the country, Edward is not about to change his mind. He has declined the petition, and will not turn. Not even for me."

I curled my fingers around the stone, which felt strangely like a mirror image of what was happening to my gut. Anne Neville had been a constant presence in our lives for some years and was, it could be argued, overly fond of her cousin. Now it appeared that her father had decided to bargain with her affections. I wondered, somewhat uneasily, considering all the rumours, if it was only this which would buy back Warwick's loyalty to the crown.

"How do you feel about that?" He flashed an uncertain glance at me. "About marriage to Anne?"

At that moment it wasn't just Anne I was thinking about. A pair of green eyes blinked back at me from the stars which were just beginning to twinkle above the horizon. I wasn't a fool. I knew he could never marry her and I was sure she was aware of that too. Now, it seemed, I was feeling protective about another, but admittedly in a much different way.

Anne Neville had never caused the satisfying, if frustrating, stirring in my loins which Caitlin Desmond had. Truth be told, I had no real comprehension of exactly how I felt about Caitlin, only that I was experiencing feelings which I had never felt before.

Not to say that carnal yearnings were unknown to me, just that I had not as yet had the bravado to do anything about it. Rob was right, in a way. I really did need to find myself a compliant wench, it was just that the thought of that was somehow abhorrent. Even more so since I had been captivated by the fair Lady Desmond.

Richard folded his arms across his chest. He began biting the inside of his bottom lip, obviously troubled. For a while I thought he would not share his thoughts with me, and in a way, that was exactly what I was hoping. But I was destined to be dashed.

"Anne is very sweet. She seems to know exactly what I am thinking and just when I need a friendly word, or comfort."

"Like a sister?" I offered, thinking his feelings must be pretty much the same as mine but he looked uncomfortable with that word.

"No. No, it's more than that. It is as if we have always known each other. That when we are troubled or concerned, we seek each other out for company. We just seem to know the right words to say to each other. I am very fond of her, and could never hurt her in any way."

It was the question I had been waiting to ask, and I could hold it back no more. His answer could either raise or destroy my hopes and my heart began to thump painfully inside my chest. I didn't know what was the matter with me! It was ridiculous to feel this way and it began to make me feel somewhat disgruntled.

"And, what of Caitlin Desmond? Is that different?"

His colour rose. Something that even the fading light could not disguise. He licked his lips nervously and suddenly his features softened.

"It is, Frank. I have always known the earl's hopes for his daughters, and for my part I cannot lie and say I have not been agreeable to that, had Edward approved. Yet, Cait..."

"Kate?"

He smiled then, the look in his eyes warmer than I had ever seen.

"I know! It sounds very English doesn't it, considering her Irish ancestry? Yet, when I first saw her, I had a sensation that just would not leave me. A need, somehow, to seek her out. To listen to her voice and gaze into those remarkable eyes. Then, one night, she had fallen foul of the queen's temper, so much that she had suffered hurt because of it. That was it! I can't explain it, but that night, well, we..."

I held up my hand, the stone falling to the ground at my feet.

"No need for detail, Dickon!"

He grinned then, easily.

"I have no intention of giving you chapter and verse! Just to say that I have been unable to completely get her out of my thoughts ever since. It is truly a gift from God, Frank, to find such companionship in a woman's body."

He blushed again and looked down, whereas I was having

difficulty swallowing, which, to my shame, did not stop me from asking yet more foolish questions that my curiosity insisted I satisfy.

"Was she...?"

He nodded quickly, and I saw him swallow hard too. My heart fell, yet I had no idea why. I felt like I had suddenly lost something precious. Yet, it was something I had never actually owned.

"A word of advice, Frank. I was so thankful I had already bedded a maid!" He paused then, thoughtfully. "Well, not exactly a maid, but at least I didn't become a fumbling fool. And believe me, I could so easily have done!"

I shuffled my feet a little uncomfortably. Not at the subject of carnal desires, they were often the main subject of our jests, usually when more than a little ale had been consumed, and usually led by Rob. It was Caitlin that was making me feel this way. The thought of her and my friend, their naked bodies entwined, her hair providing them with a glorious counterpane....

I cleared my throat. I couldn't talk about it anymore and decided on a slight shift of subject, keeping my eyes fixed on the toes of my boots. I thought it best to appear disinterested, when in truth I was anything but. I could have talked about Caitlin Desmond all night, but these current visions were determined to disarm me, and I had a care for what I may betray.

"And what do you think will happen? When Edward refuses the earl's appeal again?"

He sighed heavily then, and his eyes hardened back into their usual steely grey.

"I don't know. He will not like it. In fact, he may well view it as the final insult. Despite my defence of him today, I am not completely convinced in his avowance of loyalty. That recent business with Wenlock had a certain smell to it. But I can't admit to that openly. Only to you, Frank."

Pride burned in my breast. It was still a matter of great significance to me that I had his trust. That we would take me into his confidence on such a matter deepened that feeling.

"My lips are sealed, Dickon. Although, I have to say, I feel the same."

He pushed himself away from the wall suddenly, running a hand through is hair, an unusual gesture for him. He threw me a rueful grin.

"I need a drink!" He took a pace forward and I fell into step beside him. "There is nothing that can be done even though I know what Edward's answer will be. I will do as asked. And the earl has confirmed that we are all to attend the Christmas court." He paused at the top of the stairs, looking back at the sky, at the rampant bear fluttering on the standard against the sky. "I think we may need to make the most of it, for unless Edward can breach the differences between them in some other way, we may be in for trouble."

With a twist of his lips, he disappeared into the shadow of the stairwell. I too looked at the banner quickly. The bear, tremendous paws stretched out to the ragged staff, looked particularly fearsome, I thought, before I shook away the image and ran down the stairs behind him.

10. MIDDLEHAM CASTLE
November 1468

Her hand rested lightly on my chest as I struggled to regain my breath. Sweat stood out on my brow and my heart was pounding fit to burst out through my ribs. It took a while to remember where I was as the last few minutes seemed to have cast me down into some other world where there was only the driving need to expel myself of the demon which had taken possession of my body. Emerald eyes had stared back at me, willing me on, smiling at me all the time, but the voice that whispered so sweetly was not hers. The eyes neither, I could see that now. It had been an illusion. A convenient one, but an illusion no less.

"Well, my sweetheart! You are a right lusty lad and no mistake! For a while there I thought'd be needing a new bed!" She spoke softly, but her words fell harsh on my ears and with mounting dread I felt her rise up beside me, her hand now reaching for my face. "Well, at least the landlord would."

Fingers traced my lips gently, tracking down to my chin, gently passing over the deep cleft there. My breathing was beginning to return to normal but my whole body felt cut loose, lifeless. It was as if I was a longbow, and had been drawn back to my maximum tension, the archer waiting some inexorable time before releasing the shaft into the air.... but when he did...

I reached up and ran my fingers through my dampened hair. It was hot, I could smell the sweat on my body, and hers of a sudden, and I wrinkled my nose in distaste. I had not noticed that before, or was that how it always was? I could not remember much. Not after drinking more than my weight in ale, and being un-nervingly attracted by two cat-like eyes dancing in front of me, above breasts which spoke of a sensuous softness. All the while

Rob had chuckled in the background and there had been the faint clink of coin. But by then, I could only think of one thing. I could see Caitlin Desmond's eyes and I wanted to possess them. Bodily.

Her hands were on my thighs now, stroking gently, I could swear she was humming a soft tune to herself.

"What is your name?" My throat was parched, and the words came out broken and harsh. The last thing I really wanted to know was her name, but I knew I had to say something, anything.

"Grace, my Lord."

"I am not a Lord; I am…" All words froze in my throat as her hand swept up and encircled my manhood swiftly.

"You are a Lord tonight…my Lord." I could hear the smile in her words but by that time my body was beginning to respond even more strongly than it had earlier. The muscles in my thighs were taut, her hands played with me expertly, bringing me to a rigid stiffness that led me to believe that my whole body would burst, eploding out from my groin if she did not stop.

"See?" she giggled artfully as I closed my eyes and pressed my head back into the pillow, no longer noticing its stale odour. "You have even brought your weapon! Now, where shall my lord wish to sheath it? Before it comes to harm?"

I tried to move but could not. Behind my eyes, Caitlin Desmond still smiled at me and I heard a distant groan. Then something warm enveloped me, silky and moist, causing me to gasp with pleasure and I looked down the length of my body from beneath barely opened lids. All I could see was her hair, the colour of summer straw, not the red of autumn fire, but somehow it mattered not. Her mouth had taken me into a cavern of pleasure and I reached down to clasp her head even closer as I began to arch my body towards her accommodating lips. I felt her smile as Caitlin's eyes exploded behind my closed lids, iridescent shooting stars, falling through the dark – burning my very soul.

Although I could not deny that Grace's skills had left me thoroughly sated, I soon began to feel somewhat embarrassed at what had just taken place. A paid whore or not, she seemed overly affectionate, and had sunk into a slumber with her arms wound around my neck. Feeling an urgent need to flee, I extricated myself as best as I could, but she opened her eyes and watched me as I picked up my abandoned shirt and began to dress in haste. I didn't want to look at her. Not from any sense of shame, just from a fear of being caught by those eyes once more. Eyes which stirred uncontrollable feelings that made me blush crimson with guilt.

My very first encounter with the female sex had been bolstered by imagining myself in the arms of a girl who belonged to my dearest friend. And whom I could see cared more for her than he was able to say. That knowledge did not make me feel any better about myself, or my actions with the young woman who lay naked and disheveled on the bed before me.

"You are a fine lad, my Lord." Her fingers played with the fronds of her hair which trailed across her breasts. "Will you be coming back? Maybe tomorrow night?" My hands trembled slightly as I began to tie the points of my hose and I reached over to pull my shirt over my head, relieved to be out of her sight if only for a breath. "My Lord?"

With some reluctance, I turned and looked at her. She was not unattractive, it was true. A mite buxom for my taste but somehow it didn't matter. She pulled up the threadbare sheet slowly, covering her nakedness, but her eyes were still roving over my arms and chest. I had never considered how I may look to the fairer sex, and for a second my thoughts strayed to Anna, my young wife. My very young wife with whom I could never imagine doing the things I had just done. It seemed like a sacrilege to even think of it!

"Maybe." I managed to murmur, pleasantly I hoped. "My movements are at the whim of the earl. We are likely to go back to court soon."

My comments were only meant to be casual, covering up a mixture of embarrassment and confusion. I wasn't entirely sure

74

how I felt. The sensation of a woman's hands, lips, tongue, were all more than pleasurable, and for a while, one could forget with whom they lay, even where they where! Lust, it seemed, burned out all conscience when it raged as hot as Hades. Now, passions spent, there was only awkwardness. Although I very much wanted to feel those feelings again, I knew there was only one with whom my true needs would be slaked. I had a feeling that no matter how many women I may choose to bed; a sense of loss would remain once the pleasure of the act itself was gone. It was only as I pulled on my doublet that I noticed I had unwittingly sparked her interest.

She sat up, leaning forwards, her breasts exposed above the crumpled sheets, her eyes shining.

"Court, my Lord? You are going in attendance upon the king?"

Averting my eyes from her gaze I managed to nod, relieved that this mis-adventure was almost at an end.

"Not exactly," I muttered. "Where the earl takes his household, I am bound to go." That still did not deflect her from her purpose.

"But, you will meet the king?"

My dress complete, I sat down to pull on my boots, nodding in assent. There was a note of expectancy in her voice that made me very sad, for some reason, because I knew what she was hoping for. Percy had been extolling my virtues earlier that evening, that much I could remember, and boasting of my affinity to the king's brother.

"Many fine Lords at court take mistresses, some say. I could give you comfort on the long journey south, my Lord. And warm your bed a' night if you should wish it? A strapping young lad like yourself could do with someone to ease the way, if you understand me. Had we longer, I could show you…"

I stood up abruptly, and fumbled in my purse, throwing two more groats down on the sheet, even though I knew she had already been well paid for her service this night.

75

"I have a wife, in the south." Instantly I regretted the terseness of my words and I turned to look at her, expecting to see her crestfallen face, but I was wrong. There was a flash of brazenness there now, a veil of determination which completely changed her face, her eyes no longer the brilliant emerald I thought I had seen. Now they were hard, flat, acquisitive.   It made my next words easier. "She will provide all the comfort I need."

I had been right. She greeted the dismissal with a shrug and shrank back into the pillows, her eyes attempting to entrap me once more, but she had betrayed herself in an instant.

"A lucky lady indeed, my Lord. I envy her her part in your... education."

My cheeks were a flaming brand as I left the shadowy room, only to find Rob leaning on the wall outside, paring his nails with a dagger.

"All done?" he asked innocently, as if enquiring of the weather. I nodded hastily, trying to cover my embarrassment but he just grinned at me, knowingly. "Our Grace is quite the tutor. She doesn't go with just anyone you know. She's a higher class of whore, for the village that is." We began to descend into the smoky taproom, the noise jarring on my ears, making me feel even more lightheaded. "She even visits the castle from time to time, to keep the earl company." Shocked by this sudden revelation I came to a halt at the foot of the stairs and stared at him incredulously.

"Please, Rob, don't tell me I have just slept with the earl's whore!"

He laughed out loud then and threw his arm around my shoulders, guiding me out of the door, into the cold stable-yard.

"One of many, Frank. Rest easy." Mollified a little, we began walking up the rise to the castle which loomed ominously above the village in the gathering dark. "How was it?"

I slowed my step, unsure if I really wanted this discussion. Rob never failed to regale us all with his latest and numerous conquests, and I had always laughed and joined in the mirth and teasing, until now. Yet, there was one burning question I needed an answer to, even though I probably suspected that Rob was not the man to provide it.

"Fine, well, I mean, it was pleasant..."

"Pleasant?" The scorn was there on his face, mixed with amazement. I think he was truly expecting me to say it had been some wondrous revelation akin to a form of spiritual enlightenment. "Just pleasant? Jesus, Frank!"

"No! I mean, I would imagine it is different, if you... if one... truly cares for someone. That surely is better than just a casual tumble for the sake of it? To actually desire the girl that lays down with you?"

We began walking again as he considered this, our footfall the only sound as we climbed past the market cross to the northern gatehouse.

"Well, I would imagine so, yet somehow I always manage to find a certain satisfaction in any pretty face and rounded body. One day, mayhap, I may find someone with whom it is different. For now, I am hoping to meet the loves-some Lady Shaftesbury at the Christmas court. Now there is someone who I surely would wish to see live up to her name." He laughed uproariously at his own joke, as I plodded on with my thoughts. It was a while before he realised I had not appreciated his jest. "So, tell me then. Who would it be? Of all the women you have met, or have seen around, who would it be that you would desire to aid you to hone your amorous skills?"

We passed under the shadow of the gatehouse, receiving a nodded acknowledgement of the guards there. Some of them were Irishmen, former servants of the king's father. I noticed one of them had the most brilliant blue eyes, which unsettled me for a second.

"No one, Rob. There's no one. At least, not yet."

"Well then, what are you worried about?" he grinned, striding towards our quarters. "Maybe the Christmas court will reveal a likely paramour!"

I followed him, my heart in my boots. This night had been a revelation in more than one way. That I had enjoyed tasting the pleasures of the flesh was undoubted. That it had also put spark to an ember deep inside of me was true. Yet if I hoped that the oncoming festivities would ease the ache that was growing deep within me, I knew I was bound to be disappointed. I could only hope that Caitlin Desmond would remain at Warwick Castle and therefore I could not be tempted by her constant presence. Somehow, I knew that hope was doomed even before it was fully formed.

11. GREENWICH PALACE
December 1468

Stamping my feet had absolutely no effect against the frozen chill which had embraced the palace in its icy grip. My hands were rammed firmly under my armpits to keep my fingers from snapping off in the freezing cold as even the thought of meeting my heart's desire could not bring warmth to my blood.

As I waited to meet her - at Richard's express request, I pondered over my most recent attempts to break the spell Caitlin Desmond had cast over me - determined that by the next time we crossed paths, it would be as meeting any other woman. That her presence would have lost its allure and have no effect on me whatsoever.

So - since arriving at Greenwich four weeks ago - I had taken a girl into my bed. Well, I say bed but in truth it was mostly wherever we could find to spend time together. Even then - I reflected - I was still fooling myself. Yes, she was a pretty little thing. Her name was Marie and she was in the service of the queen's mother, the Duchess of Bedford, but I didn't hold that against her. In fact, I was far too busy holding something else against her as I soon found that my initiation into the world of fleshly desires had awakened a whole new side of me that I had no idea existed.

What was more, Marie looked nothing like Caitlin and even though I could not understand what it was about her that caused my disobedient body to respond the way it did, I wasn't about to complain.

She had a sweetly innocent smile, which dimpled her cheeks prettily and eyes that shone like pebbles after the rain. Her hair was very dark, almost black, and fell around her shoulders in a fall of silk, not a wave or curl to be seen. And I had been her first, meaning that she had hardly noticed my own inexperienced fumblings, which, to be blatantly honest, were not as inept as they could have been. I was, it appeared, a quick study in the art of love, and the moans and sighs of appreciation which seemed to increase in intensity at every encounter only served to forge my confidence.

Until this evening in the hall.

I had already caught Marie's eye, her coy, downward smile fooling me not at all, knowing she was anticipating that we may later find a quiet corner in which to share our mutual desires, but then, all thoughts of her disappeared like a snuffed candle.

Caitlin sat across the hall, seated next to Isabel Neville, putting the aloof young woman in her shadow as she stared up at the high table, her eyes devouring Richard like one long denied sustenance.

I was truly a fool, I told myself then, I knew nothing of the ways of love. For as I stared at her, and although she did not see me, I knew that if I bedded a hundred women or more, if I slaked my lusts until I could no longer stand from exhaustion, I would still ache for just one taste of her lips. The thought made me thoroughly downhearted, a mood which had improved little when Richard called me aside later and asked me to wait for Caitlin in the gallery at midnight. My task - for tonight - was to escort a girl I had begun to believe I loved and to keep her company until my friend could free up the time to take her into his bed.

Before those particular visions could rise up like spectres to haunt me, I heard a sure, quick step coming towards me, travelling down the passage and, forgive me, but I slunk back into the shadows to watch her approach unobserved.

She was swathed completely in a blue velvet cloak, its hood trimmed with miniver and shadowing both her face and hair from my sight. What did reach me was the heady smell of violets, no matter how lightly it had been applied and I imagined her touching the fragrance to her wrists, throat, and other secret places which I could only dream about. Before my thoughts could torture me any longer, I stepped out in to her path, only to be met by a sudden flare of her eyes, which had become the light of my life.

I nodded towards her, rubbing my hands together briskly, only partly because I knew they were shaking, blowing warm air into them just in case I would be required, God forbid, to take hold of her hand.

"Dickon has been delayed." I said, securing my hands back under my armpits, almost to prevent the temptation of that touch. "He asked me to take you to his chamber… that is…. if you are happy to be escorted?" She looked up at me from beneath the shadow of her hood, her skin glowing in the light of the torch which flared above my head, and then she smiled and I was almost completely undone. Something inside me turned to liquid yet with a bravado I didn't know I possessed, I stretched out my hand, urging her to follow me through the gallery.

I thought I caught a slight nod of her head in acceptance and I stepped forwards, making sure she walked just slightly behind me as I made my way through the sleeping palace to Richard's chamber. We didn't exchange a word on the way, but I was conscious of her gentle breath as we ascended the stairs, and the delicate clouds of fragrance which sought to confound me as I led her on. For a time, I tried to stop breathing myself, only inhaling very shallowly, in a vain and desperate attempt to keep detached from her allure. It was a nightmare, and my newly attuned body began to assert its demands, determined that its arousal would not be ignored.

It was with some relief that we finally reached Richard's chamber, not only for the warmth, but for the ability to gather my thoughts in more conducive surroundings. As she followed me into the room, I distracted myself by throwing yet another log onto an already roaring fire, before almost falling over one of Richard's hounds which had already made itself at home by the hearth. I couldn't figure out which one it was. They all looked the damn same to me despite the variety of colours and a whole range of chivalric names ranging from Tristan to Arthur to Roland. It looked at me balefully before resting its head back on its paws, watching my guest, almost smiling.

I stood up, straightening my doublet, breathing in deeply before I dared to turn and confront her in the light of the many candles which kept the night at bay. She had dropped her hood and for the life of me I couldn't work out how I was going to survive this encounter. I would either end the night as a witless jackanapes or disgrace myself in some other way. Neither prospect filled me with delight, but I managed a smile which I hoped was genuine as I looked at her face, her hair, her eyes, not knowing where my gaze should safely rest.

"Please, come sit by the fire. 'Tis a truly raw night and I am not sure how long Dickon will be." That much was true. I just prayed to God he would not tarry. Or that he would never come. Which led to me silently cursing myself as the worst of friends. Before my eyes, she sank down into the chair opposite me, holding out her own hands to the fire, a gentle smile turning her lips into a sweet bow. Something inside me groaned.

"Did you enjoy the evening's entertainment?" I sat down myself now, trying to appear politely interested whilst wondering if I should also join the troupe of mummers who had played in the hall tonight, so complete was my own performance. I could see from her expression that nothing I had done or said had made her think that I bore her anything other than friendly cordiality. I had seen enough guarded expressions in my time and hers was completely, sweetly open. She fussed with her skirts a little then, covering the toes of her slippers, relaxing back into the chair.

"Not especially," she answered with what I thought was a frank honesty. "I never cared for the court. I am only here because..." It was only then she appeared to struggle for her words, her cheeks flushing becomingly. "Well, as you know I serve at the earl's pleasure and his household attend the king, so..."

I began to run my thumbnail up and down the wood grain in the arm of my chair, trying to detach myself from the power of her gaze. Her words had a certain resonance with me. We all served someone. Even the lowest of us, whilst the king also served his country and God. I smiled myself then.

"Don't we all? At least, that is how he would have it." She looked a little taken aback at my words, almost as if she had not expected her frankness to be answered in like mind. That made me smile even more. "Have no fear," I reassured her, understanding full well how difficult life may have been for her, serving our dispassionate queen. "I have been in attendance on the earl for many years now, being given in to his service. Although, to be fair, that has had more than its share of benefits." How I remained so calm as she returned my smile was a complete mystery to me, but I started to relax, beginning to enjoy her presence rather than find it a means of torture. Perhaps that was the only way to stem this tide that was raging inside me, to try and get her to like me as a friend. I couldn't do that if I was a bundle of jangling nerves.

Inanely I asked her how she was finding life at Warwick, for the enquiry only to be greeted by a mischievous glint in her eye.

"Much improved on my previous position, for which I have only one person to thank."

I could not help but chuckle softly, remembering Richard's awkward audience with his brother when trying to determine her fate.

"Dickon holds his brother's favour and asks for so little for himself that the king is attentive when he does. Even concerning one so powerful as the queen, it has to be said. I am sure the company of Anne and Isabel is much more pleasurable than those cold-faced women who trail around in her grace's wake. They remind me of geese, all beady-eyed and that incessant gaggling! Lord – the noise!"

We both laughed then, sharing a secret bond we had not suspected. A disdain of our queen. Almost a treasonable offence, if one should speak it. She raised up her hand and wagged a reproving finger in my direction.

"Careful, sire! For I was once such a goose!"

I felt my face flush but the feeling that we had just made some form of connection loosened my tongue. I felt suddenly giddy, as if I had drunk too much wine.

"But I think it plain that you must have stood out from the rest. As would a swan, maybe, caught up in the middle of such a crowd." My heightened colour was matched by her own as she began to giggle.

"You did not see me clattering about in the queen's chamber! I very much doubt she would describe me as a swan, a wild boar would be much more in keeping."

A wild boar! The significance of her choice of words made me smile.

"Aha!" I exclaimed heartily, hardly missing a beat. "An animal close to Dickon's heart! That could explain much!"

We stared at each other for the barest of moments at the reference to both Richard's badge and their relationship. I feared for a second that I may have overstepped the mark, may have embarrassed her by voicing my knowledge out loud. But suddenly, we both burst into laughter at exactly the same time, for my part releasing a dam of tension that had been building from earlier that evening as I stood on the gallery, my heart sore.

We laughed for quite a while, her eyes shining with tears of joy as we both settled into a comfortable silence, for some reason now feeling much easier with each other. Well, I certainly did, and much to my delight, I think she did too. There was some expression of fondness there, I was sure of it, and that gave me great joy.

As her laughter subsided, we looked at each other and I saw her expression change. She began to toy with the metal points on her sleeve, drawing them through and through her fingers, her eyes downcast.

"Francis, can I ask you something? You don't have to answer, if you find it difficult." Her question asked, she folded her hands together in her lap. I felt so easy in her company now, even that gave me no alarm, so I gave no answer, other than a smile and she continued, encouraged. "Did Richard...?" There was a hesitation there and I waited, hoping I would be able to answer whatever it was she sought. "Did Richard really want to wed Anne? When the earl... when he tried to arrange the marriages with George and Isabel?"

My first reaction was one of surprise, which I hoped I covered successfully. Then I became much more uncomfortable, remembering my conversation with Richard back at Middleham, and now very much aware of her direct stare, pinning me to my seat. I ran my hand through my hair restlessly. The last thing I had expected from this quiet young girl is that she would be so direct. In a way, it was quite refreshing.

"Well, you know we were all together quite a lot at Middleham. Still are when not called down to court for visits such as this." I knew what she wanted from me and although a devil deep down inside me could have told her the truth, I told her only a version of it. "After so many years, I don't doubt there is affection between them. I have seen signs of it. They are very close that much is true." I could have added that Anne had much higher expectations than Richard, who was much more realistic in this concern. But I didn't. I couldn't do that to the beautiful face that was looking at me with complete and utter trust.

"Close – as brother and sister?"

There was so much hope in those few words, and at first I was not sure how to answer her. I looked down a little, veiling my gaze whilst I composed my answer.

"Not exactly. If Anne is like a sister to anyone it is probably myself. I have sisters of my own whom I have not seen for some time, and I must admit Anne did fill that emptiness when I was first sent to Middleham."

Her frown was quick but I didn't understand it – at first. "What is it?"

She began to fiddle with her gown now, obviously uncomfortable, the tables turned now that she was asked to answer. Her next words sent me reeling.

85

"Well, Anne was talking one day about the lack of suitable matches for her... for a lady of her nobility, and, well, she seemed to imply that the earl had considered yourself as a match for her hand, since the king had refused his earlier request for the hand of a royal duke."

If she had declared undying love for me and fallen at my feet, I could not have been more shocked. Anne Neville? A bride for me? That was ridiculous! I began to chew my thumbnail anxiously, a bad habit, I knew, but the action was a nervous reflex.

"But I am already wed to the earl's niece!" The thought was still sinking in. "Although..."

In some skewed way it made sense. My marriage to Anna Fitzhugh had as yet to be consummated, whereas Anne and I were more of an age. And I was wealthy. Very wealthy. So, now that Anne had been rejected by a royal duke, did the earl consider his daughter a better bride for me than his niece? An annulment? I felt strange for a moment, caught between wanting something and not knowing what I wanted. I hated indecision. Despised it. And at the moment I despised myself. All the pleasure of the evening had gone; the room was cold. I wished Richard would hurry up.

I fixed my eyes on the fire so I didn't have to read her eyes even as I asked her.

"Is this true? You do not jest?" Not that I thought she would. Not on this. "He would annul my marriage to Anna?"

"Francis..." her name on my lips was like blossom on a breeze, but it was blown away roughly as the door opened and Richard entered with Tom, his squire, scurrying in to check the fire and refill the waiting flagons. Richard surveyed us both with his usual serious regard. He had picked up on the atmosphere and knew he had interrupted something between us. He didn't look particularly happy about it either as he returned her ardent gaze without responding before looking at me directly.

"Francis?"

It was a tone of command; I was used to it. I had no idea

what to say to what had just been revealed to me and so I stood, quickly. A little too quickly, finding I could hardly look at either of them.

"The lady is here as requested, Dickon. I'll be off to my bed if you don't mind?"

I managed a quick nod in her direction and the misery in her eyes clutched at my heart. And not only that, she also stood in some haste, her cloak pooling around her as a hand stretched out towards me.

"Francis..I..!" it was a desperate plea and I halted. I had to stop. I could not walk away from her like that, no matter what confusion now reigned in my mind.

Richard was watching me; I was more than aware of that. He had no idea what was going on and the whole situation made me very uneasy.

"No matter Lady Caitlin," I said as pleasantly casual as I could. As if my mind was not in a turmoil of confusion. "Please do not distress yourself." I looked towards Richard, a plea hidden in my words. "Dickon – if I have your leave?"

"Of course," he answered tersely, his eyes moving between us, tinged with suspicion. I felt his gaze boring into my back as I left the chamber, leaving them to their night together, where thoughts of Anne Neville would not long prevail in Caitlin's mind, that was for sure.

She wanted him, that much was obvious. They would spend the night in his curtained bed, exploring each other's bodies, relishing the feelings they shared. I felt sick. My head was pounding and there was a tight feeling in my gut. I was not quite sure what was disturbing me the most. The closeness of Caitlin, the lingering smell of her perfume, the thought of her in Richard's arms, or my future once again being decided on the whims of men.

It was not that I cared much for Anna Fitzhugh, in fact that I cared anything. What was galling was the lack of my right to choose. Right now, yes, I would willingly annul my marriage to

Anna, if it meant I could marry the girl I loved. The devil was playing a game with me this evening and I could almost feel his sting. It burned hard, hot and fierce low down in my body and my pace picked up as I headed for the guest apartments on the east wall of the palace.

She was there, I knew she would be. I had told her I would not be long and I had kept my promise. She was wearing a dark crimson gown, the folds of her skirts as black as the hair that she had kept loose, falling around her like a veil.

Marie rose up from the window seat as she saw me approach and there was no time for words as I reached for her and crushed her lips to mine in a passionate, if somewhat rough, embrace. Her lips parted to admit my tongue, which roamed her mouth, denying her the ability to speak, yet still allowing her to gasp with pleasure.

She returned my advances just as ardently, my hands curled around her back firmly as she grasped my neck. I am not sure how long we stood there in the shadows, mouths locked together, feasting on each other madly. I pulled back for a breath, looking into her eyes which were black pools without the light of a torch, but she smiled.

"Francis.." she breathed. "Oh..!"

Without ado, I caught her hand and pulled her into an empty ante-chamber. The fire was low and no candles were lit. I had no idea whose room it was and at that moment I cared not one whit as my body raged with a lust that I could not contain. I heard Marie giggle softly as I pulled her along, before turning her around, to kiss her once again. The force of my passion caused her to walk backwards until we reached a point of resistance, and before I knew what I was doing, she was lying back on a table, my hands fighting with her skirts until I felt flesh, at first cool, rounded, then deep, warm and moist.

She was groaning softly now, as I almost ripped my points apart to free my raging manhood, her own hands tearing at the laces on her bodice, freeing her breasts to the air, nipples hardening in the chill.

I had no control over my actions at that time, and can not say that what I did filled me with honour, but she clamoured out for my body as I did for hers, and as my mouth roamed across the swell of her breasts, I slid inside her with an almost practiced ease, finding a rhythm that had her moaning with pleasure.

I was silent, not a word did I speak, although the escape her flesh gave me was all that I needed just then. As I thrust inside her again and again, my mind grew vague, each arch of my body wiping out the words I had heard, the thoughts I had had and as I reached the peak of my desire, slamming myself against her, she curled her legs around my back and my whole being released.

The fears of the night emptied away, into this young girl who seemed only too happy to allow me to abuse her body. It appeared that it was only myself who knew that the taste of passion would soon fade, only to die in the ashes of disgust and despair.

12. GREENWICH PALACE
December 1468

The cold, hard stone of the chapel floor was a welcome penance during Mass the following morning.

I could see Richard clearly, his attitude seriously devout as usual, and I admit to my shame that as I looked at his clasped hands my mind envied what business they had been about the night before. Tortured by my thoughts and not a little guilt, I kept my head fixed firmly forwards and down and dare not look for Caitlin although I knew she would be somewhere in the congregation behind me. I imagined I could smell her violet fragrance in the incense which wafted around me like a mist, which did nothing to help my mood.

Although I despised myself for my appalling behaviour the previous night, it seemed that all it had done was heightened my attraction to Marie. I had already passed her that morning as we filed into the chapel, and the look she gave me was one of the most love-some I had ever seen, her eyes sparkling in a way I had not noticed before. The stark realisation that she may have enjoyed our encounter shocked me a little, but was not without some relief.

Bedding Marie was the one consolation I had, and I had to grudgingly admit it brought me both a measure of pleasure and gratification, shamed as I was at how I had used her to assuage my anger and frustration the night before. That it had not displeased her was a surprise, but then, I was hardly an experienced paramour, and I was not about to try and make sense of it by telling tales to Percy. Even if my need to understand was desperate, my skin was feeling decidedly bruised. There was no way I could bear his taunts and jests today, not even as close as we were.

With Mass finally over, I was wondering if I should seek further reparation by confessing my sins when a female voice cut through my thoughts.

"Lovell? A moment, if you please?"

Out of the corner of my eye, I saw Richard halt on his way from the chapel. It was only when I turned that I saw it was because he had recognised the voice that I had not. Cecily Neville, Dowager Duchess of York and Richard's mother was advancing towards me with a sure and steady step. I glanced at Richard quickly and he shrugged, also looking towards his mother as she approached me. She moved, I thought, like some form of avenging angel, and with rising dread I wondered if someone had told her my secret. Was I about to be chastised by the matriarch of the House of York for ravishing a defenceless girl within the confines of her son's court?

For a few moments, I tasted fear, before calming myself with the knowledge that the last thing that could be said about Marie was that she was defenceless. Her passion was as hot and ardent as mine, and my advances had been welcomed right from the start. In seeing the reaction to my behaviour last night, I had an inkling that her sexual powers were being nurtured by the day and that quite soon, she may well be a force to be reckoned with. Surely then, she had no cause to complain?

Cecily Neville was a formidable figure. Not that she was overly tall, but her whole bearing was so queenly, her presence could not be ignored. Dressed in dark grey, which only caused her stormy eyes – Richard's eyes – to stand out more fiercely against her pale skin. Her sapphire rosary beads knocked together musically as she walked towards me. They were looped around a silver girdle, one which encompassed a waist to be envied by many a woman less than half her age. As I looked at her she half turned and caught Richard's attention.

"Take this to my chamber for me, would you? I will not be more than a moment. We should then pay our respects to the countess, bearing in mind the day."

Richard took the missal from his mother's slim fingers as it was offered out to him. For a moment, he looked at it

91

thoughtfully, passing his hand over the cover. Then he glanced up and his eyes seemed to be tearful, an impression that lasted only for a second. He said nothing, but left the chapel swiftly and she watched him go before turning back to me, her expression wistful.

"Ah, how I hate this time of year." I frowned then, not quite catching why she should make such a statement. Her eyes fixed me with a direct stare, which was not ungentle. "I spent many a happy year at Sandal Castle in years gone past. I cannot visit there now. Especially not in winter."

My face flushed bright red as I remembered. The battle of Wakefield. Eight years ago this very day. Richard's father and brother slain in the snow, death turning the crisp, white flakes into a festive crimson for the most dreadful of reasons. The duke had settled in for the Christmas period, believing a truce to be in place in the skirmishes and bloodshed which were staining the families of the land. Venturing outside the safety of his fortress, he ran directly into the Lancastrian army, who seemed to have a different understanding of the word truce. To this day, no one seemed to clear as to what event had caused the duke to lead his men out of their stronghold, but the decision had been an untimely one. He was cut down by his enemies, the Lancastrian army that my own father had once fought for. Warwick's father fell beside him, and one of Richard's brothers was also killed by Lord Clifford, pleading for mercy, some said. If he was, Clifford was in no mood to show pity, too anxious to avenge the death of his father at an earlier battle. An eye for an eye. The cause of constant battles over the course of a decade.

As I looked at the duchess, I wondered how she had coped with the knowledge that the heads of both her husband and son had been chopped off and stuck on spikes over the gates of York. What strength of character did you need to see you though those events? She was looking at me sharply now, possibly wondering if I was a mute.

"I need your assistance today, Lovell." It was not at all what I had expected her to say so I merely inclined my head. "I have spoken to my nephew and he has approved my use of you."

"Then I am at your service, Your Grace," I replied smoothly, wondering what Warwick had set me up for now.

"I need you to go to the stables and see the Master of Horse. I have a gift for my youngest son, and it seems your name comes up as one of his most loyal friends." She paused. "And one has need of loyalty these days. I consulted my son, the king, also. He could think of no one better than you." She frowned slightly. "Although I know there is a Percy around here somewhere but Edward just laughed when I mentioned him."

It was very hard to suppress the smirk that threatened to crease my face in two. The thought of Rob carrying out an errand for the duchess lifted my mood. Particularly if it involved discretion.

"I am honoured, Your Grace," I replied, inclining my head in formal acknowledgement. She was the king's mother after all. "May I ask what the gift is?"

The look on her face was something to behold and my heart sank back down in my chest as it dawned on me what an idiot I was.

"Is the fact that I am directing you to the Master of Horse not a big enough clue? Dear, dear Lovell! My son may extoll your virtues in chess but it seems the true level of your intellect falls far short of what I had expected."

My utter humiliation was saved not only by the fact that the chapel was almost empty by now, but by the slight tilt to the left hand side of the duchess's mouth. It seemed she shared the same love of sarcasm as her eldest son, so any barb was slightly softened. Only very slightly.

"A horse, then?" I ventured, somewhat shamefacedly. The woman had all the bearing of a queen, and was – to me – just as formidable as the actual queen. In fact, more so. She gave an imperceptible nod, now allowing herself to smile.

"A fine steed. Brought down from Middleham just recently. I will bring Richard down into the courtyard just after Sext. Please be ready to present it to him."

"Me?" I honestly thought she was sending me to groom the beast, or indeed polish its bridle, not actually hand it over to Richard. I would have thought the Master of Horse would have done that at the very least. The shock must have been apparent on my face and her smile widened.

"You are capable of leading a horse by the rein? My nephew has, at least, taught you that much? Or do you spend so much time at chess that you fail in the most basic knightly duties?"

Her sudden change of tone had me even more confused, causing me to fall over my tongue.

"No... I... I mean..."

She laughed then, a sound as clear as a bell.

"Relax, boy. I do love to tease my son's friends, especially those who do not crumple into the ground at just one word. You are non such as that, I can see, which pleases me. I am also told you excel at the lute?"

Despite her complimentary words, I could now only nod dumbly. "Good! You must entertain me one night during the festivities. I will very much look forward to it. Now, off you go. Be ready by the chime of Sext. I don't intend to stand around in this damnable weather for too long waiting for you!" Without a further word she sailed off, her gown trailing behind her against the stone, the arc of her spine rigidly set.

Without further ado, leaving her just enough time to clear the door of the chapel, I set off for the stables, at least lucky enough in the fact that it had for the time being stopped snowing, although the courtyard was already covered in deep drifts which slewed up against the palace walls, blurring the rough hewn edges.

Sir Thomas Burgh, the king's Master of horse, was not hard to find. He was a tall, broad man, with sharp eyes, crinkled at the corners, enough to think he spent hours staring into the sun. As I entered the stables, knocking my boots against the door frame to dislodge snow from my toe caps, he turned to acknowledge the sound only, his face expressing no surprise. He knew I was coming, that was for sure.

"Lovell," his tones were clipped and tight and I nodded my head. He was not a man I knew well, but he was said to be amiable by reputation. And fond of his ale. That one came from Rob. "Over here."

I made my way across to where he was standing and stepped back, holding a stall door ajar. He said noting else, just jerked his head, and I stepped inside and whistled softly in appreciation. There before me was the most magnificent destrier I had ever seen. A grey so silvered it was almost white, and even I knew that truly white horses were the stuff of legend. There was only the slightest dark gray dappling to it's flanks, but the fringe of its hooves and the mane and tail, were darkly grey as a thunder filled sky.

It rolled one cautious eye at me and snorted, misty breath rising in clouds. Without thinking I held out my hand and it raised its head, ears folding forwards, a sign it was definitely not going to bridle at my touch. Sure enough, before long I felt the leathery, whiskered flesh nuzzle against my hand in greeting. It was only then that I allowed myself to reach up and stroke the thick, luxurious mane.

"A fine beast, don't you think?" As I nodded Burgh continued to speak. "Sent down from Earl Warwick's own stables, bred from the finest Syrian stock. 'Tis a pity though." His last few words made me start, and I turned to face him as he leant against the stall, his eyes on the animal full of grudging admiration.

"Pity?" Strong teeth nipped at my palm, disappointed at the lack of any treat there. "What do you mean?"

The sniff he gave was somewhat dismissive.

"This is an animal bred for war. It's still only a yearling, but the breeding will out. You should know by now Lovell, it's not only your sword and axe you take into battle. This ton of horseflesh is as lethal as anything you can wield in your hand. Our young duke will need all his mettle to bend this beast to his command." I passed my hand down the silvery flank and felt its muscles ripple beneath my palm. I didn't know much, that was true, but I knew one thing. Richard could, and would, be its master, no matter how difficult the task. As I was just fighting another unreasonable surge of envy, I heard the jingle of harness, and Burgh thrust a bridle towards me.

"Get on with it. You don't have long."

I frowned then, taking the bridle from his hands. Surely he didn't think I was that ham-fisted that it would take me over two hours to bridle a horse? The duchess had said she would see me again at Sext!

It was then I saw what was in his other hand and I sighed. My feet were already freezing and I had come down without my cloak, an impulse action I was now about to regret as I looked at the brush he was holding out to me. In one way, I would only be too pleased to brush the animal's coat until it shone like silver, looking like an armoured war-horse as I lead it out proudly to meet its owner, if only my feet were not already encased in blocks of ice.

13. GREENWICH PALACE
December 1468

On the first chime of the chapel bell, Burgh nodded in my direction and despite being unable to feel any of my toes, I urged the silver-grey steed forwards, out of the shadows and into the snow crusted courtyard, where large, feathery flakes had once again begun to fall. For the first time I noticed its high stepping gait and how it flicked its storm-grey tail regally, as if relishing a spell of freedom, ready, willing and expecting to be admired.

A small group, each one of them heavily cloaked, had gathered at the bottom of the stone stairs. The duchess was there, as was Countess Warwick, young Anne and the regularly insufferable Isabel. Richard was staring at his feet, looking as unimpressed as I was to be out in the depths of winter, but he looked up as the first hoof struck stone, no matter that it was covered in snow.

Richard raised his head just at the moment that I met Caitlin Desmond's gaze, with a look which began, in me, an instant thaw. Her expression was almost as dumbstruck as Richard's, but the smile which followed was one of friendly welcome and I returned it broadly, before tilting my head to look at my friend's face. To be honest, I felt a bit like a grinning idiot, but my heart was thumping so loudly at the sight of her I just couldn't help myself.

I walked the animal in a circle, so that they could all admire it, bringing him to a halt just before the small group. Isabel appeared to be trying to disappear into her furs, whilst Anne was almost jumping up and down with excitement, her eyes shining like two bright stars. Her cheeks were rosy with the cold and it struck me that she had never looked more childlike and innocent than she did then. But, to me, it was still Caitlin who outshone them all. Her eyes had a depth to them which made me long to dive in and be lost forever.

Swathed in a tawny velvet cloak, which only served to

contrast the fiery tones of her hair, she blazed like the last gasp of autumn, declaring defiance against winter's chill. Beside her, all the others were colourless shades, and Richard had not moved nor spoken, he just looked at his gift then back at his mother, who nodded her head at me sharply. It was my cue; I had been briefed.

"From the finest stables in Middleham."

Richard looked at me, then his horse, then back at his mother, his face unreadable, as if set with shock.

"He's Syrian. A fine lineage, one as fine as your own!" The duchess took a step forwards, placing both hands on Richard's shoulders. "Never forget that, my son. Always remember you are descended from the most noble of bloodlines, through two branches of the Plantagenet house, directly from the third Edward himself. This animal has a similar pedigree and will serve you well. May God be with you at this holy time."

I was just beginning to think this whole affair was woefully solemn for a festive gift-giving, when those words and the look behind her eyes laid me low. My own mother had never shown such affection for me, not even when my father died. I had the idea that my mother favoured my sisters above me, a fact borne out later by the affection she had lavished on my young bride. Although, sadly, even that had not lasted long. My mother was dead and chested only a few short months later, outliving my father by only a few weeks longer than a year.

Cecily kissed Richard's cheek, and turned from him, making her way slowly back up the icy stairs followed by the countess and Isabel, who had spent the whole time looking bored and aloof. No doubt she was missing George, as it had not escaped my attention that she had spent most of the festive season trailing around after him like a docile hound.

After watching them disappear through the archway at the top, Richard ran his hand down the beast's neck, and though I tried to catch his eye, he demonstrated a deliberate evasion and kept his face averted. Anne was still smiling and I dare not look in

Caitlin's direction, keeping my attention on Richard. I had a strange sensation that Caitlin was aching to approach us, which I knew she would never do whilst Anne was there. The snow was beginning to settle, on us mostly, and with my frozen feet now making their presence felt once again, I broke the silence.

"What will you call him?" I handed the reins to Richard and gave the strong neck a final slap. "He's a fine beast. He deserves a good name."

"Yes, name him, Richard! Something to do with snow! He is so wonderfully white -or maybe something festive for the season!" Anne's voice was almost shrill, heightened either by tension or pleasure. I could not help reflecting how different she acted, against Caitlin's calm observance. The unnamed mount snorted suddenly, nuzzling Richard's palm as if seeking its own treat for standing out so long in the cold. Richard responded, but so quietly, I had to strain to hear his words, albeit that I was standing the closest to him.

"Syrie," he said, almost a whisper. "White Syrie."

With a quick encouraging sound, he led the animal forwards and the two of them fell into step, the horse accepting his new master as if he had been with him for years. I saw Burgh in the shadows of the stable, grinning mirthlessly as he watched Richard approach and I turned back to Anne and Caitlin who were both regarding his retreating back.

I looked at Anne, agonizingly aware of Caitlin's profile caught in the corner of my eye, and she gave me a small smile, brushing a snowflake from my shoulder.

"He'll be fine," Anne said confidently, before pulling up her hood briskly. "Let's go inside. It's getting worse out here." I could think of nothing else to say but as I stepped forward, I felt a hand on my arm and even then the warmth of her penetrated the freezing air.

As I looked into Caitlin's face, it struck me that if her clothes were autumnal, her eyes were the freshness of spring, leaves unfolded to meet the sun, her skin was pale, translucent – her cheeks dusted with the palest rose. She was all four seasons standing beside me and I knew I never wanted to be where she was not, at the same time knowing that such imaginings were a folly. I swallowed hard and tried to keep my mind under control. Her voice was as soft as the velvet of her cloak, the gentle lilt more prominent in the hushed courtyard.

"What is it? What's wrong?" she asked almost fearfully, as if to hear the worst would cast her into some form of hell. "It was a beautiful gift, was it not?"

I nodded, tearing my gaze away from hers, both wanting and fearing Richard's sudden appearance. I needed him to come and be my salvation, to take Caitlin away and remind me I was a languishing dolt. Yet at the same time I didn't, I longed to spend time alone with her, no matter how short. To have her look at me, to hear her voice and inhale her fragrance. I knew that what I was about to tell her would sadden her heart, but there was nothing for it.

"It is the 30th day of December. Eight years ago on this very day Richard's father, the Duke of York was foully murdered in a snow filled field outside Sandal Castle. It has given the duchess's gift additional meaning I think." I saw her eyes melt as I spoke and I would swear on a holy relic that they darkened, or lightened. That they changed hue in a subtle shift like the sky as dawn dispelled the night. Something in them made me pause, and I found I could not tear my gaze from hers. The very tip of her tongue appeared between her lips, which parted as she spoke to me alone.

"I am so pleased that he has you for his friend, Francis, for I think there are few who truly understand his heart."

Embarrassed and touched at the same time, I finally looked away from her and over into the shadows beyond the stable doors. I had no answer for her, although I knew that every word she had said was true.

"Come." I said quietly. "He will be along soon. Don't worry."

Solemnly, she looked back at me and allowed me to guide

her inside, her eyes still searching mine.

14. GREENWICH PALACE
January 1469

"What the hell was that?"

The young freckle-faced minstrel flushed bright red and looked around the hall which was now almost empty, servants scurrying around to prepare for the night.

"My Lord?"

Rob shook his head impatiently, gesturing his cup at an older man in the group of minstrels.

"No, you there! You in the green – whatever that is you are wearing. What was that?"

The musicians looked at each other askance as The elderly man looked down at his voluminous green robe. It was of an old fashioned style, that was no doubt, and Rob was being particularly mischievous to point this out. But then, he had downed quite a lot of wine, his mood unusually terse.

"The music, my Lord?" Rob rolled his eyes and the musician swallowed hard. "My Lord...it is a tune recently brought over from the court at Burgundy. It..."

"For Mary's sake, I feel like you just used my head as an anvil. Can't you play something more soothing?" Rob cut across his explanation impatiently, leaning back in his chair. "What's that one about that woman. Bella something...is it?"

"But the king likes..." The protestation was cut short as Rob tilted his head and glowered at the older man.

"The king... in case you hadn't noticed... left about an hour ago, no doubt to save his hearing. Now, that tune.."

The younger boy brightened suddenly, seemingly happy to save the elder man his scold.

"'Oh Rosabella,' my Lord?"

"That's the one!' Rob cawed triumphantly, waving his cup triumphantly. "Play that one! It's gentler on the soul! Well," he looked into his cup frowning. "On my soul anyway."

The young man looked at me, perplexed, his brow knotted.

"Just play the music," I said quietly, knowing that this particular tune was usually accompanied by a vocalist who was in no way present this evening. And it was a lack of presence that had caused Rob to be in such a bad mood. He had hoped that the statuesque Lady Shaftesbury would bend to his advances, having accompanied the Warwick household here. It was Epiphany, and soon everyone would be departing back north. Rob had been hoping to make his own presence felt in more ways than one… but he had not anticipated the allure of John Woodville, the queen's brother, who had been swifter off the mark.

As the mournful tune filled the air, Rob threw back his head, drinking deeply and I felt I was being watched. Sure enough, my eyes caught Marie, talking with some other ladies down the hall. Talking to them, but watching me. I had noticed she looked particularly fetching this evening, a silken gown the colour of blackberries setting off the cool sensuousness that was her skin. I could not be sure but it seemed lower cut than she usually wore, revealing more flesh yet still tempting. Her slender neck was bare, aching to have her wealth of hair released to fall like a veil around her.

A welcome, familiar stirring urged me to leave Rob to his drunken musings, if I could but get away without his questioning, until I saw that Marie had conveniently provided a solution to my predicament - to leave Rob to drown himself in his cups. As the music once again soared into the hall, albeit much quieter this time, I inclined my head in Marie's direction, hoping she would understand, and of course, she did.

Without a moments hesitation she began to walk towards me, bringing her companion with her. The other girl was fair, but far too fair for my tastes. She had the silver gilt hair of a Woodville and it was only as she drew closer that I understood, with a silent groan, that that was exactly who she was. Martha Woodville had the same colourless, gilt complexion as her sister, so fair that even her brows and lashes were almost invisible.

It struck me, as the two approached, arms linked in a sisterly fashion, that she looked almost unfinished. An artist's sketch, waiting to be filled with paint and life. The girl was very slim and as far from Rob's taste in women as it was possible to get. But tonight, she was just what he needed. She was a Woodville and the look in her eyes as the two of them halted before us told me that Rob's revenge on her brother would be doubly sweet.

Marie looked up at me from beneath a curve of dark lashes, her arm still looped around that of her companion.

"Do you not dance, sirs?"

Rob rose to his feet, his expression miraculously clearing as he looked at the two women.

"Only when I have the right companion, if I may be so bold as to ask your name, my Lady." He already knew Marie, but if he had not already met the queen's sister, I could not resist introducing him.

"Rob, this is Martha. Martha Woodville, sister to our most gracious queen."

Watching him bow low whilst surreptitiously placing his goblet back on the table, I had to repress a smirk. She was pretty enough, certainly pretty enough for any man to take more than a passing interest in, as one thing that should be said is that the Woodville strain was certainly known for its grace and beauty. Only I knew it wasn't that which was making Rob's interest – shall we say – peak.

"Enchanted, my Lady,' he smiled, his blue eyes glittering with intent. Martha was, in the meantime, looking back at him with a type of shy interest which somehow saddened me. Could I really be happy that Rob would intentionally use this young girl to wreak his offended ire on? I had no doubt that Miriam would soon tire of her tiresome Woodville beau and Rob would be there as soon as she lifted as much as brow in his direction.

It was the festive season, the court glittered like a golden bauble as wine flowed like winter streams and everything seemed so beautifully gilded and bright. But I knew John Woodville. He was an interminable bore, his favourite topic of conversation was himself and knowing Miriam as I did, she did not seem the type of woman to be long enamoured of such a man.

Rob was a lot of things, but he was also charming, in a brusque way, good company and his interest in the fairer sex was just that. An interest in them and not in getting them interested in himself.

The mournful throes of "Oh Rosabella" were just coming to an end, when Rob shot a glance at his nemesis in green and threw him a covert gesture that looked like he was hurrying them along.

The elderly minstrel looked confused but happily, his son caught on and they launched into the much livelier "Petit Vriens" giving Rob the opportunity he wanted. His sore head and foul mood forgotten, he held out his hand. Martha blushed, reasonably prettily, but then I was judging her against Caitlin where there was no true comparison, and she placed her snow-white hand in his large, tanned one.

Rob drew her away to dance, his satisfied smile a blatant acknowledgement that he had already entrapped the unsuspecting woman into the lair of his revenge. Marie grinned and then sidled up to me, a waft of orange-flower water lingering in her hair.

"You are not with the duke tonight."

It was not a question and I turned my eyes away from the couple, just as Rob's arm slid around Martha's slim waist, drawing her just that bit closer than he probably needed to, yet she seemed not to mind. She was smiling at any rate.

"No, not tonight," I replied absently

Her smile was knowing and I frowned slightly.

"I thought not, "she murmured, her hand straying up to brush something invisible from my sleeve. "I have just seen him with Lady Desmond. It made my heart glad for I knew then that you may then have time to spare for me."

She may as well have punched me in the gut. Yes, I had settled myself to the idea that I would only ever skirt around the fringes of Caitlin's life, but it still hurt. If Marie had seen them together, that meant only one thing.

I kept my eyes on the dancing couple for the moment, amazed, as always, that Rob managed look so composed after downing a tun of Rhenish. So absorbed was I in my own feelings that it took a while for her words to hit home. How could she know about Caitlin? She and Richard scarce exchanged a look when in mixed company and I was often the facilitator in their late night trysts. And Marie was in the service of the duchess, the queen's mother. This was not knowledge I felt Richard would want them to be in possession of, particularly bearing in mind the queen's feelings for any Desmond. I turned a quizzical gaze on her, feigning innocence.

"Why so?"

Martha Woodville was laughing. I could hear her over the music, so Rob was obviously making an impression. With her head tilted so winsomely, Marie's eyes met mine and the look there made me bite my lip whilst my loins begin to clamour loudly, drowning out the soaring tune. I should have been ashamed of myself, but I was not.

"She was passing him a note, from Anne Neville."

I looked at her blankly. How she would know who the note was from amazed me and I wondered if she also knew what it said? A prick of conscience made me remember her mistress's reputation for being descended from a water nymph. A particularly mystical one. She caught my message adeptly.

"Martha saw Anne write it. The countess spent the afternoon with the queen to share the felicitations of the season. From what I hear there was more frost inside the chamber than there was outside. Anne was talking to Martha, they seem quite friendly by all accounts, and everyone knows how sweet the Neville girl is on the king's brother."

She began to fuss with the lace bodice of her gown, apparently for no other reason than to draw my attention to her neckline and the smooth expanse of skin exposed there. I breathed in deeply, feeling an unaccountable urge to run my fingers across the line of her gown where it restrained her breasts.

"Does he ever speak of her to you?"

"No." The answer was instantaneous and I knew I had been unable to keep the flash of annoyance from my face but she appeared not to notice. There was one thing about Marie, she seemed particularly single-minded when it came to what she wanted. And I had to admit a certain amount of pleasure, that for the moment, she seemed to apply that determined spirit to me. I softened my manner with a bemused smile. "But then, why would he, as I never speak of you to him." Martha laughed again, louder this time. "Rob, however..." I let my tone tease her and caught her gaze in mine which began to burn.

"And, what do you say?" she whispered softly, moving closer so that I could better see down into her décolleté. By now, I just wanted to peel the silk from her body and feast on her like rare fruit. Marie could stir my lusts like a cook with a stew but yet she was not a woman I wanted to spend much time with. Frivolous and loving of gossip, once my desires were sated, we seemed to have nothing to say to each other.

We were standing so close that her hand sought mine within the folds of her skirts. Her thumb circled the palm of my hand whilst her little finger toyed with the gold signet ring I wore on mine. I swallowed hard, her touch was stoking a fire that would need certain actions to put it out. And soon.

"Why," I whispered softly, "I tell him you have eyes that shine like stars, and a body that could make a man weep."

Her fingers curled around mine slowly.

"Yet – I have not done so?"

"Not yet." I murmured, lowering my lips to her ear. "But there is always tonight."

She pulled on my hand and my natural reticence held back as she smiled, exposing her neck to my warm breath.

"Then perhaps we should hurry. Martha shares a chamber with her sister, Mary, but she is with the queen this night. Would you not prefer a soft bed to our usual venue?"

Bearing in mind that most of our trysts took place either in empty chambers, window embrasures or any other quiet space we could find once the palace slept, I had to admit this was a tempting offer. Privacy was not in abundance and most of our encounters were rushed, even if satisfying.

Without another word she turned from me with a courteous curtsey and crossed the hall swiftly, but slow enough for me to see the confident exchange she had with Martha, who was now returning to sit with Rob at the board. They both approached me, Rob grinning like a fool and his partner almost becomingly flushed.

"I will bid you good night." I said, somewhat hastily, somewhat annoyed to catch the curve of Martha's lips. Then I reprimanded myself. So they had planned it. I was not about to spoil Rob's night by telling him that rather than scoring a victory over his enemy he had actually been deliberately sought out. He was hardly likely to take that well and if the Woodville girl was willing to share her body with him, that was her affair. Although with that knowledge, I felt Rob may not find her such easy prey as he suspected.

Before long, I had caught up with Marie just as she had reached the passage to the royal apartments and after following her lead, I found myself in a softly lit room which smelled of roses. Marie walked over to the sideboard and reached over to a taper, lighting another candle, so that she stood between two pools of light.

She must have seen the frown on my face as she half turned, exposing the laces of her dress, looking back at me over her shoulder. Taking the initiative, after all we were there for only one thing, I moved over and began to strip out the silken ribbons which pulled the satin bodice together around her, revealing her snow white kirtle beneath.

Neither of us spoke but once I had sufficiently freed her from the restrictions of her clothing, she turned and placed both hands on my chest, as if in protest.

"But..?" Before I could say more she placed a finger tip on my lips.

"Step back… just a little." Her voice was breathy, light as gossamer, but my blood was up now. The last thing I wanted was to step back. I could see the orbs of her breasts, her gown shadowing them, giving them a mystery that would soon be diminished, but she seemed determined in her cause, so I did as she said and widened the space between us.

Facing me, she pulled her gown down from around her shoulders, stepping out of the pool of fabric around her feet. I stood, mesmerised, as she pushed her skirts out of the way and straightened up, standing before me completely naked. As my throat dried, no doubt aided by the fierce pounding of my heart and the heat of my blood, she lifted up her arms and released the fall of ebony silk that was her crowning glory. It fell down her back like a bridal veil, only pausing to caress her shoulders which were bathed in ambient light. I looked on and my chest threatened to explode. Along with a more intimate part of my anatomy.

Her eyes were lakes of darkness as most of the light was behind her, although I could still clearly see every curve and line of her body. Against the fairness of her skin, her nipples stood out, dark and proud. Her breasts seemed to call out for the sanctuary of my hands and looking down past the plane of her stomach, I found that mysterious, deep valley into which I now longed to travel. My eyes returned to hers and she smiled.

"Dearest Francis," her voice was velvet, soft and unctuous, a quality that was almost touchable. "Now, shall I make you weep?"

It was hard to describe. My innards felt as if they were melting which was a strange sensation bearing in mind the rigidity of my manhood. I began to undo the points of my doublet, hoping my hands did not tremble either with anticipation or desire as I looked back into her eyes.

God forgive me, but for a few seconds I did see someone different standing there. The candlelight played on her hair, turning it bright as flame as it thickened and became unruly, foaming over mother-of pearl shoulders like a raging sea, the breasts were a little larger then, tipped rosy instead of dusk, and my thoughts would let me go no further as her pleading eyes flashed emerald green for the barest of seconds and I was completely undone.

Half undressed, I lunged at her, hearing her gasp as my hands and lips assaulted her body with a force of attack I normally reserved for the tiltyard. Within minutes we were on the nearby bed, her naked body writhing beneath me as she raised her legs up, encompassing me, drawing me down into the waiting, eager warmth of her. I knew I was out of control, but the gasps of pleasure and moans of gratification coming from her lips only urged me on more. Her tongue caressed mine as I kissed her between lunges, her teeth nipped my lips, her breasts brushed my chest as she arched herself upwards, each time meeting my urgent demands with a willingness to be devoured.

"Oh, Francis... Francis...my love, my...oh, please...!"

I could not say her name. It never entered my head to be truthful, yet my body slaked its lusts on hers and we both knew that this was the real reason that brought us together. No matter. As I purged myself against her willing flesh, there were many things that I could not deny. One of them was the tears in my eyes.

15. WESTMINSTER PALACE
January 1469

I left her at the chamber door, somehow feeling that Martha may be returning before too long, yet I somehow doubted Rob would be with her. Nevertheless, it had been sheer bliss to share our passions on a soft bed instead of any available surface, and it had certainly given me a full appreciation of her many charms. Yet, as we left, the kiss we exchanged was almost chaste and she had reached up and touched the cleft in my chin affectionately.

I made my way back to my chamber, but took a more leisurely route. It was long past Compline and the palace was quiet, slumbering its way out of the end of the festive season. As I turned the corner to pass through the galleried landing overlooking the courtyard, I saw a lone figure, dark, staring out at the falling snow. I could recognise him across a tiltyard in full armour so at this distance, even in the dark, it was easy. Richard stood with his hands on the balustrade, lost in silent contemplation. He didn't even hear me, I don't think, until I came to a halt by his side and spoke to him.

"We may have to delay our return north."

It was a casual remark, but I saw the muscle in his cheek twitch in response.

"We should - but it won't go down well if we do. Warwick is aching to get away from here. He's like a chained beast around Woodvilles. The countess may delay though. I am not sure if she is taking her household to Warwick or Middleham." He coughed suddenly, clearing his throat. "Even Anne isn't sure."

We stood in silence for a moment watching the landscape become increasingly unrecognisable in the new drifts which were building up against the walls like feather buttresses. I couldn't help my next question.

"And Lady Desmond?"

He looked down at his hands, his fingers, deathly white,

where he grasped the stone balustrade. For a while I thought he wasn't going to answer me, but then he sighed.

"I didn't know what it would feel like, Frank, but…" he looked up seemingly embarrassed, wanting to look at me I think, but despite that still avoiding my gaze.

"You love her." I could see his profile clearly as he stared straight ahead. It almost felt stupid making so obvious a statement. But then, wasn't love something that only our elders experienced – if they were lucky? It was never something I had anticipated, despite reading the romances of old, where maidens were fair, knights were brave and chivalry was the ultimate aim of all men. I didn't love Anna – in truth I had never expected to. One day, when she was of an age, I would be expected to perform my husbandly duties. The thought almost panicked me when I thought of my recent skirmishes with Marie.

"Does that sound foolish?"

It didn't to me I had to admit so my answer was prompt and honest.

"No. Why should it?"

He shook his head wearily.

"I don't know. I think it is because I didn't expect it. I have believed for so long that I would be married for land and power rather than have the privilege of finding someone with whom I could share my heart."

"But – you can't wed her!" The exclamation left my lips before I could mask its surprise.

"No." One word. Drenched in sadness. I hardly had time to wonder why something that was supposed to bring such joy and happiness was making us both so unutterably miserable when he turned to look at me, his eyes steely. "And if I can't, I will not be forced into any foreign marriage bed. If I am denied a path I would take because of the stain of bastardy, I will choose who will take her place." The determination in his voice was hard to miss, I had heard it too many times before.

"Do you have anyone in mind?" I knew the answer. I didn't

need to ask but I did it just to see the look on his face. He didn't say anything, but then he didn't have to. Once again he stared out into the snow. "Despite what the king may say?"

I saw his lip curl, somewhat sardonically, as he answered me.

"George is still his heir, whereas at one time there was talk of my joining the church. I do not think I was ever destined for great things, so in that respect my marriage is not of a great concern. Not as much as his. Edward only balks now because Warwick appears to see it as a reward rather than a request. It appears to be a joint arrangement which Edward will never agree to. It gives Warwick far too much power, and that is something he already has in abundance. I sometimes wonder if Edward married as he did just to spite him. If Warwick had not been so insistent on the French marriage, would his bedding of Elizabeth Woodville have remained a secret for all time?"

I looked around the darkened passage quickly.

"Have a care Dickon. That's the sort of talk which lost Desmond his head!" The thought was not lost on him and I saw his features soften.

"Poor Cait. She really had no idea. I had to tell her the whole despicable tale! I don't know if that is why we are so close. With my father also losing his head at an enemy's hands." He snorted then in derision, immediately disagreeing with his own words. "Enemies! What am I saying. Tom lost his head at the hands of the House of York, to my eternal shame! At least my father and Edmund were killed by the enemy. "

I thought of my own father, a lifelong Lancastrian, but he was such a remote figure I could not feel anything that would compare to Richard's grief.

"Caitlin asked me about Anne. That night... well... I can't believe Warwick ever truly considered annulling my marriage. The Fitz-hughs...there is a family bond..." I trailed off. That night still filled me with shame for some reason, even though it had had the opposite effect on Marie. Somewhere deep down I needed to purge that guilt in the only way I could. Honesty and be damned.

113

"I have to say Dickon, I envy you Lady Desmond. Dare I say, if I had seen her first..."

That made him smile and he turned back to me, his eyes glittering.

"As if she would be interested in you!" He reached up and thumped me on the arm companionably. "Besides, as you say, you're already a married man!"

"Don't remind me!" I groaned. "I really should visit her once the thaw sets in, I suppose. Although I can't say I am eager for it."

He turned in full to face me then, folding his arms across his chest, his expression speculative.

"And until then, you have other consolations." I couldn't help it but I flushed wondering who had told him. Rob, no doubt. I could see him grinning now. I chuckled, if somewhat uneasily.

"A mere distraction, Dickon. 'Tis you who have found true love, I think, and I wish you well of it. You are truly fortunate."

The humour disappeared for a second, and he released his arms, reaching up to slap himself on the right shoulder.

"Especially when you consider what baggage I bring with me!" I looked down at my boots, ashamed. I found it hard to imagine how it felt, to suffer from the affliction which had recently begun an assault upon his slim frame. It had begun only a year or two ago, and was a burden he bore in almost complete silence. I knew, as did Rob, and Tom his squire, but outside of his family, as far as I could tell, no one else had any idea. Life, for Richard, carried on as normal, no matter how difficult this was for him at times.

How must it feel to have your body twisting against its natural form? No matter how slowly and insidiously. He very rarely referred to it, but I managed to raise my eyes back to his now he had.

"You know, she didn't even blink. When she felt... not a second. Yet, I fear it will worsen and then what? I have seen old men bent over double with such afflictions. Is that really what God has planned for me Francis? Is it my punishment for not taking vows as should have been my destiny?"

I had no words of comfort for him, only shame for how sorry I had been feeling for myself. He turned away from me again and looked out into the courtyard. The snow had stopped falling and one by one stars were beginning to wink into life from behind milky blue clouds.

"I think Anne will understand too," he continued after a while. "She is so sweet and innocent, I hope she manages to hang on to that as these times can be so cruel, and I feel there is something in the air. Edward knows Warwick is restless. George too. Now that he has spurned his ambitions once again...there can only be trouble ahead." I watched him as the moon slid out from behind a cloud and turned the world silver. He raised his head skywards. "I am glad you feel affection for Cait, Frank. For whatever happens, I know you will have a care for her welfare when I may be prevented from it. I know I can trust you, for some reason I always have. Ever since we met in the tiltyard." He turned to me then and I swear I almost fell to my knees. "Thank you, Francis, for being my friend. I cannot tell you how much your loyalty means to me. But I hope to repay it in time."

Once again there were tears in my eyes but I swallowed them down.

Stupid! What was wrong with me.

"There's nothing to repay Dickon. The privilege is all mine."

We stood for a while longer, watching the sky clear as the moon turned night to day, comfortable in each other's company, words no longer needed.

16. WESTMINSTER PALACE
February 1469

The snow continued to fall until well after Epiphany, and it was not until the beginning of the following month that we could begin to consider returning north. During that time, although the festivities of the season had drawn to an end, many of us remained in close quarters at court, trying our best to entertain ourselves until the weather improved.

My clandestine trysts with Marie continued, often when I had left Richard after spending the evening in his company, playing chess, cards, or just generally in conversation about the latest book we had read, and the exploits of our chivalric heroes and how we wished to emulate them. Now and again, Anne would join us, sometimes Isabel and George, but on those nights, the atmosphere was a little more stilted and I often retired to a window embrasure, keeping my head down and strumming a tune on my lute. Where George was, one could never be sure how the conversation would run, and so I preferred to keep away from those difficult waters.

There was another reason for this, which was also entirely selfish. For when the Neville girls visited, their ladies-in-waiting accompanied them, and whilst Rob was only too pleased to exchange desire laden glances with Miriam, I found it hard to meet Caitlin's eye, other than to return her shy smile. These nights usually ended with the ladies retiring back to their chambers before Compline, whilst we stayed behind to continue our own pursuits.

George hardly ever tarried though, departing not long after Isabel had left, and not for desolation at the lack of her company, as I saw it. He had no interest in discussing the tales of Arthur or the more interesting principles of Vegetius, and so would make his excuses, yawning broadly, either at the prospect of our company, or to give a false reason for his sudden departure.

And most nights, as the hush of the castle descended to meet the quiet snow-filled gardens outside and Rob and I took our leave, I was aware of the shadow who waited in the darkened alcove outside the chamber. Much to my relief, Tom had taken over the responsibility of ensuring that Caitlin was delivered safely to Richard's chamber on the nights they spent together, although this change had the result that I had recently spent very little time in Caitlin's company.

Yet, I saw her all the time. In chapel, in the hall, cloaked and hooded, picking her way, warily, around the gardens, skirts trailing in the snow, leaving a path like a wake. Richard rarely spoke of her, and I no longer brought up the subject, but with every passing day, I awoke with a burning need to see her, like a hunger one has for bread or wine.

Finally, the weather had abated enough for us to make our preparations to leave, and I for one was more than glad to have something else to do, and pleased at the prospect of escaping our enforced confinement, no matter how warm and comfortable it had been. The feeling of freedom, just from being astride a horse, the comfort of its ambling gait and the feel of the fresh air in your face was something I was very much looking forward to. Richard was taking leave of the king and his mother whilst I remained in his chamber, supervising the removal of his chests and other belongings for the journey north. There were always a few regular items which he always took with him, these including his books and chess set, which had been a gift from the king himself.

I had sent Tom out with the last chest a while ago and was looking around the chamber satisfied with the task done when the door creaked on its hinges, heralding his return and the signal that it was time to go.

"That's the lot, Tom. I think we can get ourselves ready to leave now."

"Not quite all." I whirled round to find Marie leaning against the closed door, looking at me with expectant eyes. She was breathing heavily, I could see that clearly by the way her breasts strained against the neckline of her gown and I struggled to raise my gaze to look at her, suddenly more than a little guilty that she had not even entered my mind today, that I was happy to leave without even a word. Obviously, she had other thoughts. "Are you in such a hurry to leave?"

Turning to face her fully, I put on my best conciliatory expression.

"My whims count for nothing. When the earl leaves, I will follow him."

She cocked her head at me with a quirked smile and I couldn't help but return it. She had been more than conducive company during these last few weeks, but I had no qualms in leaving her behind. If anything, our liaisons had become somewhat too regular, and despite the obvious pleasure that we gleaned from each other's bodies, for me, her constant, watchful presence had begun to chafe.

"Were you going to leave without saying farewell?"

I took a step towards her and she raised her chin, parting her lips. We stood inches apart and I could feel her breath on my face. I knew exactly what she wanted and why she had sought me out.

"No," I said softly, running my finger down the intricately embroidered pattern on her bodice. "How could I do that?" It was like this, when we were alone, that I found myself most susceptive to her charms. She caught my hand in hers and held it to her breast, warm and soft, I could feel the rise and fall of her chest as she pressed it closer.

"Indeed," she smiled up at me. "I was thinking the same thing, but I also think that had I not come looking, you may have done just that. I had hoped to see you last night, but you were nowhere to be found."

Our faces were inches apart now, and she was pouting up at me, her displeasure an affectation, I felt. Despite the fact that I knew my time was short, other parts of my body refused to listen and began to make plans of their own.

"I was with the duke." I said simply. It was true. It had been a quiet evening, considering. Richard and Rob had played chess; I had been idling the time away with my lute. Richard had bid us good night as bell chimed for Compline, but I knew from Tom's guarded expression that he would not be alone for long. Which had led me to invite Rob to a game of cards, and we had played until the early hours.

"Lucky duke," she smiled, yet one side of her mouth turned down. "And now he gets to take you away and I may have to seek out other company."

If she was trying to make me envious, it didn't work. All it did was amuse me, although I found myself wondering if I had time to taste her pleasures one final time.

"There are plenty here who would be only too pleased to make your acquaintance, yet, I will be back, Marie. The earl travels to London frequently."

Her hand raised up and she began to play with the collar of my shirt, her fingers brushing my chin gently, sending shivers down my spine. Any minute, Tom could walk in, or Richard. Yet still, my body began to ache.

"Well... maybe then you should remind me why I should wait for you? Why I should spurn the advances of the queen's brother, now that Lady Shaftesbury will also be leaving court."

She pushed her body forwards then, pressing herself against me and I saw her lips curve when she witnessed the effect her advances were having on me. It was hard for me to deny. Yet, unwittingly, she had poured cold water on the flames of my desire. Cupping her chin in my fingers, I tilted her face up to mine and kissed her lips, noticing her eyes close as I did so. Her mouth was warm, inviting and she opened her lips to encourage me, but I pulled away gently. Whether it had been a jest or not, the thought of her willingness to consort with the Woodville brother who was married to a dowager duchess turned my stomach. I knew Rob liked to rise to the challenge, so to speak, but I was not made of the same mettle.

"You should not. If that is what pleases you, Madam."

Her eyes flew open and although she tried to disguise the shock there, I saw it anyway. Her hand touched my cheek.

"Francis, I didn't mean...! It was a jest. I was teasing you."

I took her hand from my face and kissed her fingers, stepping back away from her. There was something of a wanton spirit there, which cooled my ardour. Although I willingly accepted, indeed enjoyed, that side of her nature once we were in the throes of passion, to see it so boldly flaunted before the act I found somewhat distasteful.

"No, but you are right. I may be away for some time. I would not, could not, ask you to wait for me. Besides, as you know, I have a bride."

"You have a child bride," she retorted coldly, and I moved even further away from her but she followed me, only just in time as the door she had been leaning against opened and Tom peered around it, his brow furrowing as he spied Marie, now stony-faced.

"Frank, His Grace is readying to leave."

"Thank you, Tom. I am done here."

I left the room without looking back and followed Tom down the passageway, making for the stairway which would lead me down to the courtyard where everyone was assembling to leave. As I stepped down from the bottom step, it was directly into the heightened frenzy of activity which confirmed that I was late. The earl was just mounting his destrier, riding out in front of the litter which already had its curtains drawn against the cold, no doubt with the countess and her daughters inside. Rob was already mounted, as were several men-at-arms, the whole courtyard was full of the trappings of a wealthy family and their household about to embark on a journey. Banners snapped sharply in the cold wind, and the sun glinted on harness and armour alike.

Tom ran over and exchanged a brief word with Richard, as he swung himself up onto White Syrie, now bridled in studded, red leather. I turned away to where a groom was holding Fides by the reins patiently, only to spot another lonely steed behind it. A small, dappled grey palfrey. As if by some instinct, I looked back at Richard, just as he twisted round in his saddle and caught my eye. He didn't need to say anything and I saw Tom with the mounting block as I walked past Fides rear, his tail swishing impatiently.

Almost forgotten, Caitlin stood beside the palfrey, her eyes large and so lucent they looked almost tearful. It must be the chill, I told myself, for there was nothing for her to be distressed by. At least, as far as I knew, but this was the closest I had been to her for some time. Tom presented the block underneath the swinging stirrup and I knew Richard was still watching. That I had been silently requested to assist. I couldn't see Miriam and could only assume she was in the litter with the countess, Anne and Isabel. I couldn't believe that Anne would snub Caitlin so, and could only then imagine that Isabel had preferred the company of the older woman.

Looking at Caitlin standing there, enveloped in her tawny cloak, I knew that what I had felt earlier when confronted by Marie's carnal desires was lust, pure and simple. It held no candle to what was happening to me now as I stepped towards the somewhat forlorn figure, who no doubt longed to ride at Richard's side, but would be relegated so far back in the company, she would be fortunate to even glimpse the back of his head.

"Lady Desmond, may I assist you?"

The grateful expression on her face as she saw me there set my heart on a gallop of its own, one faster than I had ever experienced on horseback. I held out my hand to take hers, hoping that my fingers did not tremble in anticipation of her touch. Somehow I had to come to terms with the reality of Richard's fondness for this girl. It was a dishonour to allow myself to covet so desperately what was his. That realisation brought me up sharp and it was just as well, for what happened next set my resolve to do better, to conquer my longings for once and for all.

As she reached out her slender fingers, I saw the flash of a ring, jewel bright! A festive spark, the colour of claret. The colour of blood. As I knew all about her, whilst knowing nothing at all, I knew that this ring was new. That it was a gift, something which had only recently been acquired. It was not only Richard who had received a beautiful possession this season. I swallowed hard as I looked into those eyes which saw fit to damn me to hell for my secret thoughts.

The Master of Henchmen had it right. We were pushed to overcome our fears, thrown at the challenges which most tested us. Until the whirling of an axe, or the guiding of a horse by your knees alone became second nature. The worst that could happen was that you overbalanced, fell to the ground with your dignity dusting your arse. I could not in all consciousness stand by Richard's side, as I hoped to do, and continue to harbor this hope.

Steeling myself, I curled my fingers around hers, the chill of her skin serving further to cool my thoughts and guided her up onto the block, watching her every move as she settled herself into the saddle, arranging the folds of her cloak around her carefully.

I still loved her. I would always love her, but she could never be mine. Yet, if I set myself to serve Richard's cause, part of that service would be to guard all that was his. To ensure that they came to no hurt or harm. Never had indentured service seemed such a worthwhile prospect.

17. MINSTER LOVELL
April 1469

The sun was burning the back of my neck as I leaned forwards towards the chess board, moving the black pawn forwards. Anna sat opposite me, her golden hair pulled back in a tight braid, eyes lowered, looking at the board. She had the fairest skin, covered in a light down, like a peach. Yet she was but nine years old. A child.

Her mother, Lady Alice, sat by the mantel, her head bowed, concentrating on the embroidery frame in front of her. Our greeting had been perfunctory, considering we had not seen each other for three years, indeed since the marriage ceremony. She was Earl Warwick's sister, and it had to be said resembled him more than any woman possibly would want to, so it was a relief that her daughter did not seem to take after either of them.

I had been summoned to spend time with my bride when Lord Fitzhugh had travelled down from his family seat at Ravensworth Castle in the north, taking the opportunity to bring his daughter with her and introduce her to the home she would eventually call her own. It served a two-fold purpose as he had business to conduct with Sir William Stanley. The man had married my mother after my father's death and she had died bearing him a son, another William.

Sir William, with his brother, Thomas, held many lands and estates in Lancashire and the west and were both well known at Edward's court. I could only assume that Lord Fitzhugh may somehow be involved in completing my mother's affairs. I could think of no other reason for them to be meeting, and particularly not here.

I didn't like Stanley, from the minute I met him I just found something about him distinctly shifty. A feeling which had been confirmed the more I heard about him and his brother Thomas. It seemed they were gaining a reputation for hedging their bets.

Even so, I wondered about their games. Thomas was married to another one of Earl Warwick's sisters and his brother had been married to the widow of the supporter of a Lancastrian cause. I had to wonder at their convenient strategising, but I returned my eyes to the chessboard as Anna put her white Bishop down. I was trying to teach her how to play so we at least had something in common and I smiled as she raised her eyes at me quizzically.

"The bishop can only move diagonally. Like this." I covered her hand with mine and showed her where the piece could land and she regarded me with the darkest blue eyes.

"Oh. Thank you." Her own smile was shyly sweet, but my heart just plummeted. She seemed so very young! "It is very hard. All the different pieces."

I shrugged, moving my knight without really caring where it went. The last thing I wanted to do was beat a nine-year-old girl at chess.

"Would you prefer to stroll in the garden? By the river?" It was a hopeful plea but Lady Alice's head shot up.

"Without a chaperone? Don't ask me to go outside, it's too cold today!"

I twisted around to look out of the window at the bright sunshine. It was a beautiful day, the harbinger of a summer to come, but I doubted she had even noticed.

"I am sure you can trust me, my lady. Unless Anna would prefer to call her nurse?"

Piercing dark eyes shot me a look of annoyance. I had obviously hit a nerve reminding her how young my bride was. Not that I needed any reminding at all, it was everyone else who just seemed happy to accept it. As we rose from the chessboard, Lady Alice having given a nod of terse approval, Anna followed me from the solar, I couldn't help but wonder on what Caitlin had told me that night at Westminster.

Anne Neville was exactly my own age, so at least we would have had a chance at forming some semblance of a relationship. I was in no way forward, but even I knew it would be at least another seven years before we could even attempt to truly become man and wife. The thought made me even more irritated and I longed to end this visit and get back to the north.

Everyone was there. Including Caitlin and the whole of the Neville family. I should have been there too – but I had to pay court to this child. Resentment began to burn like a torch in my chest. It was a feeling that I tried to swallow down as we left the room, almost colliding with Sir William, as he entered the solar.

I immediately stepped back, inclining my head in deference. He was not an over-tall man, though clean shaven, with close cut hair which made it difficult to work out his true colouring. Grey-green eyes locked onto me for a second before he bowed his head and smiled at Anna.

"Now, sweetling, run along. Your husband will be with you shortly."

Her nose wrinkled as she looked up at him, but exactly what she was thinking I could not judge. With a swift glance at me she turned and walked down the passage way to the stairs as we both watched after her in silence. I waited, not a little nervously. We had hardly met, Sir William and I. In fact, I had seen more of his older brother around court, him being very highly thought of by Edward. I cleared my throat in anticipation which seemed to focus his attention.

"Very young," he remarked flatly, now that Anna had disappeared from view. He was looking at me, a searching expression on his face, as if looking for something.

"Yes, my Lord." I could think of nothing else to say.

"When do you leave for the north?" The question was direct, yet not particularly unfriendly. If he was wondering when they would have my house all to themselves, he would not have to wait too long.

"Four days only."

Raising his head, he peered into the sun-filled solar. I knew from the angle of the door that he would have a view of Lady Alice as she sat sewing by the hearth.

"I have a word of advice for you," he said, his eyes flicking back to connect with mine. "Don't come again." I could not have been more taken aback if he had punched me in the face and this no doubt showed as his lips curved in a rueful smile. "Come back when she is a young woman. Don't be around to witness the girl grow into womanhood. That way, when you do see her again, be it here or anywhere else, it will be as if you have just met, and you will no longer think of her as a child. By the age of fourteen, she may in no way resemble the child she is now."

I frowned, absorbing his words. At first I had thought he was almost banishing me, but as his words began to sink in, it made sense. In seven or eight years... I may not even recognise her. I could see a certain practicality in that, for if my thoughts began to turn to me sharing the same joys with her as I did with Marie, my stomach began to lurch and I felt sick.

"Seven years is a long time indeed," I murmured quietly. His hand came down upon my shoulder heavily, a truly fatherly gesture from someone who had held that title in law for only a short span of time.

"A lot can happen before then. Turn your mind away from it and let her bloom. For sure she is not going anywhere and she may even turn out to surprise you."

With a quick squeeze of my shoulder, he brushed past me into the chamber, leaving me somewhat thoughtful as I traced Anna's path through the hall and down into the garden. It made perfect sense. I hated to admit it, my dislike for the man running strong in my veins, but it did.

My step felt much lighter as I crossed the bailey and made my way down to the riverbank. It was something I was extremely proud of, the beautiful spot in which my family home sat. It nestled close to the sloping banks where the River Windrush swept by, clean and clear, rushing over the rocks and wherries as the graceful fronds of the weeping willows dipped in their green leaves as if cooling themselves in the heat of the day. I looked back at the tower of St Kenelm's church and breathed in deeply.

As if some spell had been cast, my spirit lifted and I was just feeling very pleased with myself about how grand my surroundings were, when a large splash distracted me and I whirled round.

Anna stood on the riverbank, watching the ripples in the water, another stone held in her hand. She didn't look at me, but her mood had completely changed, I could tell that from the angle of her chin and the pout that sat upon her lips, I had seen it all too often in my younger sister. I had not expected to see it in my bride.

"I know you don't like me! Well, I didn't want to marry you either. You are too old!" I stood looking at her in amazement but she looked so petulant that I had to grin.

"Who said I didn't like you? You're are nine years old for Mary's sake! What is there not to like?"

Without looking at me she threw the remaining stone with unerring aim, planting it directly in the centre of the free flowing river.

"I was told I must please you. I don't care if I please you or not. Why do I have to please you when you don't please me?" She sat down on the river bank then, hugging her knees, oblivious to the ruin it would cause to her gown. "And I hate chess! It's a stupid game for stupid boys!"

I couldn't help smiling, although I did my best to hide it as I crouched down beside her, pulling at a long stem of grass, and beginning to strip it into two.

"Who told you to please me?"

She hugged her knees tighter.

"Everyone. Even your step-father."

I put the fresh green stem between my teeth and began to chew, relishing the fresh, dewy taste. I was so relieved to finally be out from under the scrutiny of so many elders all watching our every move. I had begun to fear what it would be like when she was judged to be of age. Would they be listening outside the chamber door? I shuddered – suddenly embarrassed.

"What *do* you like?"

She turned her head suddenly and I was surprised to find her eyes moist with tears. The eyes of a doe fawn, if they had not been so deeply blue.

"What?"

"You don't like chess," I reminded her gently. "What do you like?"

I saw her swallow back her tears and my heart softened. After all, she was just a young girl. Much the same age I had been when fate had whisked me up to Middleham and plunged me amongst strangers.

"Dancing," she said softly. "I like to dance. And I can sew. Very prettily. Mama said I have a gift for it." Leaning forwards, she rested her chin on her knees, her eyes once again fixed on the river. "I could make you something. If you would like it?" Once again my heart constricted tightly. She was so young.

"You don't have to please me Anna. I find you pleasing enough, you do not need to work so at it. I am ashamed if I have given you cause to feel otherwise."

"No, you haven't. It's just..." I could feel the awkwardness seeping out of her. Why would she not feel strange? We hardly knew each other and I may as well have been twice her age. Looking at her innocent young face and remembering the feel of Marie's body against mine, my throat dried. How in the lord's name would this ever work? William Stanley's words began to whisper in my head once more.

"I like dancing," I said absently, at a loss for words. "And I play the lute. Passably."

I heard her sniff with some determination and she began to stand, causing me to rise quickly.

"Can we go see the doves?" I cast my eye over to the circular dovecote. It was then I had an idea. Where it came from I knew not but it just seemed right.

"Do you like birds?" Lambent blue eyes looked up at me, the shy smile was back.

"Yes. I do. Very much." I threw the chewed strand of grass onto the ground. Maybe this would just work out, for the time being.

"Well then, you can do me a great service. I have a falcon; her name is Lark. Now, she is a tender soul, and does not like to hunt. But, she flies beautifully and I cannot take her to the wrist as much as I would like." She was watching me somberly, but I could see a light behind her eyes. "I brought her here from London, hoping to spend some time flying her, but I will have to leave soon. Would you care for her for me?"

For what seemed like an age she looked down at her feet, her fingers picking at her skirts. Just when I began to wonder if she had lost her voice, she turned large eyes up to look at me.

"You don't want her anymore?"

It was hard not to smile at the plaintive edge to her words.

"No, of course I do. But she chooses not to hunt and I would no longer try to make her do so. She just likes to fly. And I could show you how –if you would like me to?"

Her small face blossomed like a flower, giving me a small sense of the woman she would become and for a second I thought myself fortunate. I also began to feel just a bit more at ease. I would spend these few days with her teaching her to care for Lark and then I would be back north. We would write to each other, tales of how Lark liked to fly, and of how the seasons flew past. I would try my best not to visit her again, not to see her now until she was a young woman, old enough to be my bride in truth. As Stanley had said, a lot could happen in seven years.

"I would like that very much Francis."

She looked up at me smiling, and curled her small fingers around mine as we walked in companionable silence towards the dovecote.

18. MIDDLEHAM CASTLE
April 1469

There was an unusual air of unease blanketing the castle which didn't take long to seep into my very skin once I returned home. I could never recall experiencing it at any time in the past as my most common reaction to passing under the gatehouse arch was one of relief and satisfaction. This time, my journey north had been peppered with memories of Anna, Lark perched on her hand like a docile pet.

The two of them had bonded instantly, and even I had to admit to a certain feeling of loss as I watched Lark soar high and far before swooping back down to land on Anna's oversized gauntlet with a delicate grace. It was almost as if the bird realised how young her new owner was and took care when placing herself back onto the outstretched hand.

These were the pictures that filled my mind in the early days of my journey but as I moved ever northwards, Caitlin's spectre began to haunt me once more. It was not that I didn't still long for just a smile or a touch of her hand, because I did, even though I had bargained with myself to become her friend and guardian, nothing more. For some inexplicable reason, I know I still just wanted to see her, as if it was a physical need to be slaked.

That was when Marie danced into my mind, leaving me with mixed emotions, knowing she was far away in London, therefore unable to satisfy my sometimes uncontrollable urges. All of this disappeared for a while as I rode over the river Cover and up though the village, glad that I would soon be truly home. Minster Lovell Hall was undoubtedly beautiful, and I was most fortunate to be able to call it mine one day, but it was within these tall, dark ashlar walls that I felt most at ease.

The first thing I noticed was that there appeared to be a lot more men-at-arms wandering around. There was always a fair contingent, the castle being the northern stronghold within close reach of the Scots border, but there were a lot more than was normal. I rode through the outer bailey and entered by the northern gate, where a burly red-headed guard stepped out in front of me, causing Fides to bridle slightly. He had a companion, taller, thin faced, who just watched from the half-shadow of the door to the guardhouse.

"Who goes there?"

It was the first time I had been challenged upon my return to the castle and if I was honest, it riled me a little. Particularly by these strangers. My reaction was therefore surly and somewhat ungracious.

"Who wants to know?"

As piercing blue eyes looked me up and down from the caps of my boots to my head, I suddenly wished I had entered by the eastern gate.

"My Lord of Warwick be wanting to know, may it please you."

It was then I heard the Irish lilt. Harsher than Caitlin's sing-song tones, but unmistakable. It seemed to me that Warwick had been taking time to embellish his forces. He had spent time in Ireland with Richard's father during the tempestuous years of civil war. That fact, that these may be Caitlin's kinsmen, warmed the ice slightly.

"I am Francis Lovell. Lord Warwick's ward by order of our sovereign lord king."

"Frank!"

An un-mistakable Percy bellow rolled across the inner bailey and the two guards turned their heads. He was standing before the keep stairs, Richard at his side, and I saw the inquisitive blue eyes register some sort of knowledge before fixing back on me.

"Then enter and be welcome."

He stepped back, allowing Fides to trot forwards but I held him back a moment.

"May I ask your name?" I ventured, twisting the reigns around my fingers, watching as a slow smile spread over this florid face.

"Why, I be Patrick Malone, young sir." He paused, almost as if anticipating my thoughts. "Lately come from Penrith." I nodded. Another one of Warwick's strongholds. I couldn't think of any thing else to say and so I urged Fides forwards and we rode into the range where I slid out of the saddle, under the watchful gaze of Richard and Rob who were walking towards me. As I handed over the reins to an eager groom, their grim expressions were not to be missed. I gave a quick glance back at the Irish guard, who was still watching me, thumbs hooked in his belt.

"Irishmen?"

It was a statement, rather than a question, but it was Richard who replied.

"The earl is arraying forces in preparation to quell more uprisings. Northumberland rode in yesterday. He has brought many men and… "

He stopped talking because he had seen the look on my face, I had no doubt of that. Just emerging from the staircase to the keep was George, closely followed by Isabel Neville. He was, to be fair, the last person I had expected to see, especially this far north. Richard looked over his shoulder to see what had distracted me and his lips tightened into a firm line. "And therein lies another tale," he murmured softly.

I turned my attention back to him but it was only fleeting as I heard my own name being screeched across the range.

"Francis!!!"

Anne Neville came hurtling towards me, her skirts firmly grasped in her hands. For a few seconds I thought she would crash straight into me, but she came to a sudden halt beside Richard, her face glowing as if she had bathed in a brackish stream. "You are back! How was my cousin, Anna? Did she send any message for me?"

I nodded my head smiling, trying to ignore the cold stare of her sister Isabel as she and George stood together watching, but obviously feeling no inclination to join us.

"She did. She sends you her greetings and hopes she will see you when next you journey south."

It was only then that I allowed myself to remember that Caitlin would also be somewhere in the castle. If the household was here, she would be with them. I wondered idly how she and Richard managed to maintain their assignations and at the same time worried that I would find out soon enough. I just hoped I would not have to be party to them this time. The visit to Anna had unsettled me a little and I wanted nothing more than to spend some time in the fresh, clear air and find some peace again. Although looking at the sheer bustle which was giving the castle all the appearance of an anthill, I began to fear even for that.

"I am so glad you are back!' Anne beamed up at me, her eyes like a mountain stream in sunlight. "We should go hunting tomorrow! Richard, please say we can!"

As her small hand reached up to his arm, he looked down at her with fondness and I had a strange sensation, as if someone was touching my head. I raised my eyes only to find Caitlin now standing beside George and Isabel, looking over at us. Her gown was the colour of cowslips, banded with summer green. Her hair seemed to be dressed differently, somehow accentuating the perfect symmetry of her face. Even from where I stood, I noticed how her bottom lip was gently held in check by her teeth as her troubled gaze alighted on Richard and Anne.

I have to admit it hurt me, to see her so clearly wounded by their obvious closeness. Isabel turned then and looked at Caitlin, exchanging some words that I was too far away to hear. She answered, but her eyes did not move from where they kept the two cousins in her sight.

"I suppose we can, after Sext?" Rob looked at me then, a wry twist to his lips. "Come on, did you bring that infernal bird?"

My smile was fleeting. I found it hard to rise to the jest when the object of my own affection looked so sad.

133

"No. I gave Lark to Anna. She loves birds, so I taught her how to handle one." The clapping of Anne's hands caused me to look back at her, hard though it was.

"Then we must pick you a new bird from the mews! I am sure father will not mind! There are plenty here to choose from!"

Her enthusiasm was infectious and I grinned at her stupidly. An expression which began to falter as I realised Caitlin had disappeared back up the keep stairs, as if she had never been there. Instead, George and Isabel were making their way towards us which filled me with dread. George was bad enough, but I was developing something an intense dislike for Isabel. She was the exact opposite to her sister. Superior, aloof and almost dismissive of anyone in whom she had no interest. Such as I.

I saw the discreet nudge that Rob gave Richard, so he was ready for his brother's voice when it sailed across the range.

"Well, well, the prodigal returns. How did you find you wife, Lovell? Was your conjugal visit to your satisfaction?" He was smirking all over his face and even though I knew I wouldn't do anything about it, my fingers curled into fists.

"My wife, and my estates, are in safe hands, Your Grace," I answered with as much pleasantry as I could muster. The man was an insufferable bore. As far as I was concerned, he and Isabel were well suited to each other and it mystified me how such a person could be the brother of two men with the qualities of Edward and Richard. My barb hit home and I saw the flash in his eyes as he felt it. Ward or no, in reality, I was wealthier than George and for him to be reminded of that fact irked him enormously. I was relishing his expression far too much to remember that you should never poke a stick into a wasp's nest.

"Brave words," he grinned, with an edge of sarcasm, "bearing in mind the Lovell line is the better for the addition of a Stanley." He looked around the castle walls, with an affected air of bored distraction. "I hope your family's loyalties are not tested and found wanting."

My face flushed bright red. He was goading me and doing it

deliberately. Richard shot me a warning glance whilst Rob merely shook his head with a downward grin.

"My family is loyal to the king, Your Grace."

"We were just talking about going hunting tomorrow," Anne interjected lightly, her face taut with tension. She hated confrontation of any sort and was desperate to change the subject.

"Excellent idea!" replied George with enthusiasm. "I was just saying the very same to your father. Some of us will need our sport to while away the time."

Richard finally raised his head and looked at his brother with a steely gaze.

"George, what are you talking about?" But he merely shrugged in reply.

"Nothing at all, Dickon. Just that life here is much more, how shall I say, relaxed. Released as we are from the frenetic mood at court, don't you think Lovell?"

I saw Richard's brow pull together and I had to admit I was as confused as he. Whatever I had done to provoke George was beyond me. I tried to read his expression but as usual he hid behind a sanguine bonhomie which was almost sickening in its falsehood. It was then that I caught Isabel's smile in the corner of my eye. She was trailing the points of her sleeve through her fingers slowly, like a cat toying with prey. I didn't understand what was going on but I felt sick to my stomach.

"If you mean the air is much clearer up here, I totally agree," I answered carefully. "The atmosphere at court can be a little oppressive at times."

George grinned even wider then, looking at me with something akin to mischief in his eyes. I was racking my brain to think what I could have done to make myself a target for his attentions, when I once again saw Caitlin re-appear. She didn't look in our direction, but was walking over to the north gatehouse. If I didn't know better, she seemed to be making for the Irish guard who had confronted me upon coming home.

As her sudden appearance distracted me, Isabel turned to see who I was looking at, and her hand went up onto George's arm in a mirror image of her sister's earlier movement. George's smile remained fixed as he placed his hand upon Isabel's fingers, the first affectionate gesture `I had ever seen them share.

"Yes, you are right, Lovell. Yet, it is not just the air though. Everything is much clearer up here."

They were both looking at me with knowing expressions, and my stomach plummeted. I heard Anne's voice, coming from a long way away.

"Good! That is settled then! Francis, let's go to the mews now and find a replacement for Lark."

Desperate to break the tension even if she did not understand where it had come from, Anne made a gesture towards the east gate, out towards where the mews sat in the outer bailey. I managed to turn away from the others, my feet feeling like lead. Somehow, I had given my secret away. I didn't know how or when, but it was true. By some means, George had discovered my feelings for Caitlin, and I had an inkling he was enjoying himself very much at my expense.

19. MIDDLEHAM CASTLE
April 1469

In the end, I didn't choose a bird. The short exchange with George played on my mind, making it difficult me to settle on a decision and for for a time, quite selfishly, I wished I had not given Lark over to Anna. Even though she would have opened me up to much more mirth during our afternoon's sport, I didn't care. I cared much more about having her familiar weight upon my wrist, in the pleasure I would get from watching her effortless flight. The inexplicable fondness I felt every time she alighted back upon my glove, no matter that she had completely dismissed what was required of her, with a somewhat admirable determination. All of this made the other birds I could have chosen seem to pale in comparison and I settled myself into just going along as an observer, happy to watch the others and keep my thoughts to myself. And many thoughts there were.

It was a clear day when we rode out over the River Cover. The earl lead our small party, his magnificent Peregrine Falcon being carried proudly aloft by his squire. Richard, Anne, George and Isabel all accompanied us, myself, Rob and the Harington brothers bringing up the rear. Rob had his dark lanner falcon, whilst Anne and Isabel both flew merlins. Both Richard and George had the much larger Falcon of the Loch, which could be said to be almost as grand, if not grander, than the earl's himself, as denoting their royal blood.

There was a strict hierarchy for falconry, and in this, I could see George gained a measure of satisfaction in that it gave him an ideal opportunity to flaunt his status to the most powerful noble in the realm. Not that there was a single person living that did not know George was the king's heir. How could they not? But today, his arrogance bothered me not at all, it was his knowledge that soured the afternoon. So it was with some trepidation that, after an hour or so of sport, I saw George urge his mount towards mine.

Richard's falcon, Tiberius, was just swooping down powerfully and as George pulled to a halt at my side, the bird snatched its prey within relentless, yellow claws.

"Good sport!" George murmured as I continued to shield my eyes against the glare. Stifling the sigh my shoulders longed to heave, I lowered my head to look at him, carefully noting we were separated from the rest of the group by a good distance. "His bird matches my own in terms of prowess, although I would rather you didn't let him know that. It should be a secret between ourselves, I think." He paused, his expression benign, as if we were accustomed to the sharing of confidences. "You do not hunt today?"

It was light, conversational, but I still didn't trust him. George gave off some sort of air that was difficult for me to breathe at times, he was so different from his brothers with whom I was always totally at ease, despite on of them being my sovereign.

"No, not today."

"Shame," came his immediate retort. "Your bird usually adds some entertainment value to proceedings from what I recall." I was used to the jibes, just not from him, and I bit my tongue. "You do still have her? Or have you had her consigned to a stew?"

My fingers tightened on the leather reins as I imagined closing them around his throat. Fides danced a little, fractiously.

"No, Your Grace. I have given her as a gift to my wife, Anna."

"Ahh..." the sound was almost unctuous in its tone. "What gallantry! Such a selfless act is sure to make a favourable impression on such a tender bride. There is, truly, no better blessing than the love of a good woman, don't you think?"

I looked over at Isabel then, who had her dark eyes firmly latched onto the pair of us. She was no more interested in the sport than Lark would have been had she been here. I just knew that it was a different type of game she had in mind, but, still, I inclined my head courteously.

"I have little experience in that field, Your Grace," I replied diplomatically. Although God forbid he also knew about Marie, court being awash with gossip at the best of times. What you believed to be secret was often known by many, yet unspoken until an advantage was needed. That was my one saving grace. If George did know about my feelings for Caitlin, there was nothing he needed of me, no reason to use my wild imaginings as a bargaining tool. At least not at present.

"Well," he grinned, watching as the bird circled around and flew back towards Richard's outstretched arm, "we all have to start somewhere. Sometimes, that can even mean that we content ourselves just worshipping the object of our admiration from afar. Filling our dreams with what we wish to become reality. Hoping that envy does not press us into actions which we may later find regretful. Much like the field of battle, I would think. Where the blood runs hot, the heart pounds and one must pick exactly the right moment to make ones move, or to not move at all." He grinned at me. I so wanted to punch him in the jaw my gut ached with the tension. "Both actions have their consequences."

Once again I flashed a look at Isabel. I could have sworn she had nudged her mount closer. I wanted to give a glib retort but decided against it. There was no point in provoking him. I would only lose in the end so I decided to play the game.

"I have as little experience in the field as I do in the sport of love." I forced a smile between tight lips. "Yet, I can see how the two compare. " I turned in the saddle better to face him fully, getting ready to twist the knife, well aware of his jealously of his brother's talents. It was something Richard had admitted to me some time ago. At the time, I remember thinking that it may not just be that which George envied, but was wise enough, despite our friendship, to keep that thought to myself. "For instance, who would not admire the skills of so great a commander as King Edward, or indeed your cousin, my lord of Warwick. And when it comes to the fairer sex, do you yourself have such a muse, Your

Grace?"

If my arrow had pierced his pride he was not about to let me savour my victory. Typical George. For a moment he looked shocked, exaggeratedly so, I thought.

"I? Well, let me see? There was a nursemaid when I was younger. Her name was Eleanor, but I used to imagine her name was Elene, and that she was really Helen of Troy." He chuckled, falsely. "I was very young. "But, other than the odd admiring glance of some lady at court, I cannot say I have." He paused then, suddenly tapping his cheek with his finger, contemplating his answer. "No. That is not quite true. Actually, I did often once think much of Katherine Desmond. You may not know her, Thomas's wife – well, widow now. I saw much of her in Ireland at one time, and she was often at court in those days. Stunning eyes. Like a doe fawn." He looked up into the cloudless sky, his lips pursed as I cursed myself for an even bigger fool. I had walked right into his trap in trying not to run into it. "Quite captivating!" he breathed on a sigh. Every move he made was orchestrated, rehearsed, I could see it now in his bearing. The man would have done well as a strolling player.

"No," I replied through an agonisingly clenched jaw. "I have never met the lady. Although, of course, I have heard much." George was nodding like a consoling parent now and the urge to wipe the expression from his face was growing stronger. My fingers were itching for the contact.

"But of course, you do know Tom's daughter. A rare beauty indeed. Fit to grace a throne herself were it not for the stain of bastardy. Of course, as you know, not that any of that matters between the sheets." He grinned at my shocked expression as I was trying to understand if he was accusing me of being Richard's cuckold in some way. "After all," he rejoined smoothly, "look at our most noble queen. Who would believe her lineage? Yet Edward is so enamoured of her as to risk the country for the sake of his lust. The things men do..."

I began to feel sick as now, not only was this treasonous talk, but it was said with much the same nature of carelessness which had led to Tom Desmond's fate. I could think of nothing to say and so remained silent.

The squires were assembling now, birds were being returned and hooded. The afternoon was over, thank the Lord. But George had not finished with me yet. He may have brought me to the ground as effectively as his own falcon, but he still chose to toy with me, until I ceased struggling, submitted, or fought back.

"Who knows?" He began to expound airily. "Maybe Tom fancied his chances with Elizabeth himself? Maybe his words were out of some form of long held admiration, or desire, of our lissom queen? It must be hard, must it not, to desire for yourself something that your closest friend holds so easily within his grasp? To watch them possess that which you burn to hold as your own?"

His eyes were now burning into mine with fevered anticipation of my reply. Richard had just turned to see us together and his brow knotted in concern. He nodded his head towards me in acknowledgement, a sign from him which I knew was his way of checking that I was alright. It was a sign he had perfected over many months in the tiltyard, and from when I had remained the butt of many a jest from my fellow henchmen.

That one, insignificant gesture began to mean a lot to me. On many an occasion in the past it had given me the strength I needed to carry on. It had always confirmed that my friend suffered the same insecurities, but that as a royal prince, no one was about to make a fool of him for it. Apart, maybe, from his brothers.

I looked back at George then and gave a quick grin, gathering my reins together as I saw Richard leap up onto his palfrey.

"I just think myself lucky in that regard, Your Grace. For imagine how dreadful it would be if the thing my friend held in his grasp was the throne."

On the last word, I dug my heels into Fide's flanks and he responded immediately, and we cantered off to join Richard as he

141

watched, turning his steed to meet mine at just the right moment.

I did not get to see George's expression, mores the pity, but Richard did, and although he had no idea what we were talking about, I knew from his face that my shot had finally hit its mark. Once again, Richard's unerring friendship had been my saviour.

20. MIDDLEHAM CASTLE
April 1469

Thankfully, Richard and Anne riding side by side kept George at a distance from me during the ride back to the castle. George had pushed his destrier forwards and was talking to the earl, whilst Isabel had to fall behind, her face downcast and glum. I was feeling particularly pleased that I had just won the battle of words with him. If he felt the need to goad me with subtle references to whatever I may, or may not, intend towards Caitlin, I was more than happy to repay the compliment with references to his ambitions.

It was beginning to be noticed amongst our company that George became more and more acquisitive, the closer he became to the earl. Whatever conversations these two were sharing in the long, dark hours before dawn, they seemed to only boost his overbearing manner. It was an unspoken fact, acknowledged only in our shared glances and Richard's careful manner whenever his brother was mentioned.

As we approached the bridge, the earl called Richard forward causing George to drop back in line with Isabel – for which he received a winning smile that seemed to affect him not at all. His eyes were firmly fixed on his younger brother's back, and as if noticing this, Anne urged her mount forwards, almost to protect him from a glance as sharp as a blade.

Before much longer, the castle walls were in sight, much to my relief as none of us seemed up to conversation, as if some damp pall had been thrown over the company. Ahead of me, I saw Richard reach up and brush a speck of dirt from Anne's cheek and she smiled at him, the fondness between them obvious to all. That simple touch set my mind to wandering once again. What if, my devil asked me, Richard could indeed marry Anne? What if... then, Caitlin was abandoned? What if... my own marriage failed due to the difference in our ages. What if a wealthy landowner with little ambition should wish to wed a nobleman's bastard? Edward had been fond of Tom Desmond. Some said like a brother. Would he, one day, make it possible for his daughter to make a handsome marriage? My devil, that small knot of burning desire inside my gut, was ever determined to torture me thus!!

I was distracted from my silent musings as two things happened which were totally unexpected. From the north gatehouse a cry rang out, loud and clear.

"Rider!"

Everyone turned to watch as a messenger, cloaked in the king's livery, galloped at speed up the incline to the castle, but it was only me who turned my head back, catching, high up, of a flash of flame that the sun had set light to. I could not be sure, there was certainly a guard on the battlement, but his steel helmet did not burn with a burst of autumn glory as I had just witnessed. I squinted as I heard George say, drily.

"Edward's man. What the hell does he want now?"

I saw it again. There up on high, a blaze of the brightest hue which I was so familiar with, yet my eyes would not reconcile what I saw. What would Caitlin be doing up on the battlements?

I had little time to think anymore as our party stepped up its pace, the earl now wanting to reach the castle before the rider did. We all set to a canter, clattering into the bailey and dismounting in the usual flurry of organized confusion which the earl's return always set in play. I found myself walking next to Richard as we all made our way across the range towards the keep, his head was bowed as he stripped off his gloves.

"Trouble, do you think?"

Richard shook his head in answer as we began to mount the stairs.

"Who knows? He is probably wondering what the heir to the throne finds so alluring in the north to keep him here so long. I must admit, I am beginning to ask the same question." He threw me an anxious glance as we turned away from the chapel into the

144

great hall. "What was he talking to you about?"

I shook my head quickly, this being no time to try and talk carefully about George's sudden interest in me.

"Goading me about my lack of skill, nothing more." Before he could ask anything else, we were in the hall where everyone was already gathering, divesting cloaks and gloves as the pages scurried frantically to and fro.

I was the only one out of our group of squires who accompanied Richard into the great hall, Rob and the Harington's remaining in the bailey. It was a distinction both my friendship with Richard and my status as a ward of the earl allowed me. The earl, still cloaked, was standing by the hearth, his head down, a letter in his hand. I hadn't taken much notice of the king's messenger once we had entered the hall, and he had come and gone very swiftly which led me to believe that the note he brought was of little significance. George threw himself into a seat and held out his hand, snapping ringed fingers to attract an attentive page who ran forwards with a wine flagon.

Isabel left the room without a backward glance, and I could only think that her ride home next to George had not been as productive as she liked and I stood with Richard and Anne, just about to take a welcome drink of watered wine myself when the earl's voice, cold as a blizzard, made the skin on the back of my neck prickle.

"Is this your doing?"

As one we turned to look at him, at first I thought he was talking to some negligent servant who may have spilt wine on his boots, his tone was so dispassionate. But it was Richard he was looking at, his eyes ice-filled.

"My Lord?" Richard answered him immediately, and with exceptional courtesy, no doubt alerted to danger by his tone.

"This!" Warwick spat, brandishing the parchment before him, the seal hanging from it like dripping blood. "Was this your work?"

The whole room seemed to shrink – become somehow

darker. I looked at George, who seemed as puzzled as the rest of us but was nevertheless finding the sudden turn of events amusing, swilling his wine around in the bowl of his cup.

Richard turned to face the earl, taking two measured steps forwards. He remained unbelievably calm. No matter that I knew he was probably quaking in his boots, as most of us did when the earl used those tones. No one ever relished being on the receiving end of his anger or scorn, and now his face was suffused with both.

"Forgive me, cousin, I don't understand. Is it bad news?"

I bit the inside of my cheek to prevent the smile I felt burgeoning as Richard reminded the earl of their relationship. No matter that Warwick was his mentor, Richard was still the king's brother, something he intended the earl to remember it appeared. I felt Anne sidle closer to me.

"This! You have been summoned back to court! Back to London! Apparently, your apprenticeship here is at an end! I repeat my question, is this at your request? Have you suggested to the king that you have learned so much here that you no longer need to waste your time under my tutelage?"

You could have heard a feather fall to the floor in the silence that followed as Richard took in the news. George swallowed noisily, before placing his cup down and flinging one leg over the other casually, surveying his boots as if he had never seen them before. Richard's utter stillness was almost as much a concern as the earl's fury.

"No, my lord. His Grace has not discussed this with me. Not at any time. He has always been most pleased at my progress here. Perhaps he now feels I am of an age to be of use to him elsewhere in the kingdom?"

The soft snort of derision which George expelled at this caused only a momentary flicker in the earl's expression.

"More than can be said for how he regards me," he murmured, just loud enough for us all to hear.

"Don't flatter yourself, boy! This is aimed at me and no

146

mistake! It is the ultimate insult. It was agreed you would be here for at least another year; Edward swore it to me himself not four months past!"

"Some Christmas present," George remarked sardonically, twisting his foot upwards, his eyes still on his boot.

"Well? What say you?" Warwick asked, his voice lowering threateningly. "Will you go?"

A slight noise distracted me then, causing me to turn my head. My own breath almost left my body as I saw Caitlin standing there on the other side of the room, looking as if she wished the wall hanging would swallow her up. She was all eyes, large, green and lustrous, yet her face was tight with tension. It puzzled me a little for there was no way she could have understood what was happening here, but I continued to watch her as Richard answered, his voice marvellously level.

"Of course I will go. It is the king's will."

"Blood of the Saints!" The curse was so loud it made me start, as Warwick whirled away from Richard and cast the missive into the flames where it crackled noisily, the acrid smell of burning wax rising through the air. "King's will? What about your will, lad? Have I taught you nothing these past years? Have I wasted my time and efforts on a mewling whelp who scuttles away to whoever calls his name? Does he whistle you like a royal hound and you scurry to his heel to grab the scraps he throws you? You sorely disappoint me Richard, I expected more loyalty from you! You of all people!"

I couldn't see his expression but I knew Richard was getting angry. I knew from the set of his shoulders, the way his arms let no light between themselves and his slim frame. His fury was rare, but frightening to behold when it did show. I had seen it once or twice, no more. That had been enough in truth. Richard cleared his throat before answering, his voice the only sound to be heard,

"My loyalty is to the king, my lord, as is yours, is it not? Am I to understand that you say there is a choice as to where my

147

loyalty lies? For if that is the case, this is not a house where I
would wish to tarry and will, by your leave, depart without delay."

By sheer chance, Caitlin and I exchanged glances just at that
very instant. It was clear that she did not quite understand what
was happening, other than it spelled trouble, yet still her concern
appeared filled with an unexpected level of anxiety. As if she
knew something I did not. I couldn't look at her for long, as the
earl was now towering over Richard's still figure, sneering at him
with distaste.

"My, my, you are exceedingly eager to return to the nest of
silken vipers that have wound their coils around this country's
hope," Warwick growled. He was angrier than I have ever seen
him and I truly feared he may strike Richard if he found him
insolent. "Did all I suffered with your father mean naught? I see
him now in you, lad, by God! I could be standing outside St
Albans, watching his futile attempts to treat with a king who was
weak as horse piss, desperately trying to remain loyal and true.
Torn between what he thought was expected of him and what he
knew was his God given right! If I hadn't ordered my men in
through the back gardens of that God-forsaken town and into the
streets, we would have been slaughtered in our sleep or taken for
traitors. I see that stubborn streak in you now, as clear as day! It
was the death of your father Richard, mark it well. Take care you
do not share his fate!"

A sob rent the air and I felt my sleeve suddenly tighten
around my arm as Anne leaned into me and I turned my head.
Her face was marked with tears, her eyes those of a trapped
animal. Scared. Helpless. But then she knew her father better
than any of us. Yet if she feared for Richard, I knew she was
wasting her time. He was more than a match for the earl, and
unfortunately, the earl knew it too, which would only fuel his fury
further. King Edward had already angered him more than he had
ever anticipated in scuppering his plans for both a French queen
and a powerful foreign alliance. For a long time, he had seemed
at peace with the decisions Edward had made on his own account,

only it seemed now, he could no longer swallow his ire. Richard nodded his head, imperceptibly. His response once again exemplary.

"I do thank you for your loyal service to my father, as does my mother and our whole family. I saw him very little, but I know that he was a brave and just man who did not deserve the desecration he suffered at the hands of a Lancastrian army. How different the outcome may have been if only your Neville kinsman had turned out to fight on the side he had declared for and not tarried in the field. My mother tells me that she gives thanks daily that you showed more fidelity when you fought with Edward at Towton. She tells me that you, too, are your father's son."

I held my breath then, waiting to see how the earl would respond to Richard's reminder that his own family had not always been loyal to the crown and Warwick looked distinctly uncomfortable. He began to back down a little, no doubt seeing his battle was lost. One thing that was as certain as sunrise, Richard would never go against his brother's wishes.

The dread calm was broken by a sudden clattering and all heads turned at the noise, apart from Richard who still kept his eyes on the earl. I stole a glance at Caitlin. She was gripping the tapestry showing the fall of Troy so tightly I feared she would bring it down upon her head. George grinned, leaning over to pick up his dagger

"Mea culpa! There was a stone in my boot!"

It was no accident, I was certain, but at least the distraction seemed to bring Warwick to his senses.

"Go then," he snarled, his brows kneading together like worried hands. "Slink back south, much good may it do you. But make sure you go well attired! The stench down there grows by the day as the rivers swell and grow ever more foul."

George laughed softly as he twirled his dagger between his fingers and Richard turned to face him at the sound. It was the first time I had been able to see his face, it was cold, white and set. He appeared to have aged ten years.

149

"Will you come south, brother?" Everyone was looking at Richard as he asked that question, except me. I was looking at Warwick's face and saw his reaction at the thought of suddenly losing both of the king's brothers. George, Edward's heir. It still eluded me why he was spending so much time here anyway. It certainly wasn't for Isabel's charms as they seemed to leave him distinctly unmoved.

George rolled his eyes and yawned, stretching his arms out with affected disinterest. It was an act; Richard knew it as well as I.

"No, little brother. I think not. I enjoyed today's hunting very much and I am sure that if I remain here taking advantage of our cousin's hospitality…. there will be a lot more sport to come."

"Very well. I will leave within the week." Richard didn't wait a beat before replying, and then nodded his head towards the earl, sharply. "My lord."

Richard turned on his heel and made for the covered bridge and I looked quickly towards the other side of the room where Caitlin's eyes almost pulled me across the floor towards her. There were so many questions there, and something else I didn't understand.

"Francis!" it was a whispered plea from Anne. She tugged at my arm insistently, showing no sign of any intention to release her claim on me and reluctantly, I left the hall.

21. MIDDLEHAM CASTLE
April 1469

About two hours later I sat in the window embrasure of Richard's chamber, kicking my heels against the wall.

I was replaying the whole scene in my head over and over, but each time Caitlin's ardent gaze troubled me. Richard sat on the other side of the chamber at a table, scribbling away, his head down. He had hardly spoken a word about what had happened, other than to assure Anne everything would be fine and that she should not worry. That bothered me in a way, as there was a lot to worry about really. From my point of view anyway. If Richard was leaving, he would be leaving without me, and I was already feeling a sense of loss. He was my friend, the one person I spent the most time with, the only one I could talk to. Then there was Caitlin. Would he – even if he could – take her with him?

Weary, even of my own speculation, I ran a hand over the strings of the lute which sat next to me, striking a slightly discordant note. I picked it up then and began fiddling with the strings on the fret, plucking each one in turn. It then occurred to me that I had not played in a while, and I ran my fingers across the strings again thoughtfully. It was at that point I felt I was being watched, and sure enough, Richard had his hand poised, still holding his quill, but he was looking at me with forbearance.

"It was bad enough with your feet beating like a tabor but if you are going to accompany them, at least make it tuneful!"

I grinned sheepishly as he resumed writing, knocking his pen against the pewter inkpot.

"Sorry. What are you doing?"

"Writing to Edward. Letting him know I will leave within the week."

My feet stopped swinging of their own accord. A week. He still meant to go so soon, even though I had hoped for a change of heart, a delay, I knew he was not made to tarry once his mind was made up.

"I wish I could come with you."

He pressed his lips together firmly as he applied sand to his signature, blowing off the residue quickly.

"Me too. But then, I could always make you my squire." I saw him smother a grin as he held crimson wax to the taper. I was glad he found it amusing at least.

"Funny! You'd give Rob a run for his money with that jest!" I watched his hands as he sealed the parchment, before sitting back in his chair.

"Actually, I am pleased you will remain here, even though I know you are champing at the bit like a horse wanting its head. It is always useful to have an ear to the ground. I, for one, am not sure what is going on here, but it concerns me greatly. George, Northumberland, the increase in forces. It is like he is building up to something and it would be good to know there is someone here I can trust. You will write to me Frank? Keep me cognisant of events?"

I nodded, biting my lip. I didn't much like being his spy, but I had to admit it may be necessary. Yet, there was one other service I wondered if he would require of me. The words left my lips quickly, lightly, almost with disinterest.

"And Caitlin?"

He sighed, heavily, and pushed the paper away from him, his fingers drumming steadily on the table.

"I really don't... "

Whatever he was about to say was never to be known as the door crashed open and Anne flew in, her face flushed and eyes full of alarm.

"Dickon! Francis! It's Caitlin! Come quickly!"

Richard was out of his chair like an arrow from a bow and I wasn't far behind him. We thundered down the passageway, towards the south east tower with Anne giving us the sketchiest of details. After the meeting in the chamber, Anne had gone to look for her and could not find her anywhere. The countess had finally found her in the chapel, unconscious, sprawled before the altar.

She needed to say no more as, rounding the corner, came the formidable form of the countess, closely followed by the Irish guard I now knew to be Malone. In his arms, he carried something that had all the appearance of one of Frideswide's straw dollies and I heard Anne gasp. I had a hard time recovering myself. Caitlin's skin, usually the pale iridescence of a pearl, was a ghastly grey, filmed with a clammy sheen, her eyes seemed sunken and one arm hung limply, swinging with Malone's every stride. Her hair, the heavy braid coiled against the back of her neck, was the only part of her that seemed to have any life. The knot in my throat felt as hard as granite. She looked completely lifeless.

Richard was quicker than any of us, reaching the countess as they turned into an ante-chamber.

"My Lady, what is amiss?"

The countess stood back and motioned Malone forwards into the chamber as she stood by the open door.

"Lay her in there, on the bed. I have sent for the physician." She turned to us then, her cool face impassive. "You are not needed here. Go about your business. I will look after the girl."

Summarily dismissing us, she turned her back and followed Malone into the room, closing the door with a dull thud. Anne grabbed hold of Richard's arm tightly, her voice breathless with alarm.

"Oh Lord! Do you think it is the plague?"

"There's no plague in Yorkshire Anne." His voice was distant, his eyes still fixed on the closed door.

"Oh, then maybe..." she crimsoned then as she suddenly realised she was about to discuss things of which her mother would no doubt have told her she should not discuss with menfolk. I flushed a little myself at her embarrassment, but Richard just bit his lip. We waited for a few moments more

153

despite the countess's direction, and before long the aged form of Jacob Higgs came scurrying towards us, hitching up his robe to prevent himself from falling. A small page hurried at his side carrying a calf-skin bag which clinked musically as he moved.

"Make way, make way," the old man grumbled as he pushed past us and carried himself through the door. Anne tried to peep inside as he entered, but the page blocked her view and she turned back to Richard.

"Do you think she will die?"

"Anne!" I was so shocked; my words came out harshly. "We don't even know what ails her!"

"I know, but…" her voice was filled with desperation and it was obvious to me how fond she was of Caitlin. The irony was not lost on me, all three of us were fond of her, more than fond in some instances.

The door opened again and Malone came out, surveying us all with cool blue eyes.

"Mi'lords. Mi'lady. Now, did not my lady Warwick tell you to go hence? There is nothing you can be doing here."

"How is she, Malone?"

It should not have surprised me that Richard knew who he was. He made it his business to know people, especially the soldiers and guards. Malone's eyes swivelled over to Richard in response to his commanding tone, smiling briefly at Anne on the way.

"She be still out cold in truth, but in good hands now."

"Did she injure herself as she fell?"

Richard's voice remained impassive, unless you knew him. I could tell he was keeping his emotions in check, keeping to short questions, asking for the facts of the situation only.

"Nay mi'lord. She is whole. If it be she fell in a dead faint, it would be a blessing. And in chapel surely the Lord himself be looking over her."

Anne pulled herself up then, appearing to take heart from his words.

"I'm going inside," she declared suddenly, and without a further word she disappeared into the chamber, leaving us all astounded at her temerity and boldness. Something the countess may not have been as impressed by. Malone shrugged then and turned on his heel with a nod of his head.

"Mi'lords." He walked off down the passageway and I watched him go, wondering. I didn't know what to say to Richard, who had begun to pace a few steps away, then back again.

"I am sure she will be fine." It was more a feeble wish than a certainty, and he knew it.

"I hope so," he replied quietly. I looked towards the closed door with unease. It was thick, iron bound oak, no sound came from within.

"Should we go?"

Richard followed my gaze and began to twist the ring on his finger slowly, deep in thought.

"You go. I will wait a little, at least until Higgs makes a re-appearance. I will catch up with you in the hall later."

That left me in a dilemma. He had told me to go when there were two good reasons I wanted to stay. Firstly, out of friendship to him, secondly, for my own selfish concern. I had heard of people dying of fever, of virulent sicknesses like the plague or the sweat. But normally these were prevalent in the cities first, spreading though more populated areas of the towns. One of the saving graces of Middleham was that it was so remote. Not to say that such places escaped their fate, as travellers moved from place to place. I just felt so protected here.

Whilst I really wanted to remain, I could see from the set of his face that he wanted to be alone, which gave me an idea. I nodded my head towards him.

"Very well, Dickon. I will see you later then."

He hardly heard me as I left, sinking down onto a nearby chair, his expression clouded. But already I was on a mission and it did not take me long to accomplish it. My quarry was exactly where I thought he would be, where I had thought I saw him earlier that day.   Where I had thought I saw Caitlin with him. He was talking to another guard, a tall, thin man at the door to the east gatehouse, but he spotted me making for him across the range and he peeled away, no doubt spotting the determination in my gaze, and we met just outside the chapel.

"Mi'lord."

His greeting was carefully reverential as he knew as well as I did that I was no Lord. It was the standard form of address for the henchmen of noble families, and could be used with as much respect as it could scorn at times. I could tell this time his address was genuine.

"Was it yourself who found Lady Desmond?"

He shook his head, blue eyes appraising, but guarded.

"No, 'twas her ladyship, the countess. I but responded to her call."

I shuffled my feet self-consciously, worried that I may give something away by asking questions, but my need was such that even this would not deny them.

"Was she breathing? I could not tell... is she...?" The thought had only occurred to me as I had hurried through the castle passages. She had been so still! Was she even still alive?

"She was, mi'lord. I think it is only a fever in truth, yet mebbe a might feisty one. She has the blood of her father in her, I wouldn't worry. Not just yet."

My brows drew together of their own accord then. It seemed a strange thing to say, not just yet. His constant gaze began to unsettle me so I swallowed hard before my next enquiry.

"Was she on the battlements with you? Earlier? When we rode back from the hunt?" He remained silent. Not a muscle on his face moved. If Caitlin had been looking for a loyal friend, in this man she appeared to have found him, for he was about to betray nothing. His stillness, no matter that it was honourable, began to annoy me. "I saw her, so you don't have to deny it!"

His response was so logical I could I have kicked myself. He almost looked as if he felt sorry for me.

"Then, why'd ye ask?"

I suddenly began to feel very foolish, which led to a rambled response as my colour came and went.

"Well, I wondered... did she... was she... feeling ill then? Only, well, it's not often you see a lady-in-waiting up on the battlements." He raised his brows, his face completely benign. "Is it?" A knowing grin spread over his face, making him seem a little less recalcitrant.

"No. That be true. But then you and I know that mi 'lady is not your usual lady's maid, is she lad?"

I had absolutely no idea what to say to that other than that he was right, but whether for the same reasons I was thinking, probably not. My throat began to feel rough, sandy.

"The duke..." He waited patiently, now obviously amused at my embarrassment. "The duke, he..."

Patrick folded his arms over his chest and grinned even more.

"Don't fret, lad. I know exactly what the duke thinks."

Stung, my retort was fast, as I was beginning to feel like an idiot. I didn't even really know why I had sought him out, other than for him to confirm that Caitlin had been fine earlier. Although even why that mattered I had no idea, it just did.

"Well, you do better than most then. The duke is not one to wear his heart on his sleeve." Malone's brows raised, but the look of amusement didn't shift from his face. I felt he was toying with me.

"No, *that* he isn't." The slight emphasis on the word was not lost on me and I flushed, trying to think of something else to say.

"So, she was well then?" I mumbled. "Earlier, when she was with you? There was naught amiss?"

Malone pursed his lips thoughtfully and looked up at the battlements.

"Be that you asking, or the duke?"

"Does it matter?"

I watched him consider my question carefully, his eyes still scanning the sky.

"It may. To her." He fell silent then, his gaze drifting back down to fix onto mine. The bluff features softened suddenly, as if his frosty outer-layer was melting. He seemed to take pity on my inability to speak.

"You may tell... the duke, that she was well earlier this day. Having only a concern for his safe return. In fact, she seemed most anxious for it, as if there were some message she needed to impart to him." He paused. "If ye be askin' my opinion, that is. I cannot say I speak for her as, to be sure, I don't. "

I nodded then, it was all I could do, and decided it was time to make a retreat. For some reason this man made me feel uncomfortable, as if he could see right through my flesh, into my thoughts and hopes.

"I will tell the duke," I said lamely and turned away, somehow feeling he had got the better of me. I don't know why I felt that way, as I had only come to see if he knew what ailed Caitlin, and I had learned nothing. I decided to go back to Richard anyway and tell him what had been said. I nodded politely and turned, only to hear his voice once again, causing my feet to slow.

"Tell him not to be a 'feared. The lass is Desmond blood. She'll recover, and much to his pleasure I think."

I turned back, a further query on my lips, but he had also decided to leave, and I saw only the edge of his cloak as he disappeared into the guardhouse.

22. MIDDLEHAM CASTLE
April 1469

Three days later I stood in the bailey as the ducal party prepared to leave for the south. Richard was pulling on his gloves, his brow drawn, his face set with a grim determination. I had watched earlier as Warwick and George had ridden out of the castle, totally ignoring the small travelling party which had begun to assemble, obviously not intending to play any part in Richard's departure. He was leaving under a cloud, the earl seemingly caring not to bridge the chasm which had opened up between them. In obeying Edward's summons, Warwick felt himself betrayed, and even though I knew Richard cleaved to his brother without question, the manner of his departure was causing him great grief, and for more than one reason.

Caitlin still lingered in the chamber where she had been taken on the day she collapsed in the chapel. Surprisingly, the countess seemed to be in constant attendance, along with Anne and Higgs, the physician, who merely came out of the room on occasion clucking under his tongue as if he had no idea what was wrong with her. Richard stood vigil outside the chamber at every available opportunity, and on occasion I had sat with him as he turned his finger ring silently. We had spoken little, each frightened, I think, of what questions we should ask of each other, neither wanting to talk of what we feared.

I had seen the countess look at him each time she entered or departed from the chamber, and even Anne had not seemed to want to approach him, but her own face was drawn and troubled too. From what I could ascertain, whatever was happening inside that chamber, it was not good.

When he could finally delay his departure no longer, Richard had stood up as the countess had left the chamber last evening, and cleared his throat awkwardly as she waited for him to speak.

"My lady," he had said somewhat forcefully. "Tomorrow I

must leave at the king's behest, and being aware of his affinity to the Desmond family, I know he would be most vexed to know that Lady Desmond was ailing. Can I give him any message of comfort that she will recover?"

At that moment, her eyes had appraised him with a cool assessment which told me, and him, that she knew exactly whose affinity this particular Desmond had. I wondered how she was reconciling this with the fact that the earl, if not herself, had ambitions for her daughter in this respect. The countess had flashed a cold glance in my direction before setting her attention back onto him.

"The fever has broken, but as yet Lady Desmond has not fully revived. According to Higgs, once her overheated blood has begun to cool, her humours will balance and she will be well. It is just now a matter of time."

"She will be well cared for?" Richard had drawn himself up to his full height so as not to be intimidated by the countess, which made him a braver man than me.

"You doubt it?

Richard had been taken aback and flushed a little, no matter how hard he had been trying to remain detached.

'Well, no, that is..."

The countess had waved a hand before him impatiently.

"Be assured, what care Higgs cannot provide my daughter is only to happy to fulfil. I can't drag her away from the bedside for fear she misses a single blink of an eyelid. The – king – can be assured of her good health. "

Those words seemed to be the catalyst for the change that had been coming and now I watched as he made ready to leave, wondering what would happen once he had gone. Now, it would not be long before I found out.

What was more, I had even more grief to add to my mood as Rob was going south with him. To be fair, the whole matter twisted me in half, for as much as I desired to ride south with the pair of them, the fact that Caitlin still lie within the chamber, to all intents and purposes still somewhat absent from this world, also pulled at me. Even then, if Richard had but given me the slightest nod, I would have been packed and horsed before he could have blinked an eye. Apart from my concern for Caitlin, there was something amiss within the castle confines which was beginning to leave a prevailing odour that was not at all pleasant.

I busied myself with the leather girth on his horse, pulling on the buckle tightly hoping to keep my wandering thoughts to myself but it was to no avail.

"I was joking about making you my squire." It was spoken softly, but Richard looked up with a wry grin. "Sulking doesn't suit you, Frank. You'll end up with a cleft in your forehead to match your chin."

I stepped back, mildly rattled it had to be said, folding my arms across my chest.

"I'd be more use in London than I will kicking my heels here. I thought you might speak to the earl..." I voiced the dim hope I had harboured inside, but he didn't even flinch. Richard slapped the rump of his palfrey, pursing his lips as if considering how he would break the news to me that he hadn't been prepared to do so. "It seems I will spend my evenings playing my lute whilst Isabel makes cow eyes at your brother and he continues to pretend she doesn't exist."

"Anne enjoys your musical abilities," he replied, his face betraying a feeble attempt to mask his amusement. "She would never forgive me if I took away such a source of entertainment." The jest soured in my belly and I kicked at a stone.

"I may as well take up needlecraft at this rate!" Richard laughed then, a rare sound from him it had to be said, but then all amusement fled from his face. Taking a quick look around, he caught hold of my elbow and drew me a few paces away, towards the priest's lodgings.

"I know this sits ill with you Frank, but my need for you here is greater than it is in the city." His intense gaze burned into my eyes with purpose and I felt his fingers grip my arm like a vice. All

I could do was frown, but in a way, I knew what he was about to say, for our feelings on matters at the castle were much in accord.

"I need eyes and ears here. Someone who can write the odd, casual missive to his good friend in the city. A lively letter, peppered with all the usual gossip and goings on of the castle. How the earl does, how often George goes hunting." He paused then, rolling his bottom lip between his teeth. "Whether the frost on the relationship between my brother and our fair cousin Isabel ever melts." I swallowed hard. So, still his spy then. He cleared his throat, fiddling with the enamelled dagger at this belt and I saw Rob watching us from across the bailey. "And, if you would be so kind, to keep the king informed of the recovery of Lady Desmond."

Those words pulled my attention away from Rob who was now scowling at me for some unfathomable reason.

"The king?" I couldn't keep the scorn out of my voice, gentle though it was. I knew it was a ploy he had tried to use on the countess, but I had believed we were far beyond such subterfuge. Richard's head came up defiantly, although he was having trouble holding my gaze.

"At such troubled times, I think the king would not wish to have to convey bad tidings to the Earl of Desmond in Ireland."

If James Fitzgerald even knew she was here, I said to myself, although kept my own counsel. If Richard wanted to downplay his attachment to Caitlin, that was fine by me. It may work for everyone else but the countess had seen through it. We both knew the truth. I nodded my head obediently.

"Of course, Dickon, if that is what pleases you."

His grin was quick, and he raised a hand, placing it on my shoulder with a quick squeeze.

"I know I leave her in good hands, Frank. You will…" I stopped him mid sentence, knowing he was finding this hard. Probably also knowing that I was finding it harder having to stay behind and play a cross between nursemaid and spy.

"Yes. Be assured. My own welfare will become secondary to

her own."

"Do you have any messages you would wish me to take south? To your family? Anna?" He quirked a mischievous brow. "Anyone else?" The expression on my face caused him to laugh once more, which filled me with both pleasure and surprise. I could already witness the lightning of his mood which was taking place at the thought of returning to his brother's side. It was certainly a change, as it was usually the thought of coming north that made him happier. But I could not blame him. Things at Middleham were far from normal these days. I grinned back, but my expression clouded as I thought of Marie. Her dark hair, pale skin… her eager hands.

"You know," Richard interrupted my thoughts, "it may not be such a privation staying behind. Although, you do need to start raising your eyes from your boots." As my brow furrowed, I could see Rob swaggering towards us, no doubt sick of waiting for our conversation to end, or wanting to know what it was we were so closely closeted on.

"Have you told him then?" Rob was grinning all over his face so I knew this was going to involve some jest at my expense.

"I was just about to."

"Tell me what?" I asked with some impatience. At this rate, I thought, the sooner they went the better, as my mood was growing increasingly fractious.

"Just a little going away gift for you!" Richard now at least had the sense to look a tad embarrassed at Rob's words, but of course that emotion was something completely alien to a Percy.

"Gift?"

"You have an admirer! Of course you wander around with your head in the clouds half the time so you were bound not to notice, the poor girl is almost panting at your feet half the time and we thought it best to put her out of her misery."

My heart sank as my face reddened.

"God, Rob, not that woman…the earl's…"

Richard shook his head as Rob spluttered, both of them

seemingly enjoying my discomfort, until Richard stepped in.

"That's enough Rob. We should be off!" Richard turned on his heel, suppressing his smile, as Rob clapped him on the shoulder in a brotherly fashion. Rob shrugged then, hitching his belt and giving me a wide grin as he went to follow him.

Typical, I thought! The pair of them would now ride off into the sunset laughing at my expense. It was a camaraderie which only existed in Middleham, when we all seemed to act much like the children we once were. It was a hard habit to break.

"My gift?" I called sarcastically, as Rob strode away. He looked back, throwing me a wink.

"Jane Cooke! She likes the way you hold your sword!"

With an explosive burst of laughter, he hurried off to catch up with Richard towards their waiting horses and I caught sight of Anne, who came flying out of the stairwell to the keep to say her own farewell as I turned away.

23. MIDDLEHAM CASTLE
April 1469

Jane Cooke.

It took me a while to recall who she was, whilst all the time Richard was riding south and I was still struggling with my disappointment at not leaving with them. So, then. Jane.

Small, a bit frail looking, she was somehow similar to Anne Neville, who now sat looking at me pointedly across the chamber as I tried to read my book. It was a military treatise, lent to me by Richard, who always, helpfully, seemed to like to write his name in his books. It seemed an odd habit to me, but I had seen for myself how precious his books were to him and I knew he set great store by them. It was, therefore, somewhat of an honour that he had left this one with me, knowing the value he placed on such possessions.

Two days had gone by. Rain had set in with a vengeance and was now pounding on the windows fit to shatter the glass. But one thing was for sure, Anne seemed loath to leave me out of her sight for long and had attached herself to me like a veritable shadow, so even if I had been desirous of it, seeking out Jane to discover exactly what Rob's parting shot had been about would have been almost impossible.

So we made a bit of a strange group. Me, not reading, Anne, not sewing, and Isabel not speaking to either of us. Rob's lady of choice, Miriam, had been in residence since I returned back from Oxfordshire, and she sat playing cards with Isabel, both of them murmuring quietly so as not to disturb the peace of the room. And then there was Jane – sitting with Anne on the raised dais in the window embrasure, where the meagre light was at its best, working attentively on her own stitch-work.

The day was dragging on, and I closed the book, staring into the flames instead. Only yesterday I had been in the tiltyard, thankfully besting James Harington at the butts, only to find Anne and Jane watching from the sidelines. At the moment it seemed that I couldn't turn around without finding her there, and I wondered now if she had been trying to find some time alone with me. It had only just occurred to me that this may have been why she was never more than four steps behind me most of the time.

My reverie was interrupted by a huge sigh, which, on reflection, was hugely exaggerated. It was designed to provoke a reaction and of course, it did. I looked up and saw Anne, squinting into the light, her brow deeply furrowed.   Jane had also raised her head, revealing unremarkable grey eyes which flashed my way quickly and just at speedily returned to Anne, as if she was frightened to look at me. I remembered Marie's openly ardent stares and suppressed a grin.

"My lady?" It was Jane who responded first to her mistress and, in truth, it was the first time I had ever heard her speak.

"This light is so poor!" exclaimed Anne. "I can hardly see to thread my needle!" Jane had no sooner held out her hand to assist, than Anne looked in my direction, her face coyly innocent, which immediately alerted me to the fact she was up to no good. "Francis? Could you help? Your eyesight was so sharp yesterday – for sure you beat everyone else in the field! A needle should be no competition for such a foe!"

Whilst I accepted the studied flattery, I rose from my chair, reflecting that I had been joking to Richard about the sewing, but I climbed up the three steps to the raised window with good grace and sat down next to Anne. She smiled winningly, satisfied with her strategy, handing the needle and silk over to me while Jane lowered her head, avoiding my eyes.

With no difficulty at all, I threaded the blue silk through the needle Anne had given to me and handed it back, which she accepted with a nod of the head.

"I wonder where Dickon is right now? They should be well south of York, I think."

166

"Well south," I agreed, unable to think of anything else to say, I just looked out of the window at the rain soaked fields. It would have been a miserable journey for sure, but I still would rather have been with them.

"Did you have chance to speak to him much – before he left I mean?" The question was couched in innocence, but I knew she was after something.

"Not much. He was too busy getting ready to leave. Then there was..." I bit my tongue. I had almost referred to the amount of time he had spent outside Caitlin's chamber. "A lot to do." I recovered myself with a grimace. "He was not happy to leave in such difficult circumstances."

Her hands dropped into her lap, her expression folding in on itself. I knew that the rift between Richard and her father would trouble her, as for so long he had been such a part of their family. Now it seemed it was George who held favour, much to her sister's non-evident delight, I imagined.

"I am rather hoping that Edward allows him to come back, after he has seen Dickon and he has been able to tell him how he loves it here." It was a vain hope and I think we both knew it even as she spoke the words.

"Well," I began, as a form of solace and explanation. "He is of an age now where the king may need him to fulfil some of his responsibilities. It is surely a credit to the earl that Edward now judges him to be able to do so. A compliment, in a way, on the quality of his tutelage." I had made that up completely on the hoof, so I was only too pleased to receive a beaming smile in return.

"Why, of course! I had never thought of that and I bet Papa has not either!" I didn't necessarily agree with that assessment but I kept quiet. "I must tell him! He has been so aggrieved and I can't bear for him to stay angry at Dickon. It is not his fault after all."

Anne picked up her embroidery again with renewed enthusiasm, that is, until Isabel gave a disgruntled snort.

167

"Poppycock! What could the king want his younger brother to do that his heir cannot? You don't see Edward sending for George, do you? He is happy for him to remain far from court. No – this is a deliberate snub. No more! Unless, that is, Papa was right and Dickon deliberately arranged his return to court. We know how much of a favourite he is!"

The heads of both Miriam and Jane dipped that bit lower to avoid the sharp edged words which had been flung across the room and I wondered how many such exchanges they witnessed between the two sisters, as they were obviously now expecting the fur to fly. So then, why did I think it a good idea to pitch in myself? But I did, of course, in defence of Richard, as ever.

"For the very fact that George is his heir, Isabel. You said it yourself. Richard is being set for a different role in the king's court. I would think George's role will change too, when the queen has a son."

If a glance could throw a lightning bolt across a chamber, I would surely have been struck dead in the few seconds that followed my words. I waited for an acid-toned response to my words, but it appeared that she had nothing to add. Not that this meant I did not know what she was burning to say, but dare not.

For any response would show her enmity of the queen, and I knew that Isabel was far too cautious to do that, especially not with things as they were. Her father could rant, and insinuate and rage at his leisure, but should his daughters deign to express a mere hint of distaste, they would be duly chastised.

Just as the atmosphere in the air was at its worst, the door opened and the countess sailed in, much to my relief. Jane and Miriam rose to their feet, whilst Anne and Isabel merely turned their heads away from each other and towards their mother who was regarding them archly.

"Any news, Mama?" Anne's voice was thin but hopeful, a question she had relentlessly asked several times every day. The woman's appraising eyes swept the room and initially she ignored Anne's question.

"Is the duke not here?"

"No, Mama," replied Isabel, her eyes back on the cards in her hand. "He is with Papa and Uncle John."

A flicker of some emotion passed behind Countess Warwick's eyes but was then swiftly gone.

"Mama?" Anne's voice was now quite urgent and the countess sighed with some impatience.

"Yes, Anne, I heard you the first time." Her daughter pouted prettily in response to the rebuke. "Lady Desmond is recovered and is now sitting up and able to hold conversation. I said you would go in and read to her…shortly." Anne clapped her hands, her sewing now abandoned.

"Our Lady be Praised! Can I go now?"

"Oh ssh Anne!" Isabel snapped, her irritation with her sister more than plain. "The girl is a servant! The way you carry on you would think *she* was your sister! She's had a fit of the vapours, it happens sometimes, to girls of a certain age."

I looked at my boot caps, wishing I was anywhere else but in this room, but I cannot deny that my heart lurched at the news that Caitlin was able to receive visitors and I wondered how long it would be before it would be considered decent for me to visit with her.

"Lady Caitlin is a good friend to me, Isabel!" Anne snapped back. "That is most unfair of you!"

Her sister shrugged, the light catching the silver thread which was woven through her gown. She was a beautiful girl, more handsome than Anne in truth, but the recent, sullen downturn of her lips took a certain amount of appeal away. It was clear that it was not just her father who was unhappy about the lack of a wedding.

"I really don't understand what the fuss is all about," she muttered, her head down once again, pretending to focus on her hand.

"Well, you wouldn't," snapped Anne shrewishly, loath to let the matter rest. "No one would want to be your tire-woman at

169

the minute!"

Isabel fanned her cards out before her, placing them on the table and I noticed that Miriam was keeping her head down. I always knew she was a sensible woman.

"You can talk," Isabel retorted, "walking round all doe-eyed until Dickon left, hoping he would take pity on you! Then ever since he left it's been "I wonder where Dickon is today? Is he here do you think? Is he there do you think?" On and on like a child! The boy's plainly not interested and you should just accept it!"

Anne stood up suddenly, her carefully stitched work now crumpled in her hand, her slim body rigid with anger.

"As you should with George! Although Dickon has more care for me than George has ever, ever, shown you!"

As I saw Isabel draw up her shoulders ready to fire back a riposte, a page stepped into the room, bowing his head to the countess, who had been watching the exchange with a steadily darkening expression.

"My Ladies. My Lord requests your presence, my Lady, and that of Lady Isabel, in the Great Chamber."

I breathed a sigh of relief as the tension was pierced and Isabel rose haughtily, sweeping across the room without so much as a glance at Anne, passing her mother to depart from the chamber. The countess shook her head slowly before folding her lips together in a thin line.

"Anne, attend Lady Desmond. I will join you shortly."

She needed no further telling, dropping her handiwork onto the small table in front of her and hurrying down the steps. Within seconds, there was only myself and the two ladies-in-waiting left in the room, where quiet had once again descended.

"Thank the Lord," breathed Miriam, finally raising her head and looking up at us. "The air in here was so dry I feared a fire would take hold!"

"Amen, to that!" I smiled at her. It was as if someone had opened a window and all of the noxious air had spilled out. Jane said nothing, but looked up at me with a shy smile. I didn't

170

respond, not even out of politeness, resorting to looking out of the glass once again.

Nothing felt right. Richard gone. Caitlin ill. Warwick and George spending hours closeted away. I bit the inside of my cheek. I knew I needed to write to Richard and tell him, at the very least, that Caitlin was on the mend. I resolved to find Anne as soon as I could, and would attend to that once I was assured she was well. And maybe also to ask if she would like me to go and entertain her during her recovery. I looked at my lute lying forlornly on the settle, but Jane had caught the movement of my gaze, and looked back at me once more.

"Will you play for us, my Lord?" There was a certain light now in her eyes, one I had seen before, but it moved me not at all.

"I am not a Lord," I answered a tad unkindly. "And no, not today."

I knew I had hurt her, could see it in the way her features folded in upon themselves. Once again, I felt a total boor, but for some reason I could not help myself.

24. MIDDLEHAM CASTLE
May 1469

Within hours, my hopes of seeing Caitlin were dashed.

Before I could seek out permission to visit with her, which would by necessity have needed a chaperone, I was myself called in to see the earl. He informed me that he was leaving that very day and I was then to accompany his brother, John, the Earl of Northumberland, to Barnard Castle the next day where he had business with the Constable. There didn't seem to be anyone else of note accompanying him, just myself and four men-at arms, including the Irishman, Malone. So as I sat astride Fides, waiting for the earl to appear, the one saving grace in the whole affair was that it had stopped raining.

I hadn't visited this particular stronghold before, but Richard had waxed lyrical about the fortress, set high above the racing river Tees. It was only a day's ride, but I had no idea how long we intended to be away, and I wasn't about to ask. As far as my duty was concerned, the earl, in lieu of his brother, held sway.

I had managed only the briefest of words with Anne, who had told me that Caitlin was indeed much better, but very tired, and somewhat quiet. This at least gave some salve to my unease, as I felt by the time I returned, she may even be up and about, making it easier for me to engage her in conversation.

As if he knew I was thinking about her, I could almost feel Malone's eyes burning into my back, as Fides gave an impatient snort and pawed the ground. As I patted his sandy coloured neck reassuringly, the earl strode out into the bailey, his face grimmer than the clouds above our heads.

Without even looking in my direction, merely sweeping his eyes over the assembled men-at-arms, he hurled himself up into the saddle of his huge chestnut destrier, and with a sharp dig of his heels, moved forwards. Biting my lip, I did likewise. His squire had not accompanied him, which meant that I would be his body servant on this visit. As we cantered out of the north gate, I prayed that whatever his business was at Barnard Castle, it improved his mood. Not that I could recall ever seeing him smile, so I had no real comprehension of what an improved mood would look like.

Northumberland kept up such a fast pace that there was no time for any conversion, not that either I or anyone else would have anything of note to talk of with the brother of our lord and master. His reputation was somewhat fearsome, and he was a staunch supporter of the House of York that was true, but in terms of familiarity, he appeared even more unapproachable than the earl. So, for hours on end, it was just a case of getting heads down, ears back and forging on through the hills and vales which took us ever north.

The sun was just beginning to set as we rode up to the forbidding castle perched on the side of the river, the long shadows giving the walls an ominous appearance. It was a huge, sprawling place, very unlike the tall, angular edifice that was Middleham. Riding through the gatehouse into the outer ward, we passed a small chapel, sitting amongst the well tended lands which kept the castle well stocked with provisions. There were a few servants milling around, but most of them appeared to have finished their work for the day, and the ward seemed unusually quiet, which changed immediately as we rode through yet another gate into an inner courtyard.

Grooms scurried out of the walls to take our horses, and the earl was immediately greeted by the Constable, and almost as quickly he disappeared through a tower door.

As I dismounted, one of the stable-hand's stepped up, but as usual I was always slightly reluctant to hand over Fides to a stranger. I knew it was foolish, but there it was. As I fussed with the reins, I sensed I was being watched, and I turned to see a stocky, sandy haired boy, in Warwick red, watching me. I turned back to Fides as he moved forwards. He was a good head taller than me, his face dusted in freckles.

"He is a grand one. Is he yours?" I turned, squinting at him for no other reason than I was trying to work out what he wanted. "I mean, rather than just one from the stables?"

It was a friendly enquiry I had to admit, and I flashed a quick look at Malone, who was retreating with his companions to the kitchens. I wished for a moment I could go with them instead of serving a noble who I knew no better than the boy who stood beside me.

"Yes. He is." It was a simple answer and I saw the waiting groom roll his eyes impatiently.

"Jack," the boy said suddenly. "Make sure he is well tended. I will come down and check myself mind!"

The groom nodded, raising his eyebrows at me. I looked back at the boy and handed the reins over reluctantly, watching as Fides was led away.

"Come with me," the other boy said. "I will show you to the earl's lodging in the Great Chamber."

Before long he ushered me up a staircase which led into a very grand room with a window which overlooked the river. There was a small ante-chamber to one side where a small pallet bed lay for myself and I threw my cloak onto it, looking around.

"I will arrange for the bath to be set up. Once you give the word." There appeared to be very little for me to do for the earl, everything he could possibly need was here, this being one of his brother's main strongholds. It seemed I was at liberty to be at my own devices for a while. Somehow, my watching friend recognised my unease.

"My name's Rob," he said. "Rob Brackenbury. I nodded in his direction, unable to think of anything else to say. "If you want anything, I will be in the Great Hall, with the rest of the squires. If you want to come and join us... there is usually a game of dice, or chess going on."

The opening of the door caused him to step back as Northumberland entered the room, giving us both a cursory glance.

" I will sup in my chamber tonight. Lovell here can serve me."

As I groaned inwardly at the prospect, Rob gave a swift bow and went away, leaving me alone with the undoubtedly surly earl, ending any prospect of my taking up Brackenbury's cordial offer. It had to be said, my preference would have been for cards and ale rather than the evening I was about to spend. Aware of my responsibilities, I moved up to remove his cloak, which he still had fastened around his shoulders.

"Do you wish to bathe now, my Lord?" I found a peg on the far wall to hang the cloak on, noting that I would need to brush the dried mud from the hem before the morning. As I turned, he was staring into the fire, lost in thought. Trying to guess his mood, I filled a goblet with wine and took it over to him, waiting as patiently as I could, admittedly more than slightly anxious. No matter how much training a boy received, even be it in the finest of houses, it would never account for the mercurial moods of the nobility. What was right for one, would be wrong for the other.

Warwick himself could be somewhat incalcitrant at the best of times, but being alone with his introspective brother was fraying my nerves. Although he was a regular sight around Middleham, he was a man I had found little reason to converse with, although his reputation was formidable amongst the squires and henchmen back at the castle. He had been imprisoned by the Lancastrians after the second rout at St Albans, but had then lead glorious victories at the battles of Hedgeley Moor and Hexham, distinguishing himself with such valour that the king had made him a garter knight.

Sometimes he was just another visitor, another lord on the high table amongst many who visited the earl. Other times, I would see him with the Master of Henchmen, watching us all at practice, discussing, pointing, no doubt considering our merits or shortfalls. Now I was closer to him than I had ever been, and to be honest, I was rather in awe, which didn't help matters.

175

He resembled his brother in many ways, yet built leaner. This earl looked like a man who spent more hours in the saddle than he did at table, and this showed in both his build and the colour of his weathered skin, which spoke of hours outdoors in all weathers. There was very little else I could do other than feel generally hapless and wait. To my relief, he eventually reached up and took the cup, sliding me a sidelong glance.

"Francis, isn't it? You've grown up. What age are you now?"

His words hit me with the shock of a slap. I had been in his brother's service for seven years now and Warwick himself had never exchanged words with me that did not focus on my knightly abilities, or lack of them.

"Fourteen, my Lord."

He took a deep drink from his cup, swallowing noisily before turning to seat himself in a chair, his eyes fixed on me once more. I folded my hands behind my back, wondering what he what else he about to say.

"And your wife, my niece. How does she?"

"Well enough, my Lord, when last I visited with her."

He took another drink, settling back with a sigh.

"You need to get to know her better. Maybe you will be able to visit her again quite soon, if events go as planned." Even as this registered on my face, I cursed myself for my inability to mask my thoughts and I immediately saw his heavy brows draw together. "Oh? That doesn't suit you, apparently. What is it? Is the girl not pleasing?" He gave a wry grin looking down into his wine. "I can understand that if she takes after the Fitzhughs." I didn't know how to answer that so I remained silent, but he wasn't happy with that either it seemed. "Does the thought of such a visit displease you?"

I gripped my fingers tightly behind my back. I had stood and lied to a king, but then I had Dickon with me and it was in his defence. There was no way I was anywhere near as brave on my own. I had to tell him the truth.

"My Lord, I was given some advice on my last visit to Minster

Lovell which I thought was most sound."

"Advice?" The one word was like a grumble of thunder.

"Yes, my Lord."

"What, advice?"

Apart from wishing for the floor beneath me to swallow me up, I was longing for someone to rap on the door and save me. But I had run out of time.

"Because she is so young, my Lord. I was advised it may be best not to visit her until she was... until she had..." I cleared my throat painfully under his merciless grey stare. "Until we could fulfil our marriage vows."

He didn't blink or move a muscle, just looked at me as if he could read my every thought. I had no inkling as to if he approved or disagreed with the idea, or it was just that I was unable to determine his thoughts, so well did he hide them.

"And who gave you that gem of wisdom?"

I closed my eyes as I said the name. For no other reason than I was beginning to feel foolish and embarrassed. I really didn't want to be discussing having carnal knowledge of his niece with him.

"William Stanley. He..."

"Oh, I know who he is!" I opened my eyes as he was pushing himself out of the chair, and he brushed past me as he walked over to the sideboard, where I heard the sound of wine pouring into his cup. "How well do you know him?"

It was a strange question, but one I could answer easily. With relief.

"Hardly at all, my lord. He was married to my mother for a short time. She bore him a child..." I hesitated just a little before continuing. Not daring to turn around and see his face but finding that only made me braver. "As Anna is so young, I believed his advice to be sound." I heard a snort of disgust from behind me followed by his footsteps as he returned to his seat whilst I stood rooted to the spot.

"Tell me Lovell, are you loyal?" That sounded to me like a

trick question, or at least one which was not quite as simple as it sounded. Of a sudden I was reminded of my chess game with the king and my wrist began to ache. I swallowed hard.

"I believe so, my Lord." A thought occurred to me which I then just blurted out without a thought. "Although, I suppose that has yet to be tested." He grinned then, tipping his cup in my direction in tacit approval.

"Well said. But, who are you loyal to?" Now it was my turn to frown.

"Why, to the king, my Lord!" A niggling worry began to nag at me. Was this what the king had been preparing me for? Had he, somehow, known that one day, I would be somewhere, being asked these very same questions?

Northumberland shook his head then, the candlelight catching the grey that had begun to thread through his hair like silver silk.

"You have been spending far too much time with Gloucester. You are even picking up his habits." Not any more, I thought grudgingly, but answered as subserviently as I could.

"I like to think of him as my friend, my Lord."

His eyes turned steely of a sudden, almost as if they had clad themselves in armour, and his lips twisted tightly.

"Royal princes have no friends, lad. That is a lesson you would do well to remember." For a second there was a far off expression in his usually implacable gaze. "You would do well to keep your affinity at arms length. By cleaving close to a cause with some distance from the throne." His thoughts snapped back into focus, pinning on me once more. "It is not too late. You're are the ward of a member of the Neville family, which could help you much. Yet, you should think on it so that your choice is clear, should the decision present itself. Which may be sooner than you think."

The earl turned his hooded gaze onto the flames and stared into them as he sipped the wine, thoughtfully. His next words came without lifting his gaze.

"I will take that bath before I eat, if you would."

It had been a warm day, and the fire still burned healthily in the ornate hearth, but the shiver of fear that trailed across the back of my neck like ghostly fingers, may as well have extinguished every last flame.

25. BARNARD CASTLE
May 1469

"Can you beat that?"

Brackenbury was smirking at me, as I squinted at the arrow which still thrummed close to its mark.

The earl had once again closeted himself away on other business and left me wondering why on earth he had brought me in the first place. Never one to lose an opportunity, I sought out Brackenbury at breakfast and asked if I could join the henchmen for the morning. He had readily agreed, and we had ended up watching the others for a while before partnering each other in competition, whilst comparing our shooting skills.

I pursed my lips, wryly, surveying his handiwork.

"Maybe."

I folded my fingers around the arrow, feeling the satisfying brush of the fletch against my palm. Slowly, I drew back on the longbow, raising to the target as I did so until I could feel the string against my chin, my thumb just brushing below. Just when I judged the pressure was right, I released, watching the shaft shoot through the air, coming to rest within a hairs breadth of Brackenbury's attempt inside the yellow painted circle.

"Impressive!" Brackenbury cocked his head appraisingly. "Middleham trains its men well, as I had heard." I grinned in appreciation of the compliment as he drew another arrow and presented the nock to the string. "I suppose you benefit much from the presence of the king's brother?" I couldn't help myself with the response.

"Depends which one!" It was almost a muttered grunt on my part but was enough to prevent Brackenbury from raising his bow as he looked at me quizzically. "No matter." I brushed the remark away quickly, hoping he would accept the dismissal, and it seemed he did, as he brought the longbow up and loosed a shot worthy of the most practiced of archers. It slammed into the centre of the target.

"Not so bad yourself!" I admitted grudgingly, and he grinned back at me.

"Well, who knows when we will be pressed into service. There's many a tale abroad at the moment. Rumblings of discontent. Have you heard of this Robin Mend-All? 'Tis said he is raising men against the king."

Foolish though I felt, I had to admit I hadn't heard of him. I rested my bow on the ground, looking at Brackenbury who was drawing yet another arrow.

"Why?"

He ran his fingers over the feathered fletchings, as if thinking deeply, his mouth puckered.

"All the usual reasons. Taxes, bribery and corruption." He sighed then. "Overmighty lords."

I knew what he was referring to. No matter who the king was, he could not rule without the support of powerful men. Men such as the earl. Men who then amassed wealth and lands, tenants and retainers, and who, within reason, could dispense rule and justice as they wished. There had been a rebellion in the days of Old King Henry, led by a Kentishman called Cade, and their protestations had been very much along the same lines.

Cade's men had laid the blame for such practices at the nobles who surrounded the king, and, so the tale went, they had been very much in support of Richard's father, a royal duke who was prevented from taking his place on the king's council. It didn't surprise me that the common man had found much to admire I the Duke of York, from what I had heard, and a shiver went down my back as if winter had returned.

A king surrounded by evil advisors? How many Woodvilles were there at court these days?

"It's probably much exaggerated," Brackenbury mused as he readied to draw up his bow. I wanted to agree with him, but the recent atmosphere at Middleham suddenly took on a new significance, and so I didn't answer him at all.

"Rob!"

The shout came from behind us and although I turned, Brackenbury loosed his arrow with unerring accuracy again, despite the distraction. He almost sliced his previous shaft in two and I didn't know whether to be depressed or amazed. It was only then that he looked around himself, as a dark-haired youth around our age came sauntering towards us.

He was swarthy, the tone of his complexion almost foreign. Young as he was, he looked like he would sprout a beard overnight if he did not submit to the barber's blade, but his eyes were sharp. Almost disconcertingly so. I doubted they missed much.

"Dick? What's the panic?"

Black brows over penetrating eyes drew together as he looked at me with a somewhat hostile interest.

"I take it your name is Lovell?" Rob cocked his head at the question and answered before I could.

"Yes, Francis Lovell. He's Warwick's man. From Middleham."

"He's not the only one," the one Rob called Dick replied curtly. "A troop of Northumberland's men have just ridden in. One of them had this, amongst other missives." I looked at his outstretched hand which held a letter sealed with red wax. I didn't need to see the script to know it was from Richard. I took it from him quickly.

"Is something amiss?" My question seemed dreadfully formal in the circumstances. The boy, Dick, gave a slowly growing grin.

"Now, that depends on your meaning of the word – amiss."

Brackenbury shook his head with amused impatience and leant on his bow.

"Lovell, meet Richard Ratcliffe. Eyes of a hawk, ears of a priest. Sees all, knows all, says bugger-all!"

Ratcliffe grinned as if Brackenbury's assessment was a

compliment. I was pleased, as it made his face a little less hard to look at and I reminded myself never to accept his invite to play cards. He didn't look like he ever gave much away.

"They bring more letters for the earl. No-one is saying anything. At least not to anyone here."

The stygian eyes alighted on me and I took the hint. What he meant was that Northumberland's men-at-arms were not about to tell tales to the guards at Barnard Castle. But to the earl's men who were already known to them...

I turned the letter over and over in my hand. It felt quite bulky, as if something was enclosed within and I raised my eyes to see them both looking at me inquisitively. I knew Ratcliffe would have seen the seal, so I couldn't hide anything.

"It's from Richard. The Duke of Gloucester."

I saw them exchange a glance.

"You keep exalted company," remarked Ratcliffe frankly. "What's he like?"

Making an instantaneous decision I snapped the seal with a satisfying crack, answering him as I did.

"Serious. Quiet. Nothing like the king." It had been a matter of fact remark but once again I saw them look at each other. For a moment I felt a little ashamed, as if I was boasting of my royal privileges. "I'm sorry, we have become friends over the years. And I have had occasion to play chess with the king, so..."

They both looked at me and I couldn't tell if their expressions contained amazement, respect or disbelief. Maybe a little of each, but my attention was back on the letter in my hand. For before I could read the text of Richard's letter, there appeared to be another folded inside of it. It was smaller, and just had one word on the front of it. A name. I moved it aside to read what Richard had written for my eyes as they watched me in silence.

"Are we allowed to know what he says?"

It was Ratcliffe who spoke, obviously not a man who held back from seeking opinions even if he kept his own close guarded, whereas I had already judged Brackenbury to be much more circumspect. I folded the letter back over the one addressed to Caitlin and looked up with a sigh.

"Nothing much. Warwick is expected at court where there is a delegation from Burgundy attending to witness Duke Charles receiving the Order of the Garter. Then he is to accompany the king's grace on pilgrimage to Walsingham."

"Any mention of this Robin fellow?"

I shook my head.

"Not directly. Just that Northumberland has been charged to calm the north, which he believes he is well equipped to do, both in men and arms."

"Men?" Brackenbury was studying his longbow now. "Does that include us do you think?" From his averted profile I could not work out if he was eager or reluctant to take part in any forthcoming skirmish.

Malone's face rose in my mind. He knew just about everyone back at the castle, and would no doubt have made himself known to Northumberland's men. He would be able to tell us what we wanted to know, although he had proven to be a somewhat hard nut to crack.

I had already warmed to Brackenbury, who had shown me nothing but friendliness since I arrived, and now his fellow henchman was looking at me expectantly. Don't ask me how I knew, but my gut told me that these were people I could trust, even though I knew them hardly at all. Some ingrown instinct which I had only ever experienced once before. It came from nowhere, but I knew it all the same.

"Well then," I shrugged with affected disinterest. "Maybe I had better go find out if my services are required?"

Rob's hand came up and clapped me on the shoulder. It was an unexpected, brotherly gesture, but I felt completely at ease with it.

"Then, we will see you later in the hall and you can share an ale, or two!"

As quickly as that, we had a silent pact. I could only hope

Malone would play his part.

26. MIDDLEHAM CASTLE
May 1469

As soon as we arrived back at the castle, it was obvious that a significant force was on the move.

Unfortunately for my new found friends, Malone could offer little insight into what may be going on. He had merely looked at me for a while with studied concern, whilst I instead told him what I knew, before he shrugged his shoulders and turned back to his companions. What knowledge he did have, and my instincts told me had had some, he obviously preferred not to share with me. In a way, I had to admire his loyalty, even if at this stage I was not completely sure who it was he was loyal to! Some men, it had to be said, served only one master in the end. Themselves.

Nevertheless, this had only served to stir our curiosity. Ratcliffe, Brackenbury and I had spent the night huddled together talking of rebels, battles, the victories and defeats experienced by the two Warwick earls set against the many stories of life at a court peppered with Woodvilles, as our experiences of life both in the north and south, converged.

Whilst feeling extremely comfortable with my new friends, and they ate up my stories of court life with avid interest along with the stewed partridge, once again, this only made me conscious of my family connections as I witnessed more than one raised eyebrow amongst my companions as we argued over the merits of one view or another. I had never been one to make friends easily, which had made my close companionship with Richard all the more unusual. Now, even though I could see they were in turns impressed or sceptical of my knowledge, somehow, I had felt that same bond again.

We parted with firm handshakes, and a sincere wish that we would at some stage meet again. As I had ridden out of the castle grounds, I felt a sense of loss that I could not really explain. Deep down, I just wished that they were travelling back with me, which seemed odd on such a short acquaintance. But there it was.

The outer bailey at Middleham was crowded with sumpter wagons, harnessed horse and men-at-arms dressed with a grim cloak of determination. I rode past the cushioned litter which the countess and her daughters always travelled in on longer journeys. Usually, this was when she was going back to Warwick, rather than any of the closer, northern castles. To me, these preparations had all the appearance of a sojourn south, no doubt to move away from any rebellious activity which may have been discovered.

In one way, I mused, it made total sense, but only if there was a danger, surely? Middleham was a fortress! A band of disorganized, rag-tag rebels trailing along behind a disgruntled merchant under a fanciful name would have no chance in breaching its formidable defences! Unless... A gnawing sensation began low down in my gut. Unless, the rebels were being arrayed by someone else?

I threw myself off my horse as it came to a halt, looking around at the frenzied comings and goings, and watched as Northumberland dismounted himself. It was then I heard a voice in my ear. A voice with a distinct Irish lilt.

"Looks like someone be on the move."

Malone stood behind me, his mount's reins still in his hands. The man obviously had the gait of a cat, as I had not even been aware of his approach. By now, the earl was surrounded by men, and was pushing his way through towards the keep.

"Is this to do with Robin do you think?" I whispered, my eyes still on the earl's hawk-like profile, but all I heard was Malone's soft chuckle.

"You be asking me that the other night, and I know no more now than I did then. Maybe you should follow him." He jerked his head towards Northumberland and without a further word, I handed Fides over to a stable-hand and followed, taking the stairs two at a time.

The great hall was all but deserted, the trestles cleared away, only two lone servants were left feeding the central fire with wood. Everything else had an almost vacant air about it, which confirmed the frenetic activity below. Northumberland had disappeared through to the great chamber but I could hear his voice even if I could not see him.

"Is all ready?"

"Yes, as my lord husband commands." The countess sounded her usual composed self and it was only as I heard her voice that my thoughts returned to Caitlin and I looked around, almost expecting to see her, but there were only the servants, now turning their attentions to strewing fresh rushes around the floor.

"Well, almost..." it was George's voice, with its recognizable, sardonic edge. "Your youngest daughter appears to be missing." I couldn't tell what happened next, but can only assume that Northumberland had not been too impressed to hear that the plans were not quite as ordered as he expected.

"I will find her." It was the countess's voice, tight with anger. "You were earlier than expected, that is all. There is other business for your attention and by the time you..."

"Lovell!"

The roar was one of a lion, and almost shook the walls, causing both of the industrious servants to raise their heads nervously. To be fair, Northumberland sounded exactly like Warwick and the servants had heard that bellow so many times before they knew what it usually signified. John Neville, it appeared, could be every bit as commanding as his brother.

Pulling my shoulders up, I passed through the doorway into the chamber where the earl stood waiting, stone-faced. I glanced over his shoulder and took in the countess's strained expression and even though I saw George and Isabel were there I ignored them completely.

"My Lord." I bowed deferentially, waiting.

"Find my niece and get her back here and ready to leave

within the hour." My eyes flicked back to the countess, who had not moved an inch. Without speaking, I turned on my heel and departed, wondering immediately where to start! It was hard for anyone to hide for long in Middleham. Large it may be, but not in a rambling, sprawling way like Greenwich or Barnard Castle. I had my head down, thinking furiously when a gentle voice caused me to raise my head.

"My Lord?"

I saw her blue skirts before my eyes met hers. Jane stood before me, her pale gaze seeking mine. For some reason the sight of her made me impatient.

"I told you..."

She said nothing to interrupt me but held out her hand, and it was what she held made me stop. I looked at the small square of parchment dumbly.

"This came today. Lady Anne asked me to keep it for you in case you returned and she was no longer here. I don't know why."

I took the letter from her. It was not addressed to me. It had Caitlin's name on it and was an exact partner to the one I held close inside my doublet. But, why would Richard send what appeared to be the same letter to both of us? Was he expecting one of his messages not to reach its destination? I frowned for a second, but tucked it inside my doublet all the same.

"Thank you." I mumbled and felt slightly awkward. I had no idea why she made me feel so uncomfortable, apart from being the guardian of the knowledge Rob had given me before he left, but it was still an odd feeling to have and I knew my cheeks had coloured as I met her eyes. "My apologies, my lady. I..." My words trailed off as I could think of no acceptable excuse I could give for my attitude towards her. To my shame, she gave me the gentlest of smiles.

"I am not a lady either." I found her total innocence quite disarming and began to fumble my words. As usual!

"Then, maybe, you should be. And no matter what, I should

189

treat you as such."

It was her turn to blush, quite prettily as it turned out, and for the first time, I noticed how shy she truly was. Her eyes sought to fix upon anything but my face.

"Lady Anne has gone out riding. I heard her say she wanted to go down by the river."

Finally, her wandering gaze rested on my face and for the first time my heart warmed towards her, but possibly not in the way she may have been hoping, yet I only had Rob's word for that.

"Thank you. I had better go. The earl is waiting." I inclined my head as politely as I could, and began to cross the hall. As if she knew she would be throwing a knife into my back, she called after me as I left.

"Lady Desmond is with her."

27. MIDDLEHAM CASTLE
July 1469

It took hardly any time at all to saddle Fides as I did it myself, and before long was galloping out of the gatehouse and through the outer bailey without a backward glance. And yes, my heart was racing for more than one reason. Northumberland was waiting on me, and I didn't have long, but more importantly, I was about to see Caitlin once more. It had only been a few weeks, but it felt more like years since Richard had left. Since I last saw those luminous green eyes regard me from across a room.

I saw them as I approached the bridge at some speed. They had pulled in to the riverside and appeared to be talking, but it was Caitlin who turned as the sound of my hasty approach became more than apparent. In fact, I was travelling at such speed that I had to pull Fides up sharp in order to stop, causing him to rear up, almost throwing me out of the saddle. Not exactly the entrance I had been planning!

No sooner had his hooves touched the ground than I found myself as breathless as he, for there she was, and although I knew she was looking directly at me, I had to force myself to focus my attention on Anne, who looked rather forlorn, as if she had been expecting me and knew my purpose. It was then I realized this outing was no accident. She had purposely taken herself away from the castle, maybe troubled by what she had seen, or heard. None of this made me feel any happier but I settled Fides back down and nodded to Anne's troubled face.

"The countess requests your return to the castle. With all haste." Those words spoken, I steeled myself and turned towards Caitlin, my throat drying by the second. "Lady Desmond. I am very pleased to see you so recovered." She gave me a small smile in response and my stomach lurched into my throat. She was very pale, but other than that her recent spell of illness seemed to have affected her not at all. Her eyes still had the power to strike me dumb, and her lack of colour gave her hair an added depth and although I longed for her to speak to me, it was Anne whose words came next.

"Francis, what is it? There is something amiss, then? Do you know what is happening?"

I knew. Of course I knew, and I suspected that she did too. Only she appeared not to want to acknowledge it, either that, or she thought I knew more than she and that I would betray myself if she acted the innocent. I shook my head, keeping my thoughts to myself. This was Anne, but she was also Warwick's daughter and being in his service was suddenly feeling a somewhat insecure place to be. I remained neutral as I replied, imparting only what I knew for certain.

"All I know is she was insistent. I would not tarry if I were you. It would appear you may be leaving. Sumpter wagons are being loaded. The bailey is awash with banners."

Anne pulled her mount around in silence and guided it towards the bridge, leaving us both watching her go and I saw Caitlin gather up her reins to do likewise. She was mounted on her silver-grey palfrey and although she did look just a little different to when I had last seen her, somehow a little drawn around the eyes, just to be in her company still warmed my soul.

I reached out without thinking and laid my hand on her arm as I pulled one of the letters out of my doublet, beneath my cloak. I cannot say why I did not give her both. The main thing was, the letter had reached her, which was Richard's firm intention. If the sadness in her eyes was because she had recovered to find Richard gone, I knew I held that which could return the joy to her face. At least, so I hoped.

"I wrote to Dickon to let him know you had recovered. This arrived today." Her response was immediate and I watched helplessly as tears filled her eyes, just at the sight of that small missive.

"Oh Francis!" she sighed, her words whispered on tremulous breath. "You are such a true friend."

Her words were so heartfelt, I knew the heat had rushed to my face and I grinned, hoping, in vain, she would not notice. If this is how just having her friendship felt, the Lord could only guess how it would feel to have her love! But my next words were just as genuine.

"I know he was concerned that he had to leave before you recovered. I promised I would let him know how you fared. It is no hardship and thankfully my letter got away before the current activity began. I am as good a friend to him as he has been to me." I drew my hand away and looked around. The gravity of the situation washed back over me. There was mischief afoot. I was sure of it and it made me feel sick to the pit of my stomach. I could only hope that either I was wrong, or if I was right, Edward and Richard were on their guard. "I hope to serve in his household one day, once my wardship is at an end. God willing."

The look she gave me then was so enigmatic, I could not for the life of me work out what she was thinking. Some sort of shadow passed behind her eyes, but it was gone in an instant and she smiled as we turned our horses back towards the village.

We rode briskly, but in complete silence, and I had no doubt her thoughts were on the contents of the letter which she now held secreted in the pocket of her cloak. Although I dearly wanted to speak to her, my mind was also distracted by what we were to confront when we arrived back, and so it seemed both of us were more than happy to absorb ourselves in our own concerns.

The bell for Nones rang out as we dismounted in the bailey and even as I turned to Caitlin, she had already spied her prey and was hurrying towards the east gatehouse where Malone was conversing with Sir John, the Steward. Whatever he felt about me, it seemed she had a complete confidence in the man, and maybe, with their shared Irish lineage, she was right to do so, it was hard for me to say. There was certainly some form of kinship there, and it warmed my heart in a way that she did have someone in whom she could fully trust, as I knew not at all how she really felt about me.

I heard her call his name as she disappeared into the throng and I stood for a while, my hand stroking down Fides neck gently. Anne's palfrey was just being led into the stables and I assumed she had already hurried into the keep to answer her mother's wrath. I supposed, I should make my way there also, and find out exactly what my own instructions were.

I hung around for what I thought was a decent interval, before crossing through to the inner bailey, hurrying past the shadowed figures of Malone and Caitlin as they stood in the doorway of the gatehouse. I kept my head facing forwards and didn't even look at them as I made my way towards the keep. It was so calm in this inner sanctum, that is made it difficult to believe the bustle that was taking place mere feet away, I was also desperate to find a few moments to read Richard's letter, but that would have to wait.

As I entered the Great Chamber, Anne motioned me across to where she stood with Isabel, and I complied, even if a little uncertainly.

"What's happening?" I whispered, as they were both looking apprehensive, although there was a hard glint in Isabel's eye which I did not miss. Anne turned to look at me, her soft grey eyes large and troubled.

"We are leaving." It was all Anne could say before the countess swept into the room followed by Northumberland, at the same time as Caitlin entered the room from the other entrance. She stood aside as Northumberland crossed the room directly, heading for the stairs, leaving us all behind watching. Sir John followed closely behind him.

The countess watched him go and then looked at her two daughters, her expression impassive.

"Anne, Isabel, we leave tomorrow for Warwick to join your father." I had my gaze firmly fixed on her and as if she could feel its force, she flicked a glance my way, but it was only for the briefest of seconds. "A garrison of men will remain here. The land is particularly restless at present and your father feels it necessary to keep a force here ready to venture out and crush any rising that may occur. Similar actions are being taken at Pontefract and Sheriff Hutton. We cannot be sure where rebels will strike, if at all! Our Percy neighbours are subdued at the moment, but are never still for long and your father is prudent as ever. He knows the Scots are always on the look out for any weakness and would not hesitate to cross the border if they thought our position weakened by attack."

So, the household was indeed going south. A demon began to prod my gut and I was determined to make sure I was not left behind this time. If the family were going south, anywhere near London, I had to make sure I was going too. I had no intention of being left behind with a northern garrison. I may even be able to meet up with Richard on his way to Walsingham if I could get a message to him. I cleared my throat a little nervously.

"My lady, would I be able to travel south also to see ...?" My words failed at the last moment as I knew I was speaking a lie. "My wife and family?"

Her reply was instant, making it clear she was not even prepared to consider it.

"I am sorry Francis but, no. The earl has commanded that you remain here and continue your training." I was biting my tongue so hard now, I almost didn't see her turn her attention to the other side of the room.

"Caitlin. It is not seemly that a lady of your stature be left within a garrison. Therefore, you will go to the convent of our Sisters of Mercy near the coast until we return north. Then we shall see. The earl has been kind enough to provide you with a corrody, should the need arise."

Even my heart froze at those words, so I could only imagine what Caitlin was feeling, apart from the horror that was writ large all over her face. She lost all the colour that the ride had painted on her cheeks and her eyes seemed to widen even more. I didn't know what Richard would have put into his letter to her, but the simple fact that he had chosen to send two copies to ensure it reached her made me feel certain he would not want her walled up in a nunnery, no matter what the Earl of Warwick may wish. Once again, I had to step up, where Richard could not speak for himself.

It also seemed a strange thing to do! She had been given into Warwick's service by the king! Would they no longer need companions in the south? There had to be some reason why she was not accompanying the household, why she was being dealt this particular fate. For a moment, my mind could not make sense of it, after all, she had not long ago been consigned to her bed, dreadfully ill. The clouds cleared, and it became apparent with the clarity of the sea shining on water.

Richard!

This was the countess's way of separating Caitlin from her daughter's intended husband. She was using the threat of rebellion and the upheaval of the household to immure her as far away from any further contact with Richard as she could. Bile began to rise in my throat. Not if I could help it!

"My lady, Lady Desmond would be welcome in my wife's family at Minster Lovell, or even Ravensworth, I am sure - if the earl is concerned for her safety during this time. I know...my wife would be only too welcome of the company." There was no time for her to give any answer to my futile attempt at gaining control of the situation as Anne's cry cut across my words. As I spun my head around in the direction of the sound, Caitlin's eyes closed, and she crumpled onto the floor, lifeless and pale as death.

28. MIDDLEHAM CASTLE
May 1469

As one, Anne, the countess and I lunged forwards, but I reached her first. Caitlin lay in a crumpled heap on the floor and without thinking twice, I scooped her up in my arms. There had been no time to think about my own ability to lift her weight, but I need not have worried, for she was as light as a feather. My only difficulty was in the nearness of her face to mine as her head lolled into the crook of my neck, releasing a wave of fragrant violet scent which threatened to be my undoing.

Anne was wringing her hands in despair, but I ignored her and glared pointedly at the countess, who met my gaze without an ounce of embarrassment.

"Thank you Francis, will you carry her to her chamber please. Anne, stop whining and go find Higgs. I think it was far too early for her to be out riding since her recovery. Sometimes these things take time."

She turned on her heel then, and I followed her, still aware of the closeness of Caitlin's body to mine and I felt a sweat break out on my brow. As I walked past George and Isabel, who had been completely unmoved by the whole thing, I heard George murmur.

"How gallant! I certainly do think what ails Lady Desmond will heal itself in time, don't you Isabel?"

I didn't know what he meant and didn't care. I still had not managed to find out how he had discovered my fondness for Caitlin, but at this moment that was the last thing on my mind. I heard Isabel giggle, but I was so intent on carrying my precious burden that I ignored both of them and followed the countess over the walkway to the private apartments.

Not without some relief, for many reasons, I finally laid Caitlin down on her bed. She was deathly pale and clammy, and made a soft, moaning sound as she rolled over on the counterpane, curling herself into a ball, her eyes still closed. I stood back, looking down at her, a deep, burning anxiety in my stomach. I spoke to the countess without turning, which was the height of bad manners, but I could not look at her at the moment for fear of what my face may betray.

"What is it, my Lady, that could ail her so?"

I heard a resigned sigh from over my shoulder and it was only then that I summoned up the courage to face her, and in doing so I saw a countess I hardly recognised. Her features were softer, the usually hard eyes reflected an affection I had not seen before as she also looked down at Caitlin lying on the bed.

"Well, as I feel our original plans are about to change, it is probably time to tell you. Lady Desmond is with child." The voice that then came from the doorway must have echoed the shock that registered in my own face.

"With child? But... Mama... whose child?"

Anne stood just inside the room, her eyes full of disbelief at the news she had just heard.

"Never you mind!" The countess returned in a flash, making what I had just witnessed seem all the more remarkable. "Go and finish your packing. We will have to delay our departure until the morning, as this – unexpected - situation will need to be resolved. Did you find Higgs?"

"Jane has gone for him." Anne's eyes now also peered at Caitlin with increased curiosity until she looked back at her mother's face. Bowing her head, she retreated from the room, closing the door.

There was a brief moment of silence before the countess spoke to me again, and I could have placed a wager with Rob, had he been here, on what she was about to say.

"I believe you already know who the father is."

I had no idea if Richard even knew that she was to have a child, if so, he had not spoken of it to me. Perhaps, it had been too sensitive, too delicate a subject, or...he had been embarrassed by it. I swallowed hard over a knot in my throat. This was one development I had certainly not foreseen in all my talks of rebels and troubles to come. I felt a sudden surge of sympathy for the young girl lying unconscious on the embroidered damask, trying to imagine what torture she may have endured these past few weeks. No wonder she had seized on Richard's letter as she had.

"I believe I do." I answered simply, and was surprised to see her smile gently.

"Then you know more than he does, or anyone else for that matter, even Anne. And I would very much like it kept that way. If the girl wants His Grace to know, I am sure she will say so. Once she is able."

As we both looked back at Caitlin, it all made sense, the sneering aside by George as I had hurried past him. Isabel, laughing. They knew. Somehow, in the same way that George had homed in on my affection for Caitlin, they had also uncovered what, for her, must have been a dreadful burden to carry alone. Now, even after watching her faint away, to them it was still a source of entertainment.

"I think you may find that Isabel already knows. George too." I saw the countess raise eyebrows to her hairline. "They must have noticed something. I doubt very much that she would reveal to them what even Dickon does not know."

I watched as her eyes registered this news and her face hardened. If I had not known better, on that day, I clearly saw exactly what the countess thought of George Plantagenet, and it was far from flattering.

"You need not worry about them. Whatever they know will remain unspoken, I will make sure of that." I felt the retort rising, as echoes of George's voice now repeated in my mind, and for a few seconds I forgot myself completely. All I could think of was Richard, of his feelings for this girl. This girl who was now carrying his child.

"Best you do. I cannot imagine what might happen if George should goad his brother with this news."

I almost flinched as she blanched at my outburst, but at that precise moment I didn't care. One day, and not too distant in the future, I would command lands and men of my own. I would own property and be able to dictate my own future, well at least I hoped I would. God and the king willing. For the moment, I stood my ground stubbornly. Her answer was perfunctory and cool, but she did not rebuke me. At least not outright. Her censure was more subtle.

"I see your affinity extends beyond the person of His Grace to his chattels. Let us hope that your investment is not ill founded, after all, you saw with what coin he repaid the earl for his good lordship."

"I did," I retorted quickly, although keeping my voice low. "I saw His Grace remain loyal to his king. I was surprised that my Lord Warwick would have expected him to act otherwise, for would that not be treason?"

If she had been pale before, she now looked as if every drop of blood had drained from her body. I had dared to answer her back. Not only that, but I had also inferred that her husband may be inciting treason. As my newly found confidence began to falter, the door swung open and Higgs bumbled in, tutting under his breath as he bent over the bed, peering at Caitlin's face inquisitively.

"At last! Wait outside!"

The command from the countess came with a terse change in tone and I was grateful to get out of the room, only to find myself occupying the seat outside, where Richard had formerly stood guard. I could have hardly been there for half an hour when the countess came out and stood before me.

To my relief, she seemed to have decided to ignore my outburst. Just as well, I thought grudgingly, as I was in no mood to apologise, which could have earned me a beating. Instead, she folded her hands before her, surveying me somewhat archly.

"Lovell, you have a new charge. One that I think may please you. Higgs has advised against Lady Desmond travelling anywhere, no matter how short the journey. I will therefore have to comply and leave her here, at least for the foreseeable future. I can leave at least one servant with her, and will arrange for one of the midwives from the village to attend, but for her daily needs, I feel I must ask you to have a care for her welfare. As much as you feel appropriate, of course."

I had stood as she appeared before me and though I tried to look past her into the chamber, it was impossible. The irony in the situation could not have been more apparent to me. Not only now was I to ensure that Richard's mistress was cared for, but his unborn child as well. I felt both honoured, perturbed and slightly uneasy at the same time. Yet, if it kept Caitlin from being confined to a nunnery, I felt sure my efforts would be for the good.

"I will do my best, my Lady." I replied courteously, trying in some small way to make the peace between us. It worked, partly, as she nodded in satisfaction, but she could not keep the sarcasm from her reply.

"Oh, I am sure you will. Now, you will be pleased to hear that Lady Desmond has recovered and is sitting up. I must return inside for the moment. Would you please go and find Jane Cooke and send her to me here?"

"Jane?" I sounded somewhat dumb.

She nodded briefly before turning away.

"I need to let her know she will be staying behind."

29. MIDDLEHAM CASTLE
May 1469

Anne's face was still troubled, and it occurred to me that the last time I had seen her smile was when I returned from Minster Lovell, quite some while ago now. She was twisting her gloved fingers together as we stood at the top of the stairs outside the chapel, and her eyes were seeking mine in a way which made me wish she would leave, and quickly.

"Do you know who...?" In the end, she could not bring herself to ask the question, her cheeks flaring with the effort. God forgive me, but I knew not how I found the strength to lie. Only that I felt an ingrained sense of loyalty to Richard, and so to Caitlin. I shook my head.

"No. She has said nothing to me." That at least was the truth. "But, then why would she? I hardly know her, other than as your servant." Again, that could not be denied. I began to relax a little, but it was a brief mercy.

"I can only think..." She paused, looking up at me uncertainly. "Could it be Rob? Tom? One of the other squires, or..?" Please, please don't say Dickon, my inner voice was pleading silently whilst my Demon chuckled devilishly. "Maybe, one of the guards? I know she is friendly with the Irishmen. Maybe one of them was of comfort to her, as I know she misses her homeland." I stifled a sigh of relief. Anne obviously never even considered that Richard would sleep with a servant, no matter how noble. She seemed to retain a form of innocence which added to her charm.

"Maybe." I left it with that, not wanting to begin to talk about any Irish guards in case Anne decided to try and seek out Malone before she left. "Maybe we will never know."

"Will you ask her?"

"It is not my business. I will do as your mother charged and, with Jane, make sure she has all she needs. Hopefully, we won't have to bother the earl too much as I am sure that is the last thing he would want."

Anne nodded sagely and threw a look down the stairs. I could tell by her demeanour that she didn't want to leave. She loved Middleham after all, as much as I did, and it was her home.

"I had better go," she said sadly, and gathering up her skirts, she turned away and went down the stairs. I didn't watch her go, I was already anxiously anticipating my next conversation and I almost ran across the great hall, breathing deeply to recover myself as I came to a halt outside her chamber door.

I had no idea if anyone was with her. I had seen Jane flitting about, but not to talk to, and the countess had sent over a midwife, who had visited Caitlin and pronounced herself more than happy with her condition as things stood. For myself, Jane and I had been introduced to her and knew where to find her should the need arise. Exactly what would happen after the most urgent need arose in a few months' time, God only knew. I could only hope that by such a time, events were much more settled.

For a few moments, I remained still, gathering my thoughts. The letter from Richard held no news which I could impart to her, and I hoped that she would not ask if he had also written to me. He confirmed he had received my note telling him Caitlin had recovered, but said nothing more on it. But then I could only guess at his movements and what may have been concerning him when he was able to find time to write back to me.

One other thing was obvious from his words. As one rebellion was quelled, another seemed to spring up from the ground like bindweed, and would continue to do so until its roots were firmly ripped from the ground.

As I turned the latch before me, I cautioned myself to be careful and not refer to the letter at all, lest she was further distressed that he had not asked after her health. Which, strangely, he had not, for reasons only known to himself. I entered the chamber, inhaling deeply as I did, and just as well, for whatever ailed her now was surely only adding to her radiance. Either that, or the sunlight which pooled around her as she sat by the window was the culprit for such exquisite beauty. I found her hard to look at and my heart began to betray me once more. She was looking down into the bailey and I walked over to her, swallowing hard to overcome the sudden dryness in my throat.

"Well, that was somewhat fortunate." I blushed as she started visibly and glanced up at me. "If you know what I mean." I muttered apologetically. I had hoped to strike both a friendly and light tone, and obviously got that wrong within a few words. Her eyes returned to the travelers who were now on their way and she rested her head against the stone of the wall, closing her eyes. "Are you well now?"

"It was nothing." I was stung by the coldness of her response as she opened her eyes and I busied myself by brushing some dust off the window embrasure, to hide my uncertainty. Our conversations had always been so friendly, so this sudden change was taking some getting used to, and I prayed that it would be short-lived, that it was only her embarrassment making it difficult for us to talk, but I was desperate for her to understand that I did not judge her. That to me, it made no difference. Some of the dust from the stone had worked its way beneath my nail and I tried to dislodge it with my tongue, making my next question muffled.

"Is it not true then?"

"What?" Her eyes were wide, bright, green gems, sparkling with an inner sorrow and my heart began to melt. It was hard for her, I could see that. Her hands were clasped tightly in her lap, almost fused together so still were they.

"Anne tells me you are to have a child."

Somehow, those words burst the dam of her despair and she bent forwards, covering her face. I looked down at her head, the tightly coiled braid of fire threaded through with soft, blue silk. It took all my willpower to stay my hand as I longed to reach out and stroke her hair.

"Caitlin?"

She sat back then, slowly, resting a hand above where Richard's babe undoubtedly lay and I caught the fierce glint of the jewel on her hand, yet, thankfully, her eyes no longer matched that cold, hard glimmer.

"So...no Lady Caitlin now? Am I no longer a lady?" My answer was as quick as the flood of pleasure that flowed through me as I basked in the warmth of her words. They were hesitant, almost frightened, but they were Caitlin's, not the cold, impassive effigy she had been but a few moments ago. I answered her as honestly as I could.

"You are to me. I just thought now that we are on our own here, we wouldn't have to be so formal." She was still looking at me, expectantly, a small, worried crease between her brows, as I kept my voice deliberately solemn. "But if you insist...I could even call you...Your Grace!" I was rewarded at my attempt to humour by a further softening around her lips. "Have you written to Dickon?" She would no doubt have read his letter by now, but she shook her head gently and I sighed. "Well, I doubt we will get anything sent out of here now for the foreseeable future, certainly not without Northumberland's permission."

The tension between us seemed to be easing and so I sat down in the window seat next to her, as close as I dare, but she didn't move, which made my heart skip a further beat. She was all I could ever wish for in a girl and more, but I had to remember to whom she really belonged. It was hard, no matter how much I told myself it could never be, I still could not prevent the way my whole being reacted to her presence. All I could try and do now was turn that into a force for good. To help her get through this in any way I could.

"I wish I could get a letter to him though," I sighed. "He sounded so vexed the last time he wrote, and there is certainly something afoot. I don't know that I really believe the reason we were given for all these troops being garrisoned here."

I had thought she may answer by talking about the letter

205

Richard had sent to her, but she didn't.

"Did Anne not say anything else?" Her voice was very low, almost a whisper, but much more companionable than it had been earlier. I couldn't think what she was referring to so I looked up at her, frowning.

"Such as?"

"Such as…. George and Isabel getting wed?"

I had to laugh at that, only something in her expression cut me short. Surely, she was not suggesting that the earl was about to disobey the king? And George! If he married Isabel, Edward's anger would be a sight to behold. I decided she must have it wrong. I couldn't think either of them would be so foolish, but still I knew my answer did not belie that confidence, which was beginning to slip away the more I thought about recent events.

"That was expressly forbidden by the king. The earl would be mad to…. George would not…" She was looking at me, her bottom lip captured by her teeth. As if she could not believe it herself, but knew it to be true. "Jesus! He wouldn't dare! They wouldn't dare! The king will be furious! We must get a message to Dickon. He needs to know what they are planning! He must be told of this!"

I had sprung out of my seat now and was pacing backwards and forwards, thinking. What were Warwick's plans? To have George married in secret, and then what? There had to be a reason for risking the king's anger, so what was it? What did he expect to happen when the king found out his heir had married, not only without his consent, but to a woman who had been forcibly denied to him?

Then there were the recent risings, all of them based in the north. Percy lands, yes, but Neville lands too! Were people that unhappy with Edward's policies? He had brought stability to the realm after decades of turmoil and strife. I halted, my feet coming to a sudden stop. Well, he had. Until he had married. In secret, and to a woman unknown to anyone, but who would anyway have been deemed unsuitable. Suddenly, Warwick's revenge seemed clear. But, how far could he, would he, go?

Caitlin was looking at me and smiled sadly, looking out of the window once more.

"Amongst other things," she murmured and my head had been so full of thoughts I had forgotten my last words. It was Richard, we had been talking about getting a letter to Richard. "Besides, you said yourself, it won't be easy to send any letters now. We will just have to wait it out and see what happens. There's nothing else we can do."

As if she herself felt in danger, she began to stroke her stomach with one hand, and I almost felt that I should do the same with my own, for surely the acid of fear that was beginning to burn there was hotter than the fiercest flames.

30. MIDDLEHAM CASTLE
August 1469

I flew down the keep stairs, hurtling into the bailey just in time to watch as the earl tried to assist the king to dismount, no mean feat with his hands tied. Edward, however, shunned the offer of assistance and dismounted athletically, and with ease.

To be honest I still couldn't believe it. The king. Here at Middleham, accompanied by the earl, George and a troop of armed men. I had been passing the time away with Caitlin in her chamber when we had been disturbed by the arrival of unexpected guests, without even knowing at the time exactly how unexpected they would, in fact, be.

The summer months had so far been long and indolent. In between training, Latin, scripture and other lessons, I had spent as much time with Caitlin as I could and our friendship had blossomed into something warm and comfortable. I thought I could tell her anything, and I hoped she felt the same, and we had spent many an hour talking about our hopes and desires, or sometimes she would just read whilst I strummed away on my lute, hoping my efforts would at least entertain her during the endless, airless days.

The child inside her had begun to grow, yet surprisingly, Caitlin still retained a somewhat slim figure, when compared to some of the more matronly women I had seen who travelled the journey to birth a child. It didn't surprise me that even in this, she would surpass many others. Alice, the midwife, came and went, and Jane was often in attendance, even though she was now somewhat surly of mood most of the time, although, to be fair, I hardly gave her a moment's thought. All of my devotions were directed in ensuring that Caitlin was well cared for and entertained, and not a day passed when I did not spend at least an hour in her company, now and again with Jane in attendance, a brooding shadow sitting by the fire.

That was until today.

Edward and Warwick were now standing toe-to-toe and the grooms led their horses away. George was stripping off his gloves as he walked towards them, smug self-satisfaction wiped all over his face. As if in a conscious effort to avoid talking to his brother, Edward turned to me, and immediately grinned broadly.

"Lovell! Well, at least I have the solace of one friendly face during my captivity! That is, as long as your affinity has not fallen subject to treachery since we last met?"

Warwick and George were both now looking at me too. Somewhere in the back of my head, I heard John Neville's words. The fact that it was the earl's brother who had been giving me advice made the matter all the more important to me. For, as I saw it, if I was reading his words right, it meant he was also aware of what had been about to happen, and not entirely supportive of it. Now was the time to find out if I was wrong, but all I could do was go with my gut.

"You are still my king and I am here to serve you. As such, you have my sword."

Edward's grin widened as the same time as George rolled his eyes even as the earl's expression darkened.

"And I thought Warwick was supposed to be teaching you! It seems the tables are turned in more than one way and now the servant educates the master."

George snorted dismissively.

"If you relying on Lovell's sword, you wont get very far. He's a boy, Ned. You are in dire need of men at the moment, and look! I don't see many of them around here. Not wearing your colours anyway."

Edward continued to look directly at me, choosing to ignore his brother completely, even though he had heard his word as clearly as I had.

"No matter his age, if Lovell is half the man our brother Richard appears to be, I think I will not need fear a few minor

209

rebellions. What say you then Lovell? When all this current –
disaffection – is resolved, how would you like to follow
Gloucester's banner?"

He could not have said anything else that would have been
such music to my ears. At the end of the day, I served Warwick
only because Edward had granted that it be so. He could reverse
that grant in a heartbeat and no one was more aware of that than
the earl. There were benefits to being a royal ward, on both the
part of the ward and the lord he served.

"Nothing would give me more honour, Your Grace."

George moved forwards then and gave Edward a sharp
shove towards the keep stairs.

"I have heard enough of this nonsense. Dickon's sword may
as well be made from wood for all the good it is going to do you.
Move, damn you!"

Edward stumbled forwards, but took this insolence with
remarkably good grace. Yet, even the earl was shocked at
George's insolence.

"George!"

Edward looked over his shoulder and smiled as he moved
into the stairwell.

"That's it Warwick! Control your son-in-law. I have spent
years hoping he will not disgrace me in public. You can have that
burden now with pleasure." He laughed loudly. "Where is your
new wife George? I would like to offer her my sympathies! I did
try to save her from this fate, I would like to assure her of that!"

So, Isabel had got her wish. And against the kings express
command. The world truly was going mad.

I watched George's face go puce with rage, but so did the
earl who stepped between him and the king as we all made our
way up the steps to the Great Hall, where we came to a halt
amongst a startled group of servants. Before they could even
decide whether they should show deference or not, a curt shout
from the earl gave them something else to worry about.

"Leave us!"

His voice almost made the windows rattle and before long we were alone in the hall, with me wondering if I should even be there at all, but I had no intention of leaving. And it would appear I still had my uses.

"Lovell. Untie his hands."

With consummate ease, Edward stretched out his arms, exposing his wrists. Checking his face carefully, I could see he was still smiling quite genially, but there was something in his eyes which led me to believe he was more than a match for the two men who felt they had him under their control.

"Careful Lovell," he murmured as I removed the dagger from my belt, "one slip and you could find yourself paying obeisance to my brother." He raised his eyebrows quizzically. "And I don't mean the one that is significant by his absence."

I thought I would be nervous, releasing my king from his bonds, but my hands were remarkably steady as I sliced through the rope in one smooth action. The rope fell to the floor as Edward rubbed his wrists, more a reflex action than because of any tension in the rope, as I had noticed it had been quite loose, considering. I was beginning to wonder exactly how serious the earl was in his efforts to rebel. Was this just all for show? A warning to Edward of what he could do, should he decide to exercise his power and influence? My anxiety increased but I kept my eyes and ears sharp.

"Well, what now?" Edward looked at his captors with a mixture of contempt and amusement wreathing his face as Warwick and Clarence exchanged pointed glances. "Come on, George, don't fail now! Pembroke, Rivers and his son are a head shorter thanks to your ambitions after all. So, I ask again, what now?"

George took a step forwards and for one moment I thought he was going to lash out at his brother. Edward squared up to him, smiling dangerously. He was taller than George by more than a head, and broader too.

"You will listen to us now, brother," George snarled, wisely

211

keeping the space between them. "We will give you time to clear your head of the insidious whisperings of your wife's family, and then, you will hear us. You will hear us very clearly."

Although I heard this exchange, sensed the danger in the room, I felt as though I had been hit around the head, the words rang hollowly in my ears. My eyes flew to the kings, seeking confirmation of what he had just revealed, and everything I needed to know was there.

This was not some whim, some tactic to get Edward to take notice of how disgruntled Warwick and George were about the rebutted marriage plans. This was no small, rag-tag band of men rising up to air their grievances with their lord. This was serious.

However Edward himself had been taken, blood had been spilt. Men had died. Men I knew. Baron Rivers, the queen's father, and his son. Which son? I was desperate to ask, but before I could even begin to think, Warwick grabbed hold of my arm and pushed me towards the door.

"Go to the steward. Tell him to report to me, now. And be quick about it."

I stumbled forwards a couple of steps, flashing a quick look in Edward's direction. I could see Warwick was as rattled as George was smug, but it was the look in the king's eyes which made my blood freeze to ice.

31. MIDDLEHAM CASTLE
August 1469

Two days later, I sat astride Fides looking over to the small hillock which was all that was left of the old castle. Not two feet away from me sat Edward, the king, once again completely at ease and mounted on Warwick's midnight black destrier. Not that we were completely alone, being followed as we were by four men-at-arms who, despite being under orders to guard the king closely, were keeping a discreet distance.

Not a lot was happening, in fact, now that the earl had his prize, he seemed to have no idea what to do with it. Edward appeared to be very much at his leisure, he often invited me to play chess with him, and Warwick had released me from my training to attend upon the king as he wished. But I was not the only one. Patrick Malone has also been put in charge of the king's security, almost like a personal body servant, and was one of the group of men now behind us, watching his every move.

Edward had also been re-introduced to Caitlin, and was also now more than aware of her condition, and of Richard's indiscretion. He had taken it remarkably well, in fact. He had even argued with the earl that she be allowed to return to Ireland, to her mother, once it was obvious that the plans to send her to a nunnery had resurfaced, something I secretly believed George had a hand in. Yet, those plans were going ahead. Jane was helping Caitlin gather together her belongings, and from the look of her, it may be she had been told she would be going there too. Either that, or something else was causing her to walk around with a face like sour milk.

Yesterday, I had been kicking my heels for most of the day as Warwick and George had locked themselves away with Edward in a privy chamber where no one was welcome. Not even a cupbearer. Because now Warwick's plan was falling apart at the seams. Rumours of more rebellions were on the rise, and this time, orchestrated as a direct result of the earl's actions and not by his will.

Edward pulled his mount up and leaned forwards on the pommel of his saddle, looking around at the rolling hills and vales. The sun dappled them with racing shadows as the scudding clouds followed the path of the breeze across the sky. It was a beautiful day, and the sun was warm on my back.

"Now, I see."

"Your Grace?" my question was swift; I knew how to be attentive to a royal prince. It was only in later years that my friendship with Richard had become more relaxed. At the very first, I had always been only too aware of his station, a fact he constantly tried to dissuade me of.

"Why Dickon loves this place. I knew he wouldn't want to leave, but I had need of him." He paused, thoughtfully, his eyes on the clouds. "Never more than now."

"Maybe he will be able to return some day." I said pleasantly, hoping to elicit some reaction, but his expression remained pensive.

"You are Dickon's friend." It was a statement, and I frowned. He knew that all too well, at least I hoped he did!

"Yes, Your Grace."

"How close a friend?" I didn't answer immediately and he followed up his enquiry as he turned sun-filled eyes to mine. "As close as a brother?" I still wasn't completely sure until his next words. "You've shared a chamber? Stripped down after arming?"

I swallowed hard then. I knew. Richard's letter had contained other news that I had kept to myself. It was something rarely discussed between us, at least since Richard had confided in me about the changes which had begun to affect his body a few years ago. Its progress had been slow, but determined. And particularly of late, it seemed. All I could do was nod somberly. I did not know what else to say, but I heard Edward's heavy sigh.

"Even my own physician can't help. Mind you, Dickon's so

stubborn I almost had to lock him in my chamber to get that far!"
He brushed away a bothersome insect distractedly. "He tried
poultices. Rancid smelling things, you can imagine they didn't last
long!" He turned to me with a smile which creased his eyes with
sadness. "For the rest of the time, you would never know." It was
something I was well aware of, but it didn't make it any less hard.

"I know, Your Grace, and particularly not in the tiltyard. He
is somewhat of a force to be reckoned with." It was a truth I had
no trouble voicing. His melancholy melted away as he grinned
back at me.

"True! If I didn't know better, I would say he was born for
war!" He looked back quickly over his shoulder, at first I thought
to ensure he was not overheard, but he actually raised his voice.
"And it may be that his chance comes sooner rather than later.
There is unrest on the Scots border I hear. Yet more Nevilles,
forgetting which side their coat is turned. These ones seem to
think the country would be better with mad old Henry on the
throne. Much good would it do them if he was! They must be as
deranged as he is!"

Pressing his heels into his mounts flank's, he moved forwards
and I followed him, wondering if this latest rising had anything to
do with the earl, although it seemed unlikely. Edward was right!
Only an imbecile would want to see King Henry back on the
throne, from what I had heard. Even those in my own family who
favoured the Lancastrian cause had admitted it. The man was a
weak king. Frail. It was his qualities, or lack of them, I had heard,
that led to the rise of the House of York.

Yet, more rebellion could only mean more trouble and I
wondered who would quell this latest rising if the king was a
prisoner. Northumberland? He had not been back to the castle
since July when he rode out to York. As I saw it, Warwick now had
both of his hands full, one with a Lancastrian rebellion and the
other with a captive king. Which left him with no free hand to do
combat with either!

My musings were soon interrupted, only now Edward had

lowered his voice.

"Francis, I need you to do something for me."

"Anything, Your Grace." I answered before thinking - only when the words left my mouth did I remember that I was still very much within the earl's power. I could promise much, but in reality may be able to deliver little.

"It's Lady Desmond. I have no intention of letting the mother of Dickon's child languish in a northern abbey." I frowned, secretly pleased as it was indeed something that I would break any rule to accomplish. I had been dreading her departure, dreading saying goodbye. Even if I knew Richard would eventually find her again, who knew when that would be with things the way they were? "Luckily, the earl has acceded to my request to allow her to travel with her own countrymen. Malone back there being one of them. The most important one, as he will handpick the others." For a while the only sound was the plodding of hooves on the hard packed ground as I waited in silence.

"Of course, these are dangerous times. Bandits and rebels are abroad in this country and allowed to wreak havoc, attacking innocent travelers. Many do not reach their intended destination. Others, those wiser, take different paths. Even if it means they do not necessarily end up where it was intended."

I considered these words carefully as we moved on, thinking hard as he continued. So, Malone had not wasted his time and had quickly shown his colours. Even though I knew he had a certain fatherly affection for Caitlin, he was taking a huge risk. For if I understood correctly, they would leave Middleham, and as soon as they could, change direction. For where? I could see Edward giving me a sidelong glance, obviously aware of the questions swilling around in my mind.

"I would like you to assure Lady Desmond, as I am sure she will be rightly vexed about the journey. Warwick tells me she has been ill, and so was not able to travel before as he had planned. Would you tell her that I intend to right my previous wrong. That her king has realised the error of his ways and will ensure reparation is made."

I nodded in acknowledgement of his words.

"Of course, Your Grace. I will tell her, and also do all I can to reassure her of your care for her, and her child."

Edward smiled, it seemed my answer had satisfied him.

"There will be more for you to do, if you would, but not just yet. I think you will understand, being so skilled in chess as you are."

I was still none the wiser, other than a strategy was afoot. He had decided that, for the moment, this was all I needed to know. That to know more exposed me, and more importantly, his plans, to greater risk. As I looked at him, he winked.

"What say we give these men a bit of a scare?" Without even waiting for my response, he kicked his heels and the horse he was riding took off at great speed, increasing the distance between himself and the bemused men-at-arms, and in less than a blink of an eye, I followed suit.

32. MIDDLEHAM CASTLE
September 1469

"Right trusty and wellbeloved, I greet you well and I hope that this letter reaches you in good time. Since my last letter to you, which it pleased me to hear you had received, my lady of Desmond has continued to gain in health and strength. Yet, I have other news which I need to tell you. She is to bear you a child. My lord of Warwick has made arrangements for her to be sent to an abbey, but His Grace, your brother, who by the Grace of God is kept safely here, has secretly arranged for her return to Ireland. By the time this reaches you, I trust she will be safely back with her family in Drogheda, as is the king's intent. I trust, once things are more certain, that you will know best what actions to take in her regard.

Written in haste at Middleham, your true friend,

Francis Lovell"

33. MIDDLEHAM CASTLE
September 1469

They had been gone a week when the whole farcical plan, which had been Warwick's ill-advised bid to bring the king back under his control, fell apart. And when it did, it happened with spectacular speed.

It was raining. Day after day, messengers had been arriving with news of the northern rebels, and leaving again with summons from the earl for the nobles of the land to raise their men in defence of the border. London was descending into chaos as old enmities rose to the surface, tensions reaching boiling point in the absence of any firm authority.

It was just the same outside the city. In Gloucester, an old feud between the Berkley and Talbot families began to stir, and in Lancashire too there was trouble between the Stanleys and the Haringtons. Even Richard appeared to be entering into the fray, unable to allow the persecution of a family who had long supported the House of York. Something the Stanleys continually failed to do, their affinities changing with the seasons.

The king's staunch supporters, Lord Mountjoy, Lord Ferrers, Sir John Dynham and Jack Howard were all adding to the instability of the situation, as they remained in the capital, making life as difficult as possible for those who supported the earl, such as John Langstrother, the new Treasurer, appointed by Warwick to replace the executed Rivers.

I listened with mounting interest to every bit of information I could pick up. Edward told me only what he wanted me to know as we played chess night after night, other news was general gossip running amok around the bailey. Everything was just about as uncertain as it could be, and all the while, Edward relaxed, drank, played chess, and read each missive with eyes which made me determine never to take him on at cards.

I sat strumming my lute, picking out the notes of an old Burgundian song I knew Edward was partial to, whilst he sat before a table, turning cards over as if expecting to see his fortune in them. I had earlier asked him if he wanted a game of chess, but he had refused, preferring to drink from the goblet at his elbow and keep his thoughts to himself. There was a sense of change in the air, of a restless energy. As if the oncoming season would bring with it a certain inevitability, one way or the other.

Then the door crashed open and the earl entered the chamber, clutching a sodden parchment in his hand which dripped water on the floor like blood from a wound.

"Well, I suppose I should have seen this one coming." Edward raised his head and my hand hovered over the strings, the last notes thrumming in the air. Warwick didn't look angry, just weary and resigned. Neither of us answered him, I merely rose to my feet, in acknowledgement of his presence. "Strangely enough," he continued, looking at the missive in his hand as if he had written it himself, "our party of Irish travellers have not reached Scarborough. I have heard from the Abbess, wondering when they are going to arrive." He paused and crossed to the fire, throwing the damp parchment into the flames, where it hissed and crackled. "In order to answer her, I feel I need to ask you. Where are they Ned?"

Edward pursed his lips carefully and swept up the cards from the table, gathering them together in his hands. I smiled at the irony. From what I could see of events over the last few days, the king did seem to be holding the best hand in this game of power. As I had told myself, a master at the table.

"Lady Desmond is on her way to a more fitting place than a nunnery. At the very least, they should have reached Nottingham by now." He looked up, green-gold eyes ablaze with warning. "Don't try to intercept them, Richard. Hastings is mustering forces there, as is my more steadfast brother. You will fail, and I don't think, at this moment, you can bear the consequences that would bring." I gripped the neck of my lute tightly. Warwick seemed to

220

take that without argument, although his attention was focused on the flames rather than Edward.

He cleared his throat, although I found it hard to believe he was nervous. More likely, he was giving himself time to consider. There was a lot at stake here, for him, and his acolyte George. Both of them had defied their king, and may now be looking at a dark future. I felt my own throat begin to close nervously. At the moment my own future was closely aligned to the earl's. I could only hope that my recent actions had shown Edward where I saw my future. Admittedly, my only role in what had recently occurred was to inform Caitlin of the plans Edward had made, to ensure that she was ready to leave when required, fully understanding what would happen and when. And to write to Richard.

Very little was required of me in the end, at least as far as actions went. I had helped save Caitlin from a fate worse than death, as I saw it, but to do that, I had betrayed the earl. I could only wait and see how my fate would be determined by this struggle between courtier and king.

"We will be leaving for York tomorrow." Only now did Warwick fix his attention on Edward, who was leaning back in his chair, shuffling the pack through his hands expertly. "I need you to help me raise the men of the north to quell the trouble on the border."

Edward gave a wry grin.

"The Percys not co-operating, Dick? You really *should* have seen that one coming." He shook his head, his eyes on the cards. "Northumberland, able as he is, can only do so much. You have spread him far too thinly." I could almost hear the grinding of Warwick's teeth as he knew the king spoke the truth.

"I don't need lectures from you in strategy, Ned. I think you are forgetting that you are still my prisoner, and not even now at liberty to move around your own country. There are still things to be agreed, before you can win your freedom."

"Such as?" The coldness that accompanied these words was

enough to turn the rain to hail, certainly enough to cool my skin and I suddenly felt that they had both forgotten I was there.

"Such as the power you have delegated to the queen's family. It has to stop. There are noble men who are being disenfranchised because of your enchantment by that woman! Sometimes, I think you have made such decisions especially to anger me, Ned, and I didn't think you were capable of such underhand behaviour. Certainly, the boy I knew in Calais would not have stooped so low. York must be turning in his grave."

Even the flames in the hearth guttered, their light seeming to lose ferocity. Edward's face set like granite and he laid the cards down on the table with exaggerated care, before raising his gaze to Warwick's still figure. I could not see his face, but I knew he may feel he had finally gone too far.

"And your father, Dick? Will he not be doing the same?" I saw the earl's shoulders stiffen and his next words were an animalistic growl.

"This solves nothing! We will go to York and raise men, then we will come to an accord. I have had to cancel the Parliament originally intended, but another date can be set. We can remain in York until that time. If you see this as a victory, you are much mistaken. You are still the king, I can see that men of a certain affinity will not raise their standards for me alone, but once this current situation is resolved, you can be sure we will return to this matter."

Edward arched an eyebrow casually, and spread his hand over the cards, forming them into a perfect fan shape on the table.

"Will George be accompanying us?"

"Of course." The terse note betrayed the earl's anger. He was being totally outplayed by Edward and he knew it. Even I knew it would be very hard for him to retain power once the king was in York. There were too many other factors to take account of, Richard and Hastings being just two of them. They would hardly sit back and watch Warwick tug on the strings of a puppet king. And Edward was no Henry. He would not be restrained for long.

"Good!" Edward smiled, finally leaving the cards alone and folding his hands in his lap. "Then I had better make ready. As I am for the lack of my usual body-men, Lovell can assist me there, I think, with your permission?"

The earl turned and they both looked at me, one pair of eyes full of sanguine humour, the other hard and cold.

"Well, as he appears to have done such a good job in fulfilling your wishes already, it would be churlish of me to refuse, would it not?"

I flushed to my hairline, not really knowing if the earl was referring to my clandestine efforts in Caitlin's escape. Yet, I suspected he knew. There was not much that escaped him, and the fact that he was fast losing hold of his prize possession would be another harsh reality he was having to face. In spite of everything, my heart began to soar, for there was one thing I did know now. I would be riding south with the king.

34. YORK
September 1469

We were in York by the middle of the month, Edward receiving a rapturous reception from both the citizens and Sir Richard Yorke, the very aptly named mayor of the city. By sheer chance, I found myself in close proximity to the king most of the time, stepping in where his servants of the body would have done had he not been separated from his usual household.

I helped him bathe and dress, served both his food and wine, and generally kept in close proximity to him throughout the day, becoming, at times, almost invisible. It not only gave me the chance to use many of the skills which life at Middleham had taught me, but to witness first hand how the wheels of royal government drove the country. I watched, and listened, and generally kept my head down and my mouth shut, understanding once again how fortunate I was.

At night, as I lay on my pallet in the king's chamber, sometimes kept awake by snoring that was as loud as the bells of the nearby Minster, I was almost ashamed to admit that neither Caitlin, or even Anna, occupied much of my thoughts during this time. Somehow, the excitement of the situation took all of my energies during the day.

It was only then that I wondered if Caitlin was yet in Ireland, reunited with her mother. Richard, by now, should have received my letter which included her news, and I wondered idly how he would have taken it. He was seventeen, a bare two years older than myself, and about to become a father, for I knew the babe was due to be born the following month.

Even then, though I knew it was inappropriate, my body began to respond to memories of Caitlin, and from there my thoughts turned to Marie. It had been too long, and I began to regret, for the first time, that I had not pursued the interest that

Jane Cooke was supposed to have had in me. But it was too late now, there were other things happening which were more significant than my carnal needs.

Edward had indeed summoned the forces needed to quell the northern unrest. To Warwick's helpless dismay, he also summoned Hastings, his brother-in-law the Duke of Suffolk, Norfolk, Arundel, Essex and Mountjoy, all steadfast supporters, as well as the majority of the council from London. And of course, his younger brother, Richard.

It was, therefore, with a great sense of satisfaction and pleasure that I stood next to the king as Richard rode into York, Lord Hastings at his side, and his banner with the white boar resplendent against the sky. I never felt more proud to be a supporter of the House of York than I did then, despite the narrowed glares of Warwick and Clarence who stood a few feet away, watching their arrival with trepidation.

Richard dismounted within seconds of his huge, white destrier coming to a halt and although he made to kneel before his brother, he was at once enveloped in a warm embrace, his metal breastplate, notwithstanding. I knew I was grinning so much that my face threatened to split into two as the two men parted, both smiling at each other. It was a sight I had longed to see and I could not stop myself from grinning like a fool.

"Brother!"

"Your Grace!"

Edward cuffed him lightly on the shoulder, brushing against his steel pauldron as he stepped back to allow Hastings to greet his king. It was then he turned to me.

"Francis! How pleased I am to see you here! Although I am not sure how you managed it!" This last was quieter, but his eyes were smiling and I bowed my head. It seemed an age since we had spoken together and nothing I could say would fully express how pleased I was to be here.

"Your Grace," he pulled a face at my greeting. "Dickon." I knew when I was bested. "Neither do I to be truthful! Fortune seems to be smiling on us at present."

He glanced over my shoulder then at George's glowering expression as he watched the men summoned by Edward troop under the gateway.

"God be praised!" he exclaimed, his face falling slightly.

Rob Percy's face appeared over his shoulder and as we also moved inside, he slapped me on the back.

"Lovell!" he grinned. "Been keeping busy?"

I had no time to respond as the assembled nobility began to cram into the hall and I found myself running backwards and forwards like a hare, serving more than just the king and assisting the many squires and servants who had ridden in with their lords. It became more and more apparent as the day progressed, that Edward's swift actions had effectively restored him to full power and within the hour he had announced his intention to return to the city as soon as the northern rising was dispelled. Quite unwittingly, or so it appeared, those who had hoped to take advantage of the precarious situation by restoring King Henry, had in fact allowed Edward to retain his grasp on his throne.

After Compline, I found myself suddenly at a loose end as some of Edward's regular servants had ridden in with members of the council. Relieved of my duties, I found my way to Richard's chamber and knocked lightly on the door, having to wait only a moment before it was opened by Tom.

"I was wondering where you were!"

The voice drifted over Tom's shoulder as he shrugged and grinned, motioning me inside.

Richard was seated at a table, writing, but he lifted his head and smiled, before returning his attention back to his task. "I won't be but a moment. Tom, get the man a drink."

Tom scurried to the sideboard and I heard liquid pouring as I moved over to a chair and sat down, feeling strangely nervous. My good friend of so many years seemed older, more assured. I noticed he was still wearing his breastplate as he bent to his duties, but his hand was moving swiftly over the parchment, as if he knew time was of the essence, and true to his word, within seconds he was sanding his signature, placing the quill back in its pot.

I watched all of this in silence, taking a cup from Tom, who disappeared into the inner chamber, leaving us to talk. I sipped my wine and waited anxiously as Richard applied his seal to the letter and rose, picking up his own cup and drinking deeply. It was only then that he turned his full attention to me, and once again I felt unusually nervous.

This man was new to me. He moved differently, with a quiet confidence. All around him now were the trappings of a noble, hardened now to so many experiences I could only guess at. With the difference in our lives these past months, I wondered if we would still be able to pick up the traces of our old friendship? Would he even want to? The gap between our ages seemed a chasm at this moment in time. I swallowed my wine quickly.

But, thankfully, his next words allayed my fears and I relaxed instantly, feeling the tension drain from my limbs.

"Thank you, Frank. I knew I was doing the right thing leaving you behind. I hate to think what would have happened had I insisted you came with me."

I shook my head slowly. I didn't see that I had done anything that Edward could not have achieved alone. Malone had done much more than me, or so I hoped. I had so many questions and it was now my opportunity to find out exactly what had happened, and I took a deep breath.

"Did she make it to Ireland safely?"

His next word made my heart lurch painfully.

"No."

Tom returned at that moment and began to unbuckle the straps on Richard's shoulders, releasing him from the breastplate and stripping off his arming doublet. For a brief moment he was naked from the waist up and I suddenly averted my eyes from the visible evidence of my conversation with the king.

There was a slight tilt to his torso, one that I had either not

227

noticed before, or that had changed so much in the past months that it was only now apparent. Tom slipped a linen shirt over Richard's head and it was gone, I felt safe to raise my eyes, although my heart had begun to beat a little more rapidly at both his last words and with what I had just witnessed.

As if nothing at all had taken place, which was truly a testament to his trust in me I was pleased to acknowledge, he moved over to the chair opposite me and sat down, relaxing back into the chair with a slight grimace. Tom picked up the discarded armour and once again made himself scarce. I sat forwards, eager to hear the rest, my heart beginning to race.

"No? What happened?"

Richard sighed and took a deep drink from his cup, his eyes seeking solace in the flames.

"Malone got her to Nottingham where news was received that her mother had died. With no other recourse, and with the unrest at the time, Will thought it best to return her to London. To the queen."

I whistled between my teeth. The queen. I could imagine Caitlin's fear. Or maybe I couldn't. I felt a quite unreasonable surge of anger.

"What the hell did he do that for?"

Richard pursued his lips, looking slightly taken aback, now regarding me intently.

"Be fair, Frank. He didn't know. It was either that or a nunnery, and she had already escaped that fate. And I was a few fair miles away at that time. Even then, had I been there, I would probably have had to do the same. London was the best place for her."

I thought back to the stories Caitlin had told me during the hours we spent together that summer. She was convinced the queen hated her, because of whose daughter she was. From the tales she had told me of her treatment, I had to agree.

"I hope she is alright." I said meekly. "She was so worried, Dickon. After the news from Banbury, she thought you might be

228

dead."

He lowered his dark head, crossing himself with his free hand. The ghosts of Pembroke, Rivers and Woodville filled the room. It was John who had met his end, I had later found out. John, who robbed Percy of his night with the statuesque Miriam. I didn't much care for the Woodville clan myself, but that thought still made me sombre.

"Warwick overreached himself there. Ned will not forget it." He looked up again but his face remained solemn. "Malone was waiting for me at Nottingham. He's here, somewhere, with my men." My men. My stomach began to burn. So many things were changing. Richard was now fulfilling the role he had been trained for, but what of me? I shook the thought from my head quickly.

"So, Caitlin is in the queen's care?"

"Well, that depends…"

I raised my head and Richard smiled, toying with his cup.

"What do you mean?"

"Malone knew one of the queen's men. Knew he had been brought up at Ludlow. He asked him to let my mother know as soon as they arrived at Westminster. I had already written to her and taken responsibility for Cait's situation. I know she will do what is right."

I considered this for a moment, swilling my wine around in my cup. So. The Duchess of York. Could she be Caitlin's saviour? The chamber was very quiet. I felt as if he was waiting for me to ask.

"Dickon?"

"Yes?"

"Your mother doesn't think much of the queen."

"No, indeed she doesn't."

"And, she had a lot of time for Tom Desmond."

"Yes, I believe she did." We both looked up at each other smiling.

"So…"

"So?"

"I don't think she will be lodged with the queen for very long, do you?"

I saw his shoulders move as he took a long pull on his wine.

"Not very long at all. In fact, with luck, no more than an hour or so!"

I drained my cup, placing it back down on the table at my side, pleasure and a new admiration for a blue-eyed Irishman mingling warmly with the wine.

"Handy man to know, that Malone fellow."

"Indeed." Richard grinned at me and finished his own wine, sighing with satisfaction. He looked around the chamber, as if it was suddenly all new to him too. Once again we were at our ease. It would not have surprised me if Rob had come stumbling in, all the worse for wear.

"What now?" I asked simply. "Do you know the king's intentions?"

Richard stretched his arms out wide and yawned, but the smile remained on his face. I had not seen him smile so much in a long time.

"We deal with the unrest, then ride for London. Edward has a kingdom to govern." He paused, and I saw a new light dawn in his eyes. "And, God willing, I will have a child to raise."

BOOK 2
Service and Suspicion

1. TOWER OF LONDON
February 1470

"Yield!"

Sweat was rolling down my face, pooling inside my helm and running into my eyes as I looked down through my visor slit. The point of my sword was resting on the steel gorget of my adversary who was lying beneath me, his breastplate firmly trapped under my knee.

Grinning, I pushed myself to my feet, releasing the pressure on Rob so that he could roll over and get up, leaving his dignity in the dust. Finally! It had been a hard fight. He was taller than me and built like a barn, but on this occasion my speed had outwitted him, much to my relief. I had been practicing hard since the recent risings, determined not to be looked over should skilled men be needed in the field again. I was barely a man, I knew that, but if reports of my ability reached the ears of those who may overlook my youth, then all to the good as far as I was concerned.

Pulling off my helm, I threw my head back, shaking it vigorously to release the hair which had stuck to my skin and I breathed in deeply. It felt so good! Victory always felt good, just as there was no taste more bitter than defeat.

My lungs were aching with the effort of our final exchange, but all that mattered was that I had managed to find a weakness in Rob's overconfidence, and eventually felled him. Admittedly, after quite a bit of effort. Rob was an able soldier, but he was off his game today and I had shown no hesitation in pressing home my advantage. I now intended to revel in that glory, much to his chagrin.

He was on his knees as he pulled his own helm off with effort and sitting back on his haunches, he exhaled loudly.

"Jesus, Frank! I may be the worse for wear but something certainly has you on your mettle! I'm not going to ask what has got your blood running hot, I saw that much for myself last night."

I avoided his eyes quickly, sliding my sword back into the sheath with a satisfying, metallic ring. I loved Rob like a brother, and like a sibling, he always seemed to know how to bring me down a peg or two.

"What would that be?" Despite my affected innocence, I knew what he was going to say before he said it, but I also knew he was wrong.

"I blame myself," he grinned wryly as he clambered to his feet, wincing slightly at some pain it appeared I had caused him. "You've been a changed man since I did you that favour back in Middleham." He laughed out loud as I shot him a curt glance and shook my head disbelievingly. "No, please!" he held up a gauntleted hand, his features a mask of deprecation. "Don't thank me! The pleasure was all mine! So to speak!"

We both walked back towards the armoury where there was a brimming water butt and I plunged my head into the cool, clear rainwater, relishing the damp trickle that snaked down my neck, crawling in beneath my backplate. As I straightened up, I reflected on all that had come to pass since we returned to London five months ago.

Edward had returned to the city in glory and for certain it was not Richard who had become lost in the shadow of his brilliance. Rewards were heaped upon him, most notably many offices in Wales, where he was just about to depart, resulting in Rob's thick head this morning. Despite my increased diligence, once again, I was to stay behind, another reason to relish my grim victory. I just felt slightly disgruntled that Richard was not around to witness me grind Rob into the dust and see what use I could be to him, despite the fact that I was still considered to be too young to join his service. It rankled, like a sore that refused to heal.

I longed for Wales. Well, for anywhere really. It was totally disheartening to think they would all be marching out of here tomorrow on the king's business and all I could do was watch them go. I shook my head again, pushing my wet hair back from my forehead.

"That will cool your ardour!" Rob jibed as he followed suit, the water turning his midnight hair slick.

He was talking about Marie of course, who, on my return to the city, had slipped back into my bed with an eager familiarity which was at first more than welcome. For a few hours at least, it allowed me to escape from thoughts which both worried and confused me. It was a fact that I spent far too many an hour these days being either worried, confused or disappointed, yet still the feelings were hard to shake off. For more than one reason.

Whilst we were travelling down from the north with the king, Caitlin had borne Richard a daughter and they were now both comfortably ensconced at Baynard's Castle in the care of his mother. I could still see the look of amazement on his face as he had been given the news he had become a father. It reached him only minutes after he had been basking in his brother's triumph, riding at his side through the gates of London to a cacophony of cheering, applause and the deafening clarion of every bell in the country. Or so it seemed. I felt more than a little deaf for days after that was sure.

After Caitlin had been churched, I was once again introduced to a somewhat changed world. Richard had invited me to see his baby daughter and the experience was both strange and profound. Caitlin herself sat in a chair by the hearth, and although the winter afternoon had been dull, and the chamber bathed in the light of a dozen or more candles, I was sure it was not just that which made her appear to radiate a sublime glow.

Her gown was demurely cut, dark velvet, the colour of sable, and above the neckline her skin seemed to shimmer like a heat-haze crossing the moon. Soft tendrils of flame-coloured hair framed her face as she looked up at Richard, her face full of an emotion I found hard to name, having not seen anything quite so intense before. She had blossomed since I last saw her all those months ago at Middleham and to me, she was no longer a young girl pining for her lost love. She was a woman.

Although she smiled at me with genuine pleasure, her emerald eyes moved on quickly to fix on Richard with a force that made me catch my breath. He had crossed the room swiftly and dropped a gentle kiss on the top of her head, before leaning further down to peer into the small, snowy linen-wrapped bundle cradled within her arms.

At that moment, such had been the intimacy between them, I had felt that I should leave. It was as if I was a child, watching two people much older than me and I had no place here, intruding on their privacy, shuffling my feet and no doubt looking as awkward as I felt. Just at the moment I decided to move and make my escape, Richard had looked up and beckoned me over to join them. Somehow, I forced my feet to cross the floor, aided by the fact that Caitlin had lowered her own gaze, for I knew I would have been frozen to the spot had she so much as looked at me just then.

Even as I stood before her, I could smell her subtle, violet fragrance, and on the hand which lay against the swaddled linen, the crimson jewel of her ring winked brightly. Everything about her was so familiar, yet in every other sense, she had become a stranger. Now she held in her arms the physical evidence of their bond and as it had drawn them even closer together, for myself, I was now more of an outsider, looking in on their love. Still a friend, undoubtedly, but one who recognised the undeniable shift in the ground beneath my feet.

"Francis," Richard had breathed in a voice softer than I had ever heard. "This is my daughter, Kathryn."

A small, peach-skinned face lay in peaceful slumber, crescents of fire-tipped lashes shadowing perfect cheeks. There was just the hint of a silken curl of hair. Not fiery, but warm, like roasted chestnuts. She was truly beautiful and even though she did not open her eyes, I knew without a doubt what colour they would be when she did.

"She is truly fair." I had whispered, my voice full of an awe I could not disguise. In truth, I was finding it hard to believe that these two people had created something so small, so perfect. "You are both blessed."

Caitlin's smile at those words almost brought me to my knees and it was then that I did make a hasty exist from the chamber, mumbling on about some chore I had yet to complete. It was a lie, yet a convenient one. No matter how steadfastly I had pledged to be true, the tableau before me was more than I could bear and I had departed as fast as I could, leaving them alone with their joy.

Rob was still regarding me archly, his breathing now returned to normal. I was just hoping that he didn't ask for a re-match as I didn't want to let him know that beating him had taken every last bit of strength I had. Even my legs felt slightly unsteady.

"Jealous?" I threw him a smile loaded with sarcasm, hoping to distract him and knowing that Rob would be smarting that I had bested him never mind that I had taken up with Marie again with such ease. He pursed his lips then, wiping his gauntlet across his forehead, water droplets collecting along his brows.

"Well, actually, no. After all, I am a respectable married man now." He paused, his eyes glinting with mischief. "Just like you!"

I could have punched him right between those eyes! A few months ago he had indeed married. Ellinor. The daughter of Sir Ralph Bewley. He had met her some months ago during the troubles and had become so completely infatuated by her beauty, he had married her with almost indecent haste. It had sounded most out of character for Rob, who certainly like variety in his choice of women, yet he had offered no explanation other than being totally smitten by her charms. I had wondered, but not dared to ask him, if she had been totally dismissive of this, which is why it had taken a ring and a dowry to make her his.

I had not met her, as he had never met Anna, but at least his bride was the same age as him and they had already confirmed

235

their marriage vows, a fact he had not been shy in sharing. Whether this would have any effect on Rob's roving eye, time would only tell. But for now, I could only feel more envy at my friend's fortunes whilst Marie's abundant charms had begun to pale in my eyes.

"Thanks for reminding me!" I said churlishly as I began to pull at the straps of my breastplate. To be fair, he had not needed to. That very morning I had received a letter from Ravensworth, the Fitzhugh family seat in the north. Just seeing the name made her small, innocent face appear like a ghost.

Rob slapped me on the back heartily before looking round for a squire to assist with his own armour.

"Ah well, at least you have some solace whilst she grows. By my faith, though, I had hoped to snare Lady Shaftesbury, but it appears my ambition was only to be thwarted." He threw me a quick grin. "Not that she can compare to my fair Elinore. But...well, 'tis still a shame." Lifting two fingers to his lips he whistled at some young lads who had just appeared out of the stables and they began to hurry in our direction, eager to help us disarm. "Yet it will be a while before I see her again now, so it is just as well I managed to get my fill before I came south."

The smallest of the grooms was now helping me out of my breastplate and I flexed my shoulders which were beginning to stiffen up already. I would certainly pay for this brief victory that was for sure.

"Well, if it's any consolation, I have been told my presence is required at Ravensworth, with my father-in-law, although God knows why! Anna's father has also written to the earl, so it would appear I will be leaving here soon too."

Rob rolled his broad shoulders with a sigh as he was freed from his own plate.

"You don't sound too happy about it I must say. Will Anna be there? I thought you had made some sort of pledge not to see her for a while?"

I shrugged diffidently, remembering William Stanley's words.

It still made me decidedly uncomfortable to think of Anna, and I didn't thank Rob for making me do so once more. Just the vision of her flooded me with a fresh wash of guilt which always made me feel somewhat sick. I had, so far, successfully managed to forget about her father's letter, feeling confident that, with things as they stood, there is no way I would be given leave to go north. Today I did not feel so confident.

"I did. I don't know where she is. Last I heard she was still at Minster Lovell. Her mother was keen to introduce her to the place which will eventually be her home."

"Ah well," Rob exclaimed, turning away from a reedy, red-faced squire who was now struggling under the burden of discarded plate, "I would make sure you take full advantage before you leave. For sure, I know it will be a long time before I lie in a soft feather bed warmed with perfumed skin. There's one thing I do know and that is that our friend Dickon frowns on camp followers."

We began to walk back towards the kitchens then, both silently acknowledging that the recent skirmish had left us both famished and hoping to persuade some friendly kitchen maid into parting with a chicken leg or two. I frowned at his words though, which struck me as more than a little odd.

"Camp followers? You're hardly going into battle."

"Aren't we?" Slightly distracted, Rob threw a wink at a young, greasy-aproned girl we both knew as Aggie. Wiping her reddened hands on her skirts, she disappeared through the door as I remained in wonder at his ability to charm any female he met. Sure enough, even before I could answer, she had reappeared with a folded linen cloth in her hands, no doubt concealing exactly what we hoped it would. "We always seem to be going into battle for something these days. If it isn't rebellion, it's general unrest over the treatment of tenants. Far too many of our esteemed nobility can't share a flagon of Rhenish without falling out over who should serve it and sure you can bet that Lord Stanley is far from happy about recent events. If Dickon thinks he will spend

237

his evenings putting his feet up with one of those books of his or playing chess, I think he may find himself sorely disappointed."

With all the charm of a practiced courtier, he leaned forward and placed a chaste kiss on Aggie's cheek before relieving her of her burden. Lifting the cloth slightly, his brows lifted in surprise.

"Game pie! Excellent!" Blushing, she scurried inside, her face now as red as her careworn hands.

2. RAVENSWORTH CASTLE
NORTH YORKSHIRE

March 1470

Rob had been right. Probably more right than he had even known himself. But if he had expected trouble from the Stanleys following Edward's granting of the honour of Clitheroe and Halton to Richard, lands which had once been held by the Stanleys themselves, he was wrong. They had not long departed London before the all too familiar grumblings of dissent rolled down from the north. This time from Lincolnshire.

It started with a dispute between Sir Thomas Burgh, my old friend the Master of Horse, who still retained his position as one of the king's close friends. His family home, a manor house in Gainsborough, was ransacked by men named Dymoke and De La Launde, who also carried off much of his property. But these were not just any men. They were relations of Sir Robert Welles, a man not only held estates in Lincolnshire, he was a man with known Neville and Lancastrian connections. With this, and other risings in the West Country, the whispers began to rise. The old spectre of Robin of Redesdale raised his head and with that, once again, the names of Clarence and Warwick seemed to be intertwined with these men who were implicated in events which challenged the peace of the realm.

By the time I was riding over the moat and passing through the northern gatehouse of the rambling northern castle at Ravensworth, the king had taken decisive action. He dealt harshly with what he obviously saw as a blatant attack on his friend, executing the uncle and father of the main protagonist, Welles. Sir Robert, however, refused to lay down his arms and met the king's forces at Empingham, where he was soundly defeated.

Tales abounded of men shedding their colours as they fled in fear for their lives and had led to the battle being called "Lose-Coat Field."

Welles himself was eventually executed, and shortly afterwards, George and Warwick finally decided to give up the game in which their hand had been so clearly revealed. They took ship for Calais, but once again the earl's formerly astute instinct seemed to be lacking. His deputy there, Wenlock, turned him away, pinning his own banner firmly to the king's mast, and Warwick had no option but to turn tail for France. The gossip I heard the further north I rode had me grinding my teeth in my sleep.

Richard had, once again, been called to the king's side, had indeed been with him as his brother and cousin turned their tails and hurtled into exile. In the same month that Richard held a commission of array, raising men from the counties of Gloucestershire and Herefordshire, Clarence and Warwick were attainted by the king. He was still with him a few weeks later in Exeter, whilst the acid of my disappointment ate away at my insides as I heard news of events in which I had no part.

Not only had I missed all of the action, it almost seemed that I had been completely forgotten about. Before he had showed himself to be a traitor, my lord of Warwick had not only approved my journey north, he had insisted on it. Events had moved on so quickly, that I was half-way to Ravensworth before it was apparent that my lord and master was now an enemy of the king. I saw no other course of action open to me other than to continue as I had been bid. With Warwick gone, I was sure the king would turn his attention to the affairs of my wardship once the realm was more settled. I had to settle for that, there was nothing else I could do. Maybe then my fortunes would change.

I was welcomed at Ravensworth with brusque formality by my bride's father, a bewhiskered, morose figure of a man, but with a little more warmth and civility by Lady Alice his wife. She was Warwick's sister and as imposing and handsome as her brother and it was her voice I heard ringing around the chamber as I was shown into the solar.

Anna wasn't present, much to my relief and as I stood before them, trying not to shuffle my feet, I was also trying very hard not to look like someone who not only had no real station in life, but who also harboured a lost, unattainable love, whilst sharing my bed with a wanton. To me, impossible though it was, I felt that they could both see right through me to the reprobate I – on that day – felt I was. I had been feeling completely out of sorts from the moment I rode out of London, and nothing had changed along the journey. In fact, I now felt even worse. I felt useless.

Lord Fitzhugh, from what I had heard, remained a steadfast Lancastrian at heart and he paid me hardly any attention, seeming to prefer to focus his thoughts on one of the two letters he held in his hands. Letters which I had been charged to deliver. Lady Alice, however, was a different thing altogether and it was her piercing stare which was making me sweat around the collar.

"Francis," she announced flatly just as I was beginning to wonder if I had wandered into the wrong room, "my how you have grown! You are quite the young gentleman now! Don't you think, Henry? Such an elegant, handsome husband for our young Anna?"

As I blushed fiercely, Fitzhugh's straggly brows twitched as he looked up briefly with a "humph" sound, before looking down again, not caring to mask his complete indifference.

"Thank you, my Lady," I replied as graciously as I could before forming the words I didn't want to ask, but felt obliged to. "Is Anna here? It is a while since I have been able to enjoy her company."

I held my breath as I waited for the answer I was praying for.

"No, she and Elizabeth are visiting with their sister Alice in the south. We thought it best they remain there, with the current unrest." There was a delicate pause, where the all-seeing gaze became even sharper. "However, her continuing residence in the south was intended to make things easier for you to visit and form

241

a... friendship over the years. That, it appears, has not worked out quite as we anticipated."

My flesh prickled as I felt that I was being accused, no matter how politely, of neglecting my bride. Notwithstanding that I had heard nothing of her movements since I had last seen her at Minster Lovell. I pondered for a moment how they would react if I told them I was following my former step-father's advice, but decided against it.

"Unfortunately, until much recently, I had been in the north myself. At Middleham, my Lady. I was there when the king was in – um – residence."

That provoked a bark of laughter from Fitzhugh who looked at me properly for the first time.

"Residence! That's a new name for it! What I'd like to know is..." his voice was stilled by the sudden appearance of his wife's hand on his arm, which seemed to take him by surprise and his brow creased deeply, accompanied by a further unintelligible grunt.

"Now, my dear," Lady Alice purred with consummate condescension, "why don't you go and attend to that correspondence that has you so vexed? I know how anxious you get when you have urgent matters to see to. You can leave Francis with me. I am sure he will be in no way offended if you leave us alone to talk."

She looked at me archly, her eyes daring me to contradict her, but to be honest, I felt a huge sigh of relief as he heaved himself out of his chair and ambled from the room. Lady Alice watched him go, almost fondly, an expression which had completely disappeared by the time she looked back at me. Now, she was regarding me more like her brother than ever, which increased my levels of anxiety markedly.

"Now, I don't know what proclivities you have taken to whilst wandering aimlessly around a Woodville court, but you can be assured that you will hear no such niceties here. We still hold fast to old loyalties, and are not afraid to say so!"

I stepped back a little, shocked to the core. That declaration was far from what I had expected. I felt I had been slapped, and with a hand as cold as winter. The complete change of tone and attitude had taken me aback, and I swallowed hard.

"I... I am sorry my Lady, I don't understand."

"There is nothing too understand," she replied icily. "The only chance for this country to thrive with a Yorkist king was if he married a French bride and of course his dalliances with a common widow prevented that!"

"A Lancastrian widow..." I murmured softly before I could prevent myself. I felt the air freeze, I swear it. Her reply was swift.

"A Lancastrian widow who sold her soul for what the king of England could offer her. Do I take it you have done the same to glean favours from the brother of the king?"

I had to sink my teeth into my tongue to prevent me from biting back the response that was fighting to be free of my lips. My blood began to run cold, despite the heat flaring in my cheeks. This was Warwick's sister, so how deep did treason run in the veins of this family? The Neville clan were huge and powerful; Warwick's other sisters were married throughout the highest nobility in the land. Arundel. Hastings. Oxford. Bile burnt the back of my throat.

John De-Vere, the Earl of Oxford had certainly never given up his Lancastrian cause, having been both imprisoned and pardoned by Edward, before deciding his fortunes were better served elsewhere and departing for France last year. I clasped my hands behind me tightly and raised my shoulders up, a little defiantly.

"His Grace of Gloucester has been very kind to me, at a time when I was thrust into a Yorkist household with no thought to my Lancastrian connections. Had he shown me any especial favour, I doubt I would be here now, my Lady. I would be with him in Wales, serving at his side with my fellow henchmen."

Lady Alice drew herself up then, determined no doubt to cast down my impertinence, no matter what truth it was founded on. She was quite tall, for a woman and must have been very beautiful when she was younger, only not in a traditional way. There was just something about her face which made her very compelling to look at. The same inner force which gave her brother such a commanding presence apparent from her stature.

"Oh, I have no problems with young Dickon! It is just a shame he chose to turn his back on the earl at a time when his support could have made so much difference. Clarence is a fool and a popinjay, even if he is heir to the throne. But it is Richard that Edward would listen to out of any of them. My brother mishandled the boy, to his cost."

She saw the curve of my lips then because I was completely unable to prevent a smile forming. I looked down at the floor to try and avoid her gaze but when I dared to look up again her brow was furrowed, making her look even more Warwick than Warwick himself.

"What?"

I shook my head slowly. I could not tell you why but for some reason I began to relax. Everything I had heard so far should have had warning bells ringing so loud and clear any words I spoke would be drowned out by their sound. There was treason here, and, for my sins, I found myself in the middle of it. Yet, whatever their reasons for dragging me north, I had no intention of making it easy for them.

I was no longer a Lancastrian. Mad old Henry meant nothing to me and would be the ruin of this realm should he ever again be allowed to warm the throne.   And as for George, well, as far as I could see he had only one priority. Himself. Neither of them were a match for Edward, either in prowess or politics.

"Have you lost the power of speech boy?"

Her voice cut through the air like a blade and I looked back at her, remaining completely composed.

"No one handles the Duke of Gloucester, my lady. He may be young but he is very much his own man, so no matter what my lord of Warwick thought he could make him do, he was always

244

bound to be disappointed."

It was her turn to smile then. A hard, frigid smile.

"You are fool, Lovell." My retort was speedy, and a mite too glib, but pleasing.

"Better a fool than a traitor my Lady."

"We shall see, Lovell, we shall see..."

With those words she sailed out of the room, leaving me alone in the waning sunlight.

3. RAVENSWORTH CASTLE
July 1470

A few months later, I stood in the gatehouse tower with Anna's older brother Richard, watching a steady stream of tenants from the outlying villages trail into the castle.

Although Edward had effectively crushed the aspirations of his wayward brother, things were far from settled and as we went into the burgeoning summer, the air was as dry as tinder, ready for the smallest spark to set the country ablaze. The last I had heard, Richard was back in Wales, whilst the king continued to dispense justice to those who had foolishly been drawn to George's false allure. Not that anyone with any sense believed that it was George the rebels followed. He had, despite being a royal prince, neither the power or the influence of Warwick.

Now, so the story ran, the pair of them were seeking support in France. Some said, unbelievably, that they may even approach mad old Henry's queen who still haunted the French court, a spectre of long lost Lancastrian hopes. As I wondered what Richard and Rob were doing over these weeks while I kicked my heels idly here in the north, I could only imagine how he was feeling if that tale was true. It was Margaret, Henry's queen, who Richard held responsible for the death of his father and brother at Sandal, not her threadbare king. My musings left me with one distinct conviction. The power of a woman, be she queen or noble, should never be underestimated.

Caitlin's face rose in my mind. Her own father had lost his life for being the friend of a king, albeit a more faithful one than Warwick was turning out to be. I spent many an hour wondering how she was getting on back in Baynard's, alone with a growing child. Unless Richard had been able to visit her on occasion, although I doubted it with what had been reaching my ears of late. I felt a pang of regret then. I missed her sorely, but then, I missed them all, and what was happening here made those feelings even more keen.

"That's Richard Salkeld, Constable of Carlisle Castle," Dick Fitzhugh murmured into my ear as a dark-robed horseman appeared below us, emerging from the shadow of the tower. I grunted back as I watched him dismount. Another northern lord riding in to Lord Henry's call. Or was it Warwick's call?

"This is ridiculous Dick. What exactly does your father think he is going to achieve? Clarence on the throne? Really?"

Dick sighed heavily. He was heavy-set, fair haired and around my age. We had made friends on my first evening here, when it had become very clear that he neither approved of, nor supported, his parents affinity. He had tracked me down at supper, plying me with questions on my time at court, at Middleham with Richard and with Edward during his captivity.

He wasn't a bit like his father and had an open, enquiring expression, with honest dark blue eyes. I liked to think he favoured Anna in that, although I was finding it hard to even bring her face into focus at all these days and remained relieved that she was still in the south. I was having enough trouble coping with the rising tide of doubt about her kinsmen, without having to see her witness that in my eyes each day. I didn't need that adding on to the troubles I saw mounting up for our future every day.

"It's madness!" Dick exclaimed, more than a note of frustration in his voice. "With Warwick in exile, surely that should be an end to it? Oh, I know Mama is offended for Uncle John, but the king didn't leave him totally penniless. And his son is betrothed to one of the Princesses of England! Surely that has to be reward in itself?"

I continued to watch the line of men shuffling forwards into the hall, ready, or more like duty-bound, to pledge service to their good lord. My throat dried up and made it hard to swallow. Much like John Neville must have felt when the king released Henry Percy from his captivity in the Tower and reinstated his Earldom of

Northumberland, giving John a Marquisate in return. Along with a promised betrothal of his son George, to his younger daughter, Cecily.

But, John Neville was a proud man. All the Neville men were, but this one was also an able commander and to this point had been unerringly loyal to his king. I couldn't help but wonder how he felt now, with his brother in exile and his own status reduced, despite his unerring loyalty over the fast few months.

I had seen others visiting the castle over the past few days, Scrope of Bolton and I suppose unsurprisingly, Sir John Conyers, riding over from Middleham to immerse himself in this foul stew of fermenting treachery. Conyers had looked slightly alarmed to see me standing by the stables as he rode in. It seemed I already had gained a reputation as a solid supporter of the House of York since accompanying the king down to London and I was the last person he had expected to see. He was right, and my loyalty was something I had no intention of surrendering, no matter what. Not for any man.

"Some men seem never to gain enough reward." I remarked bitterly, still watching the activity below, resenting each new arrival, even those I did not know. "I have seen more than enough of them here this week."

Dick snorted in assent.

"I wonder where Thomas Stanley is?"

We flicked each other a quick grin. We had both heard the story brought in by one of the many riders who were thundering around the north bringing news of the king's progress as he came north to crush the rebellions. It was old news now, but still entertaining, as was anything which showed a Stanley for what they were. Before the battle at Empingham, Richard had been bringing his men up from Wales to join the king's forces and had come face to face with Thomas Stanley near Chesterfield, who had been riding south to meet up with Warwick.

The story had it - possibly embellished from mouth-to-mouth but who knew? - that Richard had stood his ground and had told

Stanley to either stand aside or he would ride over him. Even the mere thought of that confrontation made the hairs on the back of my neck stand up. In my version, sitting directly behind Richard was Rob, grinning mirthlessly, praying for Stanley to make a fight of it.

"Keeping his head down, I would imagine." I replied, still smiling. "Neither of them have declared for Warwick, as I hear it. Not him, or my former step-father."

"Well, as we know, even some of Warwick's own men turned on him. When Wenlock refused him entry into Calais, he must have been puce with fury!"

I had no difficulty in picturing that. Just as I had no problem imagining George's anger – no doubt blaming Edward for the loss of his baby daughter as the ship was buffeted and tossed in the channel. Poor Isabel. I didn't like the girl, but to lose her first child n such circumstances was truly dreadful. She had attained her hearts desire, against the will of the king, and they had both paid a heavy price. Now they were all exiles and I was almost hostage in a Lancastrian household planning to raise arms against the king. I could almost hear the Wheel of Fortune creaking as it moved with unerring determination.

I turned away from the sight below, flinging myself onto the nearest seat and set to chewing the flesh at the side of my thumbnail. It was a nervous habit I was trying to break. And failing. If I stayed here much longer I doubted I would be left with a thumb at all! Dick took up my place at the window, but had fallen silent whilst my thoughts were in turmoil.

"I can't ride against the king, Dick." He didn't answer me, but I saw his shoulders move. "And – I can't stay here. Not any longer. Not now I know what's going on. Will you help me?"

Again, there was silence. I knew I was asking a lot, but I had made my mind up. I wanted no part of what was going on here, not even by association. Even being married to Anna tied me to the Fitzhugh and Neville families. My wardship was supposed to bind my family's loyalty, not turn it against the realm. Surely, I had my own voice? I did not have to follow the path that Warwick appeared to have chosen for me? Warwick was an exile, the king was my master now!

"Dick?"

With visible reluctance, he turned to face me, leaning back against the wall.

"I know I haven't known you long, but I like you Francis. I really do."

I shrugged airily, feeling more than a little frustration at his words.

"That's very decent of you Dick, but that doesn't get me out of here. Will you help me?"

He glanced out of the window again, his profile stark against the glass. It began to rain as he turned back to look at me, and the depressing sky was reflected in his eyes.

"For Anna's sake, yes. Yes, I will."

4. RAVENSWORTH CASTLE
July 1470

Once my mind was set upon its course, Fortune seemed only too happy to step in and intervene, making it virtually impossible for me to make the move I so sorely desired. As if he could smell my intention on the air, Lord Fitzhugh then decided to keep me close by him. There was almost a dogged intention to keep me engaged in some task, no matter how trivial, at every moment of the day.

I was either reckoning up the lists of his tenants and their rents due, calculating wages to be paid to his retained men, or serving on him at table as he welcomed yet another local magnate, every one of them very well known to Earl Warwick. Then there was the full gamut of other services, helping him dress, arranging for his bath to be drawn, running backwards and forwards between barber, physician and priest. It seemed there was no chore he was loath to give me.

It was on one such errand, taking his shirts down to the laundress, that I saw a familiar figure loitering by the stables. It was enough to have me diverting from my intended path and crossing the courtyard with an eager anticipation. I didn't know many people here, and trusted fewer, so there was no possibility that I would miss an opportunity to greet a friendly face.

"Rob? Rob Brackenbury?" There was undisguised amazement in my voice. The sandy head turned my way, his face splitting in a broad grin as I approached him.

"By God! Lovell, what are you doing here?"

His eyes roved over the linen bundle in my arms ruefully. "Or would you rather I didn't ask?"

It was impossible to stop my face flushing even as I smiled. I couldn't believe how good it felt to see a familiar face, despite the somewhat embarrassing circumstances. Rob was a squire himself, and I knew he would understand that we were at the mercy of our masters and had no choice but to do the jobs we were given, but all the same... I felt I had better explain.

"Fitzhugh is my father-in-law. Only I think he may be getting me confused with his daughter. He will have me mending his hose next." We both laughed, and I felt genuinely pleased to see him again, and comforted that we were able to resume what had begun to grow into a warm friendship. Rob looked around the bailey, his expression betraying his complete distaste for the situation he found himself in.

"I'm here with Thomas, the Constable. There is something going on and that is no mistake. The whole place is like a hive, and its much the same back at Barnard Castle. It stinks of rebellion to me, or the makings of one."

I looked around hesitantly before I replied. The courtyard was far too busy where we stood and I gestured with my head for him to follow me, moving us over to the chapel walls where it was much quieter. Not many residents of the castle seemed much concerned with their mortal souls at present.

"From what I can gather," I whispered hurriedly, my head bent towards his, "Warwick is behind it again, despite the fact that he skulks in exile. If the plan is to draw the king north so they can attack from the south, you would have thought Edward would have learned that lesson well after last year. Fitzhugh could find his head on a pike next to Welles if he's a mind to it."

Rob shook his head in disbelief.

"Where will all this leave you then, being married to his daughter? In fact, where does it leave all of us? I've no quarrel with the king, and that's a fact. There's more bloody trouble in these parts between the Percys and the Nevilles than any harm the king has ever done!"

I adjusted the pile of shirts under my arm, feeling so disgruntled with my father in law that I wanted to cast them down into the dirt and grind my heel into them.

"And now Henry Percy has his earldom back, and all his

lands. With Warwick in exile, the north is his to take." I swallowed nervously. "It is far too soon to be assured of his allegiance."

Rob looked over his shoulder then and lowered his voice.

"While Warwick tries to take the crown? For Clarence?" He spat on the ground angrily. "I've never met the man but anyone who can turn on his brother like that deserves to be horsewhipped." He paused then, his brow furrowed and he stared at the ground.

"Rob?" His sudden silence worried me and he raised his head as I hissed at him urgently. The look on his face made me feel a bit nauseous.

"Francis, what are you doing here?"

I was taken aback for a while and laughed.

"I told you, I'm..."

He was shaking his head vehemently, the expression on his face devoid of all mirth.

"No. I know that. I said what are you doing here? Whose idea was it for you to visit?"

I began to feel a cold sweat along my spine as I answered.

"I was sent for."

I watched his throat move as we locked eyes on each other.

"Are you still close to Gloucester?"

I hadn't seen it and it had been right in front of my eyes all the time. I had assumed if I was too young to serve with Richard, I would be treated with like consideration here. Yet, was I not now acting as Fitzhugh's very squire? Would he not, if he was readying to ride out against the king, take his squire with him? Squires could be killed in battle, not one man was safe when the melee of armed conflict descended. Whatever happened to me, if Warwick won, my lands were free to be granted to whomsoever he felt fit. So what if his young daughter was suddenly bereft of a husband? I could see it would matter not to him.

Yet for me, there was something that scared me even more than death. If I was at his side when the rebellion broke out, I would be implicated in the king's eyes. And Richard? What would he think? Would he trust me enough to know that I had been duped into going north? What sort of idiot was I? If the worst came to the worst, I could end up on the wrong side of a battlefield. I could lose my life, but worse than that, to me, would be to lose my friend's trust.

"I'm getting out of here." I said with more conviction than I had previously felt. A dousing of icy reality had suddenly made matters much clearer. If I intended to go, I needed to go soon. Very soon. "Dick Fitzhugh said he will help."

Brackenbury looked back at me, his thoughts busy behind his eyes.

"Can you trust him?"

"I don't know. He offered to help. I know he doesn't agree with what his father is doing, we have talked about it a lot. I have to trust him, there is no one else! I need to find a way to get out of here and reach the king before its too late!"

I had no idea how I was going to achieve it, but as soon as I spoke the words, I knew that saying soon meant I had already left it too long.

Brackenbury was thoughtful then for a while. He looked up at the sky, squinting.

"You know," he remarked, as casually as if he were talking about the weather. "I quite fancy a ride south."

5. NORTH YORKSHIRE
July 1470

So, it appeared I now had two adherents who were happy to rebel against the gathering forces in the north. All we had to do was find the right time to escape. Preferably before Brackenbury was hauled back to Barnard Castle. Easy, if you said it quickly without thinking of the many obstacles! These thoughts played on my mind as we accompanied Dick on a hunting trip to the forests south of the castle.

It had been a pretty ordinary, if uneventful trip. Dick was totally focused on his sport, and even the bird I was flying was pulling in its fair share of bounty. There were only the three of us, with very few servants, a couple of whom I knew were Dick's familiars. It had been good to escape the confines of the castle where the walls reeked with treachery, making every word dangerous. Especially if those words showed any dissent of the events which were moving forward with inexorable inevitability.

As the sun reached its zenith in the sky, I passed my small falcon back to one of the handlers as Dick turned his horse and came towards me where I sat with Brackenbury, who had remained decidedly thoughtful and unhelpfully silent for the last two hours. I was just beginning to feel sad that the morning was over, meaning we had to go back to the oppressing confines of the castle, when Dick arrived before us.

"Father has gone to Richmond today, and won't be back until tomorrow." It seemed a totally unnecessary announcement and I shrugged my shoulders, watching as my bird was skillfully hooded, blinding him to any more sport.

"More plotting?"

Dick gave a wry grin.

"It appears all is ready. He plans to move south in two days'

255

time." He nodded his fair head in my direction. "You, apparently, are going with him."

I could feel the blood drain from my face. I had been right; it was actually going to happen. Talking about raising arms against the king and actually being part of it were two distinctly different things. It hadn't seemed real until Dick confirmed my deepest worries.

"He hasn't told me that," I grumbled, trying not to look at Brackenbury, as I was more than aware I sounded like a sulky child. "But I was beginning to suspect as much." Thanks to Brackenbury, I added silently.

"He doesn't have to," said Dick in a matter-of- fact tone. I could tell he wasn't being dragged along just by the tone of his voice, Fitzhugh obviously wanted to keep his own heir out of harm. "He is acting on Warwick's orders so even if he wanted to keep his daughter's husband safe, he has no choice in the matter." He paused then and looked over his shoulder where two horses were standing to one side, having been used by the handlers. "You, however, do."

Brackenbury marked his gaze but said nothing.

"I don't follow." I was following the path of his gaze, but had no idea what he was talking about.

Dick sidled his own mount closer, leaning towards me.

"Those two mounts over there carry food and ale, not much mind – just some bread, cheese and whatever else I could scrounge without suspicion. Ride south, cross the Swale, keep your head down. Head for York."

"What – now?" The shock in my voice was harsh even to my own ears. Dick was nodding determinedly. I heard Brackenbury's horse utter a soft whinny.

"Father is away, when he comes back I will tell him you had a fall on this trip. Taken to your bed. By the time he has discovered you were not quite as injured as you made me believe, you should be well on your way."

I began to recover my senses and could see Brackenbury

pondering this out of the corner of my eye, but still he said very little. So, just like that, we would leave. It was what I wanted more than anything, so why did doubt now flood into my gut? I would turn my coat against Warwick, much as Patrick had done when he took Caitlin south. But he was a hardened soldier, much braver than me. I began to feel a bit uneasy, despite the small voice inside me telling me to just go.

"But, Lady Alice? It may be that your father doesn't miss me as he is away, but your mother? She will expect to see me in the hall and if you tell her I am injured…"

Dick's voice lowered then, his expression lightened like the sun emerging from clouds.

"Mama has had a change of heart. She was never completely convinced, but her dislike of the queen coloured her actions. Yet, recent news has caused her to reconsider. Warwick has married his daughter to Prince Edward of Lancaster, in France. Mama, as a Neville, was truly hoping that these rebellions would make Edward see sense in the end. That although he would hardly put his Woodville queen aside, he may stop showering her kin with half the landed estates in England. But this, for her, is a step too far. The king will never reconcile with Warwick now that he has hitched his cause to the woman he holds responsible for the massacre at Sandal. And of course, my grandfather's death too. Discontent is one thing; outright treason is another."

If I had any blood left in my body, it departed on those words. Anne, married to a Lancastrian prince?

"I…" I don't know what I was planning to say next but whatever it was, the words dissolved at the sight of a small purse held out towards me in his gloved hand.

"There is not a lot there. Just enough to get yourself out of trouble if needed, but to me, you are better staying off the beaten track. Keep out of the inns, you never know who is wandering around at the minute. If you get going now, you can make good time. The king may even be in York by the time you get there."

"Makes sense." Brackenbury finally spoke, his voice flat.

257

Suddenly, despite my desperation not to raise arms against Edward, to fight on a side directly in opposition to my best friend, I began to waver. I almost began to look for other ways out which didn't mean me throwing myself into the fray in such a dangerous way. But as my mind whirled, I knew there was no other course of action. Richard was the man I hoped to ultimately serve. That would be lost to me if I stayed here. How could he ever trust me again?

Then there was Caitlin. What would be the look in her eyes if when next I saw her, I was a traitor to the Yorkist cause? In the end, there was only one course of action, and only one other difficulty in my mind. One I knew made no sense, but it was there just the same. I looked down at Fides, his golden, sand- coloured ears pointed forwards as if listening intently to the discussion, eager to be off.

"You said, those horses over there..." I swallowed. "They are just a couple of nags. Surely..."

Dick nodded. I knew he would.

"You don't want to be riding about on thoroughbred horses, that will only draw attention to you. Also, if your horse is stabled, Father will believe you are still inside the walls, if he decides to look. I don't think he will, having more than enough on his plate at the moment, but this is a precaution, and could buy you some time. It is the sort of thing he may notice when he comes back from Richmond. That horse of yours is so pale it draws the eye."

I passed my hand down the long muscular neck, and Fides tossed his mane in response. So, I would leave Fides. Stupid though I knew it was, a solid lump formed in my throat.

"You will take care of him?"

Brackenbury chuckled softly then.

"Lovell, you are priceless! Horses are ten a penny when a man is in your position."

I glared at him angrily, acid beginning to boil in my gut.

"When you have had everything that should be yours taken away from you, you treasure what is truly yours! Fides was given to me by my father, everything else was granted to Warwick. Everything! Even the right to name my bride."

Brackenbury raised his brows in surprise at my outburst, but his eyes fixed on mine steadily.

"Some of us had very little in the first place, nor even now. Think yourself lucky. I probably won't even be missed."

I felt my cheeks burn and knew he was right. I was being ridiculous, and even childish. But still, I could not help feeling stupidly upset at handling Fides over to someone else and then leaving him behind. Would I ever get him back? My throat hurt, I couldn't swallow.

"He will be fine," Dick smiled, placatingly. I could see from the expression in his eyes that he agreed with Brackenbury and thought I was either being foolish, or a coward. Using a horse as a reason not to follow my true affinity. "When this is all over, he will still be here. After all, my father doesn't want me to go with him, thank God, so I will care for him as if he was my own, for I surely know you will lavish true care and affection on my sister, once she is truly your wife."

For a second, his gaze hardened, and I was unsure of his meaning, but the moment passed quickly and his smile returned. I felt another stab of guilt as Anna was the last thing on my mind, in fact, she was very rarely on my mind at all. I felt as though he knew that, somehow, even as the inevitability of my situation dawned.

"It goes without saying," I murmured, passing my hand down Fides strong neck once again. "Of course, that situation may depend on how the king views your father's actions." I saw his brows fly up quickly and I hid a smile of satisfaction. I liked Dick, he had shown me nothing but friendliness, but that last barb had stung deep, even if that was not his intention. The fact that he seemed to feel I owed him some sort of familial favour after having to flee the treasonous actions of his father just left me feeling more than a little irritated. Besides, he would have my horse.

"Don't forget," I continued, fixing my eyes on his face, "I am Warwick's ward and Warwick is in France. In exile. Should he never return, I wonder if the king will allow my marriage to his niece to prevail, once he has dealt with this rebellion."

Dick shrugged, somewhat embarrassed and I began to feel a little churlish. It was not his fault that any mention of my wife had an unsettling effect on me due to my affections for Caitlin. The bald fact was I hated being reminded I had a bride.

"I hadn't thought of that," he said quietly. "I would hate to see Anna treated so, but who knows what will happen." He looked up, his expression clearing. "Especially if you don't make a move soon."

"I know, I know," I said hastily. "I am sorry Dick, I did not mean to bite your head off. It's..."

He waved his hand before me, cutting off my pathetic apology, a little red-faced himself.

"No matter. I understand. But you really should get on now, if you are to get a good head start."

"He's right," Brackenbury spoke from behind me. "Come on Lovell. Let's get away from here while we can."

I had no choice. With reluctance, I slipped from my saddle, and with a final pat of the broad, sandy neck, I walked away from Fides and didn't look back.

6. NORTH YORKSHIRE
July 1470

The rain set in at sunset and made its presence felt, falling in thick, heavy sheets. With little breeze, it was like riding through walls of water and it became completely obvious that we would be unable to find a dry camp site, never mind light a fire. After a brief agreement, we decided that if we were going to spend our meagre allowance on lodgings at an inn and that it may be more prudent to do so on the first night, before anyone even knew we were missing.

We wanted to push on, skirting Middleham, but in the end had to settle for a small, somewhat ramshackle place at Witton, on the edge of the hills and just south of Castle Bolton. For once, I was relieved we both knew the area well.

The inn was warm and dry, and not overly full, but with enough occupants so that we did not attract undue attention. At least, not by anyone travelling the roads. For my sins, it was not just the rabbit stew and ale which warmed my belly as the young serving wench, with hair the hue of a fox pelt and eyes like acorns, climbed into my bed as a distant bell struck away the hours and rain hammered down on the roof. Her name was Jane, which made me smile as I thought of shy Jane Cooke, for her namesake was in no way shy and I allowed her hands to travel over my body languorously, as I took my fill of her eager mouth.

When I broke my fast with Brackenbury the next morning, he shook his head at me in wonder as he nodded towards the un-shuttered window, where weak sunlight was creeping in to lighten the shadows. I knew what he meant. Our money was gone, so all we could do was be thankful for the change in the weather and pray it would hold.

We rode beside each other with ease, at least now able to hold up our heads which had been impossible the day before, and so it gave us the opportunity to pass the time, even if I was initially somewhat self-conscious of my nightly endeavours. I knew it was pointless to ignore what had happened so I decided to try and find out more about my companion, to make the conversation easier as the day passed.

"Do you have a girl, Rob?"

The question caught him by surprise and I saw him start a little. He probably thought the last thing I wanted to talk about was women.

"Well," he began unsteadily, "in a fashion. A young girl from the village. She comes to the castle now and again."

"Will you wed her?" It was an innocent enough question, but it made his cheeks burn, a sight that offered me some relief.

"I think not." We rode on in silence for a while before he spoke again. "What do you think your duke will make of the French marriage? Didn't I hear that the earl had wanted him as a husband at one time? Although, you could say a prince is a better catch than a duke, apart from the fact that he's in exile!"

"Which is where he will stay!" I retorted heatedly, completely forgetting his question. "Warwick's lost his mind, that's all I can say. Been spending far too much time with Clarence! The man is ambitious and untrustworthy. It fair pours out of his eyes how keen he is to unseat his brother's birthright." Brackenbury seemed to consider this for a while, string ahead at the road. Never having met the duke, Clarence or the king, he had only my word to go on with regard to the events I had witnessed and the characters of those involved.

"Is it true Gloucester has a bastard child? I heard mention of it at Ravensworth."

I nodded carefully. We were heading on to even shakier ground here.

"'Tis true. A girl, Kathryn. Born last year."

"What's she like?"

"The girl?"

Brackenbury barked a short laugh

"No, you dolt! The mistress. Word has it she is an Irish Princess. Surely that cannot be true! There are no Irish princesses – are there?"

Two glittering green eyes rose up from the depths of my memory. The smell of violets, a flash of fiery brilliance caught on the battlements. She always returned to haunt me at the most unlikely moments, but had now been summoned up by my companions words.

"Well, if mindless gossip eases our path, she's the bastard daughter of a nobleman. Irish it is true. Tom Fitzgerald, Earl of Desmond, as was. That's his sons title now since he was sent to the block. And yes, she is beautiful, and charming, with flame coloured hair, skin like mother-of-pearl and eyes which glow like fireflies on a summer night."

There was silence for a while as he drank in my words and I tried to dispel her vision from my mind, efforts which were not at all helped by his next words.

"And, maybe you are just a bit in love with her yourself?"

My head shot round so hard it nearly flew off. What had I said to make him think that? I hardly knew him, and he had uncovered my secret! So, why had no one else? Or had they? My horse bridled a little at the sudden tension in the reins as my fingers gripped tighter around the damp leather.

"What!!?"

He was laughing at me, his grin so broad his face nearly split in two as he ambled along on a horse he was almost too big for.

"God's Blood, Lovell – I've heard you talk about the Neville girl, the tavern wench and your wife, and at no time has your voice betrayed a single emotion until those last few words. Are you going to deny it?"

For a while, I couldn't think how to answer him and just sat forlornly on my borrowed horse, who to be fair was behaving just as well as I could have expected from Fides. I looked down at the bay ears, only then getting a sudden flood of longing. Was I really so poor at masking my feelings? For sure, George had also spotted my secret, and now Brackenbury, who I knew hardly at all. And now he sat waiting for my reply. I couldn't lie, in fact, I didn't want to lie.

"No, I can't deny it." I sighed heavily, my shoulders suddenly feeling encircled by a collar of lead. "I fell for her the first time I saw her, but by then she was already his." I turned to look at him guardedly. "And no, he doesn't know! Neither does she. It is my burden to bear." He returned my pointed stare with a sanguine expression as we rounded a bend in the road, passing underneath low branches which were still dripping the odd drop of rain from the deluge of the previous day.

"Well, I am hardly likely to tell him, am I? Never even met the man, or likely to." He clucked under his tongue as his mount hesitated at a particularly large, muddy crevice in the road. "Your secret is safe. With me, at least." There was only the sound of our horses' hooves for a while, sucking in the mud as we plodded along, both of us apparently lost in thought. In a way, it had been almost a relief to admit how I felt.

"It has not been easy feeling envious of someone you really like. He's a good friend."

Brackenbury drew in a huge sigh.

"Bad luck." He said finally. "But at least you have a wife. Is that not some compensation?"

I grunted then, still thinking of Dick Fitzhugh.

"She's young. Too young yet for us to even be bedded. And as for compensation, well, not to put too fine a point on it but the compensation is all hers. She will benefit from my inheritance. It is the reason Warwick arranged the marriage I think."

"I didn't realise you were such a catch!"

I could hear the amusement in his tone and I had to grin myself. It was ridiculous! Here I was, not a groat to my name, fleeing from the service of the most powerful noble in the land. If this plan failed, I may not see a single penny of my much vaunted inheritance.

"Go on then," my companion continued, his voice mirthfully

taunting me. "Impress me. Though I should warn I am easily impressed. I may be the son of local gentry, but you know what that can mean in the north." He paused to underline his point. "Very little."

I whipped my head around so quickly my neck almost snapped.

"What? You never said! I thought you were just a…" my words failed me then. I didn't want to call my new found friend a commoner. Especially now it was becoming clear he wasn't.

"Oh, my family own a couple of manors. I am almost embarrassed to bring it up as Dick was enlightening me on your vast holdings. No wonder Warwick wanted to harness you to his family. What was it now, Baron Holand?"

Damn Dick Fitzhugh! Did the man have to gossip like a girl? I had spent the last few years trying to hide my title from the eager, pricked ears of the henchmen at Middleham. It wasn't something which sat comfortably with me, although I had no idea why. At that precise point the heavens opened once more, which, to my complete dismay, would only hamper our journey further. We were still not in sight of the city walls. The rain began to pelt down relentlessly, the sheer noise of it making us raise our voices to be heard.

"Over there!"

Brackenbury pushed his horse towards what appeared to be an abandoned barn, surrounded by the dilapidated ruins of what was once a farm. Keeping still for the moment, I squinted up at the leaden sky, my eyes instantly being battered by the sheer force of the rain as it began to hammer down with all the strength of an advancing army. Although I dearly wished to reach York before nightfall, I knew it was impossible and even if we still had money left, which we didn't, we were no were near any hostelry to offer us shelter from the oncoming storm.

With reluctance, I turned my bay's head toward the blackened ruin. My declaration of innocence to the king would have to wait.

265

7. YORKSHIRE
July 1470

We managed to find shelter for the horses under a nearby tree and we were lucky enough to find use of the collapsed roof timbers to provide us with our own temporary lodging.

Crouching within their shadow, we were able to avoid the worst of the downpour, although, particularly to my own disappointment, we could both see the foul weather was set in for the day. Leaving as we had, the one thing we were bereft of, apart from money, was proper riding cloaks, ones which would repel at least some of the deluge. Grudgingly, I had to count us fortunate in that at least the horses had been well fed the night before, as had we, and our wineskins were full. So apart from being cold and wet, things could have been a lot worse.

By dusk, the storm began to recede and although the rain had lessened into a fine, if constant, drizzle, the ensuing dark along with the sodden state of the road, made us decide to stay where we were. Particularly when we discovered that our shelter was so effective, we were able to light a small, but comforting fire.

Brackenbury crouched next to the sputtering flames and cocked his sandy-coloured head for a second, before turning to look at me, his eyes bright with the heat.

"I could just eat a nice, roasted rabbit right now."

I grunted in partial assent. To be honest, I was not that hungry, but I saw him smile. "And a good ale!" It was then that I discovered he had similarity to his namesake and I shook my head in amusement at the thought. "What, then? Are you so partial to spiced heron that you can't face a common coney?" It was exactly the sort of comment Percy would have thrown at me, and I suppressed a further grin.

"I like a good rabbit pie as well as the next man. I just had my fill last night."

He began to chuckle throatily. I groaned inwardly, having walked right into his next jest.

"I am sure that young wench is saying just the same." He shrugged, throwing another few sticks from the fallen timbers into the flames. "Depending on her appetite of course."

"Funny!" It was just like being with Rob Percy and I was both pleased and astounded that I had found a companion who was so easy to talk to. I hoped that whatever happened, we would remain friends.

It was then we both heard the noise. It was a sort of scraping, rustling sound and at the same time as one of our horses snorted loudly. My hand shot to my dagger, beginning to loosen it from its sheath.

"I think we have company."

Brackenbury reacted like a spooked cat. Jumping up on his haunches, impressively bearing his sturdy bulk, he swung himself round in the direction of the sound.

"I thought I heard something earlier," he whispered. "Unless it's a hart or something? The hunting around these parts is supposed to be good."

From between the timbers I could clearly see a pair of muddy toecaps. Someone was close enough to hear us breathe.

"Do harts in these parts wear boots?" I could hardly hear my own whisper.

"You there! Show yourself!"

We looked at each other quickly. His mouth formed the question "How many?" silently, and I shook my head. I had no idea. Hopefully one, maybe two. If so, we may have a chance of either talking ourselves out of trouble, or taking them on.

"What is it, Tom?"

A second, gruffer voice called out from farther away, but not that far. About where our horses were, I guessed. So, two men, minimum.

"Have we snared ourselves some rebels?" A third voice

then, confirmed our fate. Brackenbury had been ready to pounce by the look of him and I shook my head again, sliding my dagger back home, although ensuring it remained loose enough to release should I need it. We were not equipped for a fight, either in numbers or weapons, we would have to take our chances. Inhaling deeply, I clambered out of our makeshift shelter, and he did the same, although it took him longer to unfold himself as he was much taller than me.

I was wrong. There were four of them. Heavily cloaked and hooded against the elements. All I could see was a glimpse of unshaven skin and dark pools for eyes, now and again flashing in the torchlight held by one of their group. It was impossible to tell who they were or what their business was. Whether they were yeoman, common brigands or soldiers, although my gut told me that they were the latter, even though no livery was visible under their heavy outer clothing. One of them had a drawn sword and the blade flashed in the flame.

The one with the torch grinned toothlessly from beneath his sodden hood.

"Where do you think you two are headed?"

"That's our business," I replied calmly. "We are troubling no one."

"They've a couple of nags back here! On their last legs if you ask me!" A voice called out from behind us, as the other three men closed in. I bit the inside of my cheek. Dick had been right to insist I left Fides behind. The taller man with the drawn sword moved closer threateningly.

"My friend here asked you where you were headed. There's trouble abroad in these parts, no doubt you know?"

I pursed my lips, trying to keep my heart from jumping up into my mouth. I had no idea if these men were friend or foe. We just had to try and get rid of them, and quickly. The best way, as I saw it, was not to appear too weak. Or too aggressive. Once again I thanked Dick silently that Fides was not here for I would have fought to keep him from the hands of these scavengers.

They could take the horses if they wanted. As long as that is all they took.

"I do. And we are trying to avoid it."

"And doing well until you appeared on the scene." That one came from Brackenbury, who was just as tall as our latest interrogator, only broader.

"You're armed?" He had obviously spotted my dagger and may have believed I had a sword as well, as I should have done had our departure not been so hasty. I shrugged, casually.

"No more than you are. As you said, there is trouble abroad. I could as well ask you if you are royalist or rebel."

"All cats are black in the dark," Brackenbury quipped – once again reminding me of Percy and I smiled.

"And dogs."

"Loyal and treacherous alike."

The toothless one spat on the ground, unimpressed at our discourse. Rain had begun to fall once again, not as heavy, but enough to cause their torch to gutter.

"For fuck's sake, are we going to get drenched again whilst these two fools fuck us around? Let's round these bastards up and get them back to camp. They won't be our worry then. Old Bill can 'ave em! We could use their horses too!" He hawked again. A disgusting habit, I thought. "Just about."

With that, the remaining member of their elite group appeared, leading our horses towards us. The taller man sheathed his sword.

"Are you going to come quietly or do we have to tie your hands?"

I looked at Brackenbury who shrugged again. We were outnumbered, it was dark and wet. The only thing we could be sure of was that these were not Fitzhugh's men, they didn't have a clue who we were and were obviously not on the hunt for two missing henchmen.

"Where we are going?" It was a feeble attempt but I had to try and one of them cackled.

"You will find out soon enough," the tall one said over his shoulder as he looked for his own mount. "And it's not us you'll be explaining yourself to."

It seemed fruitless to resist further so as our makeshift shelter was destroyed and the fire kicked out, we mounted our rain slicked horses and headed off with our captors. No one spoke, there was only the relentless sound of hooves splashing through mud and water. With the rain and the dark, it was impossible to tell what direction we were going in but we went on for about an hour. It was then, with my soaked clothes sticking as close to me as my skin, I smelled pungent, wood-smoke, the rising aroma of damp campfires. A lingering tang of roasted meat, the twinkling of torches and the unmistakable stench of the latrine trench, told us we were approaching a campsite.

I began to feel slightly sick with anxiety and cursed the foul weather under my breath. That, and myself. If we had pressed on further yesterday, even not lingered so long this morning to break our fast, we may have made it. We couldn't be that far from the city walls. It was only a good day's ride from Middleham to York, although we had skirted the village, which had taken us longer, that was true. But Conyers knew me too well and had already seen me at Ravensworth. It had seemed too risky, until now.

Very few looked up as we trudged into the camp, most men still huddled around fires which were struggling to remain alight in the constant rainfall. Dark, cloak-swathed bodies crouched beneath what shelter the trees afforded and as we forged deeper into the confines of the site, we saw the tents. There were standards, but sodden and flat as they were, it was still frustratingly impossible to work out exactly whose captive we had become.

As we passed one of the smaller, guard tents to our left, the flap lifted and a dark shape emerged from the dimly lit interior.

"Ye Gods, Jim, what the hell have you got there? A nice shank of venison would have been more welcome!"

It was then that the growing tightness across my chest finally released as Rob Percy took a step closer to my horse before squinting up at us, at me, his jaw falling agape.

"Jesus and all the saints! I must be dreaming!"

8. YORKSHIRE
July 1470

It was only once I had slid out of my saddle and clasped Rob's hand firmly that our captors seemed happy to relinquish their charges. The taller soldier of the group also dismounted, and pushed down his hood, his gaze still undeterminable in the shadows.

"You know these men?" His words were still leaden with suspicion.

Rob looked up at his namesake, who was also now cautiously dismounting, following my lead.

"I know one of them well enough to know that he will account for the other, although what the hell he is doing here is a mystery!" He turned back to me. "You don't know how glad I am to see you; I had heard…" As if only just aware of the watching audience, he stepped back and lifted the flap to the entrance of the tent.

"Tyrrell, will you hand over your charges to me?" At the authoritative nod of Rob's head, the tall man waved a hand at his companions who melted away into the camp as he ducked under the canvas, where Rob then directed us to follow.

Inside, although dimly lit, the tent was warm and dry. The man named Tyrrell pulled off his cloak as he strolled over to a table where a flagon of wine stood next to the remnants of a meal. He poured himself a drink noisily before turning back to Rob, who was now studying Brackenbury closely, just as he was returning the favour.

The man called Tyrrell wiped his lips with the back of his hand. "Well, Percy, I was intending on taking these men to Hastings as they were found skulking around in the undergrowth like rats, so if you wouldn't mind explaining?"

Now in the light, I could see his face clearly. He had hard, rough hewn features, as if his face was carved out of rock. Even his eyes had a granite like quality. The overall impression was of a man who was somewhat formidable. He had the sort of nose my mother had liked to call 'strong.' I had a different name for it. Long.

But Rob seemed easy in his company

"Faith, James, this man here is one of Gloucester's closest friends, although his companion is not known to me."

"My name's Brackenbury. Robert Brackenbury. From Barnard Castle."

I glanced at him quickly as he said these words, marking the set look upon his face. He was as tall as Tyrrell, and it was him that he had fixed in his gaze.

Rob reached for the wine himself then, but genially poured two more cups which he then left sitting on the table as he took a deep draught of his own drink.

"Well, that fits. We had heard that you had joined forces with Fitzhugh, Frank. I must admit it was a surprise, but our informant was reliable."

It was just as I had feared. I knew I had been right to take the risk once I heard his words and I cleared my throat which had begun to dry as the implication of his words sunk in.

"Does Richard know?"

Tyrrell snorted and swilled his drink round in his cup.

"His Grace knows who his friends are."

I shot him a sharp look. I had no idea who this man was but he was not about to offer me a treatise on friendship.

"Then His Grace also knows that this friend remains at the mercy of the whims of the Earl of Warwick, who, presently, is my lord and master."

Tyrrell shrugged as if he cared not at all.

"And possibly using you as a spy?"

It was Rob's turn to snort now as he swallowed his wine, almost choking, his eyes sparking bright.

"Lovell? A spy! Now there's a thought to make my day! Unless he traded in his infernal honesty with his marriage vows, I very much doubt it. His friend, however..."

Brackenbury took a step forwards then, his face suffusing with colour which could be determined even in the half-light. I stretched out my arm in panic. I had never seen Brackenbury anything other than genial and mild-tempered, but with his size, I didn't want to find out now that it masked a devil's temper.

"Rob, don't be daft." I said quickly. "That's the main reason we are here. Neither of us had any intention of being implicated in Fitzhugh's treason. I can't believe that you would even think I was!"

"You don't know how pleased I am to hear that!"

The voice that answered my question was not Rob's, but was as well known to me and even hearing it after so long caused my head to swim.

Richard paused under the tent flap, a disembodied hand holding it back above his head. He was still in half-armour, but bare headed, and he looked older. Much older than I remembered him. Even as our eyes met, it seemed that he had increased the two-year gap between our ages. But it was a maturity of knowledge and experience, all youthful naivety fled with his experiences of the last few months. I desperately hoped little else had changed.

My obeisance came automatically and out of the corner of my eye I saw Brackenbury follow suit, after a slight hesitation, as his attention had still been fixed on Tyrrell. Richard continued into the tent, followed by Tom Parr and another henchman I recognised from our days at Middleham, but for the moment could not recall his name. Even in my surprise, I wondered how in all the hell he had ended up here from Middleham.

"Dickon." I breathed. "I count myself fortunate it is your men that found us and not Fitzhugh's."

He smiled at me then and I could see the genuine relief behind his gaze.

"Then I thank God what I heard was untrue. I had hoped it to be so, but other than my own instinct, I had no cause to disbelieve it." He glanced at Tyrrell then. "You need to check your informers, James. I did tell you they had this one wrong!"

Tyrrell gave a small bow, his smile tight.

"Even good men make mistakes, Your Grace. He witnessed this man squiring Fitzhugh himself. He was told they were close in all things and would be riding south together."

I didn't see Brackenbury grin, but I heard the amusement in his words.

"Well, if your spy was Dick Fitzhugh, he was covering for us. He helped us leave unobserved." He faltered hardly at all as Richard swung a dark, questioning gaze in his direction. "Not all the men in Warwick's service endorse his actions, even though they are paid to serve their lord and master and can do no other."

"And you are?" Richard's voice was quiet as he took in these words.

"Robert Brackenbury, of Saleby, Your Grace."

"Warwick's man?"

"The king's first."

I smothered a smile, remembering my own words to John Neville some time ago. After a few reflective moments, Richard held out his hand to me and we clasped hands tightly, his fingers gripping round mine with a tension that almost broke my bones.

"I thank you once again for your loyalty, Francis." I could see there was something else on his mind even as he spoke. Not for nothing had I been his close friend for the past few years. Even if events kept conspiring to keep me from serving him, it didn't stop me from knowing his thoughts as well as my own. He bit his bottom lip before looking around the tent, then back at Tyrrell.

"James, would you take care of Robert here. See he is fed and given some dry clothing." As James placed his cup down, Richard turned back to Brackenbury. "As the king's man, would serving his brother suffice? I have need of good men and these days it is hard to know who to trust. If you have won Lovell's friendship, that is as good as account as I could ask for."

I could not deny the satisfaction that flooded through my veins. Finally! If he was taking on men to fight the rebels, I would now get a chance to hone my craft at his side and not in the tiltyard. Surely, I had proved myself now?

The look on Brackenbury's face showed the sheer amazement at his turn in fortune and he glanced at me quickly in disbelief.

"I would be honoured, Your Grace!" he breathed and as Richard nodded his approval, Tyrrell picked up his cloak and gestured for Brackenbury to follow him, which he did without a backward look, leaving me alone with my two friends.

Rob passed me the waiting cup and poured another for Richard, who accepted it thoughtfully. Pleased with myself, I downed mine in one, feeling its welcome, spiced warmth fill my belly.

"Do we make for York tomorrow? Is the king already there?" My words were eager, perhaps foolishly so as they were met by a deafening silence which should have warned me what was to come, but the thought of riding north among the assembled men and showing Richard what I was made of filled my mind – and the quiet.

Richard took a delicate sip from his cup and placed it down again. I waited, in anticipation, looking first at Richard, then Rob, who seemed to find his own cup of great interest, he stared at it so intently.

"We do." Richard answered finally. "Edward is expected there by the end of the week. We will then all move on, possibly to Ripon. We have heard the rebels are ready to move."

I threw back my head eagerly. No wine had ever tasted as heady as that and I began to feel lightheaded.

"Well," I grinned, a little shamefacedly, "someone may have to lend me a breastplate at the very least, but if..." His next words fell like an axe.

"I want you to continue on to London, Frank."

I knew my mouth was gaping before he even completed the statement. Fully aware I looked like a fool, but he couldn't have been talking to me? Surely, he could not have been talking to me? There were Robs, Toms, Edwards a plenty around any camp, there must surely be another Frank! Until I saw the look in his eyes and I knew.

"Dickon..." it was almost a groan of supplication. I knew it and so did he.

"I am sorry Francis. But my relief at your steadfast service has cheered me for more than one reason. Not only because I could not brook such betrayal from a friend but also because I have a quest that only you would know how to fulfill. God has smiled on me in truth by reuniting us again in this way."

Rob gave a discreet cough and turned to Richard.

"I'll go check on the men, if I have your leave, Dickon? I need a few of them to walk the camp perimeter."

Richard didn't answer as Rob threw me a wink and left the tent, leaving us alone in an awkward silence. When they left London I had only hinted at my desire to accompany them, this time I had no qualms at all about being more direct.

"Why, Dickon? I was going to be dragged into battle by Fitzhugh, and it's not for fear of fighting that I made myself scarce. It's about who I prefer to fight for! You need men, I heard you tell Brackenbury. Am I not as good a man as any?"

For a few moments he could not meet my eyes, preferring to look at his feet, as if fascinated by the mud that caked his boots. He looked weary, yet not in a way that made you think he was not completely alert to everything that was going on around him.

"I trained with you," he sighed finally. "No one knows your worth more than I. To be honest, I don't think we will fight, not here in the north. I think the danger will come from the South, so we need to deal with this rabble and turn back towards London as soon as we can. Warwick could land anywhere now the French have backed his cause, but my money is on Kent. He is well liked there and has many of his affinity who would rally to his banner

277

without question."

It was only then that I remembered. Anne.

"Do you really think he wants to put that God forsaken Lancastrian Prince on the throne of England? Is he completely mad?"

He looked up then, the Richard I knew.

"You heard then?" I nodded in assent, finding no words I could say to him, sadness pooling in his eyes. "Poor Anne. I cannot imagine how she must feel. But there is one thing I do know, and that is that he may be able to manipulate his daughters into doing his bidding, but he will find my brother Clarence a different matter. You can be sure this is not why he turned against his blood kin – to see the spawn of those responsible for our father and brother's deaths crowned."

I could hear the emotion tightening his voice, yet if it related to Anne or George I didn't know. He swallowed with difficulty then, surveying me carefully from under lowered lids.

"Yet, I feel there is a reckoning coming. If it does, I need you to be where you can help me the most. I need you in London, Francis, with Caitlin and my daughter."

9. BAYNARD'S CASTLE
August 1470

Summer peaked in a blaze of glory and if I was initially heart-sore leaving my friends behind outside York, the sight of Caitlin in the courtyard of Baynard's Castle as I rode through the gate banished every last vestige of disappointment from my soul. Dressed in palest lavender velvet, she was completely unaware of my arrival, and I was thankfully able to drink my fill of her before she even knew I was there.

Her face was hidden from sight at first, as she was bent over, completely focused on her daughter. As she picked her up, she rose, turning, settling the small, auburn haired child on her hip with a smile. My hands tightened on the reins, making the leather creak unwillingly, causing my borrowed mount to a sudden halt as two pairs of malachite eyes fixed on me, and once again, I fell hopelessly in love.

Kathryn Plantagenet was the most beautiful child I had ever seen. Without a doubt she had her mother's eyes, lit from within like stained glass with the sun passing behind it, and her skin had the same pearly sheen, although flushed with the blush of youth. Yet everything else belonged to Richard. The veil of her hair was auburn, falling in rippling waves onto her shoulders, and I had often looked at strikingly similar, straight, dark brows, albeit then above a storm grey gaze.

I had never dreamed that a young child would ever hold my attention for as long as Richard's daughter did, and as she looked at me, it was almost as if we had met before, as ridiculous as that seemed. But as Caitlin walked towards me, her head level with her daughter's and both faces wreathed in smiles, I truly knew my heart was lost. Within a few more steps she was by my stirrup looking up at me, and it was with gratitude that I noticed the unbidden pleasure in her eyes.

279

"Francis! I can't believe you are back! I am so pleased to see you! Can you stay long?"

With my hands trembling, I dismounted, trying to remain casual, to ignore the effect she once again cast over me like a cloak. Time apart from her had in no way lessened my feelings, which were just as intense as the last time I had looked at her face. I prayed I would not make a fool of myself for she was as good as married in a way. More so. As I gained my feet, I turned towards her, returning her wondrous smile.

"As long as you like! I have no where else to be now that my lord has fled, and so here I am!" She frowned a little, her brow creasing, even as the smile stayed in place, but I turned my attention to Kathryn, who was regarding me solemnly. "Now, who is this beautiful princess?" As if she understood my pathetic attempt at flattery, Kathryn beamed at me and reached out to me with tiny fingers, which made me laugh in response. "Ah! She even agrees!"

Caitlin giggled, and caught her daughter's errant hand.

"Don't encourage her! She is completely pampered! Joan and the duchess's ladies pander to her every whim. Never have I seen a child so spoiled!"

My eyes met hers then in all seriousness as the stable-hand appeared to relieve me of my horse. As it was not Fides, I surrendered the reins willingly.

"She deserves it. You both do."

Blushing, I could tell she was anxious to change the subject and she nodded her head towards the horse as Kathryn began to gurgle loudly.

"Whose horse is that? Where is Fides?   In fact, where have you been all this time? Patrick told me he had heard you had turned your coat and joined the northern rebels but I told him he must have heard it wrong! That you would never turn against the king!"

Her utter faith in me caused my chest to swell, whilst also causing a warm flood of pleasure to burn there.

"Fides is still in the north. I…" The sight of a familiar figure striding across the courtyard distracted me from whatever I was about to say. The very same Patrick Malone was approaching us, the falcon and fettlerlock emblazoned proudly on his chest. Kathryn saw him too and I swear she grinned and clapped her hands as he came to a halt before us.

"Beggin' your pardon Mi'lady," he began, addressing himself to Caitlin with a bow, "but Her Grace requires this young man's presence without delay."

I noticed that he completely avoided any eye contact with me as he spoke. He still believed I was a traitor it seemed, despite any protestations she may have made on my behalf. Caitlin looked at me, her eyes large and concerned.

"Will I see you later? I wondered..?" she paused, hesitant, biting her lip. I knew what she wanted of me, what she would always want of me. That certain knowledge both disappointed and pleased me at the same time. It was obvious she was more than happy to see me, I only wished it was because it was me she really wanted to see.

"You will indeed," I replied as graciously as I could. "I was with Richard in York and it is by his will that I am here."

Had I been versed in all the chivalry in the world, I could not have said anything else that made her light up more than those few words. As I bowed my head to take her leave, I could not miss how her eyes welled with tears of joy.

10. BAYNARD'S CASTLE
August 1470

As I entered the solar, the beams of sunlight filtering through the windows and warming me with the welcome of a familiar friend, Richard's mother looked up from the book she was studying, a prayer book it looked like. Her two ladies, seated by the window, continued to attend to their sewing ignoring me completely. I had a particular talent, it seemed, for being ignored.

Duchess Cecily's gaze was as hard and shrewd as ever, and I halted a few feet away from her, aware that she was studying me intently. I had not seen her for some time, in fact since the day I presented Richard's Christmas gift, but she had not changed at all. She had as much composure and regal bearing as the queen, more so, in fact. In all, an audience with the king's mother was more intimidating than one with her eldest son.

"I heard you had arrived. Do you have something for me?"

Slightly taken aback, I fumbled inside my doublet for the letter Richard had given me before I left, although how she knew I carried it was a mystery. I stepped forwards and placed it on the table by her chair, falling back into place once I had done so.

Without taking her eyes off me she rested the open book down in her lap and picked up the letter, snapping the seal between her finger and thumb with a resounding crack. Only when she had unfolded the letter did her eyes finally leave me be. The room was silent for a few minutes as she read the words on the page, and I caught one of her ladies looking at me from beneath lowered lids. I didn't smile, but the fact that I had caught her looking caused her to flush with colour and her companion nudged her gently. They were both young, and very pretty, far too pretty to be in Cecily's service and I wondered how they coped with her pious lifestyle and formidable manner. The blushing girl looked at me once more and this time her eyes held.

"Well, that clears up a few things!" Cecily's voice caused me to start a little, and I turned back, connecting with her satisfied smile. I didn't know what to say to that so I said nothing. Richard had not confided in me as to what he was putting in the letter so she had the advantage of me.

"One should always expect their sons to be loyal but can not necessarily expect as much from their servants. In this case, we seem to have been outplayed." She must have seen my brow crease in puzzlement and the thin smile tightened, although not in anger. "What made you of all people, the son of a man with known Lancastrian leanings, turn against the lord who had given you a home, put food in your belly and turned you into a knight?" I began to feel more than a little annoyed. Why was everyone always questioning my loyalty?

As far as I could, I had been subservient to Edward's rule from the day of my father's death. I had no choice in truth, but still, I had not railed against my fate. So why was it always a surprise whenever the subject came up?

"Edward is my king, Your Grace." I tried to keep my tone patient despite my inner frustration. This was the king's mother after all. "My father may have had different loyalties but I was too young to cleave to them before he died." Her lips pursed in what I swear was suppressed amusement. It was almost my undoing. Diplomacy was never my master.

"So, we made a Yorkist of you?"

"Apart from my Lancastrian bride." The words were out before I could stop them and the chamber plunged into silence. "Who I am very grateful for." I added somewhat hastily, hoping to save myself from censure.

I saw Cecily's shoulders move, although her face remained impassive. I knew I had somehow pleased her.

"I can see why Richard likes you." She waved the letter in her hand to and fro with purpose, raising a raft of golden dust motes in the sunlight. "Enough, indeed, to ask for Edward to pardon you."

If I had been feeling confident, those words doused me as effectively as if I had fallen in the River Cover. A pardon? What on earth was I being pardoned for? I had hoped my explanation back in York had redeemed me, but it seemed it was not to be that easy. My heart dropped through my boots and I was once again conscious of two pairs of eyes watching me intently from the other side of the room. I took a deep, steadying breath. I had to keep calm.

"Your Grace, I don't understand. I informed His Grace of exactly why I was in the north, and what I had done there. I thought my actions were more than clear."

Her eyebrows raised high on the smooth, unlined forehead, giving her a haughty demeanour.

"So it seems, to him, else Richard would hardly have intervened for you. You will learn, Lovell, that these days' things are not as simple as they used to be, and Edward walks a much harder path. His trust has been tempered by betrayal in the fiercest of fires. To see those closest to him turn against everything he has fought for ripped the blinkers from his eyes." She sighed then, casting her gaze over to the window, as if looking out to see the past staring back at her. "It is a lesson his father had learned well, but these past few years of peace had softened him."

She turned her face back to me. It was painted with a grim resignation.

"He tests those closest to him the hardest now and traitors grovelling at his feet for mercy may find him a changed man." The silence between us for the next few seconds was almost unbearable. "I understand he was particularly disappointed to hear about you joining the rebel forces."

My head hung down of its own accord. There was nothing else I could say that would mean anything, other than to blame those who controlled both myself and my livelihood. The memories of princes were short it seemed, as I was given no choice of which master to serve. That was Edward's choice, but in

284

no measure was I brave enough to blame the king for my misfortune. I could only hope that Richard's words would pierce the armour of the king's resolve. There was nothing else I could do but listen as she told the tale as he had seen it. How my actions had worked against me, forced on me though they had been. No matter that I had no power over them, up until the time I chose to rebel myself.

"You were at Ravensworth were you not, when the banners of revolt were raised? In the company of your father Fitzhugh, who Edward is still pursuing as we speak, their pathetic attempt at a rebellion in ruins around their feet." Her eyes narrowed. "You were called by him to go north and be at his side I understand. You acted as his close body servant and were being groomed to attend to him during his ill- advised campaign. Your wife was no-where to be seen, so it was no conjugal visit which steered you north, or am I misinformed?"

My throat grew dry. Brackenbury had seen how it would look, the day he asked me what I was doing there. I had been slow, my thoughts on other matters. A fool. For a while at least.

"Not misinformed, Your Grace," I replied with care, "but not fully informed. I left Ravensworth as soon as I discovered what Lord Fitzhugh was about. When he raised his banners, I was already riding south to join the king. There is a man from Saleby who can account for me should it be needed. A man now still with the king's army as far as I know."

She waved the letter again airily. I half expected the letters to fall from the page.

"So I see from what Richard tells me. Thank the Lord you had the common sense to remove yourself from that rabble before things went too far." She stood up then, and strode over to stand before me, rosary beads clicking together musically with every step. Folding her hands together, she fixed me with a look of determined intensity. "Don't worry. Edward will listen to Richard, of all men. Your honour will be restored in his eyes. As it has been in mine."

I raised my head then, looking up at her cautiously. Neither of us seemed to think it fit to mention that I was still Warwick's ward. Warwick, now in France with the king's brother and stirring a pot of boiling intrigue. Cecily cleared her throat brusquely, almost as if her business with me was completed. "Now he wishes me to welcome you here under my roof as I believe he has a duty for you to discharge."

I nodded, meekly.

"Yes, Your Grace."

She shook her head a little at that, registering some disbelief.

"It is unusual, but then Lady Desmond is an unusual girl." I frowned as she smiled, hiding the hidden meaning behind her words. "She does not make friends easily, and I know she will be pleased that you are here. In other circumstances, I may be concerned that a young man is seen as a suitable companion for someone so close as you are in age." Her smile disappeared, at least from her lips, but no matter how she tried, I saw the pride in her eyes. "Yet, handsome as you are lad, I am fully confident that her heart is already wed."

11. BAYNARD'S CASTLE
October 1470

It was a sublime summer. There seemed to be no end to the long, warm days where the blue canopy of the sky reflected on the river, turning it into a silken ribbon, which rippled in the balmy breeze and parted passively, lapping around the bows of barge and boat alike.

Mostly, my duties consisted of keeping Caitlin company, and in doing so, entertaining her winsome daughter. On occasion, I accompanied the duchess on her almsgiving and charitable works around the city. She frequented many parishes, St Faith Under St Paul and St James Garlickhythe, being the two closest, but on one morning I accompanied her to All Hallows Barking, huddling in the shadow of the city walls.

Her dedication and care for the poor never ceased to hold me in awe. I had often ridden through London and knew that each time my eyes had been wide open, yet even though I saw the crowded streets steeped in mire, redolent with the pungent smells and raucous sounds of closely pressed men and animals, I may as well have been blinkered like a mare. Only on these visits with the duchess did it become clear to me how much poverty there was, sitting incongruously beside the dwellings of the wealthiest merchants and the grandest of churches. It was the first time I felt ashamed of the wealth which although I did not personally possess, I surely reaped the benefit.

Worthy though these visits were, no doubt both good for my soul and for my reputation which had been temporarily tarnished in the eyes of the Yorkist matriarch, the best hours that summer were those spent with Caitlin and her daughter, both of whom now had a firm claim on my heart. Where I could not show my feelings for Caitlin, I could thoroughly indulge her beautiful daughter and I did this unashamedly. In one sense, it was a form of blessed relief, to finally be able to shower some of the love and affection that I had managed to keep hidden deep within my soul.

During long, hot days at Baynard's Castle, with Caitlin watching nervously, I supported Kathryn as she rode her first horse, an experience which caused her to throw back her head and release a peal of musical laughter which almost caused the animal to start across the courtyard. She showed no fear, her father's daughter in every way, and afterwards she leaned forwards and laid her head down on the animal's neck, cooing softly, her fingers sunk deep in its mane. I am sure the horse fell in love with her itself.

Then there were lazy afternoons where she perched upon my knee, her hand resting on the belly of my lute as I plucked the strings, to the accompaniment of a gaggle of musical noises in her own attempt to rival my meagre skills. As the sun set, turning the river crimson, her nurse Joan would carry the sleepy child off to bed, and I would sit in the window embrasure, content to be alone with Caitlin for a while.

Sometimes I would read aloud as she sat with her needlework, knowing that she would never see the irony of my reciting passages from "Tristan and Isolde," of one man's love for an Irish beauty who belonged to another. Why would she? Friends though we were, I was as certain as I could be that she didn't suspect a thing.

They were moments I knew I would remember for the rest of my life. The wide-eyed emerald innocence of Kathryn's curious stare, the downy, rose-tinted peachy skin of her cheeks, the graceful curve of Caitlin's neck as she bent to her stitch-work, unaware that I had learned my passages by heart so I could watch her whilst I told the tale. The subtle fragrance of violets that filled the air as the warmth of the day cooled and the stars peeped out above us, shyly, one by one. I watched her so closely, knew her so well, that somehow I recognised that she was transforming before my eyes.

As her daughter changed, so did she. She grew rounder, her

skin became even more radiant, glowing. A sheer joy shining out of every pore. Yet other mornings, in chapel, she was wan, the skin around her eyes bruised, her clear brow folded into a delicate knot as she bowed her head, thoughtful, her eyes remaining open, fixed on the floor. Now and again her hand strayed to her waist, halting there. Sometimes she would depart the chamber swiftly, declaring that she had left something behind. Usually something trivial. A glove she wanted to repair, one of Kathryn's bonnets. A book she returned with only to place it on a table unread. There was a look about her, one I remembered well, for I had seen it before. In Middleham.

Caitlin was, if I was not mistaken, once again with child.

I kept my own counsel until one clement afternoon, where Kathryn had decided to practice her new found wobbling skills – for it was hardly walking. Barefoot, she padded across the chamber floor, flitting between Caitlin and myself, uttering loud squeals of joy each time she reached one or the other of us. It mattered not to her. The happiness I felt as that young child wrapped her arms around my neck, her auburn curls like silk against my cheek, emanating waves of her mother's fragrance, was dimmed only by the dull stab of envy that prodded my gut.

Reluctantly, I released her once more and watched with pleasure as she toddled back over to her mother, launching herself into Caitlin's arms as she sat on the floor, her silver gown pooled around her like a molten lake.

"Oh, I so wish Richard could have been here to see this!" she smiled, regarding her young child with a beaming pride. "She changes more and more by the day now and I fear he will hardly know her by the time he gets back!"

I picked up my lute then, more for something to do than any need to play it and began to fuss with the strings, watching from beneath my lids as she pressed a hearty kiss onto her daughter's forehead, causing another wave of laughter. I kept my head down, knowing what I was going to say, I had been waiting for the chance.

"I think there is one other major change he will not fail notice when he returns, if I am not mistaken!"

I spoke softly, hoping against hope that she would not take offence at my words, but desperately wanting to share this secret with her. As the duchess had said, she had very few companions, only one of Cecily's ladies, Joan, seeming to be able to get close to her at all. As I waited for her to answer me, Kathryn wriggled free from her mother's grasp and made her way back towards me with a determined grimace that I recognised well for I had seen similar on Richard's face often. Putting down the lute, I slipped down to the floor and held out my arms, which made her totter even faster, her face wreathed in smiles.

Catching Kathryn quickly, I swung her upwards, reveling in the simple joy of her youth. Keeping my gaze averted from Caitlin, I landed her on the padded cushioning of the window seat, where she immediately latched on to my lute. As we both patted the strings, I heard the rustle of velvet when Caitlin stood, but I still couldn't look at her. Fortunately, Kathryn was demanding all of my attention, which I was only too happy to give. She had the cutest feet, and I found it difficult to believe they were so small and perfect. I tweaked one of her toes, if only to change the subject and breach the silence. Kathryn shrieked with pleasure as I shook my head laughing.

"Where are her shoes?" For a few seconds I thought Caitlin may not answer, but I heard her sigh softly.

"She hates shoes – pulls them off at every opportunity." I looked up as she answered but she was now avoiding my gaze, her fingers playing with the polished coral pendant which lie around her throat. Her voice caught on the next words she spoke. "How did you know?"

How did I know? Because I watched her every minute I was with her. Because she did not make one move, one glance, undergo a change of expression that I did not mark and commit it to my memory. I could not tell her the truth so I lied, shrugging lightly, as if it were a matter of no consequence whilst my gut tightened.

"I lived in a household completely surrounded by women at one point in my life. That may be why I noticed. I just felt there was something... different about you." Kathryn had gone quiet, her thumb now firmly fixed in her mouth, usually a sign that she was about to fall into sleep. "Does Dickon know?" She nodded lightly.

"He has requested we go to Ludlow before the weather closes in. Once the duchess gets back from Berkhamstead."

The duchess had been at her country home for the past two weeks and was due back any day. Malone had gone with her, now a constant presence in the York household, one she seemed to trust implicitly. Malone had also brought his young son over from Ireland, and he was now serving in the duchess's household, having completed his training in his Irish homeland. The boy was his father's image, a younger copy, and the same age as Richard.

Ludlow, I mused in silence. So she was leaving? I swallowed hard, watching Kathryn as she fought an ongoing battle to prevent her lids from closing over agate eyes. All I could do was try and make a jest of it. How could I ride to Ludlow each day to read "Tristan and Isolde?" To teach Kathryn how to play the lute as she plucked the strings making her own tune.

"Well," I smiled tightly, swallowing down my despair, "I am not...."

A sudden commotion arose in the bailey outside. It was the noise of a returning army, at least it resembled it in its chaos. Dogs barked, bells rang, horse hooves clattered against stone. The unmistakable slither of metal against metal. Footsteps and shouting. It sounded like commands, or orders. A rumble of thunder rolled overhead.

Caitlin moved over towards me, her eyes fixed on the window, but we could see nothing. Just the river, flowing endlessly on its way to the sea. I knew it could be Edward, returning from the north, and not before time to be honest, but something told me it was not. Some strange feeling that had the

291

hairs on my arms standing up as if an early winter chill had reached into the chamber with searching fingers.

Whatever it was that I felt, I knew she felt it too. We would know if Edward was returning, we would have had word. The duchess would have been here; I was sure of it. Chambers would have been made ready. Besides, his first visit would have been to Westminster. To his wife, his queen.

"You don't think..?" Caitlin whispered quietly, her eyes fixing on mine, almost black with fear.

The door opened then, and two figures entered, neither of them known to me. Their faces were strangers, but the black bull badge they wore on their sleeve was all too familiar. It was the badge of Richard's brother, George, and before either of us could draw another breath, there was the man himself. No longer in France, no longer an exile, George of Clarence stood in the solar as the rain began to pound against the windows and something told me his visit was neither wanted or welcome.

12. BAYNARD'S CASTLE
October 1470

Instinctively, I moved forwards to protect the sleeping form of the child from his sight. The last time I saw George he had made it clear he knew of my affections for Caitlin, and now he had found us together. Whatever he was up to, unless he had turned his coat once again and returned to his family's affinity, I wanted to remain on guard. As usual, George acted as though he was a genial, benevolent host, which for the moment, allayed my fears somewhat.

"Lady Desmond! What a surprise! You really have turned into the most resourceful of young ladies, I must say. Is there any noble residence in the land that you have not yet graced with your presence?"

Caitlin looked back at him, doing a damn good job of masking her shock, her face betraying only the mildest of surprise. My attention meanwhile was on another man who had just entered the room, motioning for the door to be closed behind him. He looked travel stained and grim, hard faced. His cloak was dirty and he appeared to have been riding hard and for more than a few days. I had no idea who he was and he wore no identifying badge. Not even Clarence's bull.

As we stood dumbfounded, George was completely at ease and moved further into the room, a sneer covering his lips as he looked at me, well disguised though it was.

"I was hoping to see my mother. This is still her home and not a refuge for waifs and strays I take it?"

I swallowed hard then, my fists clenching involuntarily. He didn't like me, I knew that. Somehow he resented either my wealth or my position, for I knew of his greed and ambition, Richard had spoken of it now and again. I wondered where Warwick was, for if George was here alone, had he turned his back on his mentor, now that the earl was backing a Lancastrian prince? George had gambled all and lost. It almost made me smile despite the circumstances.

Caitlin stepped forwards, her demeanour as noble as any titled lady in the land.

"Good day, Your Grace. Duchess Cecily has taken herself to Berkhamstead for a few days. She is expected back any time now and will, I am sure, be very pleased to see you. Can I bring some wine or other refreshment, for you … and your companion?"

George threw his gloves down onto a nearby settle with an air of careless abandon and crossed over to the fire whilst his silent friend remained by the door like a sentinel, watching the scene play out in a way that did nothing to ease the growing tension. George's smile was full of condescension, his hazel eyes alight with some inner pleasure that he appeared in no real hurry to impart.

"Why not?" he exclaimed jovially, making his own way across to the sideboard where a wine in a covered flagon stood waiting. He offered a cup to his silent friend who ignored him, causing George to chuckle.

"Your loss!" George grinned at his truculent companion with a shrug. "We do, after all, have something to celebrate, do we not my friend? And despite her piety, my mother has a well stocked buttery."

The man regarded him wordlessly, his face not moving a muscle. I heard noises outside. More men? Edward? Warwick? My throat began to dry up but I managed to challenge him on one word.

"Celebrate?"

George threw his head back to drink, swallowing deeply and noisily. He was totally at ease, and enjoying our discomfort no end. The man was intolerable. It would not have surprised me to hear he tortured small animals.

"Why, of course, you don't know! We have a new king! God save King Henry!" Once again he raised his cup and drank thirstily as Caitlin and I exchanged glances.

"God save the king!" His friend finally spoke to repeat the refrain. His voice was heavily accented. Welsh. I was sure he was Welsh. Suddenly, Caitlin blanched white and I thought she would faint, just at the same time as Kathryn began to cry, awoken from her slumber no doubt by George's booming cheer. Although I wanted to comfort Caitlin, I dare not, and so stooped to pick up Kathryn, holding her small, warm body against my chest as she whimpered softly into my neck. Caitlin sank into a nearby chair.

I knew what she was thinking. King Henry. Old, mad, King Henry. Where was Edward? Where was Richard? Kathryn began to cry more steadily, silver tears squeezing from beneath her lids, sensing the charged atmosphere in the room. Or maybe her mother's anguish.

"Sshh! Hush now..." I tried my best to offer comfort, rocking her to and fro and I heard George laugh.

"So! Dickon's whelp is it?" He was still drinking, looking at me with undisguised dislike. "Well, it will be a cold day in hell before you will be seeing him again! Or my dearest older brother - your erstwhile king. Last seen, they were both running east like scared rabbits. Heading for the coast, no doubt, hoping to escape to Burgundy. But we will find them. They are both traitors to the crown now and we all know what happens to traitors."

Caitlin reached out her arms as George's words unfolded, and I stepped forward to pass Kathryn into her care. Her face was a mask of worry, so tight I feared it would crack apart should she be delivered one more blow. Nothing had prepared us for this. Nothing. Suddenly, she found some inner resource of strength and jerked her head up, eyes blazing as hot as a wildfire, fixing on George as if she would scorch him where he stood.

"What happened?"

His every movement was casual and languid as he filled his cup again, pursing his lips in reflection.

"My brother needs to choose his allies more carefully. He thought he could meet us in the field but when John Neville

295

decided to support his brother Warwick, it both turned the tide and paid Edward back for his poor judgement at the same time. Only now, as he cools his heels in whatever God-forsaken bolt-hole he has found, will he regret taking away the Northumberland title from a man who was unerringly loyal. Typical Edward! Take away a dukedom from a tried and tested ally and hand it to a former Lancastrian. It's that sort of mindless behaviour that started this mess in the first place. Henry Percy must be giggling up his gauntlet like a girl! He gets his lands and titles back and the Neville stalwart gets a paltry Marquisate. So – John showed Edward his undoubted mettle and knowing his prowess in the field - they turned and ran! So much for Edward's famed skills in battle! But then with only Dickon, Hastings and that fop Rivers to stand by him, he could hardly hope to win at cards, never mind a fight! I always said he had gone soft. Life with the Woodville bitch has turned him into a coward. This country deserves better!"

I listened to all of this closely, my head lowered as I dare not look at him, not with the full force of my gaze, but his words forced me to choke a response.

"Better? King Henry?"

The dark stranger moved towards me before I even knew he had stirred and the first indication that he had was the myriad of bright silver spots which appeared before my eyes. He had slapped my face with some force, causing me to stagger back against the window embrasure, only just managing to keep my feet. My cheek stung sharply, my eyes now bright with tears of shock.

"Have a care, boy!" he growled, cold, lifeless eyes boring into mine. "King Henry, God save him, is the rightful king and the usurper has fled. Your loose mouth will lead you to a tower cell should you not choose to curb it. You have had one chance and that is all I am prepared to grant you. If I hear anymore filth from your Yorkist loving lips, I will drag you there myself!" He was so close to me I could smell his breath, stale from days on the road. My fingers ached to react but luckily George laughed, which distracted me, just enough to not get myself into further trouble. Not that I much cared at the moment.

"Easy, Jasper. The lad is Warwick's ward and is worth much. He will not take kindly to him being manhandled."

"There will be no Yorkist slurs against his Grace. Warwick's ward or no, it makes no difference to me." The man called Jasper looked at me, then at Caitlin, eyes which held no humanity in them at all, only a hard purpose. "Who is this woman?"

George was refilling his cup again – no doubt making up for his days on the road. Either that or the wines of France were not to his taste, like their affinity in politics.

"Lady Caitlin Desmond. The Earl of Desmond's natural daughter."

"Desmond?" The stranger almost spat the name out as if it tasted foul. Something which only served to enrage Caitlin, pulling her out of her silence. She settled Kathryn down and glared at him. A small flame of pride began to burn deep in my gut. If George thought Caitlin was some timid, retiring lady of the court, I think he was about to have his supposition disabused.

"You have the advantage sir? You know who I am now, may I ask your name?" Their glances clashed like drawn swords.

His answering tone was flat, like his gaze.

"Jasper Tudor. Half-brother to our most gracious King Henry."

Good God! My heart began to beat rapidly. Talk about a Lancastrian rising! This, surely, was not what Warwick had in mind when he set himself up against Edward? To reintroduce the whole line of descent of John of Gaunt back onto the throne, bastard and by-blows all?

"Tudor!" The word was out before I knew it.

"I warned you, boy!" Tudor spoke to me but was looking at Caitlin, and she rose slowly, adjusting her grip on her daughter as she did. I could only imagine what she was thinking, but she showed enormous bravery and confidence whereas I was trying to stop my knees from knocking together in uncertainty.

"What do you want here? You can see the duchess is not at home! Why do you not go on your way and leave us in peace? We pose no threat to you, surely?"

"The child?"

Jasper ignored her, directing his question to Clarence as if she had either not spoken or was not even there. George was also now looking at Caitlin, and if I was not mistaken, his expression was carefully arranged.

"Gloucester's bastard." George answered him curtly and the two of them continued to talk as if we were no longer there. I tried to catch Caitlin's eyes but her attention was fixed on Tudor, as if she didn't trust herself to look away from him for fear of what he may do.

"We cannot have the bastard of a traitorous exile running free in the city. Arrangements must be made to secure the girl somewhere safe."

George laughed and sauntered over to Tudor at these words, touching him on the shoulder like an old friend. Now Caitlin did look at me, and I sank down onto the cushions of the window seat, now just beginning to understand that we were living in a changed world. Without Edward to curb his brother's impetuous actions, and knowing his previous interest in Caitlin's lineage, a dull bell began to toll somewhere inside my head. George had been Lieutenant of Ireland before turning against Edward. He had friends there. Friends who used to serve his father.

Caitlin seemed to be thinking the same, or something even more dreadful. Her eyes were filmed with tears as George continued to chuckle with his new found friend.

"Jasper, Jasper, fear not.   The child is but a babe and no threat to us. Warwick will be within the city in a few days and Henry will be king for all to see! Were I you, I would give more concern to Queen Margaret's return, for she will surely not tarry in returning to rule this realm now that my brother has scurried away into the night. I will take care of our young charges here, you need not worry yourself over them, there is much else for you to do."

I swear just then that Tudor almost squared up to George, drawing himself up to his full height.

"Then, the woman must be presented to court. Her child can remain here in the care of her nurse… and your mother, should she deign to return. For all we know she could be plotting with your brothers and Burgundy as we speak."

Queen Margaret. My blood began to run cold. In all of the thoughts that had coursed though my mind these past few minutes, I had forgotten about the queen. Warwick's nemesis. Some would say, the cause of our current situation. I asked the question which rose in my mind for if anything was sure to bring murderous rage down on George's head, it was if he should dare to try and harm Edward's queen. Surely, he knew that? Surely he had understood how the board had changed once Anne had been betrothed to the Lancastrian princeling?

"Where is Queen Elizabeth? And her children?"

My question caused both of them to look at me as one. George was still smiling. I didn't think he would ever stop.

"The Woodville woman has taken sanctuary in Westminster Abbey. She can stay there until she rots as far as I am concerned, although I think Queen Margaret may feel differently. She will brook no other rival once she is back on English soil. Her fate has been sealed." It was Tudor who answered me. I rose to my feet again, feeling I may need to be poised for a fight.

"The Abbey is a sanctuary, my lord." I replied carefully. "To break sanctuary is to affront God himself."

Thunder rumbled overhead once more. What foul treachery this storm had blown in without a care. Jasper bowed his head before looking up from beneath lowered brows.

"She is a woman. She has children with her and they have certain needs. Sanctuary is not a fit place for them to be housed for long and I will repeat myself, as you appear to have an affliction that affects your hearing. Queen Margaret will not brook two queens to stay on English soil. If the Woodville whore is lucky, she may get to join her husband in exile. If not…" He straightened up suddenly, as if he remembered something. "There are debts to be paid. It remains to be seen what coin will suffice."

He paused then, as if the memory had pricked him in some way.

"I must go back to Westminster. Secure this boy until Warwick returns, then he must bend the knee to King Henry or suffer the consequences. I will recommend the girl to Lady Margaret; she can serve at court as fitting of her noble blood. Everyone in this palace must swear their allegiance to King Henry, down to the lowest cur feeding the stable dogs. See to it!"

Turning on his heel, he was gone, leaving only the silence in the room and a crusting of dried mud upon the tiles to mark his presence. It was not lost on any of us that he had just been barking orders at George as if he was the lowest servant, duty-bound to his carry out his whims.

George turned his back on both of us and went to the sideboard to fill his cup again. His thirst was as relentless as his arrogance it seemed. I walked down the two steps from the window and went to stand beside Caitlin who was now shaking visibly. Kathryn looked up at me with eyes full of innocence and smiled. A smile I returned, although it was hard to form. That one look gave me the courage to speak again.

"King Henry? Forgive me, Your Grace, but are you really going to pledge your affinity to the man responsible for the death of your father and brother?" No answer was immediately forthcoming, and I believed we were due one so I pressed on. "Your Grace?" I heard Caitlin whisper a warning just as George turned to face us. The smile had gone.

"No."

"No?" I could have laughed had I not been so taken by surprise.

His whole manner now seemed much changed, his mind visibly working as he spoke, walking across the chamber to stand by the hearth. A kernel of suspicion began to form in my gut.

"I should say, I will. But it will mean nothing. And so will you, but again, it will mean nothing. You will both do exactly what I tell you to do - for the time being. If you think either of my brothers will be content to idle long in the Low Countries, then you have seriously misjudged them. They will return. We will do what we can to aid that return, whilst we bow and scrape to the feeble Lancastrian puppet king."

Kathryn had nestled her head back into the haven of her mother's neck and Caitlin stepped up to place the girl onto the cushioned safety of the window embrasure, where she rolled over and closed her eyes. Brushing her hands down the front of her skirts, she then straightened up.

"So...you don't support the Lancastrian rebellion?" She asked tentatively.

George pursed his lips, smiling ruefully.

"Do I surprise you Lady Desmond?"

"Frankly, yes, Your Grace."

It was my turn to smile then as I watched George react in his usual ebullient manner. Throwing his hand in the air.

"I surprise myself! I am my brother's heir but I am also a realist. How long do you think it will be before they turn their attentions to that fact? Yes, they see me as their ally, presently, but I know some of this is only to be taken at face value. The danger lies not once Henry is back on the throne, but once his Queen arrives in London and resumes her place at his side. That is where the real power lies."

"And the Earl of Warwick?" It hadn't occurred to me to think where I may fit into all of this treachery and scheming. It was clear from what George had said that the earl was due to return. And then what?

"Warwick has cemented his position in the marriage of Anne to the Prince of Wales. In doing so, he disinherits me, which was not our agreement. He has of course promised me much in return, but it is as much as I could have gained anyway from

Edward. So, where is the profit for me? What was it all for?"

Caitlin seated herself once more and sat back in her chair, shaking her head at him as if he was a recalcitrant child. Which, one could say, was near to the truth.

"What *was* it all for? They are your brothers! One of them is your king!"

George leaned forwards almost threateningly, but she did not shrink, it was me who placed my hand on the dagger at my belt. I was not sure I could go so far as to attack the brother of the king, but I would defend Caitlin with my life. His voice was rasping with anger as he replied to her.

"A king who married a common, grasping witch with a family that attached themselves to him like some demonic succubi! Lancastrian to boot! What did our father fight for? What? All we wanted was for Edward to expunge the Woodvilles - annul his marriage, admit his misjudgment. After all, it was a clandestine ceremony, the Pope would have consented, and if not, well... we know dispensations can be bought. But no. Here we are! The result of his unbridled lust is a mad, incompetent king back on the throne and the woman who placed our father's head on a spike above York ready to sail back any day. You think I am content with that? You do not know me, girl, not at all!"

Lightening lit up the room which had been steadily darkening since the arrival of the storm. A crack of thunder followed, immediately above us, almost opening up the roof above our heads.

"No, Your Grace, I do not know you," Caitlin answered calmly, "other than what I have seen with my own eyes and what I have been told of you." She halted whilst he registered her words with a grudging amusement. "You do not seem a man who will be content to have their ambitions dashed, which is surely the only result of a Lancastrian king. You are Yorkist royalty, how long before that begins to chafe like a burr under a saddle. Both to them and to you. You make this sound as if it is your choice to turn against them, but I am not so sure. Then there is your mother..."

As if summoned by the mere power of speech, the door to the chamber opened as a further roll of thunder rumbled away down the river. The duchess, dry as a bone despite the torrential rain which was now weeping out of the heavens, swept into the chamber with her eyes fixed on the face of her errant son as she answered a question that had not been asked of her.

"Yes, my dear, there is. I am not about to let him forget that for one second.

"Well?"

I was trying to look anywhere other than at the glowering countenance opposite me but the force of his gaze had a physical effect. I could almost feel his fingers gripping my chin, turning my face in his direction, subjecting me to the fury that burned behind his eyes.

Exile had not changed him. Humiliation at the hands of his king piled up with the ordeal of having to swallow his pride and kneel to the Lancastrian queen, made no mark on him – at least not outwardly. To be fair, his strategy had now succeeded, and he sat before me as if it had only been a matter of time, which he had bided, and won. I wondered if he ever even considered that the price he had paid may have been far too high.

This was the first time I had been in the earl's presence since before the failure of the northern rebellion. Notwithstanding that the whole affair had been a disaster, as far as he was concerned, I should have been at Fitzhugh's side and I was not. As soon as George had pitched up in the solar a few days ago, I knew I was in deep trouble. I had chosen to cleave to the king. Well, to his younger brother, which was very much the same thing. Once again I cursed my luck. In sending me south to look to Caitlin and his daughter, I had forfeited the chance to be by his side in exile.

And no matter how uncomfortable that exile may be, my preference, at this moment, would be to experience that discomfort rather than the skin-stripping glare of the Earl of Warwick. I knew his ire would be fierce, but temporary, unless it was his intention to have King Henry declare me a traitor and take my head. This was one occasion where my age may save me, but even then, I would still rather have had the uncertainty of exile, than suffer the stain of serving at a Lancastrian court.

I swallowed nervously, trying to wet my throat enough to reply.

"I humbly beg your pardon, my lord."

"You do?" His brows met in the middle of his forehead in a worrying knot, making his stare more hawk-like. I felt like he was about to swoop down and pick me up in powerful claws before shaking me to pieces. I swallowed again, my voice breaking.

"Yes, my lord."

"What for?" He sat back in his chair, settling down the better to enjoy my humiliation. For a moment I was puzzled, until the completely expectant expression on his face gave it away. He wanted my total submission. All I could do was grit my teeth and get on with it. I was in a completely new world. A subject of a Lancastrian king. My father would have been proud.

I gripped my fingers tightly together behind my back until my knuckles sang.

"For absconding from Ravensworth Castle. For desertion of my duties to Lord Fitzhugh and by default, to yourself."

The room fell silent as he surveyed me coldly. I couldn't look at my feet anymore, so I returned his gaze steadfastly.

"And?"

He must have registered my complete surprise at this further interrogation as his lips began to curve ominously.

"I... I don't understand, my lord." My throat was closing up by the second. I began to suspect that he was setting me up as a traitor. It was only the thought of what would happen to my lands which was no doubt preventing him from turning me over to Henry. Or was it? If he was all powerful in this court, he could surely secure the transfer of my inheritance to him in perpetuity. Or was he not as sure of his puppet king as he made out to be? He broke my train of thoughts by clearing his throat loudly.

"Stealing horses? Plotting with the usurper March to suborn men in my service? Plotting to deceive me, your lord and master?" Beads of sweat broke out on my upper lip. Stealing horses I could understand. He was not about to listen to my tales about Dick Fitzhugh that was for certain, and anyway, I did not want to implicate him in this affair if I could help it. But plotting? With March?

"March?" The surprise in my voice must have been obvious. Warwick leaned forwards, his elbows now resting on the table. For some reason I couldn't stop myself looking at his hands. Thick powerful wrists, dark hairs powdering the back of his hand, heavy gold rings on three of his fingers, one of them bearing his seal. A standing bear. At this moment he looked just as threatening as that animal.

"Edward Plantagenet, you fool! Did you not collude with him to remove a servant of my household who should, some months ago, have been secreted behind the walls of a nunnery? Albeit you were assisted by one of those Irish renegades, who I have yet to get my hands on!" He snorted in derision and once again threw himself back against his chair. "Damn idiots! They always were soft for York!"

I breathed deeply, exhaling with studied care. So we were going as far back as that then? I wanted to remind him that being soft for York was the very reason he had the benefit of the Irishmen in the first place, but managed to keep my jaw firmly clamped together. That was until it became obvious he was waiting for a response.

"I believed I was serving my king, my lord."

The sneer was immediate.

"Which just so happened to mean you were also serving Gloucester." The curl in his lip grew hard. "How you have both disappointed me! I thought I had trained you better!"

From somewhere deep within me a simmering anger began to boil. If anyone had a right to be disappointed, it was Edward, for his betrayal. Richard, for his falseness. How did he dare to claim such feelings for himself? Even though I knew it was happening, I was powerless to stop it. He may be the most powerful noble in the land but he was a hypocrite and a traitor.

"Were it not for the House of York, my lord, you would not be where you are now. Is treason the coin in which to repay their trust? How bitter do you think their disappointment tastes now?"

"You have a sharp tongue Lovell, but a dull mind."

His rejoinder was quick, but my anger was now too hot to let him have the last word. I knew it was stupid, knew I was sealing my own fate, but still I could not stop myself.

"Truth, like virtue, can often be seen as simple, but that does not make it less powerful."

In the silence that followed, as my own heart pounded painfully in my ears, he lowered his eyes, lips pursing thoughtfully. There was no knowing what he was thinking, even had I been able to see into his soul.

"The truth is," he began after a while, his words pitched evenly, as if he were discussing the weather, "Jasper Tudor wants your head on the city walls. I believe you showed him much the same disrespect you are displaying this morning." I felt my gut tighten but the sheer mention of George's dour friend was enough to stoke the fire of my fury even more.

"I did not disrespect him. I do not know him."

"You disgraced yourself, and by association, me. You showed disrespect to King Henry."

I couldn't resist a swift smile myself, seeing as he was still examining his fingers.

"At that point, I did not even know if he was telling the truth. Clarence is an inveterate liar. I had only his word to go on and I had no reason to believe he was not mischief making. At that point, I did not recognise a King Henry. Edward was still my king."

He did look up then, his eyes made of granite.

"And is he still your king?" I was just about to reply, when he waved a hand before me airily, before pushing himself to his feet. "Don't be a fool! At the minute I have the means to save your hide, but if you utter one more word, you will tear that opportunity from my hands."

I had no idea what he was talking about, but I could not help the flood of relief which surged through my limbs. I had been gambling on the fact that Warwick prized me for my value to him if nothing else, and the fact that I was his niece's husband. I had not, however, considered Jasper Tudor. Warwick walked around the table towards me, adjusting his belt as he approached.

"Fortunately for you, my aunt, the Duchess of York, has petitioned on your behalf." I looked down quickly as a conversation I had recently been witness to rose in my mind. It was abundantly clear that both the duchess, and George, were in no way reconciled to a return to Lancastrian rule. Warwick seemed to have forgotten that it was not by chance that Edward had made for the Low Countries. He had blood there. His sister now sat at the Burgundian court, a marriage brokered by Edward himself in order to form a beneficial alliance. His family were no strangers there, and certainly not the unwelcome interlopers that Warwick and Clarence would have seemed in France. I could still hear the duchess in my mind, her words assuredly confident as rain drummed insistently on the windows, clamouring to be allowed in, like a returning resident.

"We play their game. We wait. If asked, we bend the knee. We give our cousins of Lancaster no cause to doubt us."

Warwick came to a halt before me and it came almost as a surprise to me as to him that I now reached his shoulder.

"She says you have been of great service to her over the past few months. In particular, in respect of her grandchild." I rose my gaze to his, feeling braver of a sudden, confident I had hidden my 'traitorous' intent. "Despite the fact that it is Gloucester's bastard she is referring to, Henry was most touched by her plea. Assisted, you may wish to know, by my own personal bond that you will conduct yourself as fitting as my ward from this moment on." He paused, his eyes searching my face as I stood before him, dumbstruck. "To which end, once you have been received by the king, you will visit your wife, who it appears you seem to have been at some pains avoid. Upon returning to court, you will attend me as a groom of my chamber, where I can keep a close eye on you."

14. WESTMINSTER HALL
October 1470

It was only a few days later we stood in the lofty confines of Westminster Hall, waiting to be received by our new sovereign lord.

The place was crammed full of familiar faces, not surprisingly, both Stanley brothers waited in grim silence, as the rest of the assembled throng milled and rippled around them like a toxic swamp. Yes, the gowns were fine, the furs resplendent and the jewels plentiful and bright, but there was a smell in this revered chamber, this place of kings, which made me want to vomit. There were too many there whom I knew, ready to bend the knee to a new king who had gained his place by treachery. I was both curious and sick at heart.

Curious to see the old man who had secured my father's loyalty and then sat back as his wife orchestrated the destruction of Richard's family. To see if he was as truly frail, and pious, as I had heard men say. To see why a king would let his wife have so much power that she had sway over the lives of those nobles whose only desire had been to take their rightful place within these halls. I turned away from the raised dais and its empty, waiting seats.

Caitlin was staring up at the roof and looking wonderfully resplendent in what I believed was a new gown. It was the colour of spring leaves, a young, bright green and figured with a tawny thread which gave the appearance that strands of her hair had been stitched into the fabric itself. I tried to catch her eye, but when she looked down again, she glanced at the duchess who stood by her side, before looking back at the dais herself, her attention now, as with everyone in the hall, caught by the sudden sound of herald's trumpets, barreling around the hall like more thunder as Warwick led in our new king, King Henry. He may as well have brought him in on a leash.

Warwick had dressed grandly, unfortunately for him, as his king appeared to hold no such store in this area. He wore Edward's crown, which had never looked so out of place before, nestling as it did on a bony head, swathed in almost unkempt, peppercorn hair. His clothes were too big for him, which made him look less of a man. I wondered idly if, had his queen been here, she would have allowed him to appear before his subjects looking so ineffective. As Jasper Tudor followed them into the chamber, his own robe a dull sable, the thought crossed my mind that Warwick had chosen his own attire carefully. There was only one man before us who looked like royalty, and it wasn't the king.

As the whispering murmur in the chamber dispersed, Henry sat and Warwick motioned to the front of the room, obviously anxious for the audience to begin. Of course, it had to be his protégé, George, who stepped up first, ready to kneel on the cold stone before the man who now replaced his brother. At that moment I was so relieved that I knew the truth, as imparted to Caitlin and myself during that stormy afternoon some days ago. We knew that he had been educated on the errors of his ways and that despite everything, he was only playing a game. It was only as he knelt before the king, his dark golden hair glinting in the candlelight, that it occurred to me that it was all he ever did. Life, it seemed, was all a game to George.

"Your Grace, may I present George Plantagenet, Duke of Clarence!"

Warwick's voice rang out as George prostrated himself and I thought I head more whispers rustling behind me. I wanted to turn my head but couldn't, yet I already knew that those voices either doubted George's allegiance or disliked it. There were many here who would only be bending the knee in fear of their lives, and others who made a career of it.

"Plantagenet?" The king's voice was as weak as his appearance, and he frowned, seemingly confused that he was being presented to a member of his own family who he didn't know. Or just confused generally. "I knew your father. A good man, although somewhat misguided. It is good to see you here at court."

I raised my brows at that. So, he did know, at least for the moment.

"Yes, Your Grace." George answered smoothly, although no one could see his expression, I knew he was smiling and my fingers itched again. Almost every time I saw George I had the urge to rearrange his features.

"The duke was instrumental in ensuring his brother, the usurper, fled into exile, Your Grace."

I suppressed a grin as Warwick frowned, trying to keep Henry's focus on the matter in hand as his royal charge began to smile inanely at anyone and everyone in sight. To all the world he looked like a simpleton and the murmurs began to swell, almost drowning his next words.

"Yes, yes, very good. May God bless you for your endeavours on behalf of my realm." Thus dismissed, George, his face carved in stone, backed away, leaving room for the next person to be presented, who just happened to be one of the Stanley brothers. In a mercifully short time I had paid my own obeisance but by then time Henry had taken to staring at the ceiling buttresses himself, mimicking Caitlin's earlier amazement. I backed away, finding myself standing next to her and whose delicious fragrance assailed me as I turned to greet her, but her face was set in stone, a hand raised in warning.

I followed her gaze to see a morose, stringy woman I knew to be Lady Stafford bowing before the king. She had a boy with her, I guessed him to be somewhere around my own age. I knew she was a woman with strong Lancastrian affinities, having been married to one of the Tudor family at a very young age. I couldn't remember the full story, but it had resonated with me in the fact that she had given birth to a son when she was only thirteen. A very young bride. My throat tightened uncomfortably as I looked at her a little more closely. Despite her slender build, she had a

312

strong, authoritative voice.

"Your Grace, may I present my son, your nephew, Henry Tudor."

Violets overwhelmed me as Caitlin leaned closer. I felt her lips brush against my ear.

"Who's he?"

"I have no idea. But that woman is Margaret, Lady Stafford. She's a Beaufort - Lancastrian through and through."

I so wanted to turn and look at Caitlin, knowing how close her face would be to mine if I did. Instead, I kept my head fixed firmly forwards. Richard may be in exile, but Caitlin was still his love and I had to remember that. Henry however now actually appeared to be intrigued for the first time that day and actually leaned forwards, a smile creasing his lips.

"God bless you my son. My heart warms to see you here. You are the true successor of this realm, the boy who will one day calm these troubled times. Welcome, welcome..."

I choked back a laugh. Successor of the realm! I heard George's hushed hiss and for once I had to agree with him heartily.

"God's blood! The man's raving!"

Caitlin still stood by my side and Duchess Cecily joined our small group, all of us watching the events on the dais with studied interest. Cecily placed long white fingers on her son's arm.

"Hush, George. He is short of more wits than he possesses, he has always been so. It is thus that he allowed the realm to descend into a stew of dissent and corruption."

Halting only temporarily, she stepped forwards as Warwick stepped down from his lofty position to make way for them and as he did, Cecily took the opportunity she had been waiting for and moved in to attract his attention. His brows were so tightly knotted he had given himself the hooded gaze of a hawk and he joined Cecily, who inclined her head gracefully, although I did not hear what words they exchanged. What ever it was, was enough to draw his attention to me and the gimlet gaze fixed on me and

313

he gestured for me to join them.

I cursed under my breath, not only for this but for the fact that George, never one to miss a trick, moved forwards with me, even though he had not been invited to do so. We stood in a small, familial group, apart from the fact that I was not related to any of them. Only by service.

"You shouldn't be surprised," Warwick was saying to his aunt. "He's been incarcerated with hardly a servant to speak to for some time now. Once Margaret arrives, with their son, things will change."

Cecily tapped her fingers against her girdle, almost as if calculating.

"And when does she leave France?"

"Soon."

George tried to suppress a snort of derision but didn't quite manage it.

"She had better hurry. It seems he is ready to anoint another Lancastrian pup as his heir to hear him today!"

Warwick glanced back at the king, who was now surrounded by a small group of people, including Lady Stafford and the boy.

"He's a nobody. The Beauforts like to take on grandiose airs."

"Quite forgetting they are bastard stock. As always. Nothing changes." There was an edge to Cecily's voice which I had not heard before. "Take care, nephew. You know the Beauforts are poison. If not for them..." she sighed then, and her hand rose to curl around the crucifix at her breast. "No matter. Much water has passed. But all the same, I will retire to Berkhamstead now that we have bent the knee. Life suits me better there. I find it easier to wear my years."

Warwick was shaking his head, his mouth forming a hard line.

"I would rather you remained here. The king must be assured of your loyalty, aunt." His head gave a polite incline which his eyes betrayed and I saw Cecily stiffen.

"Does the king command my presence here? Or do you?" The air between them was so cold I expected to hear it snap.

"It is the same thing."

"I have just given him my pledge; did you not see? My son has also turned against his own brother. Is that not proof enough that I am not his enemy?"

"Your blood is his enemy. He may not be too cognisant of it, but be assured the queen is."

"The queen who murdered my father and brother." George weighed in now and with his words I regretted my earlier judgement. I watched Warwick carefully as yet another one of his novices began to rail against him. "In fact, who murdered your father too. We both know she is not as biddable as her husband." George looked over Warwick's shoulder. "And now there is another Lancastrian cause. You would do well to be cautious, you have a snake by the tail. It may be docile at times, but it still has fangs."

George extended his hand on these words, and his mother took his arm, allowing herself to be led off across the hall. I stood awkwardly, watching Warwick fume inwardly as I waited. For a few moments I thought he had forgotten I was there, until his eyes snapped back into focus.

"I have a task for you."

"Yes, my lord." Contrite. I already had a suit of his red livery waiting to be worn. I disliked the colour red intensely.

"Make it your business to know the Tudor boy. Befriend him. You are after all very good at making friends."

I took the sarcasm and bowed my head.

"And my trip to Minster Lovell? To see my wife?"

Warwick chewed his lip furiously.

"This is more important. Your wife can wait."

With that he turned away and I stepped back, turning to face the sea of faces. Yet the one I longed most to see had gone.

315

15. WESTMINSTER PALACE
October 1470

So I had been given my task. Or tasks to be exact.

It began almost immediately as I began to serve Warwick once again in exactly the same manner I had served Fitzhugh. I was to be seen and not heard and it soon became apparent that even though I was hearing a lot – I might as well have been invisible. Those who knew of my affinity to the House of York had either forgotten about it, believed that I had turned my coat as they had or were so arrogant they felt that Edward would happily settle down in the Low Countries forever and leave them to ravage his kingdom.

It was almost laughable – particularly from those who knew Edward well. And something I knew. If Edward did return, he would spare no quarter. Especially not with his cousins, something George had done well to recognise in short order.

In the meantime, a Parliament was being organised for November where Edward was to be attainted. I assumed this would be the same for Richard as I went about my duties with my eyes lowered and my ears attuned to every word. George was to be rewarded with his father's title, the Duchy of York and Warwick was beginning to press for the queen to make an appearance in England.

Tensions were beginning to make themselves felt between the diehard Lancastrians and their new Yorkist companions. Some, like William Stanley, seemed to distance themselves from Warwick, and as I already knew, George was lost to him. I could only imagine that he felt his position would be solidified once the young Prince, with his Neville wife, arrived in England. Surely, no one would disrespect the father of a future queen? I wondered, at times like that, if Warwick remembered exactly what hand fate had dealt to Queen Elizabeth's father, Baron Rivers, who he himself had executed only last year.

I saw little of Caitlin, immured as she was at Baynard's Castle. I had a fleeting glimpse only as I was sent to bring George through to Westminster one day. She had been with the duchess and the duke in the solar and although I knew she had been pleased to see me, I could see her brilliant gaze held a thousand troubles. Of little Kathryn, I saw nothing. Our days of music and laughter in the sun had faded away. Now, as winter approached, the grey overcast sky heralded only more gloom. And when I wasn't thinking about Kathryn, or Caitlin, I wondered what Richard was doing, if Rob was with him and what had become of Brackenbury.

As for Henry Tudor, I had no idea how to accomplish what Warwick bid of me. He was nephew to the king, and seemed always to be in the company of his uncle Jasper or his mother. I racked my brain to think of what we may have in common to share an interest and could think of nothing. Nothing that I could see at least. But I thought I needed to make a start.

The opportunity came when I was collecting some letters from the Constable's lodging which needed to go to the earl. As I crossed the bailey, I glimpsed Henry out of the corner of my eye, making for the tiltyard. My immediate thought was that he was going to practice, but his attire did not seem to indicate that he was about to don a breastplate and begin swinging a sword. He was dressed a little too formally, which seemed to be his habit.

I followed him anyway knowing that I could always use him as an excuse should the earl accuse me of being tardy. I could hear the unmistakable sounds of a practice yard in full swing as I drew nearer, over-laid by the hoarse commands of the Master of Henchmen bellowing out across the yard.

Henry stopped by a small pavilion which had been set up at the entrance to the yard, its bright blue and yellow silk looking incongruous in the grey of the day. There were a group of squires, about half a dozen, engaged in swordplay, their movements ebbing and flowing like a tide with each thrust and parry. One of

317

them suddenly burst forwards, circling his sword above his head in an arc which reminded me of a move Richard used with particular accuracy and my heart saddened.

It was somewhat ironic that Henry turned his eyes to me as I felt a pang of loss for the friends who were no longer with me. I swallowed nervously as he looked at me, wordless, and formed a smile.

"Are you going to practice?"

He flicked his grey eyes back towards the squires, and back again.

"No. Not today." He swiveled his head back away from me. It was hard for me to work out his mood, other than he was surveying the ongoing conflict somewhat pensively. It occurred to me then that even if the court was Lancastrian, he was a stranger here.

"I will give you some sport, if you wish. I am sure my lord of Warwick will be only too happy to give me leave."

He folded thin arms across his chest and looked back at me. It wasn't a friendly look, nor was it dismissive. It was almost expressionless.

"I... I have an injury. I took a fall from my horse and twisted my knee this last week past. The surgeon advised care."

"Oh, bad luck." I couldn't think of anything else to say. He hadn't been limping so there was no way of telling but I had no cause to doubt him. "Maybe another day, once it has healed." I turned away from his unsettling gaze and watched the squires. "My name's Francis. Francis Lovell."

"I know." My head turned back at this. He was still looking at me. "You are Warwick's ward. Yet your family were for Lancaster. You must be thankful of recent events."

His words took me by surprise and I felt my face flush a little.

"I have not suffered at the hands of York. I have been treated well under my lord's care." My answer was as careful as I could make it whilst he watched me and pursed his lips.

"My mother tells me you have great wealth. Or will have

once you are of age. Our house is wealthy; she understands these things. She tells me I should seek out those whose friendships could be advantageous in future years." Those words took me aback.

"I didn't know your mother knew of me, much less my family." He had turned his attention back to the squires, but I saw his lips curve.

"My mother makes it her business to know as much as she can about those who may be ..." I had begun to wonder if this Henry had any emotions at all. But as I waited his smile grew. "Biddable."

I felt as if a cold bucket of water had been thrown over me. Biddable? A stir of anger began in my gut. What the hell had I ever done that marked me as the instrument of other men? Especially to a woman I hardly knew? But he was still talking even as my fingers gripped the stiff pile of parchment in my hands. "Wealth and influence makes you powerful, but vulnerable at the same time."

"Very few men can stand upright for long on shifting sands," I replied cautiously, sensing some inner veneer of suspicion in the thin young frame standing next to me. He bowed his head for a moment before turning to look at me once more, his gaze flicking down to the letters held in my hand.

"As my Lord of Worcester so recently found out."

He saw my brows draw together. John Tiptoft was a favourite of the queen, Edward's queen that was. He had a particularly bloody reputation, and had executed more than a score of Lancastrians, using cruel and unusual methods far beyond the traditions of the day. I remembered the talk amongst the henchmen at Middleham. Some of them took much pleasure in relating the gorier descriptions to me with glinting eyes. I truly thought they believed I knew every Lancastrian lord personally.

Aside from that, his reputation preceded him in other ways and my gut twisted as I remembered. Tiptoft had been Lord Deputy of Ireland. He had been Edward's Lord Deputy and had

319

presided over the execution of Caitlin's father.

"Is he attainted?" I knew my naivety shone from my eyes as soon as the words left my lips. He was one of Elizabeth's creatures. I knew his fate before Henry confirmed it.

"Dead. Executed at the Tower. He'll be impaling no more men of Lancaster that's for sure." He gave me a grim smile of satisfaction, in acknowledgement I thought of what he considered to be a job well done. "I like to hunt. We should go hunting one day."

With those words he turned on his heel and walked back towards the inner ward as I stood wondering how many men of York Warwick would now dispose of in revenge.

16. WESTMINSTER PALACE
November 1470

I began to wonder exactly how our fledgling relationship was to flourish with the announcement that Henry was soon to leave court, with both his mother and uncle. It was obviously a move Warwick had not anticipated. I mused if that in itself was becoming a pattern.

They were heading back for Pembroke, it seemed, content now that the country was back under Lancastrian rule and that surely the queen would grace our lands before too long. Yet to be fair, with the weather now well and truly turned, I don't think anyone expected to see her before Candlemas. Our proposed hunting trip never did see the light of day, although we were both more than cordial when we passed each other as we moved around the court.

Now, as some form of recognition of their departure, a feast was being held and I stood in the door way watching the various members of King Henry's elite sweep into the chamber. My jaw tensed as I saw them, the men I had been told were my enemies, that is, up until Warwick changed his mind.

Oxford, his brother Thomas, Sir John Langstrother, the Stanleys, Lichfield, Keeper of the Privy Seal, Tunstall, Henry's chamberlain. Montagu, considering his recent turn about, was nowhere to be seen, and neither was Northumberland. No doubt the two of them were keeping weather eyes on each other from opposite sides of the northern march. Waiting to see who moved first.

As my eyes swept the table, joy drenched the disappointment as I saw Caitlin, just seating her self next to George. And the space next to her was currently empty. I needed no further prompting and I kept my eyes fixed upon her upturned face as I pushed my way through the crowd, giving a polite nod to William Stanley on the way. My feet hurried as I feared some well-fleshed, sweating lord might plonk himself down next to her and it was with some great relief that I clambered over the bench and claimed that right for my own.

"Cat got your tongue?" She had not uttered a word since she entered the hall. I knew because I watched her. She was dressed in sky blue silk, trimmed with cream lace around the neckline. Her skin shimmered fit to rival the fabric of her gown and the glorious abundance of her hair added a glow to the room, one which her eyes immediately outmatched. As I settled down, her hand immediately covered mine on the damask and I looked down at her slim fingers resting over mine. My heart lurched. Would this feeling never go away?

"I am so glad to see you!" Her fingers squeezed mine gently but I had no time to reply as a harsh sound buzzed across the table like an annoying insect.

"Sshh!" Margaret Stafford and Henry were just sitting down themselves as a cacophony of sound announced the arrival of the king, causing us all to rise hastily to our feet. I didn't look at Henry, I looked only at Caitlin and unfortunately George saw just that, and I caught him grinning out of the corner of my eye. A herald's voice could be heard clearly, ringing out across the room.

"All rise for Henry, King of England, Ireland and France."

George Neville, Archbishop of York had now given his esteemed sanction to the occasion, although I had to admit it seemed to me he looked decidedly uncomfortable. For some reason I cared not to look at anyone on that high table, where better men had once taken their repast. The minstrels struck up in the gallery and a succession of servants traipsed into the hall to begin presenting dishes to the high table. Wine began to flow and conversation thrummed in the air as loud as lute strings.

Plates of spiced heron were eventually placed before us and I watched Caitlin eye hers with disinterest. It occurred to me only then that I had hardly ever seen her eat a full meal. She picked at her food as if being polite to her host and she looked desperately unhappy, which I could not bear.

"What do you think?" I whispered, attacking my own bread trencher with some enthusiasm as I was quite hungry myself. I gestured discreetly towards Henry Tudor as she flashed me an enquiring gaze, only to be met by a shrug of disinterest. That made me smile inwardly. Not that for a moment I thought she would have the slightest interest in Tudor. But I was pleased all the same.

"Not much," she replied quietly, from behind her cup. Her reaction just made me grin.

"Well, he's not worth much muster in the tiltyard, that I can tell you. And as for the butts, well, he had much difficulty working out exactly how to knock his arrow. Needless to say, if that is the standard of Lancastrian training, we don't have much to fear from this Prince Edward."

One thing I had made time to do was to watch Henry practice in the yard. He seemed to find difficulty with most things, not exactly showing a burgeoning soldierly character. My one regret, knowing he was leaving soon, was that I had not had the opportunity to face him myself.

She looked up at the high table then, examining the father of the unknown and unseen prince.

"I wonder what he will be like?" I had an answer for that, from the mouth of the Tudor boy himself. Henry had been speaking to one of his friends, and no one was averse to spreading gossip, no matter where it emerged from.

"Apparently fancies himself as a bit of a warrior. I hear he was supervising executions at the age of seven."

"The same age Richard was at Ludlow. God save us!"

Richard's name caused her fair face to fold inwards and I knew what she was thinking. I leaned towards her, as close as I could get without being overfamiliar. As close as I could get without getting dizzy at the scent of violets.

"He will be fine over in the Low Countries, I promise you." It was then my own words hit home just as hard. "I just wish I was over there with them."

One slim hand rose and began to play with the coral bead at her throat. I knew it well. Richard had given her the gift on the birth of their daughter and I had never since seen her without it adorning her neck. Now she touched it like a talisman, as if by doing so she could keep him safe.

"I pray so. I pray so much these days my knees are raw! I just hope it is enough!"

 "Prayer is never wasted where the cause is just."

At the same time we both turned our attention to Margaret Stafford who had overheard our quietly spoken words. How, I have no idea. The woman must have had the hearing of a bat. Caitlin answered swiftly, obviously rattled for some reason.

"Madam?" That one word was delivered with such disdain that I tried to kick Caitlin's ankle under the table in warning. I made contact but it made no impact on her at all. For some reason, she disliked the woman intensely, even though, as far as I knew, she hardly knew her. Margaret took the inquiry without flinching and sat back regarding Caitlin carefully.

"Prayer can cleanse the soul. I am very pleased to hear, Lady Desmond, that you attend to your devotions. Only through the Lord can you gain your salvation."

Henry and I exchanged a swift glance before he looked back at his mother as Caitlin picked up a piece of fruit and took a bite out of the flesh.

 "Indeed Madam and I am truly touched by your concern. I am, of course, thankful for the benevolence shown to me by the Duchess of York, who has schooled me well in this respect. As you are no doubt aware, there is no more pious a woman at court than she so I fear not for my salvation under her instruction."

Unfortunately, I had just taken a huge gulp of wine and almost choked right there and then. Tears sprang to my eyes making the candle flames dance as I struggled to prevent the wine making a reappearance, which I did by just taking on more and forcing it down. Either the sudden ramp in tension or the sound of my choking attracted George and he turned towards Caitlin as Margaret replied to her with frost limning every word.

"I am aware of the duchess's piety. She carries out many godly works within the City. You are indeed fortunate to have been in her care. I am sure when circumstances necessitate your departure, you will leave much improved for it and able to choose a more virtuous path."

George leaned back then, wiping his lips with an affected flourish before placing his napkin down beside his plate with a nod of acknowledgement across the board.

"Her reputation is only matched by your own Lady Stafford. My lady mother often speaks of it."

Margaret accepted this intervention gracefully and began to eat once more as Caitlin pushed her own dish away. The exchange had peaked Henry's interest and he inclined his head towards Caitlin, as if seeing her for the first time. With some relief I noticed that he never even seemed to be aware of her beauty. His look held not one vestige of interest or admiration, I was pleased to note.

"You do not eat, my lady. Is the food not to your taste?"

"I have no appetite this evening, sire," Caitlin answered politely but without raising her head. "The duchess returned from her almsgiving with a chill and I fear I may also be afflicted by the same."

"That is a shame. Do you not feel well enough to enjoy the dancing? There should be much merriment once the tables are cleared away." I was just registering some shock that he may actually intend asking her to dance later in the evening when his mother put paid to any thoughts that he may be about to pay court to Caitlin, no matter his bland expression.

"Hush, Henry," she almost hissed. "You know how the king disapproves of too much frivolity." Henry caught my eye only briefly before looking back down at his plate, and I had to feel sorry for him. Margaret Stafford came across as a controlling, shrewish, type of woman. I gave silent thanks that my own mother, although being guilty of no more than a measure of disinterest, had never seen fit to admonish me so publicly.

As everyone returned to concentrate on the food before me, I engaged Caitlin in conversation, hoping to lighten her mood. I spent some time pointing out the different nobles who now formed part of Henry's court as I knew very few of them would be familiar to her, and her eyes followed mine from each velvet clad, furred shoulder to the other. For a while, I thought she had stopped listening but then she sat back and sighed, and I knew she had been listening all too well.

"Francis, if you could be anywhere else right now, where would it be?" I smiled as I dipped my bread in a dish of plum sauce, happy to be a part of her distraction from the depressing sights around us.

"Well, that is easy!" I said, taking a mouthful of the moist morsel and chewing reflectively. "Because I am truly fortunate in that respect. Middleham was at first a fortress, but became my home once Richard became my friend. But my actual home, Minster Lovell, rivals it in beauty to be truthful. It is a heavenly place, Caitlin, set in gently weeping trees by a winding river where kingfishers play and silver fish swim. I would love you to see it sometime."

She looked at me then and I felt blessed that I was seated as my knees went weak.

"So, Minster Lovell would be your answer then?"

I took a sip of ale, well aware that what I was about to say may sound fanciful, but I knew she would understand. That, and the fact that sitting next to her in conversation was making me lightheaded, without the aid of any wine.

"No, not exactly. For all its tender, green beauty, Middleham has a stark wildness which rivals Minster Lovell in its own way. The hall is soft, sun-washed and warm, whereas Middleham is cool, dark and brooding, like an old friend who you know very well and are always pleased to meet. So, I think I can best answer your question by telling you that both have a place in my heart. And as my heart has to beat twice every time, I can truly say that they both have a home there."

My prose was rewarded with a dazzling smile, which lit her eyes like stained glass in the sun.

"Why Francis Lovell! You should surely be a poet. Now I see why you love such tales as Tristan! You have a romantic soul!"

Grinning, I did my best to perform an obeisance to her kind remarks over the board and she laughed, a truly musical sound to my ears, but it did not last long. Her eyes began to travel the room once more.

"Where is John Neville? I thought he turned his back on King Edward? Why is he not here?"

"He is in the north." I answered, looking up at Warwick on the high table. "With Henry Percy. Don't ask me who is keeping watch on who as I doubt even they know themselves. You would think someone would have learned by now. Nevilles and Percys don't mix - never have. And that was before John was robbed of his earldom." Even before I had finished speaking, her face had become troubled, and she too was looking at the high table, only directly at the king.

"So all these Yorkist lords were forgiven their allegiance to Edward?"

"All bar one."

I had not even known George was listening, so to hear him speak was a surprise which made me turn my head. There was only one execution I knew of and my eyes dared him to make an issue of it here, knowing what havoc he would wreak.

"Who?" Caitlin frowned as she looked at George, unwittingly giving him the opportunity he had no doubt been waiting for. George smiled. An oily smile, as he picked up his wine cup and tilted it towards me.

"Lovell? Do you wish to enlighten Lady Desmond?" As I continued to glare at him, he rearranged his features into a mask of amazement. "You mean, no one has….?"

327

At that precise moment Margaret called Henry away from the table, but not even that distracted Caitlin. She had scented trouble between George and myself, and she was not about to let it go.

"No one has what?" she asked angrily, her voice lowered as she looked first at me and then George. "What is it? Who are you talking about?"

George resumed eating as if what he was about to say was of no consequence. Which it wasn't, to him at least.

"John Tiptoft. Our erstwhile earl and one-time resident of your own fair country. King Henry did you a great service madam. You should thank him." He nodded his head towards the high table where Warwick was whispering into the king's ear. "Although, to be fair – it was more Warwick's whim than the king's."

I closed my eyes for a moment, but it was no good. I felt a delicate touch on my sleeve and I knew I had to tell her. If I didn't, I could be sure George would.

"Worcester. The Earl of Worcester. He was Constable of England for Edward." I took a swift drink to prevent myself from croaking I felt so nervous. "A favourite of the... of Elizabeth."

For a few moments she seemed lost in thought, her eyes far away and distant. It threw me as I tried to think what she could be thinking, and I lost my advantage. George was waiting and pounced.

'Well, if our young ward will not enlighten you, it looks like the task falls to me. But then, we are almost family, you could say. John Tiptoft, Earl of Worcester - you could call him Elizabeth's avenger, certainly in your case. He would carry out the queen's desires, no matter how distasteful they would be." He paused, drinking noisily. "For instance, the execution of members of Irish nobility." I waited, my heart pounding in my ears. "For instance, one Thomas Fitzgerald, the Earl of Desmond."

For a second, she looked completely non-plussed and cast her gaze around the room. Then, before I could move, she was out of her seat and fleeing from the hall. Several eyes turned in her direction as the meal was in full flood and no-one should leave without permission whilst the king remained seated. But despite this it took me only seconds to follow her out into the passageway, where she stood, one hand braced against the wall, her head bowed, as if she was about to faint.

She must have heard my footsteps for she turned her head, eyes brimming with tears, picked out by the torchlight above her head. Her voice was full of despair, choking with sobs.

"Francis...did you know? I can't..."

"Caitlin, I am so sorry!" It was all I could think of to say. How much I wanted to embrace her, to envelop her in my arms and let her cry until she dispelled her despair. I took a step forward but a voice came from behind me and I froze.

"Lovell?" I didn't answer. I knew it was Jasper Tudor, but still I didn't answer. My eyes remained fixed on Caitlin's distraught face.

"I am speaking to you, Lovell."

"Yes - my lord." I clenched my fists tightly, knowing that I was about to be summarily dismissed and could do nothing about it.

"Get back to the hall this minute! Think yourself lucky that the king was too absorbed with his nephew to notice you depart without being dismissed or seeking his leave. You too madam! Your behaviour is completely reprehensible. I do not know how you behaved at the usurper's court, but now you will comport yourselves as fitting King Henry's household and that means adhering to the social niceties, no matter how much you may despise them."

I turned to face him, trying to keep myself between him and Caitlin, knowing he had as much disdain for her as he had for me.

"Lady Desmond is upset my lord. You must forgive her. The duke..."

He moved forwards quickly, his face thunderous, even in the shadowed hall.

"I have already told you boy, get back to the hall before you are missed. Your ignorance sickens me. I will not tell you again!"

I cast one desperate glance back to Caitlin, who looked about to faint, but I was completely helpless and felt wretched. I strode past Tudor and made my way back to the hall. Trying not to draw any further attention to myself, I returned to my seat, keeping my eyes lowered as I knew Warwick was watching me.

George was refilling his cup as I sat down, pushing my food away and generally glaring at anyone who looked my way.

"George Plantagenet, you are a bastard!" I cursed under my breath. I know he heard me, for he smiled.

17. MINSTER LOVELL
November 1470

I was finally sent off to Minster Lovell and I had to believe it was partly due to what happened at the feast as before that Warwick had been keener for me to exploit the fact that Henry and I were of a similar age. However, with the news of his imminent departure and my recent transgression, I was packed off in such short order that I had no opportunity to find out what had happened to Caitlin in her encounter with Jasper Tudor. I looked for her before I left, but didn't see her, Warwick keeping me busy until it was time for me to leave.

I had been commanded to visit Anna, and much before I was intending to do so in truth. I anticipated that it may be a difficult reunion, and to some extent bittersweet. Yet, in finding myself so charged, was pleased to be reunited with Fides, who had been brought down from the north by Dick Fitzhugh and that in itself took the sting out of the matter. Dick had been as good as his word and Fides looked as fine as he ever had, well groomed and bright-eyed and from the way he searched my hands for treats when we were reunited, was just as pleased to be reunited with me.

Dick was also to accompany me to Oxfordshire, where, as he informed me wryly, his mother had recently taken up residence. So it was with more than a little trepidation that we rode into the walled bailey, but the anxiety I felt melted away at the sight that met my eyes. I had no difficulty in recognising Lark, as she balanced on the hand of a young woman who I knew I had never seen before, as I was sure I would have remembered her. Dressed in dark blue, topped by a fustian riding cloak, she threw her head back and laughed as I watched her, before handing over my bird into the hands of a waiting squire. So caught up with looking at her was I, that it was some time before I noticed Anna, standing by her side, though it was an Anna little changed. Taller, no doubt, and her features now beginning to show some maturing into those of an attractive woman, it was to my shame that I admitted she could not hold a candle to the girl at her side. It was then I heard Dick chuckle.

"Oh Lord! Elizabeth!"

I turned my head away from the picture I had been studying. Reluctantly, I have to say.

"What?"

Dick jerked his head forwards.

"My sister, Elizabeth." He was shaking his head in private amusement. "I warn you, she is incorrigible. Likes nothing better than causing trouble."

As I listened to his words, I realised this was something I had completely forgotten. Elizabeth, Anna and Alice had all been sent south, no doubt because of the rebellious intentions of Fitzhugh. I just had not imagined they would all end up here, in my home, but then I had to remember, Lady Alice was Warwick's sister, and I was his ward, and with Edward fled, he could play fast and loose with my inheritance as it pleased him.

By this time, our arrival was causing some attention and both Anna and Elizabeth turned to watch our approach, whilst I marked the differences in their responses. Anna flushed, rosy red, quickly ushering the squire in the direction of the mews as if she had been caught out committing some misdemeanour. Elizabeth performed a half-turn, her eyes passing over her brother quickly with the contempt of familiarity, before they fastened on me, and stayed there. Her lips were semi-parted, as if she was about to speak, or smile, or both, as she examined me down from the crown of my head to my boots. At least, that was what it felt like. A physical touch, and in response I grew warm, if not a little agitated.

I knew her not at all. Had never seen her before, yet she covered me with a gaze as all consuming as the most voluminous of cloaks. As I stared back, not even aware I was doing so, I heard Dick chuckle again.

"I warned you! Be on your guard!"

I laughed then, if a little uncertainly. She was my wife's sister, yet as unlike her as anyone could be, and I wasn't completely sure if that fact alarmed or excited me, so I covered my confusion by drawing Fides to a halt and slipping from the saddle. Dick did likewise, but no sooner had I dismounted and handed the reins to a waiting stable hand than I heard a voice directly behind me.

"Dick! About time! Where have you been? We were expecting you over a week ago! And who is this? We didn't know you were bringing a friend, and such a dashing one at that!"

Turning slowly, my first reaction was to catch Anna's eye and I smiled cautiously. She was undoubtedly still very pretty, high cheekbones now beginning to make their mark on her formerly round, childish face. Her deep blue gaze was as dark as I remembered it, but she did not smile in return, even though her colour had now returned to normal. Yes, she was older, but still a child. I couldn't help it but my heart sank.

She didn't respond to her sister's enquiry, although Elizabeth now stood before me, her gloves held in her hands, perfect brows raised in anticipation of an answer. Dick sighed heavily.

"Lizzie, this is Francis. Anna's husband."

For a moment no one spoke and I waited for her to flush with an embarrassment of her own. So her reaction was totally unexpected as she burst into a peal of laughter.

"Good Lord!" She turned to her sister and cuffed her shoulder with the leather gloves. "You never said he was so handsome! How could you not tell me, your sister, what a handsome husband you had? For sure, I thought our uncle had married you off to some oaf-faced buffoon, you talk of him so little!"

I saw Anna's throat move as she swallowed and she avoided my gaze.

"Francis and I have not seen each other for some time, Lizzie. Besides which, whatever I may have said of him to you, you would surely find some mischief in it." Having answered her sister adroitly, so I observed, she looked at me once more. "Good day, Francis. It is truly a pleasure to see you again. Mother and Lady Katherine are in the solar. Shall we go up?"

I saw Elizabeth slide a sideward glance to her brother as Anna picked up her skirts and turned towards the hall, and without a further thought I fell into step at her side.

We walked in silence – and not a little discomfort – until we reached the bottom of the stairs when Anna turned to look up at me, her face open and innocent but her expression uncertain.

"I am pleased to see you again. I thought you had forgotten us both."

"Both?"

"Lark. And myself. You wrote for a while, but then you stopped."

I began to squirm under her constant scrutiny. It was true. It was almost as if giving her Lark had absolved my guilt and once I was assured my bird was safe, there seemed no other reason to keep in touch. All being well, I had considered that a reckoning would be due one day. One day too far in the future for me to contemplate.

Whilst I struggled for an adequate response, she didn't wait and began to mount the stairs leading to the solar. I followed, meekly, feeling more than a little chastised, aware of Dick and Elizabeth's voices behind me as they drew closer.

I caught up with Anna as she crossed the threshold of the sun-filled solar, and I followed her in, immediately halted in my tracks as I saw both Lady Alice and another woman who I did not know, seated either end of the table which occupied the centre of the room. For a few moments I looked around, drinking in the beauty of my home.

My eyes fastened on my favourite spot. The padded window seat nestling within the traceried window which looked out over the winding banks of the river. In the summer, that view was so wondrous that it looked like the window itself was filled with

334

stained glass. I knew how warm and restful that space would be, light pooling over the faded velvet cushions and suddenly I longed to be seated there. Playing my lute, or reading a book, with Caitlin sitting at my feet in the sunlight.

The sound of voices broke into my thoughts as Dick and Elizabeth entered the room, and Anna crossed to take a seat by her mother's side. In the ensuing silence, I realised that all three of them were looking at me, but not Dick, or Elizabeth, who had taken herself off and was now indulging herself in the luxury that my favourite haven afforded.

The light from the window imbued her hair with a halo of gold, making her eyes appear even bluer than I had thought at first. She sat on her hands, smiling at me.

"Francis. This is my sister, Lady Katherine, Baroness Hastings." I had to stop my eyebrows from raising as Lady Alice spoke. William Hastings was currently with Edward and Richard in exile and so I wondered if the Baroness had been placed in Lady Alice's safekeeping. I remembered Richard telling me something very similar had happened to his own mother when the Duke of York had also been forced to flee the anger of the Lancastrian court.

I snapped of my reverie and moved forwards, swiftly, bowing politely to both ladies.

"Lady Alice, my lady. I trust you are both well?"

"I am," answered Lady Alice with a smile. "And I am glad to see that you are, after your rather impromptu departure from Ravensworth." I flushed slightly, Dick not being inclined to defend me as he kept his head down. He had told me that his mother approved of my actions, but it appeared now that she was not about to admit to this lapse of judgement. I felt sure it would have been different if we had met before Edward had to flee for his life. "I must say," she added as I stood in silence, "you have taken the devil's time about coming to visit your family."

Glancing at Lady Katherine, I was slightly reassured to see a much warmer smile upon her lips. Her plucked brows danced momentarily, as if Lady Alice's words amused her. All I could do was inhale deeply.

"My lady, please forgive me. The rebellion…"

"The rebellion you did not take part in." She interrupted me, her eyes sharp as knives. "So that cannot have kept you too busy! Your sisters, especially Frideswide, have been most distressed at your lack of care. As for your wife…"

At this point Lady Katherine reached out a hand across the table, placing her palm down. A pearl the size of a quail's egg shimmered in the light.

"Now, now Alice, I am sure Anna can speak for herself." She tilted her head to one side. "Should she have any complaint."

All eyes then turned to Anna, who looked up with a composed assurance which belied her young age.

"No Mama. Francis and I had an agreement that we would write little. I was to attend to my studies and my husband to his training." It was a bare-faced lie but only she and I knew it. The glance I sent her was full of admiration and gratitude. She may only have been just shy of eleven years old but she had a maturity which was totally unexpected. I had been struggling with the notion that I may have had to admit to the advice I had been given by William Stanley, but I had been offered a reprieve. It was almost gratifying to see Lady Alice shuffle in her seat, no doubt having her plan to admonish me roundly dashed. Yet I should have known better. She had not finished with me. I could tell by the way she set her shoulders and the line of her lips.

"Nevertheless. He had no such arrangement with his family. It seemed to me that your allegiance to the House of York took precedence over blood bonds."

"I was serving my king," I replied swiftly. My anger began to rise again. Was I constantly to be reprimanded for cleaving to the very house that my own family had forced me to serve? Was I now to become a Lancastrian again, my affinities changing like a weather cock?

"Have you bent the knee to King Henry?" I gritted my teeth

before I replied.

"If I had not, do you think I would be here now?"

As soon as the words left my lips I regretted them. Not that what I was saying was false, but that she had so easily been able to rattle me. I waited for the inevitable rebuke, my eyes fixed on her face, but all she did was smile. Slowly.

"Well, at least they have forged you a backbone in the north. To be honest, when I heard you had fled, I feared I still had a milksop for a son-in-law." She looked over at Lady Katherine then, her face a mask of forbearance. "I imagine it is not easy to raise a boy without a man's influence. With a house full of women, how can a boy be expected to aspire to all that he should be? Our brother's tutelage has been a Godsend. I cannot thank him enough."

Lady Katherine nodded her head, although I could see she was surveying my discomfort from beneath lowered lids. Now, I was being treated as if I wasn't even there. It appeared that even the Fitzhugh's were more at home here now as Dick had gone to join Elizabeth in the window seat, where they both sat surveying the scene in silence. Once again, my salvation was to be a complete surprise as I heard Anna speak.

"Not forgetting the king's brother, my lady. Francis wrote that he was his closest companion and that they learned much together."

I didn't actually remember doing any such thing but I must have mentioned something in my earlier letters which she had picked up on. I couldn't for the life of me think what it was, but I thanked her once again with a look, making her blush.

"Well," sighed Lady Alice, standing now, brushing her skirts down briskly, "he's long gone, so you will need to make new affinities. But there will be plenty of time for that. For now, you need to spend time with your wife and reacquaint yourselves. You need to make the most of every day as my lord of Warwick wants you back at court before the festivities begin."

If my heart wasn't already in my boots at the thought of

337

spending time with a child, no matter that she had just saved my skin on more than one occasion, the thought of Christmas as Henry's court flattened it completely. Unless…. I looked down at my feet to shield my guilty thoughts as two smiling green eyes beckoned me back to the city. There was always Caitlin, and this time there was also Kathryn, who would be witnessing her first festive season. Suddenly, the prospect of returning to court didn't seem quite so bad.

18. MINSTER LOVELL
November 1470

The next day dawned bright and clear, the trees and rushes which lined the river were rimed with frost and looked eerie, stretching spectral fingers out towards the water. After breakfast, Lady Alice decided we would all benefit from a walk in the gardens, which somehow Dick managed to avoid completely. It was therefore only myself, accompanied by Anna, with Lady Alice, Baroness Hastings and Elizabeth, following along behind at a measured distance. I had a feeling the whole outing had been arranged in order for me to spend time with Anna, which to be fair had been the main purpose of my visit. It wasn't that I minded that so much, as having an audience, feeling beady, watchful eyes burning holes in my back as we walked along.

Anna was huddled into a dark blue fur-trimmed cloak, her skin rosy with cold. She hardly looked at me, keeping her eyes fixed ahead, and I flexed my fingers inside my gloves anxiously, knowing it would be down to me to elicit conversation.

"Thank you for your kind words yesterday. I don't remember explaining about my friendship with Richard, but it was good of you to intercede for me."

"I mostly got it from Dick," she replied, to my surprise, her breath misting the air. "He wrote to me often from Ravensworth, whilst you were there." She paused, sliding me a cautious glance. "And after you had gone." We walked on a few more steps as she appeared to consider. "Why would you not fight with my father?" Although her voice did not appear to hold any resentment, I felt sure it was there.

"He was raising men against the king, Anna. I did not believe that what he was doing was right." I saw her frown, although she still didn't meet my eyes, looking only ahead.

"But, you are pledged to the earl of Warwick?"

"And Warwick is pledged to the king," I replied tersely, "so there should have been no choice to make."

She hesitated for a second, finally looking at me fully, searching my face with serious intent. My heart sank. The girl was still very much a stranger to me and I could see that she didn't understand how I could disobey her father.

"You wouldn't understand," I tried to say more kindly, but I knew I had failed completely as her face flushed.

"I understand you were my father's servant. That you and another boy took two horses and rode away when he needed you. My father is a good man. He would only have fought against the king if there was a good reason to."

I sighed heavily. All I had succeeded in doing was upsetting her, I could see that plainly writ on her face. There was no way I could explain to her about the queen, about George, she was too young to understand. I barely understood it myself. It was then that my saviour, of a form, intervened.

"Now, what are you two sweethearts whispering about?"

Elizabeth had hurried forwards to join us and once again the contrast between Anna and her older sister became startlingly apparent. Not that Anna was not pretty, it was just that her older sister was a true beauty. Her face was just a shade more heart shaped, her eyes had a delightful tilt to them, and her hair had a darkly golden thread through it that gave her an added warmth which Anna appeared to lack. Plus, she laughed often, whereas Anna was much more serious.

"Oh go away, Lizzie!" Anna scowled, without even looking at her sister, but for all her irritation, Elizabeth merely laughed.

"Oh no, I have been keeping company with Mama and Aunt Katherine for long enough now and listening to them talk about a load of stuffy nobles who I neither know nor have interest in knowing has been punishment enough. And I did it willingly for you to have some time alone with your husband!" She turned smiling eyes upon me then. "Are you not grateful?" Anna refused to look at either of us. I had a feeling she was still smarting from our earlier words.

"Eternally," I replied to Elizabeth cordially. "Although I fear your sister also finds me dull company." This was accompanied by a sharp, dismissive sniff from Anna as she turned away from us, keeping her eyes fixed on the river as if she had never seen it before. Elizabeth was in no measure so shy or difficult. She cocked her head at me, full of mischief, the marten fur of her hood brushing her pale, rose cheek.

"Then my sister is a fool!" Reaching out a gloved hand, she prodded Anna on the shoulder whilst her eyes still harnessed mine. "For shame, Anna, that you should treat your beloved so!" She paused, and her cheek dimpled prettily, causing an unwilling reaction low down in my gut. "And such a handsome beloved at that. You truly do not know how lucky you are!"

With that, Anna turned, her face pale with anger, her lips thin, bloodless. I had never seen anyone so young and tender have eyes as full as rage as hers were at that moment.

"Well, lets see how you feel when you are married off to a stranger! I hope it is one of those old, boring men who Mama was just talking about! See how much you find to smile about then!"

With her small fists gripping her skirts, she ran across the frosty grass, back towards the bailey and through the gate, disappearing from view as Elizabeth and I watched in stunned silence. Elizabeth raised her fair brows, a stunned smile still hovering around her lips, but she had no chance to say anything else as her mother and Lady Katherine drew level with us, both of them looking over in the direction where Anna had fled. Lady Alice frowned at Elizabeth full of disapproval.

"What have you said now? Can I not put you two girls together for more than the blink of an eye than you have to cause her grief?"

Elizabeth grinned and threw me a wink which made me hide a grin behind a gloved hand.

"Oh Mama! Anna is so stuffy! She is being most ungracious

to her husband, after he has travelled all this way to spend time with her." With that, she looped her arm into mine so swiftly that I had no chance to react and stood there stupidly as she sidled up to me. "You can be sure that I would never treat my husband so poorly." She was smiling up at me artlessly, so did not see the look that passed between her mother and her aunt, but I did. It was a look that told me not only that it would not be long before Elizabeth herself had a husband of her own, but that she presently knew nothing of it. I also guessed that when she found out, she was somehow not going to be best pleased.

"A good man may cure your audacity," Lady Alice remarked grimly, pulling the edges of her cloak closer together, striding past us towards the bailey wall. Obviously she too had had enough of our morning walk. Yet if she meant to scold Elizabeth, it was to no avail. The girl merely pulled my arm towards her, causing an unintentional thrill to ripple through my body. She was very close to me, and she was very attractive, warm and pliant, I could almost feel the sinuous curves of her body.

"A good man like Lord Lovell here would suit me right nicely," she simpered, and I thought only half in jest as her eyes danced. "Anna is a very lucky girl, if only she could but see it!"

Katherine Hastings drew closer, pushing her hands further into her cloak to keep them warm. She was regarding us with a fond expression and leant over in a conspiratorial fashion. Her fair face was very close to mine, her breath on my cheek.

"To be lucky in love is the very best that Fortune can afford you. Should you find it even once in your life you are truly blessed!"

With that, she followed Lady Alice and as I watched my blood ran cold. Elizabeth still clung onto my arm as we walked together, but suddenly it was Caitlin who filled my thoughts. My companion was chattering on pleasantly as we crossed the bailey and went indoors ourselves, but I heard not a word and she must have thought me dreadful company, but right then I longed to be back at Westminster. I couldn't explain it, but something deep inside me, some instinct I could not explain, told me I needed to go back, and as soon as I could.

As we entered the solar, Anna was standing by the hearth, holding her hands out to the roaring flames. She looked over at us as Elizabeth swung her cloak from over her shoulders. My own mood had sunk into my boots and I walked over to the window seat, where I all but threw myself down. This was all to no avail. The girl hated me and I – well, I could never envisage us as man and wife. Not now that I truly understood what being joined with a girl meant.

After all, she was ten years old. It would be at least another four years before... I swallowed hard and looked out of the window, at where our feet had crushed the whitened grass. I could never imagine lying with her in the way I had with Marie, the way I wished I could with Caitlin. So lost in thought was I that I didn't feel anyone sit down next to me, until I heard a soft sigh. I turned away from the window into the sparkling, blue eyes of Elizabeth, whose face was now unusually thoughtful. I looked around the chamber. We were alone.

"Anna loves our father very much and took it badly when she heard you had deserted him." In the mere time it had taken to come inside from the riverbank, she seemed to have grown in years. She still smiled, but no longer in a carefree, frivolous way. "You were quite the gallant knight before that, to hear her talk. And she talked about you every day." Her lids lowered as she blushed. "I was quite envious to tell the truth. She treated your falcon as if it was the most precious gift she owned."

Guilt rose up in me like a flood. Should I have had more care for her before I made my plans to escape the north? I hadn't given her a second thought, all my concerns had been for Richard, and for my king. Even now I hated the thought that Henry sat upon the throne, whereas everyone else seemed to accept it as the most natural of events. A cold panic gripped me then. What if he never returned?

"I am the king's ward," I answered lamely, "King Edward that is. His brother is my friend."

Elizabeth reached out and laid her hand over mine. It was warm, soft. For some reason she reminded me of apple-blossom – all light, pink and fair.

"She knows that really, but she is young. In her own way I think she is very fond of you, but she is also very scared. She…"

I held up my hand. I didn't want to talk about it, not with her. The last thing I wanted was marriage advice from my wife's sister!

"It is fine, Elizabeth. It will be fine." I gave her a rueful grin, which must have appeared more relaxed than I was feeling. "Someone told me once that I should stay away from her, until she had grown into womanhood. He thought that may make it easier…" It was my turn to colour now. The last thing I had intended was to talk so, but Elizabeth merely returned my gaze, her face now more serious than I had ever seen it.

"Whoever he was, he was a wise man."

I opened my mouth to answer, to agree, when the door to the chamber swung open and Lady Alice stood framed in the doorway. For a moment, she took in the picture as she no doubt saw it. Both of us, seated close together, Elizabeth's hand over mine, our faces close together. Whatever she thought, her face betrayed no flicker of emotion or suspicion. A parchment was held loosely in her fingers, the red seal swinging like a pendulum on its ribbon.

"Ah, here you are." Her face may have been expressionless but her voice was hard as ice. "A message has arrived from my Lord Warwick. French ambassadors are visiting court and we have all been bid to attend for the festive season."

December 1470

The palace was decked with as much greenery as in years past that I could remember, but to me, there was no colour in the court. Within a day of our arrival, I was dressed once again in Warwick livery, it having been made clear to me that my services were still required by my lord and master. So whilst Anna, Elizabeth and Dick pursued whatever pastimes took their fancy, I would be bound to serve at Warwick's whim from Mass to Compline and beyond.

My most pressing concern was to find Caitlin and assure myself that she was fine, having left her in such a distressed state over two weeks ago. Before I could complete my most desired task, I had first to report to the earl as his letter sent to Minster Lovell instructed. However, when I climbed the stairs to his chamber, I had not expected to find George lounging in a chair by the hearth, and I think he was as surprised to see me as I was him. I couldn't help notice how sullen he looked, which, considering George hid most of his emotions and intent behind the falsest of smiles, was countenance I was not used to seeing. He had an ornately decorated goblet in his hand, the flames picking out each glimmering, individual jewel brightly.

"Lovell. Welcome back to the house of fools!" A surly grin met my frown. "I am awaiting my lord's return. As are you no doubt. Why not have a drink with me to pass the time?"

I shook my head warily. If Warwick walked in here and found me partaking of his best Rhenish, I would no doubt come off the worse because of it. George shrugged indifferently.

"Well, at the very least sit down! You are making me uncomfortable hovering around like you do! And don't worry! You will hear him coming a mile off when he arrives – his entourage makes almost as much noise as a score of heralds."

I knew he was right, I had witnessed the chaos of Warwick's

arrival many times, it was almost royal. I moved over and sat down, gingerly. It was a new experience for George to be anything close to amiable with me, at any time, but I needed to take care. He was not someone who I trusted, and so I sat, patiently, looking around the room. It was one of the grandest rooms in the palace, furnished with the finest oak chairs, thickly woven rugs and a massive tapestry depicting the 'Seige of Jerusalem.' That one made me smile, as I knew it had once been the property of the queen's mother, Jacquetta, and obtained by her under means which were more foul than fair.

He sighed heavily, taking a deep gulp from his cup.

"You've been to Oxfordshire?"

"Yes, Your Grace." My answer made him smile, for some reason.

"You are lucky. You should have stayed there."

"My lord bade us return for the festive season," I answered mildly. His lips twisted in response.

"Festive! I have seen more cheer at a Requiem Mass! There's a festering stew of naked ambition here, and Warwick thinks he can hold a lion by the tail and still keep his hand." I tried not to grin even though his mood was sour. Not that long ago it had been snakes he was warning Warwick about. "His government is a sham and his hold on the king tenuous to say the least. I have heard whispers of at least one wager that has him losing his head within hours of Queen Margaret taking her first step on English soil. Thank God at least the wine is decent, for you can be sure nothing else around here is." I twined my fingers around each other carefully. The Parliament called in November had ceased for the festivities. It gave me both pleasure and unease at the same time that Warwick's grip on authority was not as sure as it had at first appeared. I sunk my teeth into the inside of my cheek, trying to appear thoughtful but in reality it was only to prevent myself saying something I would later regret. His next words caused me to taste my own blood.

"Even your Lady Desmond has fled."

My head shot up. I couldn't help myself, even as I saw his eyes flare with amusement. He knew exactly what my reaction would be. It was the last thing I had expected him to say. The last thing I expected to hear.

"Fled? Fled where?" Instantly I had vision of a remote, high-walled abbey, of Warwick finally getting what he wanted. Or worse, for me. Ireland.

"She is in sanctuary, with the queen. Playing nursemaid to our new Prince of York, although I am sure Elizabeth may well have been totally enraged by the choice of nursemaid appointed for her." I stared at him in disbelief, although unsure if it was the news about Caitlin or the revelation that Edward now had a son. No wonder George was so downcast. Whichever way he turned now, his future did not look as bright as he had hoped for. I heard him chuckle softly before he took another drink. It did not surprise me that he was now about to soothe the sores of his own disappointment by digging his claws into me. "You can thank my mother for that particular masterstroke!"

He continued to pin me with his gaze, watching my face closely, knowing I was squirming under his scrutiny.

"A grim place to spend one's own confinement, don't you think?" My expression must have given me away as his smile broadened. "Oh of course, you would have known about that! How silly of me! You know everything about her, don't you? Maybe even more than my brother, I think." My fingers gripped tighter around themselves, once more the urge to punch him made my muscles throb. His star was surely fading both in York and Lancastrian circles, but I still doubted I would have got away with it so I gripped harder.

"I don't know what makes you think that," I answered as casually as I could, hoping I was getting away with it. "I have spent a lot of time with her, that is true. Mostly at either Countess Warwick's wish, or your brothers." I had suspected he knew my secret, the way he was looking at me now confirmed it. "You forget I am in service, Your Grace. I do as I am bid."

George smiled lazily, cocking his head to on side, obviously enjoying himself immensely. All thought of the machinations of the last few weeks that had seen his own ambitions thwarted seemed to have vanished for the moment. Like a cat playing with a mouse, he was deriving a perverse distraction from his troubles by prodding me in my weakest spot.

"And you serve the House of York with particular enthusiasm, I have to say. Particularly remarkable since you were born into the household of steadfast Lancastrians! Mind you, as it was our own Yorkist adherents who did for her father, perhaps the winsome lass feels safer in the arms of a scion of Lancaster." He laughed roundly then, as my face grew puce with anger, I could feel every blood vessel dilating. "Oh, come now Lovell! Can't you take a jest in good spirit? You are fond of the girl, just admit it and move on, there is no harm done, well, at least not to Lady Desmond. Poor Jane Cooke, however, she is quite another matter!"

So, that was it! Suddenly, it all fell into place. The sly glances in Middleham, loaded with an unspoken knowledge. Jane had been Anne's companion, but she had also been Caitlin's – particularly during the months leading up to Kathryn's birth. Or at least, until she was spirited away from the north. Yet, I had not heard of her for some time, in fact I couldn't remember when I had last seen her.

"I don't understand," I mumbled, even though I suspected I did, after Rob's cryptic warning about her. George was chomping at the bit to enlighten me.

"She is one of Isabel's ladies-in-waiting now, didn't you know? She has been with us since we came over from France and was quite heartbroken for a time. It appears you never gave her a second glance, so busy were you tending to the wants and needs of my brother's mistress. At one time, she even believed you may have cuckolded him, but I assured her that dogs very rarely bite the hand that feeds them." He stood up then, unfolding himself from the chair, and stretching out his arms. "She is quite over her heartbreak now, in case you were wondering."

It all made sense then. The sullen silences, the moody glances. Her apparent reticence to engage with Caitlin, almost serving her with bad grace. So, that was what was behind it all, and that was how George and Isabel had discovered my secret. I cleared my throat, hoping I looked more confident than I felt.

"You forget, Your Grace, I am a married man."

He was shaking his head even as the words left my lips.

"A married man with a painfully young bride. A married man with a mistress, so don't play the innocent. It doesn't suit you." We were so engrossed in each others game that we didn't hear the door open.

"Or you, George." Despite George's warnings about the chaos accompanying Warwick wherever he went, somehow neither of us had heard him arrive.

I pushed myself to my feet as quickly as I could, my cheeks flaring at being caught in such a compromising position. To someone walking in the room, George and I looked like conspirators, plotting cosily by the fireside. A king's brother, and a king's ward, both of us bound by an older loyalty than the badge we currently wore.

Warwick stood before the door, the familiar knot in his brow somehow even deeper. He was another who was not wearing the ravages of power easily. His hair was greyer around the temples, the grooves either side of his mouth deeper, more pronounced. George merely took another drink from his cup and sat back in his chair, completely unruffled as my heart pounded fit to shake the walls.

"Isabel told me you were ailing. I expected you to be at my side to receive Louis' envoys." He took two steps further into the room and didn't even look at me, his hawk like stare fixed on his son-in-law's languid form. "I see all you suffer from is a surfeit of wine! I should have guessed as much!"

If I had thought the air thick with tension before, now it was so dense I could hardly breathe. George licked his lips noisily before draining his cup, in express defiance.

"I already know the terms they have come to discuss. I heard them in France. Did I really need to hear them again?" His hazel eyes rolled to take in Warwick's towering form, lit from within with a simmering anger. "You have been handed a poisoned chalice, cousin. Even if you can take most of the realm with you, the city will be a different matter."

Warwick gave a grunt before he stomped over to the sideboard where he poured himself a goblet of wine. It was only then that it occurred to me that it was my role to be his cupbearer and I stepped forward hesitantly, but he waved a gloved hand at me dismissively.

"Oh, don't bother yourself, Lovell. I can see you have no doubt been distracted by the duke's tales of woe." He threw his head back, swallowing deeply from the cup, and I watched his throat move as I also swallowed, nervously. Draining the cup in one, he put it back down, his face thunderous. "Swallow down your pride, George. I have promised you much and will do all I can to deliver it."

George's face tightened, all vestige of his earlier pleasure vanished like morning mist, but his eyes still glowed like camp torches in the dark.

"Yet, a paltry substitute for the kingdom itself. You bartered my royal lineage for your own place in history. With me on the throne, your daughter would still have been queen, but no, your old alliances were too powerful to deny. What else has Louis promised you, cousin? For I feel sure there is more to your devil's bargain than you are prepared to reveal."

I saw his knuckles whiten around the stem of his cup. For a moment I thought he was going to throw it at the wall in anger. It would not have been the first time.

"You are raving George! You should partake less of Malmsey and more of meat! Securing the future can only be of benefit to both of us! After all that has happened, you know I tried my best to give you the crown. If you want to wrap the blame for my failure around anyone's shoulders, it should be your brothers, not mine!"

George almost snarled a reply, which seemed most unlike him, usually he was able to cloak his emotions with a mask of pleasantry, or indifference. Not anymore it would seem.

"And I suppose your own brother Montague had nothing to do with it? He refused to back our rebellion, and then picked up his ragged staff when it was far, far too late, for me at least! Can you still trust him, up there in Pontefract? Can you still believe he will fight your cause again should Edward decide to return to England?"

351

"With what?" Warwick snorted with derision, his face dark with anger, his voice barreling around the walls. I flinched at the sound. However revealing this power-play was, I truly wished I could escape. All this did was fuel my anxiety, for if Warwick's allies were now his enemies, what of those who were already determined to see his wings clipped? To relish the sound as his body hit the ground and send in their dogs to finish him off. "His companion in lechery, that peacock Rivers and your grass green brother?"

"And a Burgundian army as soon as you declare war on Charles. For that is what Louis really wants is it not? He cares not one whit who is on the throne of England. You could crown one of the Tower apes for all he cares, as long as his old enemy is vanquished. So, never mind *his* army, my lord. Where will you get yours from?"

Warwick's shoulders sagged in resignation and he leaned back against the sideboard, with all the appearance of a vanquished foe. I didn't know the details of what alliance Louis had made with Warwick, there had been little opportunity for me to find out anything before I was packed off to Oxfordshire. But everyone knew France and Burgundy were mortal enemies. So that had been the king of France's price, then. War on Burgundy. The destruction of Charles, the duke. The duke who just happened to be married to Edward's sister, and who was currently sustaining Edward's small, loyal band at his own expense. No wonder Warwick was looking a lot older than his years.

"You have men," Warwick answered simply, his eyes on his boots. "You can raise the South west."

George stood up then, pulling down his doublet and adjusting his belt with fastidious care.

"I can." He said nothing else but looked at me, barely suppressing a grin. Whatever this battle of words was really about, he knew already he was going to win.

The earl raised his eyes, the eyes of a man who has seen too much and knows it.

"What do you want, George?"

George raised his hand and studied his nails as if the question was of no import. Warwick didn't take his eyes off him, waiting. Seconds later, George cleared his throat, lifting his chin in a gesture of assured arrogance.

"Only what was mine. It is only fair it should be restored." He flicked a glance at me. "It may be that it assists you in more ways than you realise." Somehow there was a hidden meaning there, but I couldn't think what it was. These were two influential and dangerous men, pulling on the rope of power equally tightly, but in opposite directions. "Ireland."

Warwick's lips twisted in a tight grin.

"Is that all?"

"For now." With that, George brushed his hands against each other as if his business here was done to his satisfaction. I knew what he wanted. Restoration of his old title, Lieutenant of Ireland. As his father had been before him. Edward had granted it to him once, and had taken it away just as easily. Fear gnawed in my gut as it came to me what he could be thinking. Warwick didn't know that not only was there a prince of England in sanctuary, but soon there would be the offspring of another attainted Prince of York. It had long been Warwick's intention to confine Caitlin to an abbey. Now, an abbey in Ireland, at George's hand, became a certain possibility, if he got his way.

Although he had stood in Baynard's Castle and told me to my face that he was playing their game until Edward returned, the doubts swilled around in my mind and would not wash away. He was slippery, deceptive and false. Who knew what he really wanted, apart from what was best for him? And who knew if Edward would ever return. For a few silent seconds, I prayed that Warwick would raise his army, would become the puppet commander of the French king. For nothing was more certain to ensure Duke Charles support for Edward's cause. But for now, there was only these two men, bargaining for their piece of power.

"Very well, it is yours."

George smiled winningly then and turned on his heel, his good mood completely restored. His former discontent vanished like rainclouds in summer.

"Then, cousin, I will wish you good day and go hence to give the good tidings to my wife."

With that he left the room, with an exaggerated swagger that shouted of victory. I watched him, feeling almost sorry for Isabel. The man was insufferable. Either that, or a lot cleverer than I thought him to be. It was more than a few moments before Warwick seemed to remember I was there, lost in his thoughts as he was. I gave a discreet cough.

"My lord, can I be of any service?"

He ran a hand through his hair distractedly. Outside it was growing dark. He looked immeasurably tired.

"You can," he sighed heavily, "but not tonight. Attend me tomorrow morning, after breakfast. I have work for you."

I knew well he had other body servants, ones whom he probably much preferred to me, knowing my true affinity, so I nodded my head sharply, trying to mask my relief, but I only made it as far as the door.

"How did you find your wife, Francis?"

I stopped, turning back. He had moved to the fireplace and was looking down at the flames. He looked beyond weary. Disappointment sat heavy on his face.

"Well, if still a little young, my lord," I answered swiftly. He smiled then, the first genuine expression I had seen on his face since he came in the chamber.

"You will never forgive me for that, will you?" He lowered himself carefully into the seat George had occupied, holding his hands out to the flames. "It is a good match."

"She doesn't like me, my lord." It was honest. He had to give me that, and he turned towards me.

"Give it time. As you say, she is still young. Once she has bloomed and her petals are ready to pluck, things will change." I severely doubted that but kept my counsel. Yet, he seemed in such a reflective mood that I dared to venture something I had long wanted to know. It was now or never as I saw it.

"My lord, may I ask you something?"

He sat back in his chair with a resigned air.

"As long as you don't want to be Captain of Calais, that post is already filled, and I don't think you would suit an ecclesiastical position," his eyes narrowed, knowingly. "At least from what I hear."

My cheeks flushed. So much for thinking I had been discreet! But I had gone too far now, and what I had to ask of him he could give freely, at no cost. I wanted nothing from him. At present, there was nothing he could give me, as long as Caitlin stayed safe in sanctuary.

"Well?"

"My lord, was there..?" Brave as I had felt, I began to falter, but I had to know. "Was there ever a plan to marry me to your daughter, Anne?"

I knew in the seconds before he pulled closed the shutters on his face that it was true. The surprise that I even had this knowledge had been mixed with an expression which gave him away.

"Briefly," he lied. "Dismissed as quickly as it was raised." There was a stilted pause as he considered his next words. "Who told you?"

"I was told that Anne herself knew of it, my lord." His eyes clouded then, and he looked down. "And now she has a Prince of England."

I could swear he looked uncomfortable, almost regretful, but by then his face had turned towards the flames again.

"That will be all, Lovell. Attend me on the morrow."

As I left the room, I almost felt sympathy for him. He looked lonely, isolated and unhappy, far from the powerful noble who strode the halls of Edward's court, parting everyone in his wake. There was one thing I could see for certain, there was little joy in being the friend of a king.

21. ST MARTIN IN THE FIELDS, LONDON
December 1470

The next morning, I found myself outside St Martin's, halfway between Westminster Palace and Ludgate, tapping my foot impatiently as a leather-skinned cleric scanned the letter of introduction which Warwick had handed me earlier, after breakfast. He was small, with sparse, grey hair barely covering his skull, and he whispered under his breath, his unintelligible words slithering like silk skirts against stone.

He read the letter twice, either that or his reading skills were sorely lacking, and after once more checking the red wax seal, he turned and went inside, leaving space for me to follow.

I closed the heavy, iron bound door behind me and stood in the south aisle, a few feet away from the font, as the hunched figure of the surly priest disappeared from view into the chancel. It was quite dark, the inside lit only by several candle sconces, giving a feeling of walled-in oppressiveness. When I had been given my task this morning, although it took me by surprise, it did not take me long to find an advantage in it, if there was to be one.

Warwick had bid me hand deliver a letter of amnesty to the Bishop of Bath and Wells, Robert Stillington. He was one of the former Yorkist supporters who had taken sanctuary in local churches, and I wondered if there was any significance in this particular mercy. I had heard, as the fish wives had it, that Stillington was a particular friend of George, but I could not be sure how many favours the duke was calling in as his compensation for losing the throne to a Lancastrian princeling. The one thing Warwick did know was that the clerics could be malleable, to such an effect that he had filled the council with them. He obviously felt this was a better option than his wary

Yorkist friends, or his equally suspicious Lancastrian ones.

The sound of slippered feet growing closer lifted me from my musings and I looked up to see a different cleric approaching. From his attire, I knew this had to be the Bishop. His was a portly figure, his dark hair showing early signs of silver scattered around his head, giving him a silver halo. His voluminous Alb was snowy white, and his waist was encircled by a golden cincture, which appeared to be made out of silk. As he came closer, his eyes fastened on me, showing no sign of recognition or concern over my scarlet livery, but no sign of fear either. Obviously, he felt safe, here in the arms of the church. He didn't say anything, just halted before me with his hands folded, his hooded eyes benign. I bowed my head reverently.

"Your Grace. My name is Francis Lovell. I bring word from Earl Warwick, Lieutenant of the Realm." I held out the letter in my hand, but he didn't take it. I looked up, to find him regarding me steadily.

"What would the king's Lieutenant want of me?" His voice was deep and rich, well suited to the lectern. I didn't answer, just held the letter out steadily. Eventually, he took it from my hand and cracked the seal, which echoed like a sob around the walls. I stood with my hands behind my back as he scanned the contents quickly before folding it in two and looking back at me impassively.

"Lovell? Of Oxfordshire? The king's ward?"

I nodded, shocked that he would know of me, before recalling that he had until very recently been Edward's Lord Chancellor.

"My lord of Warwick's ward, at the king's command."

"And not too happy about it, it would seem."

He appeared to be smothering a grin, making his face soften. I didn't seem to be doing very well in hiding my feelings of late. I needed more practice it would seem.

"I was more than content until two months ago. I serve at the pleasure of the king."

This seemed to amuse him and the grin broke into a questioning smile.

"Ah, but which king?"

I looked around the nave quickly to make sure we were still alone. It was a strange thing about churches, you felt that no matter what you said, someone heard. If not God himself, one of his servants.

"The true king, Your Grace."

He nodded sagely, his eyes lowered.

"Being a king is a transient state."

"As is being his ward, presently." The last thing I had anticipated was to be sharing the musings of fortune with a man of the church, but for some reason, I quite warmed to him. "Will you come out of sanctuary?" We both looked at the letter in his hand at the same time and he ran a thumb carefully along the crease, as if expecting it to be sharp. He arched a brow, inclining his head.

"You have been at court. Do you think I should? Is it safe for those who enacted King Edward's will to have unfettered access around Westminster?"

I grinned at him, pleased to at last have found someone with a sense of humour, even if he was closeted in this dark place.

"Well, on that I am probably not the best judge. However, Richard Woodville has also been pardoned, although no doubt the earl thinks he may be able to coerce the queen and her newly born son out of the abbey. After all, two queens in England..."

I stopped babbling as his expression darkened. The vision of anyone facing up to Elizabeth's white hot fury melted away as his face crumpled, his eyes looking away, as if seeking something in the shadows.

"A son? The queen has had a son?"

I shivered, right down to my boots. The air, and his manner, suddenly turning decidedly cool. I had been pleased that he had been so amenable. After all, I had a favour to ask of him, but now I seemed to have overstepped the mark. Although I was unsure

exactly how. Surely it was glad tidings that Edward had a son?
For once that news reached him, nothing would keep him from
taking back his throne. Yet, did he even know? For certain,
Bishop Stillington was only a mile or so away from Westminster
and it had come as a shock to him.

"Yes." My voice was unsteady as I answered. "All Souls Day,
last passed."

The Bishop seemed to lose himself in thought, taking a pace
or two away from me, turning his back on me. He fixed his eyes
on the altar for a while, if I had not known better I would have
thought he was saying a silent prayer. I waited, the minutes drew
on. The shadows seemed to gather.

"Your Grace?"

He turned then, his face re-arranged to hide his innermost
thoughts.

"Forgive me. Thanks be to our blessed Lady for his safe
deliverance." I frowned as he crossed himself, as his benediction
was performed more by rote than with any sincerity, but I copied
him nevertheless. "Could I ask something of you?" I bit the inside
of my lip. I had imagined my saying that to him. "Would you
convey a reply to this letter?"

I nodded. What he could have to say to Warwick I couldn't
imagine, but that was none of my business. Besides, a favour
begged a favour, so I waited once more as he disappeared back
into the chancel. The silence was eerie, and I took a few moments
to kneel by the altar rail myself and pray for the safety of my
friends across the sea. And for others I loved who may be absent
from me.

I rose as the Bishop reappeared, a new parchment clutched
in his hand, yet suddenly, he stopped by the altar rail and became
hesitant.

"Can I trust you I wonder?" It was my chance, and
shamelessly I took it. The things that love can make you do!

"You can if you would also return the favour that I am about
to grant you. I swear on my life."

360

His lips thinned visibly, but I could tell he was not angered. His eyes crinkled at the corners, giving him away.

"What is it you need from a penniless man in sanctuary? Absolution?"

I shook my head. I knew he was teasing me.

"Do you know Abbot Milling? At Westminster?"

He nodded sagely, his brow creasing.

"I do. Very well." My throat began to close, and I swallowed with difficulty. Why did I always find it hard to ask for things for myself?

"Would you recommend me to him?" His eyebrows raised. "There is someone I wish to visit in sanctuary there."

The Bishop chuckled softly, looking down at the letter in his hand.

"Do you wish to deliver more good tidings there? To the royal guests?"

"No. To a close friend who has also been forced to take shelter there." His eyes met mine as he heard the sincerity in my voice. "The queen is no friend of hers, and I would like to assure myself of her comfort." I could never be sure which word it was but something I had said caused his expression to soften.

"Ah," he sighed. "I see." He appeared to ponder for a while, and then held out his hand, the letter face upwards, the words unclear in the guttering light.

"Come back tomorrow. I will ensure Brother Browne admits you. Deliver this safely and I will happily petition on your behalf."

I took the letter from his hand, and he waited no longer, walking around the rail, where he bowed before the altar, falling to his knees.

I left him to his prayers, and walked out into the chilled air, which felt warmer than it had inside for some reason. I looked down at the parchment in my hand, at the words which I could now read all too clearly.

I had a letter to deliver into the hands of George, Duke of Clarence.

22. WESTMINSTER PALACE
December 1470

It seemed to be my destiny that whenever I thought I had made progress, fate stepped in to push me from my intended path. Pleased with the bargain I had struck with the Bishop, I returned to Westminster to seek out George and had to admit to the novelty of actually looking forward to seeing him for once. Quite how I was to arrange a return visit to St Martin's the following morning, I had not yet worked out, but in my current state of anticipation, I was not above asking George himself to help me achieve my aim.

As it was, the first person I collided with as I pushed into the crowded hall was Dick Fitzhugh. He was garbed in a coat of rather fine, claret coloured velvet, which made me very conscious of my despised Warwick livery. He smiled broadly, clapping me on the shoulder with gusto.

"Francis! Where have you been? I thought we would catch you around here somewhere. Anna asks me every day if I have seen you."

That I did not believe, for it would have been a huge turnaround in her view of me, but I let it go unchallenged.

"Sorry, Dick, but unlike you I am not free to spend my day at leisure, dicing or lounging with the ladies of the court." I looked around the noisy throng, almost everyone vying for time with Warwick or one of the officers of the realm. It was a mass of seething anticipation. "Have you seen the Duke of Clarence anywhere?"

Dick was nodding as we pushed our way past two well-fed merchants, their faces puffed with indignation, one of them muttering unrepeatable curses about French varlets.

"He's just ridden out." My heart sank but I kept my expression hidden from him as we emerged into the cool quiet of a side passage, the growing crowd ebbing and flowing like a river.

"Where?"

Dick cocked an inquisitive brow.

"Who knows?" He looked over his shoulder at the gathering which was growing noisier by the minute. "Warwick knows, no doubt. Mama seems to think that there is very little he can do with Clarence now, aside from lock him up if he wants to be sure of where he goes and what he does. No one trusts him, they feel he pays lip service to the new king only for what it can profit him. And only for as long as it continues to do so."

I could feel the stiffness of the parchment inside my shirt where I had enveloped it to be safe. It had not really occurred to me what Stillington, who found it necessary to flee into sanctuary, would have to say to his former king's brother. I had been far too concerned with what he could do for me. I began to consider if this had anything to do with Edward's return, although I didn't know how. But then, I didn't know much.

"I had better go," I replied, avoiding his eyes. "I have been gone far too long as it is."

Dick shrugged, and not for the first time I envied him his carefree life.

"I'll see you at supper? I believe we are to be graced by the French envoys." He grinned, his eyes merry. "No wonder Clarence has scarpered!"

He turned away and soon disappeared in the crowd. Unconsciously, I checked that the letter was still safe next to my skin before making for the stairs which would lead me to Warwick's privy apartments. Upstairs, the atmosphere was a lot calmer than it was in the chamber below and as I turned the corner I came across Will, one of my fellow body servants, carrying a large flagon of Vernage.

"Is that for his lordship?"

Will nodded, his flaxen hair falling over his eyes, which sat in an unusually flushed face.

"He's in a particularly foul mood. He's been barking at me since Lauds. Christ knows what has him in such a temper. Where

363

have you been anyway? We could at least have shared the scorn he had no problems heaping on my shoulders." He was pouting, like a sulky child, his bottom lip dark pink and moist. I held out my hand for the flagon, which he passed over with a look of relief and grudging thanks.

"He sent me on an errand, but it took longer than expected. I'll take this in. Is he alone?"

"No, he is with my Lord of Oxford."

That knowledge did little to lighten my mood, as the day was just going from bad to worse. John De-Vere was a staunch Lancastrian, serving in the armies which had fought long and hard for King Henry against Richard's father. Once Edward was on the throne, the earl was allowed to succeed his own father, who had been executed by the Earl of Worcester. It was therefore no surprise that Worcester had met his end not so very long ago. However, he had also supported Warwick in the rebellions last year and had fled to France afterwards to sit at the feet of the exiled Queen Margaret, where Warwick had no doubt joined forces with him.

He was a formidable figure, tall and steely eyed. Being exactly the same age as Edward and only just slighter in build, I could only imagine what the outcome would be if they were to face each other across a battlefield. From what I had heard of Oxford, he had as much of a feel for combat as Edward, with the added driving force that he had lost both a father and brother at Yorkist hands. Exactly the same fuel which drove Edward forward with a burning ambition for the English throne. They were certainly well matched.

Will pulled at the latch and swung the door open for me to enter as I balanced the heavy flagon in both hands.

"....far too generous." It was Oxford who was speaking as I entered, walking over to the sideboard without a glance either way as the door closed behind me. The conversation continued as I poured the wine into two waiting cups.

"It is a small price to pay, John. And at least somewhere the

364

man holds a modicum of respect."

This was followed by a grunt.

"Which is more than can be said for anywhere in England."

It was the usual fate of the servant to be seen, and not heard, providing a silent service and remaining available to either anticipate or fulfil the whim of your lord and master. I delivered one brimming cup into Oxford's hand and he never even looked at me, his concentration still on the man who sat opposite.

It was Warwick who flicked an uninterested glance my way, as I retreated to deliver his own cup before standing in the shadows, my back to the wall.

"If it keeps him onside, it is a small price to pay. The place is full of tribal loyalties and separated from us by a sea. As soon as the queen arrives, we can pack him off there out of the way."

I couldn't see Oxford's expression, but the distaste in his voice was for more than the wine.

"Ireland is a hotbed of Yorkist affinity, not least the Fitzgeralds. They've blood in the game, after all. How they never seemed to blame York for what happened to Desmond still eludes me. Even that was blamed on the vanities of a dead Lancastrian's wife. No doubt the charges against him were trumped up. It was a bad business all round."

My gut clenched as Caitlin's family was mentioned. I wondered what she would feel when she heard this news, locked away in the bowels of the abbey. She was ever afeared of Clarence.

Warwick was swirling his wine around thoughtfully, looking into the depths of his cup for an answer.

"I know more about that business than I care to know. Edward was and remains a fool. His common sense gets irrationally blurred by a rush of blood to his balls. Its not the first..." he broke off suddenly, his mood decidedly irritable. "No matter. That business is done." He finally took a drink from the cup in his hand, throwing his head back as if the wine would drown his troubles. Which, from the permanent knot in his

365

forehead, were many.

There was an uneasy silence for a few moments, where all that could be heard was our breathing. Well, theirs. I was holding mine.

"And, where is he now?"

Warwick stood up, abruptly, no doubt in an attempt to bring an end to the audience, something Oxford seemed to pay little attention to as he remained seated, sipping from his own cup with ease.

"He has gone to visit his mother at Syon." He pursed his lips. "He will be back the day after tomorrow, but in the meantime I have a plethora of stubborn city merchants to deal with."

"His mother?" The scorn drenched Oxford's tone and he sat forward, his earlier calm disturbed. So, the duchess worried them more than George? I tried not to smile. "Richard, are you completely sure you can trust him?"

"God's blood John, it is through his mother's enmity of the queen that I managed to get George to turn his coat my way in the first place! She is my aunt, she had remonstrated long and hard over the way Edward has allowed his queen to whisper her desires into his ear night after night. To addle his brain with lust."

John finally stood, almost squaring up to Warwick, albeit in a most subtle way. They were eye to eye across the hearth.

"Yet, what will the old duchess think when you declare war against her daughter's husband? If her alliance is as true as you believe, she may live in faint hope that her son can return to England and resume his father's title. Can take his place at a Lancastrian court, although I have to say that seems as likely as the sun rising at midnight. There is one thing, Richard, to rid the country of a troublesome queen, quite another to attempt an attack on the whole York dynasty. You forget, I also know Edward. He is a shrewd man, despite his poor choice in bedmates. Then there is his younger brother, of whom I know very little."

Warwick's grin was hard, his eyes narrowing.

"You don't need to worry about him. He's loyal as a dog to

his brother. If Edward returns and bends the knee, his brother will do likewise. If he chooses treason, so will he. They can both follow each other to the block if they so choose." He dug his thumbs in his belt with determination. "If we can bring Charles to heel in Burgundy, we can force him to return the exiles. Edward may find he does return to England, but not quite in the way he desires."

Oxford turned, so I could see his face in profile, saw the curve in his lips.

"First, you have to declare war on Charles, Richard. Louis is waiting, and will not fulfil his part of the bargain until you do. Margaret and her son could linger around his court for weeks. You don't have that luxury. Your power without the queen at your side is fragile, and all know it. There are as many who distrust your motives as do Clarence's. You have to act – quickly. For all our sakes!"

Warwick took a step forwards, placing one heavy hand on Oxford's shoulder, his face relaxing for the first time since I entered the room.

"First, I have to convince the city. Many here still hold fast for Edward. He flattered the merchant's wives and filled their husband's coffers. Once the talking is done, we can raise hell in Burgundy. But the talking must come first. Without the city at our backs, we would be foolish to launch an invasion. It would be just the move Edward is expecting. We need to thwart that ambition."

Oxford seemed to acknowledge his words, but still looked distinctly unimpressed. Something told me that had he been in Warwick's position, things would be moving a lot faster than they were, and he found this current strategy hard to swallow. But then Warwick was older, more experienced in both the politics of power and the rigours of warfare. Somewhat mollified, Oxford smiled, if a little tightly, and they both turned to leave the room.

It was not at all as I had thought that day back at Baynard's when Clarence swaggered into the solar, so confident and overbearing – with Jasper Tudor at his side. It seemed that Warwick had struck a devil's bargain with the French spider, one he may now be beginning to regret, no matter how boldly he strode these halls.

I had heard how peasants had risen in revolt against the king, in the time of my own father and before. The merchants could do much more damage if they chose, even I knew that. They could place a stranglehold on the country from which it may take years to recover. No trade, no money, no wages for men to either make war or defend the country against others.

It was beginning to come home to me how hard it was for even the most powerful to follow their own will. Fortune was certainly a cruel mistress, that was sure.

23. WESTMINSTER PALACE
December 1470

It was a further week before I saw Clarence again, and the duchess had accompanied him back to court for the festivities which now began in earnest as the snow began to fall.

I had been given no other course than to keep Stillington's letter close to me, not having had any opportunity either to hand it personally to the duke, or, more frustratingly, to return to St Martin's to collect the missive that would allow me access into the sanctuary at the abbey.

The French ambassadors were present at this evening's feast, and included an urbane Scot, William Moneypenny, who it appeared was highly regarded by the French king. Despite the usual adornments and the glitter of a thousand candles on silver, to me, there was a lack of light in every chamber. A spirit haunted me. I expected to see her around every corner, hear her laughter behind every door, smell her fragrance on the winter air. Even the music failed to cheer my mood.

I had been seated at the board with the Fitzhugh family, Dick, Anna, and Elizabeth, who kept smiling at me beguilingly over her cup. Anna paid me no attention at all, remaining close to her mother, and ignoring my presence as if I was invisible, a trick she seemed to have picked up from her father who was employing the same tactic.

Totally disgruntled, I retired to the back of the hall leaning against an archway, watching Dick, who was throwing himself into the merriment with unusual abandon. He was dancing with one of the ladies who had accompanied the duchess of York to court, a tall, dark-haired girl who looked far too aloof for my tastes, such as they were.

My eyes were fixed on Clarence, who was paying his usual lip service to the festivities, draped in as much gold as the high table, smiling at all and sundry as usual. He nodded to the nobles,

Oxford and Stanley alike, both those who had served his brother and those who had risen against him. His duplicity sat as lightly on his shoulders as gossamer, and he breezed through the swelling throng with ease. All I could do was wait, with the parchment still tucked inside my shirt, for the opportunity to complete my task. As for Caitlin, I was even beginning to think I no longer knew what she looked like.

"You don't dance?"

I knew it was Elizabeth as I could smell orange blossom, a scent which I remembered from before. I smiled, watching Dick now lead his young sister out to dance, noting how she smiled at him almost adoringly. It seemed that I was not to match up to her vision of manhood as seen in her own family. In her eyes, I was sadly lacking, and a coward to boot. Her sister seemed not so sensitive.

"No," I replied, giving her a quick glance, not wanting to take my eyes off Clarence for a second. "I prefer to play the music rather than perform to it."

Chance would have been a fine thing, I pondered. My lute lay abandoned in my chamber. There was very little time, or purpose, for me to indulge my whims at present. Undeterred, she sidled closer to me, her fragrance becoming heady, reminding me of summer.

"I would like to hear you play. Very much."

"If only that were so," I murmured, watching Clarence bow over Margaret Stafford's hand, his head cocked as if he was enthralled by every word she said. Which was hardly likely.

"Can it not be? Everyone is so engrossed in the festivities. No one would miss us, I am sure."

She was right. Even the king was not present. The story being whispered that he had caught a chill, he had made only the briefest of appearances before retiring, leaving us all to our leisure. Warwick stood by the high table, his head closely bowed to Sir Richard Tunstall and the London merchant Sir Thomas Cooke. Across the room, Lords Stanley and Oxford stood, appearing to all to indulge in pleasant discourse, but the guarded look in their eyes was unmistakable even through the smoke and torchlight.

Every thing, every movement before me seemed dry, stiff and formal. I was expecting sparks to fly each time the skirts of the dancing ladies brushed each other as they passed, fueled by the simmering suspicion which lay an invisible veneer over all. It was then that I felt her hand steal into mine, her fingers curling around my palm with a firm insistence.

"Come on," she whispered, her lips close to my ear and before I knew quite what her intention was, she was pulling on my arm. After a slight hesitation, and one last glance at George who was holding out his cup for an attendant page to fill, I gave in.

I don't know what I was thinking, apart from that I wasn't thinking. Before I had chance to even reconsider where this was leading, Elizabeth had reached her destination, the door to a private chamber, which she opened, pulling me through firmly. There were candles burning, and the faint smell of incense from somewhere, and a fire bathed the room in a golden light. There was a flagon of wine, cups and a bowl of what looked like figs and nuts. If I hadn't known better, it almost looked staged. Like someone had carefully prepared for a private feast.

Elizabeth was leaning against the door now, looking at me from beneath lowered lids with a strange light emanating from her eyes. I had seen it before and my chest tightened. It was the look that Caitlin had often thrown towards Richard, when she thought no one was looking.

I had suspected she liked me, just not this much, and I smiled, somewhat nervously, looking around me. I wasn't sure whose chamber we were in, but I had to say it looked very inviting.

"Now what?"

She walked towards me as my body began to betray the best of my intentions. She was very, very pretty, her hair was a warm, tawny blonde, and in its intricate braids it resembled skeins of silk, waiting to be stitched into some glorious tapestry. Her eyes were an intriguing mix of blue and grey, resembling the sea on a stormy day, neither one colour or the other, reflecting flashes of both as the light touched upon them. She stopped within inches of me, and I could see her chest rise and fall, the curve of her breasts so pale and smooth. My fingers began to twitch, wanting to reach out and see how it felt.

"How ungallant!" she grinned mischievously, before affecting a look of mild shock. "I thought you knew I liked you. In fact, that I liked you very much. I thought," she reached up one hand and touched the cleft in my chin gently, her amusement disappearing, "you liked me too."

My throat was parched, as my blood began to heat up. I knew what she was doing and no matter that my mind was conjouring up images of Anna's fresh face, of Caitlin's lustrous gaze, my body was stirring up a whole vision of its own and I had very little power to prevent it from running its course.

"I do," I croaked helplessly, as her finger began to track along my jaw, before she withdrew it and played the same finger sensuously across her bottom lip. She took a step closer, our mouths were inches apart. She needed to do no more as the devil took my arms and slid them around her waist, holding her there, her breasts pressing against my doublet. "It is... this is wrong, though."

With that, she stretched her neck forwards and her lips brushed mine. A shock, like lightning, shot through my body and I barely stifled a groan as my groin stiffened.

"Everything is wrong at the minute, though, isn't it?" she breathed softly. "The wrong king sits on the throne. It is wrong that we are spending this Holy time surrounded by so many men who hate each other so openly. Wrong that you should be wed to a girl almost half your age when there are so many others who could be a true wife. Wrong that you have to wait for the pleasures of the marriage bed."

My head began to spin. The smell of oranges, warm and

citrus, like summer. I lowered my head and pressed my lips into the curve of her neck, hearing her sigh, gently, my own nerves beginning to thrum like harp strings.

"What would you know of the pleasures of the marriage bed?" I murmured.

Her hand began to play with the collar of my doublet, seeking the ties of my shirt, loosening the points. I continued to kiss her neck gently, a long line of kisses from beneath her ear to the silk trim on her gown, my lips brushing velvet.

Her hand slipped beneath my shirt, her fingers cool on my skin, making me intake my breath sharply.

"I was rather hoping you could show me," she whispered, and finally our lips met, gently at first, before the kiss grew more passionate, her mouth parting naturally to admit my tongue. Her body pressed up against mine, willingly, making me pull her tighter, knowing she would feel the hardness she had caused. Not caring if she would understand it, by that time I had lost my mind and all I cared about was devouring every inch of her.

My own hand stole up to her neck, pushing under her hair, forcing her lips even harder against mine. For a young girl who, to all intents, had no experience, her passion was something to behold. She was neither fragile or nervous, and seemed to know that her body had a power all of its own, and one she knew instinctively how to use.

I reached for the laces of her gown just at the moment when she paused, as her hand came into contact with the secret held against my skin. I felt her falter, but it was too late, and her fingers withdrew the letter from its hiding place as she pulled away, a half-smile on her lips.

I opened my eyes and she was looking at me with a puzzled expression, and she leaned back.

"What's this?"

I released her waist, covering her hand with mine, all desire suddenly ebbing away like rain down a roof. I curled my fingers around the parchment.

"It's nothing." But it was too late, she had taken a step or two backwards and was now looking down at her hands.

"It is something..." I couldn't think how to explain it; my cheeks began to heat up for a different reason. She was still looking down, biting her lip now. That plump, sensuous lip that had been mine such a short while ago. My heart began to pound and the only thing I could think to do was fasten up my doublet, at least I could appear decent even if I didn't feel it.

"Why do you have a letter for the Duke of Clarence?" Her eyes looked slightly crestfallen, which hurt me more than I expected. "Who is it from?"

I stood there gaping like a fish. From what had been a pleasantly surprising evening, events were going downhill fast. Even faster then as the door opened and Lady Alice entered the room, thankfully alone, but that did nothing to eliminate the shock on her face.

"What are you two doing here?" She looked around the room quickly, her face darkening all the more as she realised we were alone. I gave a silent prayer that I had shown the foresight to fasten my clothing as the whole affair could have ended up a worse than it already was. A lot worse. I didn't know where to put myself, in the most literal of senses.

Elizabeth's eyes widened in alarm, as she tried to hide the letter in her hand, pulling it close to her waist. But it was too late. Lady Alice was as eagle eyed as her brother.

"What do you have there?"

The silence seemed to last for year, and as I began to envisage that I was about to be dragged before the earl in short order and accused of treason, Elizabeth became my saviour, ensuring at once that I forgave her for putting me in this situation at all.

"It's a poem, Mama."

"A poem?" Disbelief was writ clear across her mother's face, but Elizabeth held out her hand, thrusting the letter towards me, forcefully.

"Yes. Anna has written Francis a poem, and she was too embarrassed to give it to him. And I am thinking now, Francis is too embarrassed to take it."

Recovering myself, I took the letter with a grateful glance, my mind whirring.

"And," Lady Alice looked around her quizzically, and not at all convinced by Elizabeth's explanation. "Why did you have to come here to deliver it? To Baroness Hastings chamber?"

So that at least enlightened me to where I was. Deep down I almost began to wonder if the enigmatic Baroness had a hand in tonight's mischief. Elizabeth's eyes grew wide.

"I was looking for Lady Katherine, and Francis happened to walk past. I wanted to give him the letter in private."

Her eyes narrowed suspiciously, but my earlier hunch was vindicated as the door opened again and the Baroness herself entered, taking in the scene before her. The first person she made eye contact with was Elizabeth, and a knowing look passed between them. It had indeed been planned. Thanking the Lord for the sudden distraction, I spoke up.

"I think it is my favorite poem," I tried to fake a different type of shyness, and looked at the paper in my hand, hoping that from the distance she stood by the door, Lady Alice would have no idea of what was written. The light was shadowy, and to be fair, her eyes were not young. "When the Nightingale Sings." I told her about it at Minster Lovell." With considerable aplomb, if I say it myself, I looked at Stillington's writing on the letter and began to speak from memory.

"Sweet leman, I pray you, give me one love-speech, while I liveth in the world so wide, non other will I seek,"

Lady Alice rolled her eyes, but her face showed she was far from displeased.

"The sweet child!" interjected Lady Katherine quickly. "Her shyness is to be admired, but I am sure she will grow out of it soon. Now, go on the pair of you, you should be downstairs with the dancing and merriment, not hidden away up here. Besides, the noise has finally given me the headache I have been avoiding all day, and I wish to take some ease."

I bowed politely to both of them, still aware of Lady Alice's keen eye, and ushered Elizabeth out of the chamber, closing the door behind us. Once outside, we almost ran down the passage like a pair of children after playing a prank on our nurse, finally reaching the bottom of the stairs by the hall, laughing and breathless.

Elizabeth's eyes were shining brightly, her face glowingly beautiful.

"You are a dark horse indeed, Francis. Who knew what a romantic soul you are!"

Grinning, I leaned against the wall to get my breath back.

"I aim to please!"

She had a laugh like a bell, and I heard it clearly above the music.

"To think, I was so close to finding out if you could. Please, I mean!"

Still feeling giddy from my close encounter, I reached up and touched her cheek, brushing my thumb across her lip.

"Maybe another time? The festivities are far from over."

She placed her hand over mine, her lips twitching in amusement.

"Far, far from over."

With that, she almost flounced away, sailing gaily into the hall which was still a long way from calling it a night. I watched her go, stopping to laugh at a remark from Sir John Plummer, Keeper of the Royal Wardrobe. It was then I felt someone was watching me and I was right. Anna stood a few feet away, her face impassive, but her eyes as large as a doe fawn's and full of hurt.

I cursed myself for seven kinds of a fool and made towards her, just at the moment when Clarence detached himself from the crowd and made his way towards the stairs where I stood, no doubt to retire to the privy apartments.

Anna stared at me in horror, before picking up her pink silk skirts and hurrying away. George passed before me without a word, momentarily blocking Anna from view, but I could still see her as he mounted the stairs. I could have caught up with her, tried to explain, tried to banish the pain from her face. But how?

Thoroughly dejected, there was only one thing I could do. I followed Clarence up the stairs, knowing this may be the only chance to fulfil the task I had been given.

24. WESTMINSTER PALACE
December 1470

I caught up with George just as he crossed the long gallery which led to his chamber, although I had the strangest feeling that he had known I was following him and just chosen not to acknowledge it. His gait had gradually slowed, narrowing the distance between us, so that by the time we were level, I could see the smile of anticipation on his face. He knew all right!

"You will quite wear yourself out, Lovell, if you carry on at that pace, and what would the fair ladies of the court do for entertainment then?" I let him pass through the doorway without comment, leaving him to turn as we both reached the ante-chamber to his apartment. "What do you want?" This time his tone had a more impatient edge to it, as if the mere sight of me made him annoyed.

"Your Grace, I have a message for you."

His eyes narrowed suspiciously, before he reached for the latch, pushing open the door, but not before he had glanced over my shoulder, to see if there was anyone else around. Satisfied we were unobserved, he crossed the threshold, with me close behind him.

I should not have been at all surprised to see that the rooms he occupied were furnished every bit as sumptuously as the king's had ever been, and to crown it all, Isabel sat by the fire, a small prayer book in her hand. Dressed in pale blue silk, she looked as if she had dressed to attend the evenings festivities, only to change her mind and linger in her chamber instead. It was only when she looked up in some surprise that I noticed how her eyes looked slightly pink, maybe a little swollen. I could have made a wager that she had but recently been weeping.

She didn't say a word, but her dark eyes passed over me quickly, fastening on George, scanning his face anxiously as if striving to judge his mood. He, meanwhile, merely strode over to a gilded wine flagon and poured himself a measure of what looked like Malmsey, taking a long draw on the sweet liquid before he addressed either one of us.

"My dear," he drawled pleasantly, and which was definitely not aimed at me, "you did not come down for the dancing."

Isabel folded the book together, resting her hands over it as it nestled in her lap. I couldn't help thinking how stiff and formal she appeared, so different from her sister Anne. Well, at least the last time I had seen her, for who knew how she was now, married to her one-time enemy. Isabel's lips were pressed in a tight smile which was undoubtedly forced.

"I decided against it," she replied quietly. "I felt a little tired." At these words, George glanced at the prayer book in her hands.

"Are you... unwell?" The conversation between them was so stilted that I felt my skin begin to crawl, regretting my decision to follow him. But if I didn't do this, how was I ever to get to see Caitlin? I swallowed deeply and bit my lip, hard.

Isabel stood up, averting her face away from me so that I could no longer see the look which passed between them. The silk of her skirts rustled as she moved towards the inner door.

"No, not really. As I said, just a little tired. I will retire, if you will excuse me." It was only then that I spotted the small parti-coloured dog at her feet, which skittered across the floor, following her progress. George lowered his eyes to his cup in answer, although I knew his mind was working hard, I could almost hear his thoughts. It was then I remembered what I had heard. About the child they had lost. A girl, born aboard ship on a storm tossed sea as Wenlock, one of Warwick's own men, cleaved to his king and refused them entry into the port. It was not that long ago really, and now Isabel's demeanour made more sense to me. It seemed the loss still resonated with both of them deeply.

George drank again before raising his eyes, a wry smile on his lips.

"Our friend Lovell has a message for us. Do you not want to stay and hear it? If only for the entertainment value?"

She didn't even look at me. All I could see was the back of her neck, where her hair was coiled into a tight braid. I mused how dull it looked compared to another, fiery skein.

"I doubt anything he has to impart will be of interest to me. I will bid you good night."

Without a further word, she passed through the doorway, closing the chamber door behind her, as George made his way across the room, sinking into the seat she had just vacated. For a few moments he stared into the fire, but then he stretched out his legs, crossing them at the ankles on the hearth, the flames turning his silken hose to molten gold.

"Your message?"

Jolted into action, I reached into my doublet and strode forwards, holding the letter out towards him. He took it from me, frowning slightly at the sight of his name, before unfolding it, and scanning the words quickly. For a moment, I thought his face lost some colour, and he glanced back at me, reading it once again, before folding it up, his face thoughtful. No, more than thoughtful. Behind his still expression, I could hear the thunderous hooves of his thoughts.

"Well, it is turning into quite a month," he intoned quietly. His mouth curved as he saw my own confusion, waving the letter in the air dismissively. "Gold angels dance with St Michael. Merchants hold the city to ransom. St Quentin falls and the court dances to music from across the sea." He leaned forwards suddenly, tossing the letter into the flames where we both watched it curl, crackle, blacken and burn. "And now the heavens fall."

I remained silent, as for the most, I had to agree. Warwick had recently commissioned, in the king's name of course, gold angels bearing St Michael, the Patron Saint of France. Louis had invaded Burgundy already, had taken St Quentin and was marching on Picardy, trusting he would soon be joined by an

English host. All along the Thames, cranes languished limply, for lack of the plentiful supply of bales to swing onto the usually teeming banks.

Whatever coin was being spent this holy period, there seemed little chance of anyone's pockets being replenished any time soon at this rate. London had always been Edward's city. It would never be Warwick's. Or Louis's.

George emptied his cup down the back of his throat, before lifting it up before his eyes, scrutinising the elegant scrollwork on the metal.

"Did you know, there is even a rumour that Edward is soon to return? That his plans are well laid. That those who turned their coats should perhaps make sure that they still have the ability to effect a reversal of fortune."

I cleared my throat carefully.

"Where would such a rumour come from?"

George raised his eyebrows, and looked at me with a pursed smile, portraying an affected innocence.

"I wonder? Such an unlikely prospect, you must admit. Whoever would believe such a thing could happen?"

I shuffled my feet self-consciously. This George I could almost like.

"I would, Your Grace."

George pushed himself up from the chair, sweeping up the cup as he did so, returning to the sideboard to refill it.

"Well," he began, waving his brimming cup in the air, "strange times bring strange events, of that you can be sure. Fortune has a way of raising up and casting down with alarming regularity. What we often believe to be a certainty, can often be no more solid than ice in the sun."

I had no idea what he was talking about and suddenly, I didn't want to. All I wanted was to see Caitlin once more. The mention of Edward's possible return had brought her face to mind with a crystal clarity.

"Did you have a reply for His Grace?" I asked my question

381

tentatively, hoping to bring an end to this evening. Hoping there would be a reason for me to return to St Martin's, no matter what lie I had to tell Warwick.

George smiled. A smile which unnerved me for some reason.

"No. No reply is necessary, and even if I did, I have no need of your undoubted skills as a messenger." I frowned at him, watching his smile broaden. "After all, I can tell him myself tomorrow, when he arrives back at court."

George was examining my face as if expecting a reaction, even though he could surely not have guessed my ultimate aim. How I managed to stop the pleasure I felt at his revelation, I do not know, but it took every fibre of my being to remain totally disinterested in what he had just said.

Fortune was at least my leman for now, for surely all I had to do to was bump into him. And in a Christmas court packed to the rafters with clerics and nobles vying for favour, nothing could be easier.

25. WESTMINSTER PALACE
January 1471

By Epiphany, the game of cat and mouse that Elizabeth and I were playing had begun to drive me almost insane. Even as the halls became more and more crowded, she was everywhere at once. Everywhere I went. Each feast grew ever more frantic with a joy which seemed almost forced at times, as if those who celebrated felt they needed to throw themselves into events with abandon, should they never be able to do so again.

And amongst it all, glances sharp as steel, whispers silken with danger. The rumours that Edward may be poised to make a return were spreading and had now breached the walls of the palace. Whilst Henry, in his best, festive garb, appeared totally unaware and mercifully unperturbed by the imminent return of his nemesis, the rest of his court simmered with unrest.

Outside, the snow lay deep and cold, but inside, a fire was burning with enough heat to rival the devil himself. On one side of the hall, Oxford, Tunstall and Tudor glowered magnificently, whilst on the other, Plummer, Cook, the newly pardoned Duke of Norfolk and his friend the Earl of Essex mouthed silent words to each other, spitting like fat on a fire.

Where Elizabeth seemed to be my shadow, I saw very little of Anna, who now avoided me at all costs. She appeared at Mass, her small head bowed low, her dress demure, usually blue. She broke her fast, sitting with her mother and Lady Katherine, and afterwards I saw her not at all. For the evening feasts, she had become a ghost. If present, she went unseen. At least to me.

Tonight would be the last feast of the season, and it was almost as if everyone would not only welcome it, but be relieved by it. No more bound by the convention to be civil to those who they suspected to be their enemies, each one could return to their own circles, form their own alliances, lay their plans for the future when Queen Margaret finally arrived to prop up her faltering king.

I had helped Warwick dress in the finest tawny damask, a colour he seemed to favour, and which complimented the dark sable of his collar and the glimmering gold of his chain of office. He looked almost kingly himself, seated at the high table, his eyes steely, chin set in a grim determination to get through the meal, if not the night.

Further down the hall, I saw Oxford his lips pressed to the ear of Lord Stanley, whose expression showed no indication of the words he was absorbing as he stroked his chin. Never had I seen a man better at hiding his true intent. If Oxford thought to keep him on side in any conflict to come, he would need to ensure that he locked his brother, my erstwhile step-father William, in a tower somewhere.

A troupe of traveling minstrels had been invited to play for the king, and their music throbbed around the room – and at times some of the players themselves, dressed in green woolen gowns with red girdles, wandered between the trestles, for the pleasure of those dining. At one point the youngest among them who sang like a choirboy, strolled in between the tables, entertaining the nobles as they ate, followed closely by a tall, blonde-haired man playing the lute. As one song came to an end, he plucked a piece of mistletoe from his gown, where it had been pinned to his shoulder in an attempt at festive finery and he handed it to someone I could not see.

He bowed courteously, as those around him applauded his gallantry and it was as I glanced around the room then that my heart skipped a beat, and for the most innocent of reasons. I caught sight of the bishop's hat, and the snow white Alb of Stillington before I saw his face to confirm it was him. But it was. By some twist of fate, he turned his head as I looked at him and our eyes caught across the smoky, candle-rimed haze. He smiled and nodded his head genially. I made myself a promise not to leave the hall before I had spoken to him, for surely he still owed me that favour.

As the evening drew on, everything was cleared away for the dancing and I was just about to seek out Dick Fitzhugh for a game of tables, when a hand laid itself on my arm. I turned, and was not at all surprised to find Elizabeth, smiling at me. But it was what was in her hand which shocked me even more, for it was a lute, and from the marks on the fret, I knew it was not any lute, it was my very own.

"What are you doing with that?" I know I was abrupt, but not only did her constant attendance unnerve me, for more than one reason, but I had no idea what she was up to. All she did was smile at me demurely.

"I said I would like you to play for me and now you have your chance." I stared at her stupidly and she began to laugh. "One of the minstrels has been taken ill, and the king has asked for 'Le Souvenir' – apparently a favourite of his from some time ago – and of course, that tune needs a lute player. A good lute player!"

She held out the instrument towards me and I felt myself begin to blush. Over her shoulder I could see the minstrels assembling again on the dais, the young singer looking nervously at the king, and then back to where Elizabeth and I stood, before turning back to talk to his fellow performers anxiously.

"I – I can't...!" I stammered, looking at the lute as if it was some offensive instrument of torture.

"You can. Of course you can!" I began to look around the room with alarm. There were far too many people who knew me here, and I in no way wanted to draw attention to myself. But she took a step forwards then, in a waft of orange-flower water, somehow spiced with cinnamon. "Just imagine you are playing for me."

Now Henry was seating himself back down after mingling with some of his nobles, and, in an unusual spate of clarity, was looking towards the musicians grouped in the corner. It was then that the portly man with a sackbut held out his hand to me, and my fate was sealed as a few heads turned, including that of Warwick, who was seated next to the king.

"Oh Lord!" I breathed, hardly knowing what I said over the hard beating of my heart. I took the lute from her hand and wove my way through a sea of interested faces to take my place, somewhat self-consciously, with the troupe of players. Ignoring the murmuring which had begun to rise, I silenced them with a nod, which was returned by my green-gowned comrade who was readying himself to sing and I took a deep breath, and curled my fingers around the fret.

"Le souvenir de vous me tue, mon seul bein, mon suel bien, quant je ne vous voy…"

It was only as the words soared to the heavens, that I calmed down enough to recall how bittersweet this moment was. Le Souvenir. A song of unrequited love. I managed to keep my attentions focused on my finger-work, the careful, taut pluck of each string, each note, until the final refrain, which rang all too truthful in my ears.

"And so I shall suffer in silence, until your return."

It was Caitlin I was playing to, not Elizabeth, but as I looked up to a ripple of polite applause, it was Elizabeth's face which caught my eye. The stout, red face man with the sackbut was grinning all over his face, and he leaned close to me with wine-coloured breath.

"That was bloody good! Do you know 'Fortuna Desperata?'"

I nodded, and before long was once again lost in the music, the crowd now forgotten. Besides, most of them had turned back to their drinking and conversations, the initial novelty of one of their own entertaining the king with the commoners having been short lived. To be fair, I felt more comfortable up on the dais with them than down in the hall. So comfortable, that I stayed to play "Danse de Cleves" only making my excuses to depart as the dancing and merriment was reaching its height.

As usual, with the increase in noise, the king had retired, and it mattered little whether the musicians played well or not. Wine was flowing, there were card games and bantering all around the chamber, some conversations were overloud, whilst others, such as Thomas Stanley, sat staring moodily into their cups. George was, however, enjoying himself, and Isabel was this time, at his side, if looking like she was too noble to truly show happiness of any sort.

I slipped out of the hall, only to find Elizabeth waiting, her face wreathed in smiles, her eyes shining like torches in the shadowy passage.

"You were wonderful! Truly wonderful!"

Lord forgive me but all thoughts of Caitlin were gone. Of Anna in truth, had I any thoughts of her at all. Elizabeth stepped towards me, and with the neck of the lute grasped in one hand, the other slipped around her waist and our lips met with a burst of passion which was, in some senses, fueled for me by a strange heady joy.

My tongue roved her mouth as she cleaved ever closer to me, aided by my arm which pulled her nearer. Her hands were on my face, one on either side, keeping my lips fastened to hers, not that I had any intention of letting her go. Only to breathe!

My body, denied for so long, was now demanding with an urgency which made my head spin. That, and the scent of her, overwhelmed every fibre of me. It was wrong, I knew it was wrong, but I could not help myself. We finally parted, her hand lay on my chest, both of us panting – and smiling.

"Francis…" she whispered huskily, her eyes dark pools as she looked up at me.

"Elizabeth…" I breathed back, unable to stop my heart pounding.

"Lovell!" It was Dick's voice, and he was close by. Biting her lip, Elizabeth stretched up for one brief kiss and then she was gone, hurrying down the hall, skirts in her hands, almost gliding.

"Lovell?" This time closer. I stepped out of the shadows, only for someone to halt my progress, and it wasn't Dick. Bishop Stillington stood before me, his tall, well-built form blocking my way, his hands folded before him, and a knowing smile on his face.

387

"Your Grace, I..." my face burned. How much he had seen I had no idea but guilt was poured all over me like a stain.

"You are a talented boy," he said smoothly. "Take care you use that talent only for good." He lifted a hand and revealed a small parchment square which he held out to me. "Go with God, my son."

As I took the missive from his hand, he turned and was gone.

26. WESTMINSTER ABBEY
January 1471

Stamping my feet against the cold, I waited outside the towering walls of the Abbey. My heart was beating erratically, making me feel slightly sick.

Sick that I may not be given entry. Equally sick at the thought of seeing her again, knowing the sin I had so recently almost committed. Even as well wrapped up as I was in my riding cloak, the winter snows had brought with them a biting wind which was making itself felt against my bones, whipping around the corner where I stood, trying to be patient. Snow began to fall again with a vengeance and just as I thought I may be turned into a frozen block of ice before anyone came to admit me, the heavy, iron bound door opened with a loud, grating creak.

Abbot Milling, his grey visage looking even more washed out in the morning light, beckoned me inside without a word and I accepted gratefully. Knocking the snow off my boots, I was more than dismayed to find it was not much warmer inside than it was without. I could only hope, for Caitlin's sake, that their lodgings were providing more adequate shelter against the winter chill.

"Thank you, Your Grace," I said, keeping both my voice and my manner deferential. He looked at me with some interest.

"My charges receive few visitors. It is a sad business, but not unremarkable bearing in mind our current troubles." He coughed gently. "I did have to consult Her Grace, but it seems she knows your name, and was assured of your affinity to her house. If she had objected, I am afraid I would have had to refuse you entry. Despite your credentials."

I nodded, half expecting that would have been the case. I could imagine that there were many who Elizabeth would rather tear her eyes out with her bare hands than look upon at present.

"If you will follow me?"

He led me down a long passage, and then through a small door into a chamber which was thankfully much warmer than anywhere else I had been that morning. The chamber was warm, dry and well lit. The fire in the hearth was roaring well, and there were sumptuous furs on the chairs and settles, which I found a little odd, bearing in mind this was sanctuary. But then I looked a little closer. The candlesticks and wall sconces appeared to be gold. The furnishings rich and well made. It appeared to me that I could only be in the Abbot's lodgings, surely no sanctuary could be as grand as this?

I was just imagining Caitlin coming in and sitting on one of the chairs by the fire, wondering if she would have Kathryn with her when the door opened and my heart plummeted. It wasn't Caitlin, it was the queen herself, Elizabeth Woodville.

Dressed entirely in black velvet, but cloaked in sable, I had to admit she was as flawless as I had ever seen her at court. Her skin was as pale as the snow outside, with the quality of alabaster, which unfortunately made me think that it would be chill to the touch. No matter how beautiful the queen was, it had to be said that it was a cool, if not cold, allure. Even her hair was an impossibly radiant gilt. I remembered that her name was Rivers before it was Woodville and it was that which she reminded me of.

There were days when the Windrush next to my home lie calm and still, even as it flowed with an endless elegance. On these days, when the sun shone, it was a strange meld of blue, silver and gold and it looked as if you could slide your hand along the surface effortlessly, and enjoy its undulating smoothness. The name Elizabeth Windrush popped into my head and despite my anxiety I had to suppress a grin.

She did not look at me until she had lowered herself into one of the chairs, and adjusted the furs around her upper arms, exposing a swan-like neck, bare of any adornment. Then she raised her lids and almost pinned me to the door, eyes as sharp as arrow points.

"Francis Lovell." It was a statement, not a question.

I made a low obeisance and kept my hands clasped firmly behind my back.

"Your Grace."

The fire began to crackle loudly, almost in reassurance to tell me that there was still heat in the room, her greeting had been so chilled.

"Do you come on behalf of Earl Warwick or the French woman?" She paused then, holding a slim hand out to the flames. "Oh, I forget. Margaret has not yet arrived in the city has she? She always did have a habit of leaving her husband to the ministrations of others as I recall."

My heart began to thump loudly. I had not for a minute thought she would think I was here on official business. I had told the Abbott who I was here to see, but either that message had not been passed on or had been completely ignored.

"My apologies Your Grace, I come only on my own behalf."

Her expression did not change. She remained completely still, other than the sinuous movements of her fingers outstretched before the flames, almost hypnotically.

"Yet, you were recommended by Bishop Stillington were you not? The same Bishop Stillington who has recently been granted an amnesty by Warwick?"

I was impressed! Obviously her intelligence was better than Stillington's as he had not even been aware of the birth of a prince. Not that the woman before me looked as if she had given birth such a relatively short time before. Or ever, the devil inside me sniggered.

"Yes, Your Grace." Some inner instinct told me that the less I said the better.

"And what does the good Bishop want with a captive queen of England?"

I found her tone slightly odd, as Stillington had been Edward's Chancellor, which is exactly why he had found the need to immure himself in a place of safety. I cleared my throat, hoping to mask my nervousness. I wondered if Caitlin even knew I was here? Was she standing the other side of the door, listening, but unable to enter?

"My apologies, Your Grace, I did not mean to disturb you. I only wished to enquire after the health of someone who shares your sanctuary. The Bishop was kind enough to recommend me."

Her lips finally made an attempt to form a smile, almost managed it.

"Oh, I know who you wish to see. I can assure you Gloucester's mistress is safe and well. But I am much more interested in why Stillington in particular would recommend you. After all, I hear the court is awash with clerics just waiting to bend to Warwick's wishes."

"Lord Warwick does not know that I am here, Your Grace."

One fair eyebrow arched.

"Do you expect me to believe that? You are Warwick's ward. You serve at a Lancastrian court. You claimed to have been a friend of the King Edward and his family, yet you fawn at the feet of his usurper! The girl fled here in fear, yet where were you? Why have you not been held to account for your servitude?"

She held all the cards, and although anger was bubbling low in my throat, I swallowed hard, determined to keep myself in check. I could not throw away this opportunity.

"I am of no account to anyone, Your Grace. Apart from my lands, which provide a livelihood for many."

"Yet you were active enough in the last rebellion for Edward to issue you a pardon, so how long ago did you turn your coat?"

To me, that was the ultimate insult and my hands gripped each other rightly behind my back.

"The king was under the impression that I was still in the north with my wife's family, Your Grace. He did not know that I had chosen to desert them when I found out Lord Fitzhugh's intent. The Duke of Gloucester will account for me. I met with him just outside York when he was on his way to meet the king."

"How fortunate for you that I cannot verify this tale with the

duke. He is unavoidably detained in the Low Countries.
Conveniently for you."

"I would willingly have been at his side, Your Grace, but he
bid me come south to ensure Lady Desmond was safe."

"And so she is, but that is no thanks to you. Once again my
husband's family stepped into the breech."

"I was not at court when that happened. I had been sent to
Oxfordshire..."

"Once again you seem to be in the wrong place at the wrong
time! What an unlucky boy you are!"

"I have no control over Fortune, Your Grace. I wish I had."

She withdrew her hand from the fire, placing it in her lap,
seemingly considering my words.

"Truly said. So." She had not taken her eyes off me for one
second since I entered the room. "How do you come to know
Bishop Stillington?"

Her interest in the Bishop seemed to be quietly relentless.
Even though she had seemed earlier to dislike the man, he also
seemed to hold some sort of fascination for her. Either that, or
there was something else. Something I didn't know. I had
thought the best policy was silence, but the urge to see Caitlin was
now becoming a real need. Elizabeth was so cold, I had to make
sure she was not in any distress. That the queen who had seen fit
to treat her ill as a servant, was at least treating her well as a
captive. Richard would never forgive me if I didn't try my best. I
would tell her all, well, as much as I felt she needed to know.

"I was asked to deliver the news of his pardon to him by the
earl, Your Grace."

"At St Martin's?"

"Yes, Your Grace."

The pale lips pursed.

"And he was so grateful to your efficient delivery of your
master's mercy, that he offered to recommend you?" Her head
inclined. "For you would not have been admitted to sanctuary
any other way."

Could I miss out the message to Clarence? Surely, it would only enrage her if she thought her husband's Chancellor was passing secret messages to the brother who betrayed his king? Or did she know that Clarence was also playing his own game? Should I tell her, or was she already aware? She seemed extremely knowledgeable of affairs at court, did she also know about him?

My palms began to sweat, and I looked anywhere but at her face, something she obviously recognised as my thundering uncertainty.

"You may as well tell me. I may not be able to leave here without fear of jeopardy but I can always ask Abbot Milling to enquire why the Bishop would so favour you."

I had no choice. I had never been good at deceit; my face always gave me away.

"He asked me to do something for him, and in return, I asked if he would recommend me to Abbot Milling. He kindly agreed." My heart was beating so loud I was surprised the windows were not rattling in the casements. I could almost hear the throb in my voice as I spoke. "He wanted a letter delivering to the Duke of Clarence."

I could have sworn I heard the ice in her eyes crystallise. The air in the room grew cold as death. There was no colour in anything, even the flames lost their fiery glow.

"Clarence." It was not a question. It was one word, spat out with disgust and disdain, as if the taste of it was abominable.

"Yes, Your Grace."

"Do you know the contents of the letter?" For the first time, I thought I saw her composure crack. Something made her expression ripple, as if she had received news of the worst kind, but was doing her best to mask its impact. It was only temporary, but I saw it all the same.

"No, Your Grace. I handed it to the duke and was not in his presence when he read it." I swallowed hard. She had even stopped looking at me which was just as well as I had chanced a lie. Her eyes were lowered and she seemed to be staring at the coronation jewel on her finger which was glimmering darkly. "But, you should know, that the duke is not at all happy with his place at court." I truly did not know how much I could or should say. Could I really tell her that his whole affinity to Henry was a sham? Yes, she was my queen, but that did not mean I should trust her confidence, in anything. If nothing else, the fate of Caitlin's father should have showed me that.

"Maybe it was a plea for him to make his peace with King Edward?"

It was the best I could do, and Elizabeth finally raised her eyes. I wish I could say she looked convinced by my explanation, but there was now something else which seemed to be distracting her. I could not swear to it, but the ice-cool composure seemed on the brink of submitting to a thaw.

Suddenly, she rose, in one fluid movement, pulling her furs back up around her neck, as if a cold wind had blown its way through the door.

"Let us hope so, for both your sakes." With those final words, she crossed the room, her ravens-wing, velvet skirts trailing in her wake, only to stop just short of the door.

"Oh, forgive me. You wanted to speak to Lady Desmond did you not?"

"Yes, Your Grace. I did, if it please you."

She was smiling now. A painted smile, with no sincerity in it and my heart was almost bursting, so long had it been thudding against my ribs.

"Lady Desmond is indisposed. Her condition has not been easy to bear in these poor surroundings. She has been ordered to rest by the physician who your king allows to visit. I am so sorry your efforts have been in vain. I bid you good day."

I watched her walk through the door leaving me in the chamber alone. My head was spinning, and there was a bitter taste in my mouth. I had ruined the only chance I had of seeing if Caitlin was alright, and it was all my fault. I should have lied. I should have told as tall a tale as a mummer at a Mayday fair. I should have told her anything that did not include the name of George of Clarence.

It was only as I stood in silence, waiting for the Abbot or a priest to come and guide me from the lodgings, that my mind restored itself to sense. She had no intention of letting me see Caitlin. I don't know how I knew it, but I did. She had been intrigued by my visit, and wanted to know how it had come about, which could only mean that she suspected Stillington was up to something. But what?

January 1470

"Francis!"

As the heavy, oaken door closed with a dull thud behind me, I heard my name being called out. I looked up from my boots where my eyes had been during the short journey through the reverent passages and saw Elizabeth, hurrying across the yard, taking care not to slip on the icy ground. Something in her manner made me also quicken my step. She still looked rosily fair, but her hood was askew, her hair a little disheveled, and the look on her face was one of sheer panic.

"Elizabeth?" I frowned, and she held out her hand, fingers pink with cold, dropping her skirts onto the frosty stone.

"Oh Francis, thank the lord! Anna has fallen ill! Mama asked me to find you, but no-one knew where you were! Come, come quickly!"

I caught her hand in mine and we both almost ran across the inner ward and through the palace arch, and I took the stairs two at a time, Elizabeth struggling to keep up with me. Our pace slowed as we hurried down the passage to the privy apartment.

"What happened?" I asked breathlessly, trying to slow my racing heart down before we reached their chambers.

Her eyes were full of worry; it was the first time I had ever seen her look so sad.

"I don't know. She was very quiet at Mass this morning, and ate only little at breakfast. But then she was sick, and her skin was flushed, but all over, not just her face. Then she began to be sick again and..." She swallowed hard. "She seemed to be in awful pain!"

I reached for her hand again, unconsciously, as I knew that what she was describing sounded awfully like the sweating sickness, which in itself was odd, as I had heard no mention of it being present in the city. Anna led such a cloistered life, I couldn't think that was what she had.

"Don't worry," I said, hopefully sounding a lot more confident than I felt. "I am sure she will be fine."

We had reached the door to the chamber now, and I couldn't help thinking back to when Caitlin had been so ill back at Middleham, although that was hardly likely to be Anna's malady. It struck me that although I was concerned for Anna's welfare, in no way was it the same gut-churning anxiety I had felt before. That only added to my already weighty burden of guilt.

The door was closed shut, and although we could hear mumbled voices beyond, and despite the fact that I had been sent for, I doubted we should just enter. All I could think to do was give a discreet knock and wait.

After a few moments, Lady Hastings appeared, her fair face pale and drawn.

"The poor girl," she sighed, looking first at Elizabeth and then at me. "She has taken a turn for the worse. I don't think you should go in at present. We are not yet sure if what ails her is infectious."

"Is Lady Alice with her?" I asked, trying not to be distracted by how fair Elizabeth looked in her distress. Sometimes her overly confident air made her appear far too capricious, and so it was a relief to see that she did feel for her sister, even as she chased her husband up and down dale!

Lady Katherine nodded.

"Then, I would like to go in please. She is my wife, after all." What gave me the inking to enter a sickroom I had no idea, other than that I thought it would be expected of me. It didn't help that I then saw the admiration deepen in Elizabeth's eyes and they filled with tears. Lady Katherine sighed and stood to one side, and I pushed the door open carefully.

The room was full of burning vapours, set to aid her breathing, and the room robed in red to reduce fever. I couldn't help thinking that the physician had acted alarmingly quickly, despite not knowing what ailed her and was covering all possible causes. Lady Alice was just adjusting the final red curtain at the window as I walked in, and one of the minor court physicians, whose name was unknown to me, was bent over a table, packing away the tools of his trade into a small leather bag.

I walked up to the bed, yet remaining some distance from it, looking at the tiny figure which lie under the coverlets. Her small face was covered in a film of sweat and was flushed, or at least that was how it looked in the muted haze of the room. She was calm, and appeared to be sleeping, but the uneven rise and fall of the sheets gave evidence of her efforts to breathe.

"Lady Alice? How is she?"

Anna's mother turned to the side table where she picked up a linen cloth, dipping it into a bowl before wringing it out. She only answered after she had placed the soothing cloth on Anna's forehead, causing her to whimper softly.

"We think it to be some form of miasma. You should not be in here."

The physician looked up, dark eyes below white straggly brows.

"There is an illness which is similar to the pox, but not as endemic. Children seem particularly prone to it, and usually recover." He looked over at Lady Alice. "In time."

"Is it infectious?" I asked hesitantly, only slightly perturbed at having my wife described as a child in my presence. Even though it was true.

"Only if you inhale the same foul air that this poor girl has. I am going to recommend that she is moved away, further down the river. It remains to be seen if anyone else falls ill." He pulled the edges of his back together briskly and picked it up. "I have been asked to report to Lord Warwick. He is most concerned lest any sickness reach the king. He will want her moved as quickly as possible." He looked around dispassionately. "This room should then be cleansed."

Whilst he had been speaking, I had been watching Lady Alice, who had sunk down into a chair by the bedside. There, by the bowl, was a small sprig of mistletoe. It rang a bell with me, and it was a few moments before I remembered, by which time the physician was at the door.

"Sire, there was a minstrel, at the Epiphany feast."

"What of it?" He had his hand on the latch and looked at me with undisguised irritation.

"Well, I saw him hand a sprig of mistletoe to someone. That mistletoe there, I think. He fell ill not long after and I don't know what ailed him, or what happened to him."

"I was not here at Epiphany. Was he not one of the king's minstrels?"

"No" Lady Alice interjected, looking at me with interest. "They were a travelling troupe. From Kent I believe."

The man lifted his hand from the latch and scratched his bristly chin, his eyes clouding over.

"I see. I will still recommend she is moved away from here." Without a further word, he was gone and I turned back to Lady Alice, who looked tired, dark circles ringed her usually bright eyes.

"You should go," she smiled at me, wanly. "Perhaps take an infusion of coriander, or liquorice. To ward off any evil humours. We don't want you getting ill as well."

I was touched by her concern, as she was now the closest relation I had to a mother. I bit my lip. I wanted to help if I could.

"Can I bring you anything? Should not you take something too? After all, you have been here all along have you not? Since she became ill?"

She shook her head slowly, reaching out and placing her hand over Anna's small, still fingers.

"I am fine. She is my daughter, and this is my place. If you would be so kind as to prevent Elizabeth from coming in here for the time being. She may welcome some comfort." There was an awkward silence, where I felt she wanted to look at me but could not. "I think you will not find that difficult." Then she did catch my eye and I wished she had not. "I think she would appreciate that from you, from what I have seen."

I felt my skin heating up, and not just from the stuffy atmosphere in the room.

"My Lady, I..."

She was shaking her head sadly.

"Don't worry, Francis. I know well she has been quite taken by you. We should not have been surprised, you are both more of an age. Just, have a care, for her sake! Lord Fitzhugh and I had found a husband for her, but our plans have been disrupted by the... by recent events." She sighed sadly, glancing back at Anna. "We must find someone else now it seems." She looked up quickly then, as if remembering herself. "I would be grateful if you would keep that to yourself. And if you can, try to dissuade her from any... romantic feelings she may have for you." I stood there mute, swallowing hard. Did she know how close we had come to satisfying those feelings?

"After all," she continued quietly, in a tone which was meant to torture me with its kindness, "you surely do not want to distress your wife."

I knew she was being merciful, that she had seen through our masquerade the other night. You didn't find a young man and woman alone in a bedchamber just passing on a message and she was nobody's fool. For me, it was a double blow to the gut. I didn't want Elizabeth, not in the sense as a wife or companion, but she had stirred my body into such a frenzy that it now reacted whenever I saw her. It was Caitlin my heart wanted. Still.

That heart now ached as I looked at Anna, who appeared even younger as she lay in her bed, struggling to breathe. How long before that girl would be my wife in truth, and how would I feel by the time she was?

The years stretched out before me. I missed Caitlin. I missed Richard's companionship. I missed Rob. I didn't feel like I belonged here, and heaven only knew what it would be like when Anne arrived with her young prince. Nothing felt right, as Elizabeth had said. Feeling thoroughly disheartened, I nodded and left the chamber.

28. GREENWICH PALACE
February 1471

Two weeks later found us at Greenwich Palace. Once the earl had found out about his niece's predicament, he secured apartments for her and her family, including me, outside of the city. It was more than expedient, getting Anna away from court just in case there was any chance of whatever she had being caught by the king. Quite frankly, there were quite a few people who I would willingly have seen struck down with some malady, but that was being completely mean. Not that I was feeling very generous at this particular time.

Only Lord Fitzhugh stayed at court, Lady Alice, Elizabeth, Dick, his younger brother George, Anna and her other sisters Alice and Margery were all shipped out with us, the air chilly but fresh as we made our way down river by barge, again supplied by the earl. One thing was obvious, Warwick certainly honoured his family connections. At least, I thought to myself as I wandered through the wintry gardens, it was a temporary release from servitude, the earl judging that I should spend time close to Anna, should she recover, or not, I assumed. Whatever the outcome, he was determined that I should be close by.

As Lady Alice supervised the unpacking of the various chests and carts which had been sent ahead to greet her on arrival, I slipped out into the gardens which looked cold and lonely – much as I felt. It was the feast of St Bridget. St Bridget of Kildare, a coincidence which caused my heart to sadden. My thoughts veered again towards Caitlin, wondering how she was, what she was doing. How much more beautiful her young daughter would have grown.

It felt like years since I had seen her, the image I had of her held close was now uncertain and I wasn't sure that she even looked like I remembered her any more. Surely, she could not have been so beautiful as I remembered. My mind, in its abstinence, had surely embellished her charms. Her eyes were probably not as green, her hair not as abundant and fiery, her skin not as gleamingly pale. They were futile thoughts, but ones I had to try and lift my despondent mood.

I wandered through the gardens which were no doubt a blaze of heady colour in the summer, but were now a shadow of themselves, a spectral, shimmering ghost of what the warm sun would bring. There was a row of trees, branches stripped bare, like bones, reaching down, almost skimming the top of my head as I walked under them, my attention now caught by an open gate in the wall, the silver flash of the river beyond.

Through the archway, I could see both ways down and up river, winding back into the city, and stretching out to the sea beyond. What shocked me was how quiet it was, how the lack of trade now caused the once vibrant heart of the city to slow almost to a standstill. As I stood looking over the river, surrounded by birdsong, I heard what sounded like a sob. A cry, caught in the throat. A sound so sad I almost thought I had imagined it, but it made me turn, taking a few paces away from the gate. The bank sloped back upwards gently, into a small, wooded copse, but what caught my eye was a blue cloaked figure, standing by a large tree whose frozen fronds dipped into the waters below.

It was only as the figure moved that I recognised Elizabeth, and saw her touch her cheek, as if wiping away a tear. She had not seen me, but I moved towards her slowly and before long, she turned, and it was then I saw the total despair on her face. I was not sure what was wrong, but a sharp pain suddenly grabbed me, what if it was Anna? Had she been given some news that had yet to be imparted to myself? My throat closed and so it was that all I could do was stand next to her, watching the river flow by slowly, in its never-ending journey to the sea.

She wiped her face furiously, her colour rising as she looked at me, obviously embarrassed to be found in such distress. I tried to act as casual as I could, not wanting to add to her discomfort, and she sniffed loudly, now rubbing her nose which was a wonderful shade of pink.

"Were you looking for me?"

I shook my head, as in truth I had hoped to get away from everyone for a while.

"No. I was just walking in the gardens." I paused, feeling a little uncomfortable and now knowing I could not avoid the question. "Is something wrong?"

Elizabeth tried to smile, but failed miserably. She pulled her cloak together tighter, as if protecting herself against something invisible. But what she said took me aback.

"I wish I was older." I thought of my lands and estates, held by Warwick until I came of age. To do with as he would, no matter how I felt. He could raze Minster Lovell to the ground and I would have no power to stop him. Not for some years yet.

"You are not alone there!" I said grudgingly, causing her to glance at me quickly.

"It's different for boys. They are not treated as chattel, as bargaining chips in a game." That I wasn't happy to take, not at all.

"I think you are talking to the wrong person. Don't you?"

Tears began to roll down her face. I had never seen her so distressed.

"We are so alike, aren't we? If only it was me you had married. We are, after all, closer in age! I had hoped..." Her head dropped down as her words trailed off and I stepped a little closer, her familiar fragrance warm in the chill air.

"Hoped?"

She looked up at the sky again as if searching for answers.

"I had hoped, if you...if we..." Once again she shook her head. "No matter."

I reached up and touched a stray wisp of her hair, my fingers brushing her skin. She looked so radiantly beautiful. Some man was one day going to be very fortunate to have her as a bride.

"It does matter, to me."

She exhaled loudly, once again avoiding looking at me

directly. Her usually blue eyes were washed pale by tears.

"I had hoped that if we had lain together, my father would annul your marriage to Anna. After all," her dark eyes found mine now with an intense ferocity, "we are more suited in age. Anna is still a child. If we gave in to our desires, perhaps..."

My head began to spin. It made perfect sense in a way. She was much more my own age. If we had been married, instead of Anna and I, by now we certainly would have been man and wife in the most intimate sense of the word. I met her eyes and had to admit, the thought did not displease me at all, in fact, all it did was fan a small flame of anger. Why had I been wed to one of the youngest Fitzhugh girls? Why, when there was one readily available who was more of an age? What had been the sense of it?

Elizabeth was a beauty. Not in the same way as Caitlin, the two were totally different as women could be, but in no way would I have found myself disappointed had I been presented with such a bride. So, why had that not happened? Had someone already expressed an interest in taking her hand, and if so, who? And why was she still unmarried?

As I stood immersed in my thoughts, Elizabeth pulled her cloak closer around her and walked towards me, stopping to look up into my face with wide, tear-moist eyes.

"What are you thinking?"

For no reason other than I could, I reached out and encircled her with my arms, pulling her body close to mine. Her head fell onto my shoulder and I felt her sigh. She was so soft, so pliable, her body almost moulding to mine as we stood together in the chill of the morning. A sudden flutter of wings made me look up as an ebony raven, launched itself from the crenellations which peeped above the cluster of bare branches which waited patiently for spring to clothe them in finery once more.

"I am thinking," I replied slowly, watching the bird grow smaller against the grey sky, "that I would have liked that very much."

Slowly, she turned her head up, until our lips were inches apart, and the temptation became too much. We kissed, but it was light, gentle, almost regretful. It was probably the sweetest, most innocent kiss I had ever had, and I held her tighter against me, but having a strange feeling of wanting to protect her at this moment rather than ravish her.

"Oh Francis," Elizabeth whispered against my lips, her breath warming them despite the brisk air. "What shall we do?"

I knew what I wanted to say. Had we had the opportunity, I would have already claimed her maidenhood, I knew that for certain. It had not entered my mind that such an act may cause my marriage to be annulled, as I had no intention of letting anyone know it had happened. Only Elizabeth... carefree, reckless as she was, had obviously thought this through. Yet, I was not sure she had the full measure of it. Something told me that the shame would be hers and that my marriage arrangement would remain intact.

I didn't doubt for a second that such a prize as she would be accepted by any man worthy of the name, despite a lost virginity. But the risk was too great, no matter how much I may desire her. Suddenly, everything seemed so futile, making me feel sad and desperate at the same time. Everything was so uncertain, the cold air itself felt full of anticipation, of tremulous change.

Caitlin. She may never see Richard again. There were rumours of Edward's return, yes. But they were just that. He may never come back, or if he did, he may not succeed in claiming his throne. After all, who ever knew that Warwick had the strength of will to take it from him in the first place? Once Margaret landed, the whole situation would be different. The disaffected Lancastrians who kept an arms length from what they saw as Warwick's court, would rush to her side, confident in their power at her side.

What would happen if he failed? If Richard was imprisoned – or killed? I swallowed hard. Fear flooded my body as I allowed my thoughts to visualize things I had never considered before.

Caitlin couldn't live the rest of her life in sanctuary. Then there was Kathryn, and Richard's unborn child.

I didn't want to think about it any more, at least, not whilst I held Elizabeth in my arms.

"I don't know," I replied eventually, and somewhat weakly it had to be said. "I wish I did."

And to be frank, I was telling the truth.

29. GREENWICH PALACE
February 1471

As if she sensed what was happening, Anna began to recover. I spent two of the following three days at her bedside, reading passages from 'Tristan and Isolde," my favourite tale, as she lay beneath the coverlet, watching me with large, gentian eyes, which betrayed no emotion. She appeared totally exhausted, and pale, and although there were no smiles for me, she managed an attempt at one for Elizabeth, who sat opposite me on the other side of the bed, her head bent over her needlework.

A sleety rain had begun to fall, almost relentless in its insistence and shadows gathered in every room, despite the plentiful torches and candlelight. Fires roared healthily in every hearth and even though it was freezing outside, the chamber where we spent those days was unusually cosy, despite the tension which rippled across the embroidered counterpane, unseen or unknown to anyone but Elizabeth and myself.

Under the watchful gaze of Lady Alice and the rest of the Fitzhugh siblings, we were finding it hard not to betray the connection between us. Dick had left again for the city, to join Lord Fitzhugh, leaving only the women and younger children behind. Oh, and me of course. The days dragged on interminably, and as I was spending most of my time with Anna, and usually with either Elizabeth or Lady Alice as chaperone. I felt completely on edge most of the time which was wearing on the nerves, it had to be said.

It was therefore with some relief that on hearing his niece was on the mend, Warwick decided to send for me. It was the eve of the Feast of St Agatha when Lady Alice came into the chamber, just as Isolde was about to enter into a marriage with King Mark between the pages in my hand. I was almost relieved for the interruption as my own imagination had mercilessly replaced that image with one of Richard and Caitlin standing before the altar. Both myself and Elizabeth looked up, although Anna's eyes remained on me, I could almost feel them burning into my skin so intense was her gaze.

"Francis," Lady Alice began in her usual perfunctory manner, "Lord Warwick wishes you to attend him at Baynard's Castle. You should leave within the hour."

"Mama?" It was the first time I had heard Anna speak, as most of the time she had lain silent as if her illness had made her mute. "Must Francis go?"

Lady Alice cast a quick glance at her other daughter, whose fingers had paused over her stitch-work.

"Of course he must. He is Lord Warwick's servant and must obey his wishes."

I avoided looking at anyone for fear of what I may give away. I wasn't entirely sure if I felt dread or relief. There was an undoubted tension growing here, as Anna recovered her senses and seemed to watch me with eyes which had developed the keenness of a hawk. Then there was Elizabeth. Yet, being back at court would offer no relief.

"Will he come back?"

It was almost as if I wasn't there, so I kept my eyes down, looking at the dark leather cover of the romance I held in my hand. My Tristan to Caitlin's Isolde. The tale always rang somewhat true to me.

"That is up to his lordship." Her tone was more than a little irritable and I wondered what other tidings Warwick had sent to his sister. "You must learn to bear these absences Anna. Francis will be a knight someday, and will need to be away from home on service to his king. It is what he has been trained for."

At this I did stand, biting my tongue to prevent me from asking which king it would be. Instead, I picked up Anna's clammy hand and pressed my lips to her fingers.

"I will see you soon. I hope your health continues to improve." I tried not to see Elizabeth as I raised my head, catching only a glimpse of her golden hair. Instead I looked at Lady Alice, who was nodding, approvingly, and I left the room, clasping the book in my hand tightly, pleased to be gone.

Within the hour, as decreed, I was in a barge, surging forward under lowering skies that at least had the courtesy to stop their downpour of freezing rain. I kept my cloak wrapped tightly around me, protecting my newly donned Warwick livery, as we rounded the bend in the river and the massive edifice which was Baynard's grew larger in my sight. It was as grey as the storm filled skies. Greyer. Dark and forbidding in this weather, although I knew it as a place of laughter and joy, not so very long ago. Sun-filled and warm. A child's innocent laughter ringing off the walls.

As the boat bumped into the dock, I took the stairs two at a time and made my way through the bailey gate, immediately encountering a small party, standing by their horses. It didn't take me long to recognise them. The earl himself always stood out and today was no exception, even though he was not dressed in court finery. Clarence had his back to me, but I would have known him anywhere, and as always he was clad in fabric so fine as to shout his royal status from the roof tops. The other two men were Warwick's friend, Plummer and Sir John Langstrother, Henry's treasurer. They were deep in conversation but it did not take long for Warwick's keen gaze to spot my approach.

"Ah, at last. We can depart now."

All the men turned and looked at me as one, with only George showing the slightest grin of recognition. I couldn't help thinking he looked as if he had a secret which no one else could guess. Except it seemed so obvious that only a fool would be so transparent.

"Why have we waited for him?" That came from Plummer, who was looking at me with disdain.

"He's my squire John. And one I intend to keep close from now on."

George winked at me then, when no one could see him and I wracked my brain to think what he could mean. Was it due to my connections with the king, after what had happened at Middleham, or because Lady Alice had warned him about my closeness to his other niece? But I had hardly time to think as I was given a horse, which I mounted quickly as the rest of them made to leave, even though I had no idea where we were going.

I followed them, riding at the back, as we headed down Thames Street, keeping the river to our right, and for a while I wondered if we were making for the Tower, only to then dismiss this as I could easily have disembarked there. But as the turrets of the White Tower pierced the cloud, we turned up towards Bishopgate, and headed north. After a while we turned into a large building with a grand frontage, and oriel windows, riding under the archway, where another familiar figure stood waiting. George Neville, Archbishop of York and now Chancellor of the realm, stood wringing his hands, his anxiety plain. He stepped forwards as we dismounted, to a host of grooms who appeared from nowhere.

"Are we ready?" It was Warwick's voice, clear and authoritative.

"Well, yes," said George, glancing anxiously at Clarence. "I didn't realise you were coming accompanied."

Warwick looked over his shoulder grimly.

"I thought I may be in need of support. I don't expect this to be easy."

George Neville screwed his mouth up anxiously, but his brother laid a hand on his shoulder and whispered something too quiet for me to hear. Or anyone else for that matter, but it gave someone an opportunity.

"Welcome back!" I knew without moving that he stood next to me. "I began to wonder what the earl had done with you, till he told me your bride was ailing!" Clarence was grinning at me broadly, his eyes shining. "Is she recovered?"

I nodded dumbly for a moment as he brushed invisible dust from his sleeves elegantly.

"What are we doing here?" I asked quietly, adjusting my own

cloak as we followed Warwick into the main hall.

"We are here to offer a king sackcloth instead of silk."

I looked at him, puzzled. What exactly did that mean? But as usual he just grinned and looked around.

"I do hope they have some Malmsey! It is just the day for it!"

I gasped in amazement as we entered a huge hall with a hammer-beam roof and a fireplace almost as high and wide as the doors through which we had entered. Flames roared with welcome and candles stood in sconces in their dozens, illuminating a group of men who sat around a large table in the centre of the room.

Servants scurried around with quiet confidence, pouring wine and taking away what appeared to be the remnants of a meal, replacing the dishes with bowls of scented water and bringing in more wine, wafers and platters of winter berries and almonds.

Remembering myself I hurried forwards and took Warwick's cloak as he divested it from his shoulders, although I had no idea where the nearest coffer or peg would be on which to hold it. Helpfully, one of the other servants relieved me of my burden with a small grin, passing me a flagon. As Warwick seated himself, I stepped up to the table and poured the wine into an empty goblet, before stepping back, watching as someone else filled Clarence's goblet also. He smiled, as if waiting for the entertainment to begin. Warwick took a drink and cleared his throat.

"Thank you, my lords, for agreeing to meet me this day," He scanned the room, taking in the assembled faces, and it was then I began to recognise one or two from the Christmas court, and realisation dawned. Warwick had assembled the French ambassadors, away from the prying eyes of court, and in the presence of his closest allies. Or those he thought were close.

Each man was dressed finely, rich silks and velvets, their tones warmed by the flames. Their foreign sumptuousness gave the whole gathering the air of a fabulous tapestry, and I already knew that Frenchmen set great store by their apparel, often sniffing in disapproval at the forms of English dress.

I could name most of them. The stiff, noble profile of Louis de Harcourt, Patriarch of Jerusalem and Bishop of Bayeaux. The friendlier, high coloured visage of Tanguy de Chaslet, Governor of Roussillion. Two other no less imposing men had been sent as secretaries, although they seemed to be off duty this evening, Dr Nichol Michel and Guillame de Cerisy.

Then there was the most unusual man in the party, the Scot William Moneypenny, Seigneur de Concressault and a man I knew was a good friend of Warwick, back from the earlier rebellions. Scotland and France had age old connections, and it appeared the so called 'auld alliance' was still strong. I wondered idly if the ambassadors would be here at all were it not for Moneypenny's presence.

"Your Parliament has reconvened?" The strongly accented tones of Tanguy rang out, as he dried his fingers delicately on a linen cloth, before reaching over to select a handful of pale almonds from the silver dish in the centre of the table.

Warwick took a deep drink of his wine as everyone looked at him for his answer. His skin was amber in the flames.

"It has."

Tanguy raised his eyebrows as he chewed, but it was Moneypenny who spoke.

"Hae they an agreement?"

I saw Clarence put his own goblet down and his lips curve in a smile. A smile of anticipation. Of great pleasure. Whatever was about to happen, he was going to enjoy every minute.

Warwick cleared his throat yet again. He went to take another drink, but changed his mind.

"All is going to plan, but some – difficulties have become clear. The trade agreement remains contentious; many merchants have long held associations with Burgundy which will take some breaking. I have – there are others working on

414

persuading them that trade with France can be just as filling for their coffers." He hesitated then, his fingers fiddling with the stem of his cup. "However, council have agreed to a truce." There was a slight murmur around the room as he paused. "Ten years, lasting for five years only after either party makes a move to denounce it."

"Obviously," Clarence drawled, his voice velvet with pleasantry, "this will be a disappointment as it is no where near the thirty-year alliance which your master desires. And which was promised."

"And Burgundy?" I didn't catch who had asked that question but Warwick nodded, looking down at the table.

"Three thousand men are being despatched to Calais this next week. They will join Louis's forces, and I will follow as soon as I can with a host of archers."

"Why do you not leave with the men? Why do you wait? Surely, they would fare better with a leader of note flying banners?" Tanguy again spoke up as the others nodded their heads sagely.

"I cannot leave England until the queen lands," Warwick answered quickly. "To which end, Sir John here," he gestured to Langstrother, "will accompany the first force to Calais. My deputy there, Wenlock, and Sir John will accompany the queen to England with all haste so that our plan can reach fruition."

Louis de Harcourt fixed Warwick with a steely glare, one which Warwick matched look for look.

"This is not exactly what we came to achieve." The fire crackled with sudden warning.

"This be the best on offer fae now," said Moneypenny, his tone conciliatory. "You all nae how the man is vexed. Once Queen Margaret is here, with Charles on the back-foot, these agreements can be improved upon. There be many men who cannae find themsel' to agree with the man here until he has shown his colour across the channel. We will have the queen, her prince," he glanced at Warwick then and their eyes met, "and his princess, all

415

standing by thon king Henry. All the better if thon girl is ready to bear a princeling. Tha' be a dynasty in the making, my lords. The wheel will turn, then, be sure on it!"

Clarence had been staring into his wine, as if seeing his future there, and at this he looked up, all amusement gone from his face, but what had replaced it was just as concerning.

"And what of my brother, my lord? Do you think Charles will watch English soldiers march into his lands without hurling Edward back over the North Sea like an axe to land in our backs and prevent the advance? He can do little about a French invasion, only fight with his backs to his lands. But an English one? Can we fight a war on two fronts?"

Tanguy smirked at him.

"Charles is weak. He has already released two English prisoners as a sign of good will to the Lancastrian cause, has he not? Those men, I forget their names..."

Clarence snorted in real derision.

"Somerset and Exeter you mean? And where are they? Have they been to court to pledge their allegiance to our cause? Have they offered to raise men? Or is their silence ominous?"

"This does no good, George," sighed Warwick. "We fight with what we have. We have enough."

George pushed his cup away at the same time as he slid his chair back and stood up, his hand resting casually on the hilt of his dagger.

"I sincerely hope so cousin, for should Edward return, we will find ourselves scattered to the four winds." He took a step back and turned towards his wife's father, his face as serious as I had ever seen it. "Do you fancy your leg on a spike in Kent while your upper quarter adorns Pontefract, my lord?"

To the astonishment of the room, he turned away and left the table and the room, as each pair of eyes followed him. Warwick snapped his fingers and I stepped forwards to refill his goblet, and watched as he drank deeply.

"My lord..." Sir John had leaned towards him across the

416

table, but it was then I saw Warwick was grinning and I knew why. If Clarence was scared, he had not turned his coat and was more likely to raise more men to Warwick's cause.

Whatever Clarence thought, Warwick seemed satisfied by his display this evening. I, however, had no such confidence, for as Clarence had left the room, he had thrown me a wink.

30. WESTMINSTER PALACE
February 1471

We returned to Westminster that evening, and seemed to leave behind us a general accord. In the main, the ambassadorial party seemed to know that although what Warwick offered was far from what Louis expected them to deliver, in the current circumstances there were very few options open to them.

The fact that Langstrother was being sent to accompany the queen seemed to satisfy them, and they had decided to stay on and greet her upon her arrival in England. The way I saw it, this gave them the additional benefit that the closer it got to the queen's arrival, the more bargaining power Warwick may have, and therefore maybe the deal they took back to France could improve. It was worth the wait.

During the following week the terms were agreed by Parliament. Yet still, Warwick had also promised to send a great force to Calais, and indeed to follow it with a host of his own. It became increasingly apparent that despite the promise of immediate action to back Louis's own advances, Warwick was dragging his heels. Even I knew it made sense. The man would be mad to leave England before Margaret made land. He may even be mad to leave after it at all, for once he was gone, he no longer held the reins which were firmly affixed to King Henry, and which gave Warwick his slender grasp on power.

I began to worry exactly what would happen when the queen appeared. It was well known that her agreement with Warwick was a deal made with the devil, for both of them. With their return, would come Prince Edward, and his bride, Anne Neville. It was what all the Lancastrian lords were waiting for, and it remained to be seen what would happen next.

My mind was a tumult of thoughts, particularly one evening, as I cleared away the remnants of Warwick's meal which he had chosen to eat in his chamber, whilst dictating letters to a scribe. It was the Feast of St Wulfric, and for some reason that had been on my mind all day.

No – not for some reason. For the reason that Lady Alice, Anna and Elizabeth had returned to court. St Wulfric had been known for his love of hunting with hawks and hounds before he became a hermit. He had also confessed publicly to having experienced an unusually intimate dream. Seeing Anna, even briefly, had reminded me of Lark, whereas Elizabeth reminded me of other, more sensual pursuits. Which had also coloured my dreams!

It was as I gathered up the silver plate that the door opened and Lady Alice entered, looking as imperious as ever. Her eyes took in the chamber in one sweep, and Warwick hardly raised his head, signing the documents which the scribe placed before him, the sound of the nib scratching on the vellum overly loud in the silence.

"You did not eat in the hall?" It was an obvious statement, and for while he ignored her words. But Lady Alice was having none of it. "You did not even appear to greet your family. Your niece, who has recovered from an ailment which almost took her from us!" She crossed herself quickly and I felt the back of my neck burn, as I am sure she was looking at me.

Warwick snapped his fingers, and I turned, as he sat back in his chair, dismissing the scribe with one casual flick of the hand. The scribe hurried from the room, giving me a quick glance as he did so. I took the flagon from the sideboard over to Warwick and poured wine into his cup and he snatched it up immediately drinking deeply. So deeply, I had cause to fill his cup as soon as he put it down.

"There is no need for me to sit in a nest of vipers to hear the sound they make. I can hear it just as well from here. Besides, there is much to do if I am to leave for the coast."

Lady Alice looked at me pointedly, and I returned to the sideboard to fill a cup of wine for her also. She took it from me without even acknowledging I was there.

"The coast? Are we being invaded?"

Warwick shook his head with a grim smile.

"Of course not. I have word that Margaret waits on Langstrother and Wenlock. Once they arrive, she will be crossing. I intend to be there to welcome her."

"And to have her ear on the journey back to London, no doubt?"

The grin widened.

"You know me too well, sister."

"Do you not think it is dangerous to leave the city at this time? After all, there are rumours, even though they have been unfounded. Is it worth the risk?"

Warwick drummed his fingers on the table, speculatively, although his expression was relatively untroubled.

"Brother George will take care of the King, Plummer and Cook can be trusted. And I have a mind to leave someone else behind who can keep me appraised of all of their movements. Particularly those of a certain Plantagenet brother."

Lady Alice raised her eyebrows high, her fingers beginning to pluck at the rosary attached to her girdle.

"Someone you can trust? Truly?"

Warwick inhaled deeply, picking his cup up once more. He seemed to have the thirst of ten men of late.

"Would you mind leaving us?"

I turned to look at him quickly, hiding my surprise.

"Yes, my lord." He next words made me stop mid-step.

"No, not you."

A slow smile spread across his sister's face and I had no idea what suddenly passed between them, but she placed her cup on the mantel delicately and inclined her head.

"Will you call and see your niece before you retire?"

Warwick nodded genially, his smile warm, his voice softer than normal.

"I will. I am pleased she is much improved."

Satisfied, Lady Alice left the room without a further word,

which for some reason left me feeling uneasy. Once the door had closed, Warwick gestured to the seat by the table and I looked around. I was, of course, the only person there, but it was still with some trepidation that I sat down before him. Nervously.

"One day, you will realise that the loyalty of your own flesh and blood means more to you than anything else. As it is now, the only bond you know is the fleshly one."

I was totally puzzled and it showed on my face, I knew it did. I had no clue what he was referring to. I was not his flesh and blood, although Anna was. Was I not being loyal to her? Is that where this was leading? He knew about Elizabeth? I said nothing.

"Not too long ago, you disgraced me,' he continued. "By absconding from the north when I was expecting you to support my cause." We had been here before so I had no problem defending myself.

"To do that would have been to rise against my king, my lord. It was a simple choice." I was almost grinding my teeth in anger.

"You have a new king now," he said curtly. "Were you in the same fix, would you take the same action?"

I frowned at him and he became suddenly impatient, his voice rising.

"If someone were to ask you to join forces with them against King Henry, would you flee rather than put your name to that cause?"

Now I saw where he was going. My gut began to tighten. How I longed to be away from this place. Back in the north, with my friends. Back before any of this had started, before the Wheel of Fortune began to spin with alarming speed. I took a deep, steadying breath.

"You are asking if I would rally to support Edward should he return."

"I am." He leaned across the table, his eyes dark, fixed on mine. "And before you answer, there is something you should remember. Your sisters are young, vulnerable. Although I was not charged to, I was happy to take them into my care when Edward fled the country. They are safe, and cared for, at Minster Lovell. The youngest girl, Frideswide? Unusual name. How old is she now, five, six?"

"Five." I could barely answer him; my jaw was clamped so tight. Was he threatening me in some way? I could hardly speak at the thought of what he may be implying. "Thank you for your care of them." I added grudgingly. "Were I older..."

"Of course!" Warwick grinned broadly now, sitting back once more. "Were you older, you could give them much. Arrange their marriages and furnish them with lands and fortune." He folded his arms across his broad chest. "But you are not. You are some years away from ministering your own lands and managing your own fortune. It is not easy, being too young to take what is yours, be it livery, lands or a kingdom. It is so easy to take a wrong turn, a mis-step, and jeopardise everything you believed was yours. Power, money... family."

I gripped the arms of the chair tightly, keeping me in my seat. I could hardly breathe! I knew what power he held over me, over all my future. But this was despicable! This was my own flesh and blood he was toying with. It all made sense now. He wanted to keep me loyal. This was how he intended to do it, by subtle threats couched in a fatherly tone.

"I can see that it would be," I replied carefully as he nodded sagely.

"I am glad we understand each other. I was hoping we would. After all, you have become familiar with my family over the months. Very familiar, some would say." My heart began to pound loudly. He was talking about Elizabeth now; I just knew he was. "Which reassures me, now that I have to leave for the coast."

I waited. I knew it had to come. He wanted something from me. I tried to keep my breathing steady.

"How long will you be gone, my lord?" I kept my eyes lowered, subservient.

Warwick pursed his lips.

"Two weeks, I would imagine, at the most. Two weeks when men can make mischief, should their proclivities change with the wind. But I am sure, close family now as you are, that should you see, or hear, anything that you know would cause me care, that you will despatch someone to me. Without fail."

"Any particular men?" I knew my voice sounded tight, but he didn't care. All he wanted was a spy. I would be free to roam about the court whilst he was away, to be responsible to no one, as long as I watched and waited. And reported back to him about anyone, any whisper, which worked against him.

"Well, I would like to make things easier for you and tell you that just about any lord of Lancastrian leanings could do something which could cause me ill will. If only it were that easy! For I could say the same about a plethora of Yorkist lords. All of whom you are more than familiar with. So, that should keep you busy." He paused, smiling. "And keep you out of mischief also."

I swallowed hard. So hard it hurt my throat.

"May I go now, my lord?"

"You may. I wish to retire soon so will let you return to your duties. But a word of warning, Lovell! You may be watching the court, but make no mistake. Someone is also watching you!"

I pushed myself up from the chair. It was as if all of my limbs were encased in lead. He knew my weak point. Knew full well my true affinity lie with Edward. With York. No matter what assurances he had given the ambassadors, it was clear he had little trust in George. In anyone in fact. Not even in me.

And he was right not to, for had he not mentioned my sisters, I would have pledged my loyalty to Edward should I get the merest sniff that he was setting out to come back to England. As I left the chamber, I still felt the same. Only now, it would have to wait. Wait until I was sure that Edward would triumph. There was too much to risk to do otherwise. I just had to hope that Richard would understand, if I were ever to meet him again.

423

31. WESTMINSTER PALACE
March 1471

Warwick left for the south two days later, and I was left to wander the halls at will, supposedly watching and waiting for someone to overstep the mark. George Neville had the care of the king, and brought him out for audiences and feasts like a hound on a leash.

Meanwhile, I roamed through corridor and chamber, listening, watching and hoping to God that I didn't miss something important, which, to be fair, was more than possible. What the lords discussed at breakfast or supper, was most probably different to what they discussed behind closed chamber doors, and these were meetings to which I had no hope of being invited. Oxford, believed to be a good friend of Warwick, was often to be found talking to Sir Richard Tunstall, and more often than not there was one or more of the Stanley brothers in their company.

The biggest threats to Warwick's power, at least in my opinion, were Jasper Tudor, Beaufort, the duke of Somerset and Henry Holland, the Duke of Exeter. Tudor had fought against Edward, and of course was the king's half-brother. But he was now holed up in Wales, taking no part in this puppet court. I had no illusions that he would be working against Warwick, only a huge relief that he was not at court and therefore none of my concern. The same could be said for Somerset and Exeter, which left Clarence as the duke's greatest risk. Warwick was no man's fool.   He knew no-one would act against him before the queen landed, even though they may be laying down plans which would strip him of his power once she sat at the king's side.

One other thing was for sure. None of them would be able to sway the king's opinion against Warwick, for Henry seemed as frail and distracted as ever. Whispering in the royal ear would advance no-one, at least not until his wife and their son appeared in the Painted Chamber. Then, and only then, would there truly be a sovereign on the throne of England.

I had never met Queen Margaret and had no desire to do so. Yet, as things were, I saw no way that anything would change, and that filled me with a deep fear. Margaret had a dread reputation. She had led armies. Edward, Richard and George held her responsible for the death of their father and brother. Warwick himself and Montagu had both fought against her and won. There were too many old scores to settle. No wonder the few Yorkist lords who sat at table as I watched and listened looked both pale and uneasy. Once Warwick returned with his prize, how long would it be before she avenged old causes?

"On your own, Lovell?"

I knew before I turned it was Clarence, both from the drawl and the smell of wine. I had been searching the hall for him, in vain, only to find he had found me first. I was leaning against an archway, and pushed myself away, bowing quickly.

"Your Grace! Can I be of assistance to you?"

Supper was almost finished; George Neville had led the king out whilst I had been thinking about the queen.

"Relax," he smiled, his hazel eyes also scanning the hall. "Have you seen my wife anywhere?"

I was somewhat surprised at the question. It only then occurred to me that I had not seen her this evening, but then, I had not seen George either, and there was no way she would be in the hall unaccompanied.

"No, Your Grace." It was a simple answer and the truth.

"Then, have you seen yours?" I had been looking away, but I could hear the amusement in his voice. I was getting slightly annoyed at being the constant target for anyone to aim at. But I kept my temper.

"This morning, at Mass, Your Grace." I had glimpsed Anna from a distance, as I had Elizabeth. I tried not to hold either of their gazes, I had enough on my mind at present.

"Pretty girl," he mused thoughtfully. "Young. Not like her sister. Now there is a woman whose blood runs hot. You can see it in the way she moves, in how she holds her head. She's more your age isn't she? Older than her sister, that is?"

Although he was a prince of the realm, I knew he was baiting me. I answered as coolly as I could.

"I cannot say I have noticed, Your Grace."

"Such a waste! You would think they could find a better match for the girl. Although, a king's half-brother is not to be sniffed at I suppose. It is just a shame he is such a cold fish!"

My breath caught in my throat and then I did turn and look at him in stunned amazement. His voice may have sounded as if he was jesting, but his face, when I turned, was deadly serious. I had to remember, after everything, the Fitzhugh's, being Warwick's kin, were now also connected to George.

Not that I would have expected that to make any difference to him, but for some reason, this did. It also made a difference to me. I didn't exactly know why, but it did.

"Your Grace?"

Without a word he retreated through the door into an ante-chamber, and I followed him, glad to be away from my post as both sentinel and spy. It was a role I felt I was not terribly well equipped for.

"Isabel spent some time with Lady Alice this afternoon. She went to enquire after your wife's health, she has been ill has she not?" I nodded, trying to keep the astonishment out of my expression that George was speaking to me in any tone other than derision. "It appears that there was a plan to marry the girl last year, but of course, recent events put an end to that. Now Warwick believes he has pulled out another ace from his sleeve. Elizabeth is of age, is a true prize that any man would cherish, and Jasper Tudor is unmarried. As a consolation prize for accepting Warwick as Lord High Chamberlain once Margaret rules the roost once again, I have to say, it is not a bad one at all. One daughter married to a scion of the House of York, one to a Lancastrian prince, one niece to a rich, landed noble, another to the king's half-brother. It is more than Warwick could achieve with my

426

brother, so why would he not relish it? His blood will populate half the land!"

I stared at him, visions of Jasper Tudor in the solar at Baynard's Castle, looking at Caitlin with his mud-flat eyes.

"Edward was a fool!" George spat, his usual mood returning. Before my eyes he transformed back into the George I knew all too well. Full of rage and scorn. "He should have let Dickon marry Anne. It was at least a salve to Warwick's wounds for the loss of the French bride. Who knows where we would all be now? Not bowing to a feeble, straw brained king, that is for certain!"

"Ssh!" The warning was automatic, but George grinned. I looked around urgently, but luckily there was no one near. The hall was emptying rapidly, only the servants and a few others milled around, taking their time. "Does she know?"

"Who?" George looked at me innocently. I could have slapped him. One minute this was like life and death; the next minute it was all a game.

"Elizabeth? Anna's sister?"

George shook his head, pouting.

"I don't believe so." He paused, momentarily, appearing to think. "My mother, the duchess, is coming to visit, did you know? She should arrive tomorrow. I think Warwick has asked her to attend to greet Margaret. Now that will be a sight to see!"

My mind was working furiously.

The duchess. Could she help Elizabeth? Is that why he had mentioned it? Then another thought crept into my head, making me flush guiltily. Could she get me into sanctuary to see Caitlin? All thoughts of Warwick were gone, of what was at stake. The duchess was a powerful, and shrewd woman. Somewhere, deep inside me, hope began to rise.

"I must go," George yawned, stretching his arms wide. "Nice talking to you, Lovell. You must visit with my mother whilst she is here. I am sure she will be only too pleased to see you!"

He strolled away, slow and easy, as if he had not a care in the world and I watched him go, my thoughts in a whirl. It was only when I turned that I saw the figure in the shadows, the figure that stepped out as I peered closer.

It was Elizabeth, and her face was swollen and pink with distress.

32. WESTMINSTER PALACE
March 1471

"Elizabeth?"

I took a step forwards, as she appeared frozen to the spot. Her hands were gripping her velvet skirts, so tightly they were bone white, starkly visible in the flickering of the torches above our heads. I could see the tears glimmering in her eyes, even the evidence of their tracks on her face. My first fear was that she had overheard George talking to me, had heard what he had said about her marriage to Tudor, that she had learned of it in the worst way.

"Did you...?"

I saw her throat move, no doubt preventing further tears from falling, or trying to summon up the power to speak the unspeakable.

"I didn't need to," she whispered, her voice trembling. "I already knew. I heard Isabel talking to my mother. I had to find you!" She took a faltering step forwards. "Is it true? Please... did you know?"

Without even thinking twice, I closed the space between us and reached out, taking her hands into mine. She clutched at them desperately, and I led her into a window embrasure, feeling her trembling as I drew her down into the cushioned seat. Everything was quiet now. Deathly quiet. Only the sounds of servants settling down in the hall, huddling around the embers of the fire. The Compline bells began to chime in the distance, calling the priests to their prayers at St Stephens and beyond. We sat very close, I could feel her leg pressed against mine. For once, it had no effect on me.

"No. I had no idea. None at all."

She shook her head wildly. Eyes, colourless in the shadows, searching my face desperately.

"But you are close to Warwick? Did you not hear of this?

429

Were you not there when the decision was made?"

The all too familiar taste of guilt rose up with a burning heat. Had I been the cause of this? Both Lady Alice and Warwick himself had made casual, subtle reference to my familiarity with this beautiful young girl. Had that closeness sealed her fate? Did they seek to prevent us from being together at the same time as forging an alliance which would see Warwick's position rise higher in the firmament of Henry's council?

My throat ached. I had a strange feeling that everything was coming to some sort of head, that nothing was as it should be. I felt like I was on a horse, galloping headlong down a hill, growing closer to a wide, raging river, far too wide to breach. And I couldn't stop it. I had no way of pulling back on the reins and avoid my fate.

She was still looking at me and I wanted to smile at her, to reassure her, but I couldn't.

"No, I didn't know. Not until the duke just told me. But it doesn't surprise me. Warwick doesn't trust anyone at the minute, and probably rightly so."

I began to feel sick to my stomach. I didn't know what to do. Anna, my sisters, this young girl before me. I seemed unable to do anything to help any one of them. Powerless. I thought of my father, a noble, Lancastrian lord, serving his king. What was I, then? A fool? A failure?

"Francis?" Her gentle voice brought me out of my self flagellation and I gripped her hands tighter.

"I'm so sorry, Elizabeth. But, maybe…" I tried to raise a smile. Failed. "Maybe it won't happen. It could be Jasper Tudor doesn't even know. Maybe he hasn't even agreed? He hates your uncle after all." It could have been true. Tudor was in Wales, he had long tired of pandering to Warwick's display of rule. He may well have other plans, have his sights set on a higher prize.

"You have to help me," she said, suddenly composed, my fingers almost crushed in her grasp. If only I could, I thought, my mind in a fog. If only I knew how. But I had forgotten. This was

Elizabeth, not Anna. From the first moment I saw her, across the bailey at Minster Lovell, she had seemed the most self-assured, the most confident girl I had ever met. Bold and beautiful, even if it had scared me a little at first, to be honest.

"Anything," I smiled sadly. "Truly, if there is anything I can do, I will. But..."

Before another word escaped my lips she prevented it. Lunging forwards, she fastened her lips to mine with such ardour, that I was pressed back into the cold stone of the wall behind me. Instinctively, my arm came up and pressed her closer. I could feel her breasts pressing against my chest, the insistent pressure of her mouth, the sweetness of the taste of her. Despite everything, I couldn't stop myself from becoming aroused, but I managed to recover myself, to grip her arms and push her away. At least for the moment.

"What are you doing?" I was gasping for breath, my heart pounding. My head trying to reason with my body that this was wrong. Fighting a battle it was on the verge of losing.

"Please," she breathed, "you said you would help me!"

"This isn't what I meant!"

"Then, what did you mean?"

It was a question I had no answer for. I hesitated, and she gave me a look so desperate I almost faltered.

"Please! I know you want me! And you know how I feel, ever since I first saw you. If you... if we..." She stopped and her hand came up to my face, her fingers stroked my cheek, her thumb brushed across my chin as light as a feather. "No man would want spoiled goods, Francis."

I knew it was wrong but the touch of her hand made me lose my head and I pulled her back towards me, our lips meeting again, my tongue finding its way into her mouth where she accepted my increased passion willingly. I ran one hand up her bodice, feeling the swell of her breast beneath the fabric, meeting the smooth skin above the neckline of her gown, yet not brave enough, or enough of a rake to force my hand down the front of her dress, even as she surged forward, almost anticipating my touch.

Somewhere in my mind I was still very much aware we were not in a private space, yet my hand longed to slide beneath the folds of her skirts, to rip at the laces which wound down her back. I was fully aroused now, my breath coming hard and fast, and when her hand dropped down to make a much more intimate contact with me than I had expected, I gasped with pleasure, and I felt her lips curve in a knowing smile.

Somehow, that brought me to my senses and I pulled away, as gently as I could. This wasn't right, no matter how much I wanted it, and I truly did, God forgive me, I did! But not here, not in this darkened corner. She was of noble blood, not a servant to be tumbled one night and forgotten. Elizabeth was still smiling, her lips parted in anticipation and my groan was now an inward one of silent despair. How easy this would be! My body clamoured for it!

"Elizabeth," I whispered, breathless, "not here! 'Tis not right, someone may come."

She reached up and ran a hand through my hair.

"But you do want me?" It was a moot question.

"I think that much is obvious!" She cast her eyes down demurely, then back up again, her hand resting lightly on the back of my neck, her fingers moving gently. Coaxingly. Threatening my fragile resolve.

"Then when?" I took a deep breath. I needed to think. My head was beginning to clear and she saw it, instantly. I think she began to fear I would change my mind. "You know, it could help both of us." Her other hand was resting on my thigh now, her fingers curved around the muscle there. God, how I wanted to be weak, in this of all things I seemed to have the strength of ten men. I knew what she meant before she said it, and the very thought made my blood begin to cool. "After all, once we confessed, as we said at Greenwich, it would no doubt end your marriage to Anna. Then there is no way Jasper Tudor would accept me. It would be an insult, surely."

432

I didn't want to disillusion her now, but as my senses returned my reason also flooded back. Yes, it was true that if we committed this carnal sin, Tudor would have little interest in her. But then, no other man would! At least not one of any standing. I was just about to voice my concerns she appeared to guess what I was about to say.

"So, they would have to annul your marriage to Anna, and let us wed instead." The last time she had said this, she had been distressed. It had been a half-formed thought, half-hearted desire maybe. Now, her recent news had solidified her intent. She really wanted to do this. She meant every word.

I couldn't think. I needed time to get my thoughts in order, and that was impossible as I was in peril of drowning in the dark, deep pools that were her eyes. I was married to Anna, Canon Law prohibited the marriage of brothers and sisters, even those made so by marriage! Or did I have that wrong? Were we only to try to prevent the actions of today by throwing ourselves into a pit of sin for the rest of our lives? Yet, I could not disappoint her, I could not bear to see her upset again.

"I know," I said feebly, "but still, we cannot do this. Not now, not here! It would be dishonourable of me, to ravish you in such a place!"

"You see," she smiled, and even in the dark her eyes glowed like candles. "This is why I love you! You are so kind and gentle, and thoughtful." She lifted her hand up once again to my face, and I kissed her fingers. "So, what shall we do?"

I summoned my best expression, which I hoped did not betray how uncertain I felt.

"I don't know, but I will arrange something. Before my lord comes back from the south, as I have no one to account to at present. Leave it with me, for a day or so. Nothing will happen quickly, not with Warwick away."

This seemed to satisfy her and she picked up my hand and kissed it in response. I was sure I felt the flick of her tongue on my skin and I shivered.

"You should go," I whispered, "before you are missed and someone comes looking!"

Elizabeth stood up then, her former despair now a memory.

"I will see you tomorrow?" There was excitement in her tone now, and I truly wished I could share it, but all I felt was anxiety.

"Yes. Tomorrow."

With that, she leaned over and brushed my lips with hers, before disappearing back out into the hall, leaving me alone with my dilemma.

33. WESTMINSTER PALACE
March 1471

The next day found me unusually restless. I rose early and attended Mass as usual, trying to avoid drawing attention to myself in any way. I saw both Anna and Elizabeth, their profiles solemn as they bowed their heads, kneeling in prayer. By entering the chapel at the last moment I positioned myself to my advantage, managing to slip away quickly as everyone trailed of to break their fast.

Memories of Elizabeth played on my mind. I had promised to see her today, but it was too early. I needed time to think. My mind was in complete turmoil. There was my commitment to Warwick, with my sisters almost held to ransom. Caitlin and her daughter, locked in the bowels of the abbey, Richard, stranded in exile and now Elizabeth, desperately relying on me to provide a comfort I was by no means sure I could give. My cares were increasing by the day and no matter how I turned my thoughts over and over, there was no way forwards where I could really be of help to anyone.

Instead of going to break my own fast, I walked around the palace grounds, taking myself away from the palace walls. My feet took me where my heart wanted to go and before long I found myself outside the Abbey, where I just stared at the tall, darkly stained windows, behind which Caitlin lived her life now. And for how much longer?

My mind shouted out a word of warning, reminding me I should really be in the hall or pacing the corridors of the palace. Listening, watching, looking for the slightest sign that even the most loyal of Warwick's supporters may be mumbling noises of dissent. What if I missed something? Something Warwick found out on his return and believed I should have reported back to him? What would he do? Would he forgive my transgression, or punish me anyway?

No answer came to me, but still I could not turn back.

I must have been wandering around in the early spring sunshine for around an hour, before I went to stand on the embankment. The sound of the river was in some way calming, watching the boats wend their way up and down, taking the city dwellers about their business, all of them getting on with their daily lives. For a few moments, I envied them. Even the humblest merchant, tavern-keeper or tradesman, plying their wares, earning enough coin to put food on the table. Good, honest work. No politics. No need to constantly have a care for who you spoke to or what you said. To know one wrong word could change your fortune.

Some activity at the end of the dock caught my eye and I walked towards it, just in time to see Clarence stepping down into a large, gilded barge. I had no idea where he was going, but my gut instinct told me I needed to know. Now. I had to take a risk, which would either pay off or not. I ran down the pier quickly, reaching the steps just as he turned back, flinging his cloak over his shoulder flamboyantly, in case anyone may be watching and unaware of his crimson damask finery.

"Your Grace?"

I called out before I had completely made up my mind what I was going to say, and now he was looking up at me. He raised a hand, holding it above his brows, shading his eyes against the early sun.

"Lovell? Is that you?"

"Yes, Your Grace?"

"What do you want?"

Good question! What did I want? I was more than aware of the boatmen, paused, waiting. One of them was holding a coiled rope in his hand, looking up at me impatiently. I had to think quickly.

"Are you for the Tower?" What if he said no? I bit my bottom lip hard as I watched him consider the question, flicking his eyes towards the boatman.

"No. I'm for Baynard's." That could only mean one thing. The duchess must have arrived! My mind went blank, yet George, the accomplished plotter, obviously saw through my ploy. "I have servants there. If you want a message taking through to the Tower, you can send a rider from there." He grinned then. "Has Warwick left you so ill served by henchmen that you have to deliver his messages yourself now?"

I saw him wink at me – or thought he did, as I pretended to fumble inside my cloak for the non-existent message.

"Thank you, Your Grace," I said humbly as I began to move further down the steps.

"Good grief man," George glared at me in his best affected horror. "I am not your lackey! You can deliver it yourself. Get in and be quick about it. Although expect to walk back for the privilege!"

I nodded eagerly and jumped into the barge as the boatman finally threw the rope onto the floor and gave a yell for the waiting oarsmen to pull away.

"Nicely done," George murmured as I stood beside him, looking out to the east, further downriver where the walls of the city sat, bathed in sunlight. I pretended I had not heard him, but was inwardly more than pleased that he had seen fit to aid me in my cause. Even if he didn't really know what my cause was, and I was not entirely sure myself. Other than some desperate hope that she may be able to achieve what I had not. Access to Caitlin and her daughter.

We didn't speak any more during the short journey to Puddle Dock, in fact George made sure of it by taking himself under the fringed canopy and lounging on a seat, ignoring me completely. He was right to do so. As Warwick had said, somewhere, someone was also watching me. The only fear I had at the moment was coming up with a reason for sending a message to the Tower. I would think of something – should I need to. I had time.

Before too long, we disembarked at the Castle, and George

snapped his fingers at me commandingly, if a little too imperiously. He was obviously enjoying himself, acting out this sham. It came all too easily to him, making me wonder if anyone ever saw the real George Plantagenet.

"Come with me!" he barked, and I obligingly followed him into the bailey, and then upstairs to the private apartments, which we quickly bypassed. I thought I recognised one or two faces as we strode by, at some speed it had to be said, only to have my suspicions confirmed as we approached the chapel. Outside the door, standing sentinel, my eyes met the solid form and blazing blue gaze of Patrick Malone, who looked at me sternly, as if he had never met me before.

As we entered the chapel, the Duchess of York rose from her knees at the altar rail, if a little stiffly, and performed a thoughtful genuflection, before moving off to the right without acknowledging our presence. I knew there was a small, private chamber there, used by the chaplain, who was notable by his absence today. George followed her, and I, being given no other instruction, followed him.

I closed the door behind us as the duchess turned raising her chin with an assured defiance. I had not seen her for some weeks, but it felt comforting being in her presence again, as if she was a well-loved member of my family who I had not been able to visit with for a long time. Even though she did not look at me, her very presence was warm and welcoming, making me feel so relieved I had taken my impromptu morning stroll. If I had not, I would have missed this whole encounter.

"Were you followed?"

George shrugged carelessly, placing his hand on his belt.

"Possibly. It is hard to say. No one knows who spies on who these days."

I smothered a noisy gulp at that!

The duchess glanced at me quickly, almost smiled. It was an economical expression, but one that showed more emotion than I had ever seen in her face.

438

"Edward has left Flushing. He will land on the East Coast, although I am not sure where. Or indeed when. I would imagine Oxford's men will roam the east, as for Percy..."

"He now has his chance to show his thanks to Edward for restoring his title. He will sit firm; I am sure of it." George's voice was almost a whisper, yet his words were no less urgent. "Warwick is on his way back. Margaret has failed to show and he has probably had wind of what Edward is up to. I will no doubt be ordered to summon my men in the south west and so could be on the road by tomorrow. Do we know who else is for us?"

"Enough." That one word implied confidence and suspicion at the same time. A certainty that men had promised to flock to Edward's aid, and a reticence even now to tell her capricious son too much. "That is all you need to know. Too much knowledge is a burden with stakes as high as they are. As long as Edward can land, the rest should fall into place. Warwick has no one he can trust to hold London should he have to move north, especially as Margaret appears to have failed him." She smiled grimly, satisfied. "London was always Edward's city."

"And we have Norfolk, Cromwell, Wiltshire and Essex."

The duchess seemed to consider, and fixed her son with a sharp look.

"We need God on our side as well!"

I listened to all of this in silence, trying not to raise hope where there may be none. I was holding on to one slim fact – Edward had always had the luck of the devil. Never had he more need of it than now. The other thing which had become startlingly obvious was my vain wish that the duchess may help me gain access to the abbey, to see Caitlin. It was what I desired more than anything. Anything, that is, apart from seeing Edward safely back on the throne. Here were two of the most royal people in the land, plotting behind the king's back and all I could think about was my own selfish desires. I hoped I was not blushing in shame.

Suddenly, I realised how quiet it had become. Both of them

were looking at me, whilst I had been lost in the fog of my thoughts. Cecily inclined her head towards me.

"My son tells me you have remained loyal to our cause," she said quietly. "That cannot have been easy. I thank you for your service."

I bowed my head, a little embarrassed, not sure what to say.

"I have tried not to do anything which would harm the house of York, Your Grace." She smiled at me then, a vestige of the duchess I remembered from last summer returning, her colour rising. "I wish I could have done more."

It was George who grinned then, paying inordinate attention to the cuff of his doublet, his eyes not meeting mine.

"Oh I would say you have done more than you will ever know. I for one am most grateful for your constancy over these last months."

My face burned hotly at his words. I was not at all sure how I felt about being complimented by someone with George's reputation for vagary. I wasn't even sure what I was supposed to have done. I had served Warwick with a quiet reluctance, but it had to be said that he was fully aware of my true allegiance. If not, he would hardly have been holding my sisters to ransom.

"There may yet be an opportunity," the duchess continued, ignoring George's words. "All I would ask is that you stay vigilant. These next few weeks may challenge the best of us." Her smile broadened. "I hear Margaret waits for the Ambassador's to return to France, and will not depart until she has first hand witness of the success of his negotiations."

George chuckled softly.

"Whilst the Ambassadors linger in London, awaiting to greet Margaret on her arrival. If my brother were here, I would hear him declaring 'checkmate!'"

Stalemate, more like, I thought to myself. Warwick's plans seemed hampered by caution and suspicion, and the responsibility for a lot of that rested on the shoulders of the urbanely garbed prince to my left. I almost felt sorry for

Warwick, despite the fact that he had brought the whole damn mess on himself.   A sharp rap on the door cut through the quiet. As one we all looked towards the sound, but it was George who moved quickly in response, going out of the door and disappearing back into the chapel.

The duchess and I regarded each other in silence. She was rolling the sapphire beads of her rosary between her thumb and finger, almost unconsciously. I took my chance. If I could not see Caitlin, maybe at the very least, I could be assured she was well.

"Your Grace, have you had any news of your grandchild, or of Lady Desmond?"

The elegant, if aged, fingers stopped their constant motion and she folded her hands before her girdle, looking thoughtful.

"I know my grandson, the Prince of Wales, thrives. I know my other grand-daughters do well, or as well as they can do in such captivity." She inhaled deeply. "Of Lady Desmond I have heard little. Although…" a small smile thinned her lips, "as the queen considers her a servant, she would not see the need on speaking of her, no more than she would a laundress." She saw my face fall as I took this in and sighed. It was true, I knew that, but no matter what status Caitlin had, Kathryn was her grand-daughter too. "I am sorry, Francis. I am sure she is well or otherwise I would have heard of it. God willing, we will all be reunited soon."

A small flame of resentment began to burn, although I knew none of this was her fault. My rising ire was all saved for only one person.

"I did try to see her myself, Your Grace. The Bishop of Bath and Wells…"

My words died in my mouth as I saw her face harden.

"What of him?"

I was once again puzzled by the reaction to his name. He seemed as loyal as a man could be to their house, yet his name provoked only stone-faced expressions. And silence.

"He recommended me to Abbot Milling. I went into

sanctuary to ensure for myself that Lady Desmond was well. Last I saw her at court, before the holy season, she was distressed." One of her eyebrows made a perfect arch, lining her brow.

"And?"

"The queen said she was indisposed and so could not see me."

There was a tense silence for a few moments. The duchess seemed to be gathering her thoughts, but eventually, she stepped forwards, and laid one slim hand on my shoulder, bone-white.

"It is a difficult time, bearing a child. Yet she is safer there than around the foul miasma which swills around Henry's court. She will be fine, Francis. The best thing you can do for her is to help Edward regain his throne in any small way you can. Once this has been achieved, Richard will take care of Lady Desmond. Of that, you should be assured."

I knew she was right. As I looked back into those eyes which so resembled her son's, I knew it. The trouble was, that didn't help me. I wanted to see her. Needed to see her, just to drink in her beauty once more, to be soothed by the balm that was her voice. I had been so bound up with Elizabeth, with her flirtatious manner and the effect that she had on my body, that I had almost let myself forget the chasm Caitlin had left in my heart.

I knew what Elizabeth wanted from me, and last night, I had almost promised I would grant her wish. But I couldn't, I knew I couldn't. If Caitlin had not been immured in that dark place, my foolish fumblings with Elizabeth would never have happened. I was sure of it. As I stood looking at Richard's mother, I knew I could not disgrace myself, or spoil a young girl's reputation. She, like I, would have to pray to God that Edward prevailed.

George entered the room again, leaving the door open and I glimpsed Malone standing behind him, waiting. A stable, dependable presence.

"We have to go. Warwick is approaching the city."

The duchess dropped her hand from my shoulder and I instantly regretted the loss of her reassuring warmth.

"Then go, and go with God. I will pray for you both."

Somehow, those gentle words in that hushed place, steeled my resolve.

We returned to a sense of chaos and urgency which was a complete reversal from the calm, sun-bright peacefulness that I had left behind me earlier that day.

I had not been back inside the palace with enough time to draw breath before Warwick stormed into the privy apartments, followed close behind by Clarence, Oxford, Tunstall, Plummer, Cooke the Bishop of Coventry and Lichfield, the keeper of the privy seal. He bumbled in behind everyone else and then hung around by the door, almost too scared to enter any further. And no wonder.

Warwick was puce with rage, and spared no time in expressing his anger, thumping his fist on the table, almost cleaving it in two with the force of the impact. The noise alone made me and Will, the other servant who had been readying his chamber, start visibly, both standing back as he reared up, like a snake threatening to strike.

"Jesus Christ! Are we so in awe of a band of impoverished Yorkists that we have taken to cowering in the shadows already? I have just heard Mayor Stockton has taken to his bed, obviously hiding under there with his piss-pot! The traitors haven't even seen land yet and already he's running scared! He better be the only one or by God, I swear to you, heads will roll!" No one dared to answer him, let alone gainsay him and point out he had no authority to order a summary execution. After all, that had not stopped him before.

"Where is the queen?" asked Oxford, looking uneasily around the room. "I thought you had gone south to escort her back?"

"Well, yes," growled Warwick, "so did I! But as I stood on the south coast hovering like a lackey, waiting to offer her wine and wafers, she's obviously decided to hold court in Honfleur for some god-forsaken reason. Perhaps her accommodations on board the fleet are deemed too shabby for a returning exile so she is waiting for them to be refitted to the style in which she has become accustomed! Either that, or the woman has turned craven at the very thought of facing York once again." A vein was throbbing in his temple, and for a few seconds I truly feared he would fall into some sort of seizure! His eyes were bulging from his head, his lips filmed with moisture as he spat out his words with unguarded venom. "I took the throne back without her help and by God, I will keep it so if I have to! She can stay in France and rot for all I care!"

Plummer glared pointedly at Oxford, willing him to intervene. There were too many ears here eager to report back his words to those whose only aim was to see him fall from grace. I knew from experience Warwick was only venting his frustration, but that would not stop those who were just waiting for the opportunity to rid the court of him once Margaret arrived.

Oxford did as Plummer bid, and stepped up towards the table, trying to adopt a more measured tone.

"I hear she was waiting for the Ambassadors to return, Richard. They have made haste now that they have had word. They left for the coast an hour ago."

"How very convenient," Clarence smiled archly, at which Oxford gave an exasperated sigh.

"This is doing us no good! My men are already keeping watch in Norfolk and Suffolk. I will leave immediately to join them. Scrope will come with me. We can cover all of the coast there without stretching us too thinly."

Warwick was nodding now, his skin returning to its normal hue.

"Have we warned Northumberland and Montague?"

"As soon as we heard," murmured Tunstall. "And Tudor Somerset and Devon. Men are being mustered all over the country."

"Then I should leave immediately," George announced, only for Warwick to turn quickly, his command flung out to anyone who was listening. It was if in speaking, George had reminded Warwick that there will still loyal Yorkists he should be wary of.

"Arrest Norfolk, Essex, Cromwell, Mountjoy, Stafford and anyone else of known Yorkist connections. Including Stillington and Canterbury!" It was then that I heard the Bishop draw air in through his teeth! Whatever their inclinations, it was obvious he did not agree with men of the cloth being immured. Despite how often it happened, especially of late.

Tunstall and Oxford left the room immediately, as I began to wonder where the Stanley brothers were. George, his departure halted by Warwick's last words, paused as a horde of scribes and officers of the court crowded into the chamber, alerted by the sudden call to action. The noise in the room increased markedly, and as Will stepped up to offer Warwick a cup of wine, I fell backwards, placing myself nearer to the door, hoping to remain unseen, a least for a while.

"When will you leave for Warwickshire?" I heard George ask.

Warwick was now looking at a letter which had been pushed into his hand by a concerned looking scribe. He raised his head, giving George a cursory glance.

"Tomorrow."

"Then, I bid you farewell. For now." George swept away from him, but Warwick was suddenly alert, the document in his hand forgotten.

"George?"

He turned back, with languid ease. Had I been Warwick then, I would have been very, very concerned about his feckless protégé.

"Do not shame my daughter." He stopped, his brows pulling together. "Or yourself."

I didn't hear what reply George gave as I took that moment's distraction to remove myself from the chamber and slip back downstairs. My aim was to get to the Abbey, just to see if there was any evidence of movement there. It would not have surprised me if Warwick decided to secure the queen by employing a guard around the entrances, knowing Edward would be hell-bent on protecting his son should he land back on English soil. The whole area was in disarray and if there was any way I could take advantage of that and get even the slightest glimpse, or word, of Caitlin, then I intended to use it!

I had reckoned without Fortune, and as I rushed out into the Inner Ward, I almost collided with Elizabeth, who had been intending to run up the stairs as fast as I had descended them.

"Francis!" she gasped. "Where have you been? I have been looking for you all morning but you disappeared after Mass! I couldn't find you anywhere."

I was desperately anxious to get away, and for more than one reason. Her face was appealingly flushed, complimenting the rose-pink and pale cream of her gown. I felt my insides turn to water.

"I have been busy," I countered, trying not to be abrupt, whilst damping down the effect she was having on me, but knowing I had failed by the confused look on her face. "Have you heard?" Her eyes were wide, bluer than a summer sky. "Edward is on his way back to England!"

As if it was the most natural thing in the world, she reached out for my hand. I could see her chest, rising and falling above the neckline of her gown, betraying how her heart had begun to race.

"But... what does that mean? What do we do?"

I let her hold onto my hand, trying to keep calm. The ward was getting busier, there were people running around all over the place, clerics, servants, armed men all mingling together, more of them flooding in by the minute. I knew it would not be long before the news of Edward's voyage spilled down the Strand and over the city walls, if it had not already.

"I will have to go with the earl, I would imagine."

Her face fell in utter horror.

"To battle? Surely not!"

447

Her very words made me angry. I knew why she wanted, or as I saw it, needed me to stay behind, but it was as if she believed I was too young to show my value, to fight for my king, even though my heart lay with the exiles being buffeted off the eastern coast. I knew differently this time. Warwick needed all the men he could get if he was going to defeat Edward. Including me. I gritted my teeth before I answered, trying not to let the tension in my throat travel down to my hand where her fingers still curled around mine.

"I am in his service. Why would I not be summoned to serve him now?" I knew my words were growing colder, I could see the hurt blooming in her eyes. She stepped closer, and I tried not to breathe in her mesmerising fragrance. Tried to pretend it was not there.

"But, I can easily get Mama to change his mind! You are married to his niece after all. He will listen to her! I know he will!" Her fingers were squeezing mine now with a reassurance I did not need. Or want. "Then, whilst he is gone..." I looked back at her blankly. "We can... you said..."

A single tear began to track down her cheek and at the sight of it, I swallowed down a lump in my throat.

"I'm sorry Elizabeth. I... "

She moved even closer, reaching her face up to mine. Her lips so close to mine, her eyes threatening to smother me in pools of gentian honey.

"Please, Francis! Please?"

I couldn't help myself. I reached up and touched her cheek. It was like silk. Velvet. I tried not to betray how torn I was. How close I was to submitting to what she wanted from me, as it was something I could so easily, willingly give.

"Edward may become king again. Then you won't have to worry about Tudor."

My words were meant to be comforting and to allay her fears but she pulled away from me as sharply as if I had doused her with ice-cold water. She took a step back, her eyes no longer fearful. They were both accusatory and shocked. They looked like Anna's eyes, the day she had berated me for not standing with her father.

"So, even if it is not him, you would be happy for them to marry me to someone else? Anyone else? As long as it isn't you?"

She had completely twisted my words, and I closed the distance between us, desperate to try and make it right. I had to make her see that we could not do what she wanted. No matter how much we may both desire it.

"Elizabeth…"

I heard footsteps behind me, clattering down the stairs in a hurry. My name being called, then Will appeared behind me, stopping short.

"Frank. Warwick is asking for you." He gave Elizabeth a quick glance. "I wouldn't tarry if I were you."

I bit my lip. It was too late. I had not intended to tell her so brusquely; I had wanted to explain. But it was all too late.

"I have to go." I said quietly. She was nodding. A frigid smile fixed itself to her face and the features I had become too fond of twisted into a mask of disgust.

'Go then!" she spat, shocking me with the sudden venom in her voice. I took another step forward but Will grabbed my arm.

"You have to come. Now!" he hissed urgently.

I turned into the doorway reluctantly, but her voice followed me.

"Don't worry about me! It is you, you should have a care for! For I will tell them you ravished me anyway, and I know they will believe it to be true!"

35. COVENTRY
April 1471

"They are withdrawing!"

For three days Edward's army had been camped around the walls of Coventry. It was the second time we had been besieged and as had happened before, Edward had eventually given up and moved on. Only this time, things were different.

Every day I had looked down on the assembling army. Looked at their banners. Edward's 'Sun in Splendour,' the white boar flown by Richard's men. The black bull of Clarence. George has been as good as his word. His word to himself of course. He had reconciled with his brothers, as I had heard it, as he came north on the road to Banbury leading the men Warwick had asked him to raise.

Edward, Richard... and George. The excitement I felt at the thought of the three brothers fighting together in harmony was only tempered by the fear I felt at what the final outcome of these next few weeks would be. For me, whatever happened, there were true concerns.

"I knew they would have to give up," Will whispered into my ear as if the departing armies may be able to hear him. "There's no food around here now. What our men haven't taken, theirs have. All around is mud and mire. There will be many starving this summer, no matter who wins."

He disappeared down the stairs then, but I stayed on for a while, watching the lines of soldiers move away, riding south. Edward would be making for London, and there was no one there to stop him. Luck, as the duchess had so long ago predicted, was shining on him once again.

After first trying to land at Cromer, he was warned by men sent by the Archbishop of Canterbury, that Oxford's army lay in wait and the next we heard, he had not only landed, but had travelled the East March unchallenged before charming the Mayor and Aldermen of York into letting him enter the city.

Word had reached us that he had tricked them. Claiming to support King Henry, and wearing white ostrich feathers to show their allegiance to his son who was as yet to land on English soil, Edward said he only wanted to claim his birth-right. The dukedom of York, his father's title. They believed him, and let him in.

After that, he had moved south, and having made his true cause clear, casting his false feathers into the dust, his numbers began to swell. Many of Edward's old friends had abandoned their false loyalty to join his ranks, and his affinity had grown the further south he moved.

Not only had Northumberland not engaged him, but after a pause at Sandal, Montague must have lingered abed as the army slipped easily past Pontefract. Before we knew it, he was outside the walls of Coventry, declaring himself king and offering Warwick a pardon - if he surrendered the city.

That had been St Akelda's day. The irony for both myself and Warwick went unremarked upon as we looked down at the Yorkist army. Both of us having said Mass at the Church of St Akelda in Middleham, with Richard alongside us, the significance cannot have passed either of us by. I had strained my eyes for Richard's banner, eventually catching sight of the boar straddling the murrey and blue. It was all I could do to restrain myself from hurtling from the castle to join him. From our vantage point, they had looked formidable. That fanciful thought had made me grin. If Rob had been surprised to see me captured outside York, I could just imagine his face if he suddenly caught sight of me racing towards the assembled army.

It was almost worth the risk to see his face!

After a few days, in fact on All Fools Day, they had a change of strategy and had moved away, only to further tighten their grip on the country. They successfully entered Warwick and many men were killed in a skirmish with Oxford, Exeter and Viscount

Beaumont at Leicester, before the army turned their attention back to Coventry once again. Now that Clarence had joined their ranks, the odds were much more even. And Edward was making that plain.

Montague, Exeter and Oxford had all arrived at the castle shortly before Edward's army surrounded it for the second time, gaining entry by the skin of their teeth. Now they all sat downstairs, planning their next move. I took one last look at the meandering stream of Edward's followers and left the wall, making my way back down to the chamber, stopping off at the buttery to collect a fresh flagon of wine, knowing it would be welcome.

War, it appeared, was thirsty work.

The four men sat around a table littered with documents. A fire smouldered in the hearth, smoke billowing into the room every time a gust of April wind spiralled down the flue. Attending to my duties, I walked around the table, refilling the empty cups. The mood of each man was equally morose.

"So, London is open to them?" Oxford leaned back in his chair, which creaked under the strain as he stretched his shoulders. He also looked much older, I thought. Tired, with deep set, dark circles ringing his eyes. "Devon and Somerset have left the city and taken their armies to the coast, to wait for the queen." This was news to me and my ears pricked up, although I kept my head down attentively, ensuring nothing was spilled. So, who was guarding London? George Neville? King Henry himself? I bit my lip very hard at that thought.

"Well, I hope they have better luck than I had," snorted Warwick with derision. "Bloody fools! They would have done better holding the city so she has somewhere to enter once she has landed!"

Montague said nothing, just stared at his cup, not even moving as I poured in the jewel-dark liquid.

"Stanley?" Oxford asked wearily, as if knowing the answer would not afford them any joy.

"Hasn't moved from Hornby Castle. It seems he is more intent on feathering his own bed than holding the throne for his king." Which king? My demon was sniggering now.

I stood back by the wall, my hands behind me, waiting and listening. Lord Thomas Stanley was besieging the home of the Harrington family, who were loyal to Edward, having lost family members fighting at the battle of Wakefield with the Duke of York. To me, it was a wonderfully convenient time to stir up an old feud. I wondered idly where his brother William was.

"I'm waiting for Percy to shift his arse," Warwick spat. "He will have to explain to me how in the hell a sparse, Yorkist rabble rode unimpeded across the East Riding! Where the hell was he? He better be moving south as we speak or he will rue the day he got his title back. I'll spread his innards all over the northern march!"

Oxford took a sip of his wine, but I saw the look he gave Montague, who had still not spoken.

"It seems the whole of the north was sleeping," he murmured softly, but all knew where the barb was pointed.

John Neville, Lord Montague since Edward relieved him of and earldom and returned it to a Percy, did look up then.

"We weren't expecting him to go west from York. Our scouts told us they were taking the eastern road. I expected Scrope or Beaumont to come across them before I did." He paused. "Or you yourself, my lord."

They locked eyes across the table. Even thought Edward had taken his title from him, everyone knew of his closeness to the Yorks. The tension in the room was rising. No doubt fear and suspicion fuelling it like logs fed flame.

"Well, we did, eventually," Oxford's voice was low, dangerously so. "Once he got past Pontefract!"

Warwick banged on the table half heartedly, trying to make light of his brother's failure.

"Well, it's too late now. Edward is making for the city and they will no doubt give little resistance. Christ knows if Stockton

453

has raised himself from his bed as yet, but I doubt it. I have ordered him and the aldermen to hold fast. The Archbishop of York holds the king. We need to follow them, leave for the city. My kinsman, Fauconberg, will move north from Kent, Tudor from Wales and with the queen, Devon and Somerset bringing what's left of the west country, we can trap them in the middle. St Albans maybe." Warwick grinned coldly. "I know well how that land lies!"

St Albans. I knew about the battle that Warwick had won there, fighting alongside the Duke of York, against the very king he was now fighting for. I also knew about the second time he had fought there. And lost.

I could hear Fortune's Wheel creaking once more. It was a sound that never went away these days it seemed.

Oxford pushed himself up from the table, his chair scraping noisily against the stone floor.

"Then we may as well begin rallying the men now. Everyone's been well rested and whilst Edward and Clarence have been outside issuing pardons and sending messages of reconciliation, my men have been aching for a fight. I intend to give them that opportunity." He looked at Warwick. "Shall we ride at dawn?"

He nodded, gravely, and the small group began to break up in response, whilst Warwick remained seated, staring at the table in front of him. Oxford and Exeter left to begin the process of mustering their men, but Montague lingered, toying with a gold ring on his finger. The gesture made me smile.

"Richard..?"

Warwick raised a hand lazily. For tonight, at least, he had the air of a defeated man.

"It doesn't matter, John." Warwick sounded weary unto death. His brother was not to be pacified.

"I didn't let him pass. You must believe me. I honestly believed he would run into Oxford's men. I was told their forces straddled the great north road."

Warwick nodded slowly, before looking up and meeting his brother's eyes.

"I know John. There are men who I am more than aware I cannot trust. You are not one of them. You are my dearest brother. I am grateful to be fighting alongside you."

Montague laid a hand on his brother's shoulder, squeezing slightly. It seemed he had nothing he could say to acknowledge Warwick's words, instead it was me who had a lump in my throat. I had no brothers. How would I be feeling if I knew I may have led one into a situation where he may lose his life? And not against an enemy in the truest sense.

"I will see you in the morning." His voice was more than a little husky, as he turned away and left the room.

That left me alone with the earl, not a place I really desired to be. But, it was my duty to clear the debris from the table and I began collecting up the cups and returning them to the sideboard. I was keeping myself busy, trying not to think about tomorrow. We were not that far from London. Fear began to rise in my gut. Fear and doubt. We could be fighting before the end of the week.

No matter how much I had wanted to ride at Richard's side, the reality of battle was now beginning to sink in. It would be a bloody business, no matter who was the victor. There were people I knew, at court and in Edward's army, who could be severely maimed. Killed. I was totally immersed in these thoughts when I heard my name.

"Well, Lovell. What do you think?"

I turned away from the sideboard, genuinely puzzled. Think of what?

"Your Grace?"

"If I was to ask you to lay down a wager, who would you favour?"

I suppressed a nervous smile. I wondered if the earl was amusing himself, attempting to lighten his mood by playing with my loyalties. I seemed to be fair game there. I shrugged diffidently.

"I have no money, Your Grace. Nothing to wager with."

I saw his lip curl, and knew at least I had not angered him.

"Humour me! Pretend, if you can, that I don't control everything you own."

I had a pewter cup in my hand, which for one second I would have loved to throw at him, but I walked over to the table instead, where he sat looking at me, his eyes unreadable.

"I don't know, Your Grace. Although trained by your tutelage, I am still a novice. Untried or untested. Of what use would my opinion be?"

He considered that for a few moments before answering.

"All that training and you turn into a bloody diplomat!" These words were mumbled, a low growl in his throat but I heard them, before he cleared his throat and raised his voice.

"Very well, then let us see how brave you are." My heart leapt into my throat. Was he going to put me in the battle array? Would I be fighting with him? His next words dispelled that thought before I could work out if I was pleased or petrified, but gave me a different concern. "In your heart, whose banner do you wish to see triumphant?"

I went to speak, to protest, but he held up his hand.

"Now is the time, Lovell, to wear your heart on your sleeve. I doubt you will disappoint me, which you will, only if you lie."

I put the cup down on the table slowly, feeling the heat of the flames on my face. Wood-smoke billowed into the room, fanned by a sudden breeze. It curled and twisted around the room like fingers, reaching out for something. Someone. Then the air cleared.

"It is an honour to serve you, my lord." I said carefully.

He raised his eyebrows, his face sanguine. He was smiling. "But?"

"God save King Edward."

36. BARNET
April 1471

The artillery had been booming relentlessly through most of the night. If its aim was to cause sleeplessness to those who were due to fight the next morning, it was surely effective. As to actually dispersing any of Edward's army – the dawn had its own surprise in store. Once more, it seemed as if the sand in the hourglass was running out. Fortunes wheel was spinning, and if nothing changed, I could see Warwick being crushed by it.

All this, of course, I kept to my own counsel as I doused myself in cold water, pulling on my clothes which were as dank and damp as the standards outside. Fog, thick and soupy, enveloped everything – seeping the light out of the world, shrouding everything in a miserable miasma of silence. Going outside to relieve my bursting bladder, I could see that even the campfires were struggling to stay alight. Feeble fireflies fighting vainly against the moist air. Voices, movements, were all muted, the usual sharp metallic ringing of an army readying for battle dampened down. Numbed. We were like an army at the edge of the world, waiting for death or glory. But which one?

I tied my points together firmly, trying not to let my stomach rise to my throat at the thought of what was to come. Somewhere out there was Richard. No doubt leading his own men. Rob too. And Tom. I thought I was going to be sick then and bent over double, retching, but nothing came up. Why would it? I had hardly eaten a thing the last two days since I realised that this was inevitable.

I had prayed to march, prayed for the adventure of riding as one of a force of men, but this is not what I had envisaged. To me, I was with the enemy! The people whose companionship I truly craved were out there, somewhere, in the rolling banks of fog. I knew I would feel braver than I did now were I shoulder to shoulder with them rather than loitering here.

Warwick had already risen when I entered the tent, and was sitting on the edge of his camp bed. I hurried in and offered him water and a towel, knowing his chaplain would be in shortly to say Mass. He didn't say a word, allowing me to dry him before holding out the padded arming doublet, flicking me a quick glance before he placed his arms into the sleeves. This was what I had been trained for. I had done it plenty of times in practice, but this was for an actual battle and I was surprised to find my fingers didn't even tremble.

As I began to clad his powerful limbs in steel plate, the tent flap lifted and John Neville, already fully armoured, walked inside, checking his brother's face carefully. Montague was an experienced warrior, assured and confident. As was Warwick, only this morning it was the latter who seemed nervous, or at the very least reflective by his complete silence. I was relived to see Montague for that reason at least.

"You can't see a hand in front of your face out there. Have you been outside?" John dropped the tent flap behind him, shutting out the clinging mist. Well, almost.

Warwick grunted.

"I don't need to stick my nose outside the tent to know how the land lies. You can feel it in the air. I hope the artillery made some headway at least!"

John walked over to the table and poured himself a cup of ale as I pulled on the damp straps of the breastplate, buckling it together on his shoulders. Warwick raised his brows as his brother turned, drink in hand.

"I've already heard Mass."

"You've been about early."

"I haven't slept."

Warwick grinned ruefully, flexing one of his arms as I fitted a pauldron, checking his movement range.

"Something on your mind, brother?"

Montague emptied his cup swiftly and put it back down on the table before replying.

458

"Apart from the prospect of meeting our cousin head on in the battle lines you mean?"

"You think Edward will be in the centre then?"

"Don't you?"

Warwick pursed his lips.

"And? Did you want to make a wager?"

"Hastings and..." John paused, frowning. "You won't like this one."

"Try me. I find myself in an affable mood today."

"Richard. I think he will have a command."

I was glad I was kneeling now to strap on his greaves, I didn't want to see his face. "I just wanted to warn you. In case you end up facing him in the fray."

Warwick made a derisory snort.

"It's that bastard Clarence I will be looking for! If I get the slightest chance to slice his treacherous throat I don't intend to miss it."

Montague looked down at his feet, his dark hair falling forwards. He appeared to be troubled, but not in a frightened or scared way. His mood was sad, regretful.

"Will you cut Edward down, should you engage him?"

Warwick ran fingers around the collar of his breastplate, tugging at the doublet underneath.

"More to the point, will you?"

Montague looked down at his hands, avoiding his brothers searching gaze. His next words sounded surprisingly gentle for such a warlike man.

"He offered you a pardon, Richard. Will you not offer him mercy in return?"

I was still fiddling with the straps, making the job last longer than it should. I just didn't want to stand up now for fear they would stop talking if they remembered who it was they were talking in front of. Unless I now mattered so little it was of no account.

"I can't John. If I spare him, Margaret won't. You know the

459

man. He would rather die on the field than suffer his father's fate. Do you think he will do any different for me? Or you?"

John looked up.

"Yes. I do. In spite of everything, I think he will."

"And we can then live happily the rest of our years under an attainder and watch our lands and livelihoods handed out to those who have played us false, for you can wager Clarence will be first in line! I have a wife, and daughters John. As do you! No – even worse. You have a son!"

I did stand up then, my task at his left leg complete, and I waited. Lands and livelihood. Warwick was happy to risk his own, and mine too. I glanced at Montague then but he seemed not to be aware of it. I was once again invisible, even as I picked up another greave.

"Richard, I came to offer some advice. Whether you take it or not is up to you, but I think you should listen to me. We need to fight in hand-to-hand combat. Alongside the men. Leave our horses in the park." Warwick was pulling on his gloves now, pushing the creaking leather down between his fingers with determination, but he didn't answer.

"Suspicion is rife through the ranks, especially with Clarence's change of coat. Besides, it is a better tactic in these conditions. Who knows what we would be plunging into on horseback."

"A pile of dead Yorkists hopefully" Warwick remarked ruefully.

The tent flap lifted again and the chaplain and a priest entered, bearing the sacrament needed for the morning Mass. John gave a deep sigh.

"Then you had better pray for it." He paused, finally meeting my eyes. "I will go rouse the men."

37. BARNET
March 1471

My first experience of a battle in which I played no part was not entirely as I expected it to be. As Warwick strode out of the tent he ordered me to remain behind, so that all I could do was watch as he disappeared into the fog, the plate of his armour dulled by moisture, merging with the mist which enveloped him. I caught a swift glimpse of his standard, hanging limply on its staff, flapping disconsolately as it followed him to the lines of battle.

If the infernal weather had not been determined to damn the whole enterprise, it may be that I would have witnessed more, but the churning in my gut twisted and tightened with a physical strength as I heard a blast of trumpets, somewhat dulled, followed by an answering blast and something that sounded like a hail of voices, shouting. It was not yet 4.30am. Only just light, if light grey.

I stood in the frame of the tent flap, straining my eyes to see the impossible. Two heavily mailed guards stood either side of the opening, one, a younger, pale-faced man, looking massively relieved that he was not part of the melee, the other, his hand twitching by the hilt of his sword as if by reflex at the sounds he could hear.

"How will we know what is happening?" I asked quietly, no doubt in one sentence betraying my inexperience. But there was no shame to be had. I had been deemed too young, or too inexperienced to join the forces, it didn't matter to me which. Like the guard to my left, I was just inwardly pleased not to be fighting against men who were once, who maybe still were, my friends.

The occasional dull thud of artillery was accompanied by the muted clash of metal on metal. Shouts, screams, full throated yells mixed with each other making an almost unintelligible cacophony of sound. They could have been a few feet away, or a few miles.

"Hard to say," grumbled the older guard. "If one of the injured makes it back to camp, or men begin to desert or flee."

That didn't reassure me at all, and I wondered how far away Warwick actually was in the wall of fog that confronted us. He was in charge of the reserves, I knew that much as I had witnessed the conversation between Warwick and his commanders the previous evening. Montague would array his forces over the Barnet road, with Exeter to his left and Oxford to his right. Who they would face as the weather hid the identifying banners, they would not have known until the hand to hand fighting ensued. The thought made me even more nauseous. Surely, fighting was better than the torture of waiting?

The noise of battle was growing louder, causing the horses in the horse park to become fractious. No doubt they could smell the blood, even if we couldn't see it. Minutes became hours and at times the veil of mist began to thin, giving glimpses of banners, shadows, a bristle of pikes could be seen, but not for long as the gauzy veil rolled back over and hid everything from view.

Then it began to change, all too alarmingly, and everything seemed far closer than it had been. I clearly heard a lone cry of "Treason!" which was then taken up by more and more throats and the shouts and screams became sickeningly bloodcurdling. Suddenly, a figure burst through the mist. He fell down in sight of the tent, scrabbling forwards on bloodied greaves in the mud, one vambrace missing, ripped from a forearm. I didn't recognise him, but I knew his colours, the gold lions on red, fleur-de-lis on blue. He was one of Exeter's men and I shot forward to grab him by the arm. The older guard helped me and together we pulled him bodily into the tent and threw him onto a coffer, where he sat, dazed. His hair was stuck to his face, there was more blood on his chin.

"What's happened?" I was calmer than I thought, even able to pour him a cup of wine which he grabbed with a shaking hand.

The red liquid dribbled down his chin, matching the blood, only darker.

"We are lost!" he gasped hoarsely. "From the first." His words were halting to begin with, gathering momentum as he gained his breath. The two guards were now standing side by side within the confines of the tent. They were swapping nervous glances, no doubt waiting to hear if they should flee. "In the fog... our lines overlapped. We were set upon by soldiers under the banner of Gloucester. They had fought up from Dead Man's Bottom, but we were pushing them back."

Gloucester! The very name made me want to be sick again. He was in the thick of it then! My friend. Fighting manfully so it sounded, despite the odds. I offered up a silent prayer for his safety.

He took another drink and I refilled his cup quickly.

"I don't know what happened next, but someone yelled that our own men had turned! Montague's men began attacking Oxford's. Damn him, he always was Yorkist!" The man spat on the ground, a glistening gobbet, blood bright!

I was shaking my head in amazement. So Montague had turned against his brother? My mind began to race. Now the man had begun talking, he seemed to be unable to stop.

"Exeter is down, mortally wounded I heard. Then, just before... I saw my friend Giles, he told me Montague had fallen also. The Yorkist had breached the centre line...everything was in disarray...Oxford...Dear God! What do we now? Must we flee?" He turned up desperate blue eyes to me, obviously thinking I knew the answer. This seemed to be his first battle too.

I had no idea what to do. I looked around the tent and found that my two erstwhile companions had made up their minds already for I was alone with the wounded squire.

"What is your name?" I asked for no particular reason.

"Robert," he answered, seemingly unwilling to give anything else away. I didn't know him nor he me. I didn't want to stay here. But I wasn't intending to flee. My mind began to boil, my thoughts in a fog of their own.

Dragging my dagger from my belt, I walked outside, my feet gradually picking up speed, taking me into a full-pelt run by the time I was surrounded in the thick of the mist. Mist which had begun to thin in places, yet not enough to see where I was, or where I was heading.

I just ran forwards, and forwards, as the noise of battle grew nearer, men began to pass me on either side, the thrum of an arrow passed by my ear, bringing me to my senses. I stopped suddenly, panting, thinking for some reason that I would have come across Warwick, holding his sword high above his head, roaring that he would win or die.

A figure loomed before me in the murk. Tall, broad, powerful, a long blade at his side. Dark, almost ghostly. The fog rolled back only momentarily, but only long enough for me to glimpse a banner, but not to recognise it. There was a shout, and the figure turned to counter an attack from behind, but as he did so, he staggered, and was so close to me as to push me back with some force.

I took a step backwards to recover but my foot slipped on something. Something wet and foul smelling, then all the world was grey. My head slammed into the ground and pain exploded in my head, I saw stars as the grey became black.

38. BARNET
March 1471

It was a dull rumbling sound which made me open my eyes. For a moment, I couldn't remember anything. There was a sharp throbbing in the back of my head, and I lay looking at the greyness above me, which was sprinkled with patches of blue. I sat up, gingerly. There was a cart beside me, and I used the wheel for purchase, gripping on the spokes to haul myself up, still dazed. I was a dead weight.

Shadowy figures moved all around me. There were groans, feeble shouts for help, cries, and oh Lord the smell! I reached up to the back of my head where the pain was and my hand came away bloodied. I had no idea what had struck me and cared even less, as I tried to take in the carnage that surrounded me. Banners lie in the mud, alongside severed limbs and lifeless bodies. Mother Nature was rolling back its veil to reveal the horror it had caused in a morning's work.

I turned my back on the field and pulled myself up straight, leaning heavily against the cart, tears forming in my eyes for some stupid reason. Blinking furiously, my vision cleared, as I finally, unexpectedly, looked upon the face of the earl I had tried to find in the fog.

He lay in the cart, once powerful limbs askew, naked but clothed in mire and blood. On his back, facing the sky, his face slashed and torn, one eye punctured, blood congealing in his nose and ears. The grand, Italian plate armour I could still imagine in my hands, gone. I pulled back with a start, gripping tighter on the rail to prevent me falling back onto the ground, only to see he was not alone.

His brother John lie beside him.

His face was unmarked, whatever wound had killed him not in evidence to my eyes. Pushing myself away, I bent over double and threw up, falling back to my knees. There was only liquid, pale and frothy, snaking down my chin. All I could do was retch, the ruin that was Warwick's face imprinted on the back of my closed lids.

"What in God's name..?"

I knew the voice. But it was only as I raised my head that I thought I must have been dreaming. Dreaming, or dead and lingering in purgatory, imagining what may have been.

A mailed hand curled around my arm and helped me to my feet. I knew I had suffered a blow on the head. That was the only reason I could have thought that Richard was speaking to me.

"What in name of all the saint's are you doing here?"

I stood up, and stared. He was dressed in full armour, but without a helm. His dark hair was plastered to his face, a smudge of blood down his cheek. He was smiling, but in astonishment. As I looked back at him mutely, suddenly stupidly conscious of my scarlet livery, of the bear and ragged staff badge, another figure joined him. Taller, broader, somehow brighter.

"Good Lord! Dickon? Is that..?"

King Edward came to a halt at the foot of the cart, looking like an iron-clad Colossus. His face also showed the results of his efforts, a mixture of mud and blood coating his usually fair complexion, but his grin was broad. Beaming brighter than the sun. He frowned then, looking at my attire. "Was Warwick so poorly arrayed he couldn't provide the lad with armour?"

Richard bit his lip, looking at me with some concern. It was enough to make me find my voice, cracked and dry though it was.

"I was not in the field, Your Grace. I came looking for my lord..." I swallowed, both faces had grown solemn. "I heard all was lost and thought he may have need..." I looked at the cart then and they both followed my gaze.

"He is beyond your help now, Francis," Richard said carefully. "I hear that you managed to serve your master well whilst not compromising your service to your liege lord. You served him well." Edward had taken a step forward, his brow knotted. I was about to answer when someone came from behind me, causing

466

me to turn as both brothers looked at the new arrival. George of Clarence now stood by the other side of the cart, his face impassive, apart from the slight curve to his lips.

"I always trusted in God you would return, Your Grace," I replied unsteadily, not at that moment certain that it was George who had spoken up for me, but I could think of no other. It didn't matter. So many things that had mattered before were no of no consequence. My head began to spin.

"Then this had been a glorious day in more than one sense!" George smiled, wiping his hand across his brow. "There is a certain sense of achievement in vanquishing one's enemies, I think. This was a vindication much deserved!"

"I did not want them dead, George," Edward remarked almost casually, but I could see from his familiar expression that not much had changed in their relationship, despite their recent reconciliation. "I had hoped they would be spared. In fact, I thought I had given orders for it."

George shrugged.

"You can't blame anyone Edward. The damned fog was so thick, only the Lord knows who was killing who half the time! No wonder Montague turned on Oxford's men. The fog was a divine providence. Like the three suns at Mortimer's Cross!"

Edward looked down at his feet for a second, no doubt to mask his thoughts, but he nodded in agreement. I looked at Richard, who was flicking his gaze between one and the other.

"What will happen to them now?" I asked quietly, still not completely believing that Warwick was dead. Richard placed his hand on my arm and drew me away a few steps, taking care not to step on the remains which littered the ground.

"St Paul's first, to display before the people. Then on to the family vault at Bisham." It was only then that I saw the blood on his own vambrace.

"Are you injured?"

He shrugged casually.

"A fleshwound. I didn't feel it at first, but it is stiffening up

467

now, I must admit. I was in the surgeon's tent when I heard we had found..." he stopped, his eyes clouded over. "I will never forget what he did for me. And neither should you!"

A sudden dread flooded me. Realisation began to clear in my fogged mind.

"Oh dear God! Anne!"

"This isn't over Frank. We heard that Margaret has left Honfleur. She could even be in England as we speak."

"But surely, she won't fight Edward? Not once she finds out he holds the king and Warwick is dead?"

I had completely forgotten how easy he was to talk to. Deep inside me, the anxiety I had felt for so long had begun to melt away, until he had mentioned Margaret. He grinned, mirthlessly.

"Edward is aching for her to challenge him. Me too, to be honest." He flexed his arm, wincing. "It is our chance to avenge our father. We may not want another battle, but at the same time we welcome it!" He sighed deeply. "It may be some weeks yet before things are finally settled. Before we can get back to where we were."

Our eyes met at the same time and a strange silence fell.

"Did you know that Caitlin is in Sanctuary with the queen?" I asked suddenly. He inhaled deeply at the mention of her name and nodded, suddenly avoiding my gaze.

"I did. I thank the Lord she was kept safe."

"I tried to see her. To make sure she was well."

"And?"

"The queen prevented it." His lips twisted wryly.

"Some things never change."

"God's Blood!" Percy's voice came out of nowhere, and before long so did he. A huge hand clapped me on the back, almost knocking me over. "I didn't expect to see you here!"

I couldn't help but grin broadly. But it appeared there had been a reason he had not surfaced earlier.

"Well?" Richard asked suddenly.

Rob shook his head.

"I am sorry, Dickon."

I watched him swallow deeply.

"So that's Miles, and Tom." Rob nodded gravely.

"Parr?" Richard's squire, flaxen headed and cheeky. I could see him standing in the courtyard at Westminster the day I met Caitlin.

"And Huddleston."

"Jesus!"

We stood looking at each other in silence. Richard looked particularly wretched. I knew Miles, and both Toms, but was more friendly with Tom Parr than any of them. I knew Richard would feel that loss particularly keenly.

As we stood, Edward gave the order for the cart containing the bodies of Warwick and Montague to roll on down the Barnet road, back to the city. That done, he walked over to us and looked Richard up and down.

"You've lost some blood. Get to the surgeon's tent and I will meet you back in Barnet." He turned, shouting over his shoulder loudly. "George! Take care of your brother. Hastings is finding accommodation in the town, which may be harder than he thinks."

George sauntered towards us, stripping off his gloves as he did.

"I'm fine," Richard grimaced, but even I noticed he was now looking paler than he did before.

"Now brother," said George easily, "the king has spoken. Percy, come with us. We passed an inn on the Barnet road, whilst we are getting his wound attended to, get yourself there and secure rooms before Hastings does."

All I could do was watch them leave as I stood in the middle of the battlefield with my king. Richard gave me a tight grin as he left and Percy threw me a wink. George, well, he had forgotten about me entirely.

I looked around. Now I could see William Stanley and Lord Howard, walking across the field, towards the king. William inclined his head when he spied me, a look of mild surprise on his face. Edward raised a hand, and then turned back to me.

"Well, what now, Lovell?"

That, was a very good question and one I had been trying not to ask myself. I had wanted to follow Richard, but once again, had not been allowed. Having just been discovered on the wrong side of a battlefield wearing the enemy's livery, I hardly thought it was the best time to protest.

"I am at your service, Your Grace."

I could see his mind working behind calculating eyes.

"Well, that is a very good idea, after all, we have been here before, have we not." So, he had not forgotten my service as we came down from Middleham. That had to work in my favour. Thinking quickly, I dropped to one knee in the mud, the dirt soaking my hose, cold, thick and wet. I didn't like to think of what else was mixed in it.

"I pledge myself to be your true and loyal servant, Your Grace. Myself, together with my sisters and my wife Anna. I ask only that you grant us your most gracious mercy."

Edward cuffed my shoulder, unfortunately with a hand which was still encased with a gauntlet. It was meant as a familiar gesture, but I knew it would bruise. One more battle wound. I was almost proud!

"Cease, Lovell! I am assured of your affinity, although for form I will need to grant you yet another pardon. For nothing else than you bent the knee to King Henry, even though I know you had no other recourse." I pushed myself up. He knew better than most. He had placed me in Warwick's care after all. "But for now, as I recall, you made an excellent squire. So, let us join the others and repair to Barnet. I need food, and wine. A lot of wine."

Grinning, he touched me on the shoulder once more, and made to join Stanley and Howard who had been standing a few feet away watching. Behind them, the cart containing the bodies of two noble Neville lords was bumping and bouncing over the field, the wheels going round like Fortune's Wheel itself. I swallowed hard, and then followed my king.

EPILOGUE
TOWER OF LONDON

May 1471

It was over.

Queen Margaret had landed the very day that Edward had been victorious on the field at Barnet. Somerset had delivered her the news of the defeat and of Warwick's death. Undaunted, as Richard predicted, she had made for Wales where Jasper Tudor had been gathering forces, but on Edward's orders, Gloucester closed its gates to her army. She had to make for Tewkesbury to cross the River Severn there, hoping to pad out her army with Tudor's Welshmen. She took her son, and his bride with her whilst the Countess of Warwick fled into sanctuary at Beaulieu Abbey. I could only think she now repented of her husband's actions and found this to be the only way to show Edward she did not support the ongoing Lancastrian cause.

Anne, of course, had no such option.

Today, I had watched Edward, accompanied with great pomp and ceremony, be welcomed back into his city, accompanied by his brothers in victory and dragging Queen Margaret behind them in a cart, parading her utter failure and capitulation to the populace. Edward's forces had prevailed in the fields before the Abbey at Tewkesbury and Margaret's ambitions, and her dynasty, were destroyed in a day. Her army was routed, with Richard once again in the thickest of the fighting, and Margaret's son, Anne's husband, was slain on the field.

The victory had been celebrated in tavern and townhouse as returning soldiers gave their own versions of the glorious victory of the House of York. It was like a feast day of its very own. Having been feted and feasted, Richard now sat opposite me on the other side of the hearth, in his chamber within the Tower. He looked tired, but relaxed, and it was the first time we had

472

managed to spend any time together since we parted company at Barnet. Spying me waiting in the household who welcomed their return, he had despatched Rob to bring me to him, but now we were alone.

A large, brindle hound slept peacefully at his feet, and although he was holding a cup in his hand he didn't seem inclined to drink. He had filled me in on all those details of the battle which I had not already been acquainted with, and some of the detail was not particularly edifying. Somerset had taken sanctuary in the Abbey, although once he heard of it, Edward dragged him out. He was tried and executed a few days later. Richard, as Constable of England, presided over his trial, gave the verdict and saw the sentence carried out.

There was no doubt we had all been trained well for combat at Middleham, but this, was something else. The power of a prince, or a noble, to enact the law of the land. It was symbolic of how far we had all come. But one thing stood out clear as a summer morn. Richard had earned his brother's respect, and a reputation as an able soldier.

It was over, yet it was not. Tudor was still raising men in Wales, a scion of the Neville's known as the 'Bastard of Fauconberg,' had been raiding and storming the south coast after his attack on London was repelled. There were rumours of unrest in the north, where the death of Warwick had left a huge chasm in the rule of the land. One I imagined Northumberland would be only too happy to fill, having had both of his major rivals in the area despatched.

"I would imagine you have some tales to tell," Richard said suddenly, looking at me with a small smile. I shrugged it off. I didn't want to speak of my time at Warwick's side. Or at Henry's court. Some of the memories were still too keen.

"Not as many as you. All I have done is kick my heels and watch Warwick try and pull on the reins of power."

Richard crossed himself, the candlelight winking on the his jewelled fingers.

473

"God rest his soul. None of us wanted that end for him."

"Not even George?" I asked slyly. He didn't answer. He didn't need to, but he finally took a sip from his wine, his face becoming troubled. "Do you know what happens now?"

He nodded, placing the wine cup on a table at his side.

"We set off south. To the coast to calm the unrest there. We hear Fauconberg has just about run his course. Which is just as well if we have to turn our attentions north."

I was shaking my head in amazement.

"Don't they understand?" I asked, mystified. "Henry's cause is lost! He's a prisoner. His wife too! There is no point in resisting any more." For a few seconds, I thought he looked uncomfortable, staring into the flames. "Dickon?"

He raised his eyes and I felt there was something he wanted to tell me, but didn't know how. There was only one thing I could think of, and as he had not even mentioned her, I did.

"Has Caitlin had her child?" All I knew was that she had not accompanied the queen out of sanctuary. I had no idea where she was, and no one to ask. He did smile then, although not enough to dispel the sudden tension from his face.

"Yes. A boy."

"Is she well? And the child?" He nodded carefully in answer. "I take it you have not seen her yet?"

He sighed.

"There has been little time. I did see Kathryn though. She is a truly beautiful child. My mother has offered to take them all under her care at Baynard's until..."

The anxiety I thought had gone since the battle was back with a vengeance. There was so much I didn't know now. Things which Richard was party to now that I had no part in, and that he obviously felt he should not, or could not, share with me. At least not yet. I would take that in matters of state, but he had charged me once with caring for Caitlin. She was different. I did not appreciate secrets concerning her care. So I pressed him further.

"Until..?"

474

"Francis…" I looked at him candidly, and he had the grace to look a little embarrassed. "There are things I have to do. Things, I never thought I would have to do, and that you may not understand. Not today. Maybe not for some time. I just have to ask you to trust me." He leaned forwards in his chair then, the firelight catching his eyes. "Do you trust me?"

I was shocked that he even had to ask me. But then I remembered. We had spent months apart. He was no longer Warwick's ward, no longer a squire of Middleham. He was a royal prince, one of the most influential and powerful people in the realm. And older. Now expected to fulfil his royal destiny.

"Of course I trust you. I am your friend, Dickon, and always will be."

A ghost of a smile crossed his lips and he sat back in his chair.

"Good. I had hoped that would be your answer. I need to know who I can trust now more than ever." Once again he looked back into the flames and his dark eyes filled with amber heat.

"Why? What do you mean?" I thought it was an innocent question until I heard the answer.

"I am going to marry Anne Neville."

Coming soon
Semper Fidelis – Volume 2

'For The Viscount Lovell…'

King Edward is back on the throne of England. His cousin, Richard Neville is dead, slain on the field of battle at Barnet. Pardoned by the king for doing his duty, Francis, still a ward of value, is given into the care of the Duke of Suffolk, husband to Edward's sister Elizabeth. With his friend Richard, Duke of Gloucester determined to marry his Neville cousin, the lives of all those he was so close to are in danger of moving on without him. The fate of Caitlin Desmond hangs in the balance. His bride is still a young child, his fortune is not his own. But he has already defied his father-in-law and survived a Lancastrian court. He has served the York princes well, and one of them is hiding something….

Author's Notes

As in 'Desmond's Daughter' I continue with the two-year age gap between Francis and Richard even though there is some evidence to say he could have been born in 1456 and not 1454. I also deliberately write his character as if he is 'older than his years' – again in keeping with 'Desmond's Daughter' when Richard would only have been sixteen at the time he met Caitlin. As I see it, it was a harder life, childhood was shorter than it is now. Young girls were considered mature at a very young age and were giving birth whilst still children themselves.

Bearing in mind the lack of actual factual information in existence for Francis, and in the consideration of the amount of dramatic licence needed to craft a credible story, I felt it would almost be pointless exercise to list every place where I have created events to fit the direction of the plot. For instance, we know Francis was pardoned in 1470, and it was assumed he was at Ravensworth with his in-laws as they were all named in the act. We know he was still Warwick's ward then, but what part did he actually have in any of his rebellions bearing in mind his age?

In considering his character and indeed some of his later motivations, it is true that within a short space of time he lost both his father and his mother, whose short-lived marriage to William Stanley may have resulted in the birth of a child but also led to his mother's death. In that short space of time did he even see William Stanley? Did they form a relationship? If so – was it a cordial one?

Like Richard, as a young boy he was visited by tragedy. But where Richard had his mother, brothers and sisters around him, Francis, heir to a fortune, found himself a hostage to that very inheritance. I found it extremely sad reading through the various entries regarding the plethora of lands and estates, used as bargaining chips by King Edward, ways of rewarding those men he wished to keep onside. Edward even paid £1,000 towards

Richard's tutelage with the Earl of Warwick from income gleaned out of the Lovell fortune.

Yet these were hard times, and treatment of noble minors in this way was not unusual. You see this pattern re-occur again and again up to 1477, when Francis finally obtains control of his own life. Although, he still has a fight on his hands to regain some of his own lands which have been granted to others, Lord Hastings being one such party. Some historians have accused him of being greedy and grasping in the pursuit of some of these land rights, but to me, I see it differently.

He waited a long time to be able to gain what was rightfully his. We have the benefit of hindsight, which he did not. He did not know that whilst still a young man, he would be both childless and a fugitive. Whilst serving Richard, surely he would have believed he had his whole future ahead of him, with sons to come after him and continue the family name. To inherit the family fortune and make a good marriage of their own.

Then, after August 1485, you see his lands being divided up and handed out again, this time after his attainder. It was therefore, during only eight short years that he lived the life he had been born to, as a titled noble of the realm. Again, not uncommon during this period of history, but it does make you stop and think, I feel, and consider what made certain people do the things they did, for right or for wrong.

With regard to his character and his relationship with his wife (who is referred to usually as Anne, Anna or Agnes – I use Anna deliberately to define her from her cousin Anne Neville). She was very young, he was young himself when they married. Can any of us really imagine what that would have been like? They had no children, but that is not to say that there was no affection between them, or that there was.

But I think a lot about this relationship can be drawn from Francis's will, made as the prospect of an invasion drew near. He made the unusual step of making a jointure settlement – this being bequests of land – on his wife. This meant, that instead of these lands reverting back to the male line after her death, which was the usual form, she would be able to pass them down to any children from a subsequent marriage. In making this settlement, Francis was directly acknowledging that if he did not survive the oncoming battle, although they themselves had no children, she was young enough to marry again and have issue. He was therefore providing for her to have children by another man.

Of course, he didn't reckon on Henry Tudor! But had Richard been the victor, which to Francis was probably the most likely outcome at the time he wrote his will, but Francis died on the field, his wife was well provided for. I think that says an awful lot about his character right there.

So, I hope the way I have written this mirrors the feeling I gleaned from reading these milestones in his life.

He was a ward of Warwick, but of the king too. Even when these men become estranged, his loyalty lies with the king. Or, should I say, with the king's brother. We may not have any real evidence of this before the Scottish campaigns in 1480, but from the little we do know, he comes across as a man who was loyal, dependable and just got on with things.

Perhaps he really was 'a safe pair of hands.'

Which could open up a whole other story...

19386197R00271

Printed in Poland
by Amazon Fulfillment
Poland Sp. z o.o., Wrocław